CIRCLE CITY PSYCHIC

STEPHANIE A. CAIN

CIRCLE CITY PSYCHIC
Circle City Magic: Book 2
Copyright 2018 Stephanie A. Cain

ISBN: 978-1-944774-02-8
First Print Edition, June 2018
Published by Cathartes Press

ALSO BY STEPHANIE A. CAIN

<u>Storms in Amethir</u>
The Midwinter Royal
Stormsinger
Stormshadow
Stormseer
The Weather War
Witchery's End (forthcoming)

<u>Faith and Fealty</u>
Sow the Wind

<u>Circle City Magic</u>
Shades of Circle City
Circle City Psychic
"C" in *E is for Evil* (Alphabet Anthologies #5)
A Stranger in Circle City (forthcoming)

<u>With Other Authors</u>
Equus (Rhonda Parrish's Magical Menageries #5)

"Prophecy is the most gratuitous form of error."

- George Eliot, *Middlemarch*

CHAPTER 1

It was the first weekend in June and Martin Cole's big sister was finally getting married.

He ran a hand through his light auburn hair and grimaced at himself in the full-length mirror of the hotel room. Why they'd had to get a hotel room when everyone in the wedding party lived in Indianapolis, Martin wasn't sure, but he'd learned two months ago to never argue with the bride.

That's not fair, he told himself. *Not like she's Bridezilla or anything.*

But there were some strange compromises involved in having his sister marry a werewolf.

"The second weekend in June is too close to the Full," Chloe had said. "I want Braxton to be at his best, but I don't want to wait until the third weekend." Her reasoning had involved the honeymoon plans, which was a two-week excursion to several of the southwestern national parks—Grand Canyon, Mesa Verde, Bryce Canyon, White Sands, and Great Sand Dunes. Apparently they had a four-night stay at the Grand Canyon, which would be long enough for Braxton to shift and recover from the full moon without putting a damper on their travel plans.

Martin stopped asking questions back around

Halloween, when he'd learned his sister was dating a werewolf in the first place.

No, the problem wasn't that his sister was getting married. Or even that she was getting married in June. The problem was mostly with the guy who wasn't the best man, but very obviously wanted to be.

Well. Problem was a strong word. Complication, maybe.

Call it what it is, dumbass, he told himself. *He's seriously hot, and he's seriously pissed at you for being the best man.*

Braxton had been great about it, all things considered. He hadn't even tried to argue with Chloe about how she'd made a promise to her brother the day he came out to her, that Martin would be her best man whenever she got married. According to Chloe, Braxton hadn't even tried to change her mind. He'd just said Elliott would understand, and Martin could even have first pick for which Ruiz sister he escorted down the aisle.

Chloe had corrected him on that right away, of course. There was no question Celi would be Maid of Honor, so Martin was stuck with her. To be honest, he was glad to have a lesbian for his escort. He'd had friends who ended up romantically entangled with their bridal party partner. Since Martin and Celi were both gay, that wouldn't be a problem.

For anyone except Elliott Blake, at least.

Martin hadn't got Blake figured out. He had dark brown wavy hair, light brown skin, freckles scattered across his nose—and a serious chip on his shoulder when it came to Martin. It had gotten to the point where Martin was almost ready to surrender the role of Best Man, but that was when Chloe dug in her heels, and no one did stubborn better than Chloe Cole.

Had someone told Elliott that Martin was gay? Maybe Elliott had just figured it out. Martin cast his thoughts back, trying to remember any interactions where he might not have been macho enough. After a moment he snorted, shaking his head at himself. *Way to exhibit your own internalized homophobia, asshole*, he told himself. He would never call his sister a bitch, he disapproved of slut-shaming, and he knew better than anyone that women weren't more emotional than men—but as soon as he worried about someone figuring out he was gay, he automatically started scrutinizing himself for overly feminine behaviors.

"Ugh. Tonight is supposed to be about cutting loose, and here you are overanalyzing again," he said. He shoved the whole issue to the back of his mind. It would suck if Braxton's best friend was a homophobe, but it happened. Martin had dealt with it before. He could deal with it again.

He heard the hotel room door open. "Dude. You ready yet?" Jake Ruiz, Chloe's partner-in-copdom, stuck his head around the corner. "Blake's about to start climbing the walls, and Braxton's starting to tell everyone he doesn't even want a bachelor party."

"What's the point of a bachelor party?" Martin said, making a face. Martin had teased Chloe for years about how she needed to find a hot partner instead of Jake, but he liked Jake. When Chloe had almost been—

scratch that, when Chloe *had* been…temporarily—killed in the line of duty last year, Jake had been there for her every step of the way. Even when shit got weird and she started seeing ghosts, Jake'd had her back. Martin had serious respect for Jake.

"I honestly have no clue. Not like wedding vows suddenly stop a guy from making stupid decisions and getting drunk off his ass." Jake grinned at Martin. "Though I gotta say, Braxton Wolfe doesn't show any signs of having a wild side."

"Dude," Martin said, looking at Jake in disbelief. "Werewolf."

Jake snorted. "Fine, fine. But that's the only sign this guy knows how to have fun."

Martin rolled his eyes and followed Jake out of the hotel room, ready for a night of…well, probably drinking by himself while he watched Elliott and Jake hit on pretty girls and Braxton wonder what he was supposed to do with himself.

Of course, he'd forgotten about Murphy O'Hare.

* * *

"Yeah? Fuck you, too!" Murphy shouted at the bouncer who had just thrown him out. He was probably the scrawniest grown man Elliott Blake knew, and he had the Napoleon complex to match. Murphy shrugged, settling his shirt back around his shoulders, and huffed.

"You could totally take him," Elliott said, smirking. He'd been dancing with a curvy redhead when Murphy's shouting caught his attention, but he wasn't that into her; it was mostly because he wanted to avoid Martin Cole.

It wasn't that Elliott had anything against Martin…exactly. It was more that he couldn't get a read on him. Elliott's best friend was marrying Martin's sister, and the guy was so closed off Elliott couldn't even figure out if he liked anything except muscle cars. Well, and his sister, apparently.

Martin Cole had decided Braxton was good enough to marry his sister, and Braxton was entirely head over paws in love with Chloe, so Elliott had to make the best of it. Not that it was a bad thing, really. Chloe Cole was a good cop, tough, strong, smart, and pretty. Elliott had known her years longer than Braxton had, since they worked together at the Indianapolis Metropolitan Police Department, but he'd never thought about introducing them. As soon as they met, though, as soon as he'd realized Braxton and Chloe's paths had crossed, Elliott had known they were right for each other.

"Mark my words, young Padawan," Elliott told Murphy about six months ago. "It's a thing." A romantic thing, he'd meant. An attraction thing. He hadn't been thinking in terms of lifetimes, because he hadn't known the identity of the girl Brax was so hung up on. But he'd known it was a thing. And he'd been right.

No matter how shit he was at finding someone to share his own life, Elliott had picking out his friends' life-partners down to an art.

At the time, he hadn't known Chloe's identity, let alone the fact that she had a reticent, broodily-handsome younger brother.

A ginger, no less.

Elliott was a sucker for gingers.

Learning Chloe was Braxton's secret crush had only sealed his conviction that this time it was for real—Braxton had found the one woman who could both keep up with him and put up with all his foibles. It hadn't been until Elliott found out Martin Cole expected to be Best Man in the wedding that he'd gone ballistic.

He was dragged back to the present—a dimly-lit alley in Broad Ripple, bass thumping from the club they'd just been thrown out of—when Murphy huffed.

"I don't see what his problem was. I wasn't doing anything."

"You picked a fight with the damn bartender," Martin Cole said. He almost sounded amused, which was more emotion than Elliott had seen out of the guy since Christmas, when Chloe and Braxton had announced in front of all of them that they were getting married.

Seriously, had this guy slept in the day they were handing out personalities?

"Oh, bite me," Murphy said, his tone casually hostile. "I just told the guy he'd barely splashed whiskey into that shot glass."

"It was almost full," Martin replied.

"Half full at best." Murphy was already walking down the street. He didn't sound particularly bothered by Martin's contradicting him. Elliott tried not to be offended, but usually he was the only person who was allowed to bicker with Murphy. What did Martin Cole have that made Murphy willing to bicker with him?

"If you didn't have the metabolism of the Incredible Hulk, that glass would have been totally full," Martin said, and Elliott suddenly realized what he had in common with Murphy, of all people.

Comic book nerd.

Okay, that he could at least understand and quantify. That meant it was something Martin and Murphy could talk about in a secret nerd language—one that Elliott didn't share, because Elliott was too busy being a damn good homicide detective and sleeping with all the wrong people.

Of course, when he put it that way, viewed in the light of a few more shots than he probably should have consumed, it didn't exactly sound like a ringing endorsement.

He ran a hand through his hair, trying to tame it. His African-American father had bequeathed Elliott dark, barely-manageable curls; his white mother had given him freckles. Elliott knew, objectively, that he was good-looking. He never had trouble hooking up for a night or two; it was hanging on to a romantic partner he'd had trouble with.

Braxton came out of the club, followed closely by Jake Ruiz, who sounded like he was apologizing for Murphy. Braxton looked half amused and half embarrassed. Elliott managed, somehow, to keep from rolling his eyes. Chloe's partner was generally a good guy. Elliott didn't have anything against him or anything. But somehow Jake had fallen into the goody-two-shoes role demanded in the wedding party. It wasn't like they even needed a damn goody-two-shoes for this particular groom-to-be. Braxton was just about as square as an alpha werewolf could possibly be.

Braxton Wolfe didn't have ego issues, didn't smoke, kept in touch with his mom, and had—for the most part—coped in a healthy manner with the death of his father last year. Sure, he might have a few lingering doubts about his own fitness to be the alpha werewolf—*oh, fine, pack leader*, Elliott amended in an intentionally snarky inner monologue—of the Eagle Creek Pack. But he was also the kind of guy who had a healthy amount of self-confidence, respected women, wasn't bigoted, and liked cats.

Essentially, Elliott's best friend was the perfect guy. The guy Elliott often wished he could be. The guy whose standards Elliott consistently failed to live up to.

Oh yeah, he thought. *That's why I was planning to drink my weight in whiskey tonight. I can't even be jealous that he's found his life-mate before me, because he's actually got his shit together.*

Yeah, this was really going to be a great bachelor party.

* * *

Martin stretched a hand out to touch the wall of their third club of the evening—just to make sure he kept his balance—and glared at Murphy. "Are you *trying* to get me murdered by my sister? She hangs out with a homicide cop. Pretty sure she could get away with it."

Murphy snickered. "The look on your face," he said, and took a long swig of his beer.

"I don't have your—constitution or whatever," Martin snapped. "Drunk is one thing, but if I get completely bombed and spend my sister's wedding hungover, she'll hang me out to dry."

"He's got a point, Murph," Braxton said. "Chloe's scary when she's pissed off."

Murphy rolled his eyes. "Lighten up. It's a bachelor party. Someone's supposed to get drunk."

Braxton turned his head to look over Martin's shoulder. "I think Ell's starring in that role tonight." Martin frowned and turned to look, not liking the concern in Braxton's voice.

What struck him first wasn't how drunk Elliott looked—it was that Elliott had his arm looped low around some guy's waist as they swayed a lot more slowly than the music demanded. Martin's stomach jolted oddly and he took a sip of his drink to hide his reaction.

Then his mouth caught fire and he coughed, remembering too late that Murphy had apparently put poison—or possibly just 150-proof vodka—in his drink. Murphy started snickering again and Jake slapped Martin on the back. Martin could feel his face getting hot as Jake fussed and Braxton fixed Martin with a long, understanding look. Shit.

"I'd better go make sure Ell doesn't make an ass of

himself," Braxton said as Martin caught his breath. "Why don't you guys head outside. We'll meet you all on the sidewalk out front."

Murphy snorted. "Remind him what happened last time he got back together with an ex."

Braxton shot a hard look at Murphy and walked away without answering.

Murphy chugged his beer and set the empty bottle on a nearby table. "You heard the boss. Down that shot like a man, Cole, and let's get out of here."

Martin glared at Murphy and did the shot. Then the three of them threaded their way between gyrating bodies to get to the sidewalk.

Outside it was probably in the low seventies, but it felt chilly compared to the sweaty humidity of the club. "We should have just stayed at my place," Martin said. "We could walk there from here."

"Or we could just get a cab and be delivered right to our hotel," Jake said, stepping to the curb to flag one down.

Martin rubbed a hand over his face and sucked in a couple of deep breaths, letting the cooler air clear his head a little. When he looked over at Murphy, the punk had a calculating look on his face.

"What?"

Murphy shrugged. "Nothing. You're pretty okay, Cole. I mean, if your sister tries to kill you, I'm totally not getting in the way. She'd mangle me. But you're pretty okay. For a DC fan."

Martin laughed and scratched a hand through his hair. "Thanks for that ringing endorsement."

"Didn't know Ell was into guys, huh?"

The way Murphy blurted it out, so matter of fact, meant it took Martin a moment to catch up. "Uh. Hadn't really given it any thought either way." *Lie.* "It's nice to know werewolves aren't bigots or anything, though."

Murphy smirked at him and turned away.

*　*　*

Elliott lifted his glass of champagne and looked around at the assembled guests. Lots of cops—this was possibly the safest wedding in the city today. Not nearly as many werewolves, but still a fair few. Braxton's position as leader of the Eagle Creek Pack, one of the two packs in the city, had meant it was politic to invite the Fort Harrison Pack as well. He saw Peggy, the leader of the Fort Harrison Pack, chatting with Martin Cole, and wondered if the guy knew he was talking to a werewolf.

He hadn't liked that Braxton told Martin about the pack, though he'd been unable to argue reasonably against it. Chloe and her brother were close, no question, and being married to a werewolf...well, some human spouses chose to be bitten and turned. Some didn't, and Chloe was still adjusting to seeing ghosts, so she might not be looking for any extra supernatural in her life. But if she did, Martin would definitely notice the change in her.

Someone jostled his elbow and he realized everyone had gone silent, watching him. Martin had done his toast earlier, but Chloe had asked Elliott to make one, too. She seemed to be in earnest when she asked, and he took her seriously enough to at least make a bullet-point list of things he ought to say. And now everyone was looking at him, waiting for him to dredge that list out of a hungover brain.

Elliott smiled. He felt charming when he smiled. Feeling charming would help him remember. He lifted his glass a little higher.

"I grew up with Braxton. Met him when we were toddlers, and bonded instantly." He paused. "Well. After he knocked me down a couple times for teasing him about being so short." He paused for laughter and his audience obliged. "We played baseball together, always striving to out-hit each other. Went on double dates together, competed for the attention of plenty of girls." He grinned. "But nothing's ever been more important than our friendship."

He looked over at Chloe, who looked gorgeous and surprisingly feminine in a simple sleeveless wedding dress. She was smiling at him, her gaze eager for whatever he would say next. Elliott gave her a smile just for her.

"I've known Cole—uh, Chloe—there for a handful of years. Not as long as I've known Braxton, but longer than Braxton's known her." He tilted his head. "We work together, and to be honest, there's always been a little bit of a friendly rivalry going on there. But Chloe's good people. She's a good cop. And I have every confidence that she'll be a good wife."

She made a face at him, but he could see the tears

glistening in her eyes. She wouldn't like it that he was getting soppy, but she'd have to deal with it. It wasn't a real wedding unless everyone cried at least once, right?

"I found out Braxton was head over heels for Chloe right smack in the middle of a case. It was one that overlapped from my job to his, and Chloe was consulting. You could have knocked me over with a feather. But as soon as Brax asked me if I knew Chloe well, I had this…this sense of…I dunno, fate, I guess." Elliott fumbled, recovered, and gave Chloe a rueful smile. "Sorry, Cole, but I knew right then there was no hope for you."

She laughed along with the rest of the guests. Braxton reached over and took her hand, and Elliott swallowed against a sudden tightness in his throat.

God, he wanted that. That certainty they had. That…that comfort.

"So, like any good best friend," he said, tearing his gaze away from the happy couple and scanning the crowd, "I started teasing Brax about it every chance I got."

Another pause for laughter. He'd originally had a couple more bullet points, but he had the audience where he wanted them, so there was no point in prolonging the toast. He shook his head and lifted his glass. "So tonight, I'd like to officially say, 'I told you so.' And I'd also like to ask everyone to join me in drinking a toast to the finest couple I have the good fortune to know. Chloe and Braxton."

"Chloe and Braxton," everyone echoed, and

drank, and the wedding singer started crooning a cover of the Muse remake of Frankie Valli's "Too Good to be True."

When he sat down, his hands were shaking. Elliott let out an explosive breath. It was stupid. He wasn't even nervous anymore, the toast was over. It had gone off just right. Why did his stupid hands start shaking now?

"It was a good toast," said a low voice to his right.

Elliott sucked in a breath and glanced over at Martin Cole. "Thanks," he said briefly.

"Better than mine," Martin went on. "You've got a way with words."

Elliott swallowed, wondering why Martin was trying to make peace now. Then he considered the fact that they were going to have to live with each other, since their best friends—their siblings, really, even if it was in two different ways—were married to each other. He nodded. "Your toast was good."

Lame, Blake. Seriously lame.

But Martin's lips twitched in a small smile. "Murphy said you're a fan of the Iron Man movies."

Elliott raised his eyebrows, suddenly skeptical. He did like the Iron Man movies, but Murphy had always given him shit for that, saying that the second movie didn't even deserve to get made. "Yeah."

Martin shrugged. "I like them, too. Stupid, maybe, but I've always had a thing for Tony Stark."

Elliott's world shifted just a little. He blinked at Martin, who nodded slightly and wandered off, as if he were oblivious to the bomb he'd just dropped. As

Elliott thought about it, he couldn't really imagine any cooler way of coming out to someone.

The music crashed to a halt. "Hey, we're going to take a quick break, and then we'll be back for another set, so get your dancing shoes on. I'm Lachlan Shaw, and we're Knot Tide."

Elliott went looking for another glass of champagne.

CHAPTER 2

Lachlan Shaw placed his guitar carefully in its case and started latching it closed. Another wedding, better than some of the others, since they'd given him a great list of songs they liked. But it wasn't like he really wanted to be a wedding singer. Knot Tide was a dumb band with a dumb name, and he only liked half of his bandmates—but it brought in some extra money, which meant he didn't have to work overtime delivering pizzas.

His keyboard player, Julie, flipped her long hair over her shoulder. "Hey, Lach, you going out after this? We're thinking about getting burgers or something."

He checked the time and winced. "Can't. Got plans with my sister. You know Ainsley; she's probably already parked at my apartment and tapping her nails."

Julie laughed. "Yeah. It's too bad she won't sing with us, now that she's back. She's got a good voice."

"Yours is better," Lachlan lied. "Anyway, she'd run practice like a drill sergeant, we'd mutiny, and someone would end up dead."

"Point." Julie smirked at him. "I know she's a pain, but you're lucky she came home at all. Lots of people didn't."

Lachlan shrugged. Somehow, as scary as it had been when Ainsley was in a war zone, it had been easier. She wasn't there every day for his mom and dad to compare his life to hers all the time. "See you at practice," he said, and headed for his car.

Ainsley *was* already at the apartment when he got there. Thank God he'd 'forgotten' to give her a key; he could only imagine her going through his stuff while she waited. Or worse, tidying up.

"I thought you said the reception was over at nine." Ainsley was leaning her lithe body against the wall next to his door, her arms folded across her chest. She looked more bored than annoyed, so Lachlan fished out his keys to unlock the door.

"It *was* over at nine. And then I had to tear down, look around for the dude who had the check, and drive out here from downtown. You know what traffic's like downtown on a Saturday night."

"Whatever." Ainsley followed him into the apartment. When he carried his guitar case into the living room, she headed for the galley kitchen.

"Help yourself," Lachlan muttered, knowing she would.

The refrigerator door closed with a slam and Ainsley came back from the kitchen to the main room of her brother's tiny apartment. He heard a can of beer *kshff* open but didn't look up from where he was settling his guitar on its stand. Lachlan shrugged out of his slightly oversized suit jacket and started rolling up his sleeves.

She exhaled and then snorted. "Really? Another tattoo?"

"Bite me, Ains."

He'd almost finished the full sleeve on his left arm, and he knew it looked good. It definitely fit the heroin-chic look he was going for. He was too skinny and lanky for anything else, so he'd decided to embrace it. Between that, the tricycle accident scar along his jaw, and the black clothes and eyeliner he affected most of the time, he was cultivating a good image for who he wanted to be.

He sat down at his computer and started working on uploading one of his music videos.

She dropped onto the broken-down couch with a loud sigh. "You know it drives Mom and Dad crazy when you blow your money on tattoos."

"It's my money," he said. "And since I'm not the one who moved back into their old bedroom, I don't think you have any room to be criticizing."

He did glance up then, just to see the flush he knew would be spreading across her cheeks. She and Lachlan shared the pale complexion, but she was a natural redhead like their mother, so she blushed a lot easier than Lachlan. Their green eyes matched, but that was just about the only thing they had in common.

Green eyes...and the music.

"That isn't fair," Ainsley said, her tone defensive. Lachlan knew without looking that she would be hunching in on herself. With just about everyone else, Ainsley was the picture of a tall, confident young veteran. With Lachlan, she reverted to the priggish older sister role—the one who was just waiting for something she could go tattle to their parents. "You know I only let my apartment go because I wasn't sure how long my deployment would last."

Lachlan had liked her better before Afghanistan, when at least he knew everyone saw the same person. He shrugged. He didn't really care. He was just glad to have one thing he could hold over Ainsley's head, since usually it was the other way around. "I'm just saying, at least I pay rent and shit."

"I'm going to move out as soon as my discharge papers are processed," she snapped. "I've already had two job interviews—with real engineering firms, too, by the way, not delivering pizzas."

Lachlan didn't mind delivering pizza. What mattered was the music.

"At least I didn't sell out," he replied, still tapping keywords into the video description.

"Ugh. Why did I even come over here?" She gulped her beer loudly. Lachlan knew he was supposed to look over and tell her how glad he was that she'd come home okay.

He didn't.

"You could at least come over for Sunday dinner," she said.

"I can't help it if work started scheduling me for Sundays." He'd had Sunday dinner with their parents every week that Ainsley was deployed. It was just the last two Sundays that he'd begged off. Never mind the fact that Lachlan was the one who went out and got a job and moved off to be a grown up; the minute

Ainsley came back, she was the only person their parents could see.

Ainsley blew out a sigh and he heard the couch creak as she leaned back. When he sneaked a glance from the corner of his eyes, he could see she was rubbing her forehead, eyes closed. His throat twinged with guilt, but he pushed it aside.

With a few more keystrokes, he uploaded his video.

He'd worked hard on this one, recording the harmonies and the guitar line and the percussion all himself. He could have done it with the band, but he was trying to build his own brand, and he wanted that to encompass the band without relying on it. He wanted the brand to be Lachlan Shaw, regardless of who else he might be working with. It had worked for Trent Reznor, after all.

"Listen, could we just start over?" Ainsley said quietly.

Lachlan swiveled his task chair so he could look at her. "Sure, if you want to start with something that isn't ragging on my tats," he said.

Ainsley bit her lower lip, watching him. She was wearing shorts that emphasized the muscles of her legs. She was shorter than Lachlan, and a heck of a lot more fit than he was. *Just another thing she does better than you do,* Lachlan thought to himself, but he shoved it aside.

"What?" he said finally, knowing it sounded grudging.

"I, uh..." Her cheeks were burning red. She bit her

lip again and looked down.

Lachlan frowned. He couldn't tell if she were faking or not. She looked more uncertain than he'd ever seen her. He watched her for a couple of seconds, then said, "What's going on, Ains?"

She sighed. "I think I'm pregnant."

Lachlan stared at her for several heartbeats before that sank in. He darted a glance at her "beer" can—and realized she was drinking Mountain Dew. His last Mountain Dew, he was pretty sure, and he didn't think pregnant ladies were supposed to have caffeine either, but even he knew he shouldn't point that out just now. Then he frowned. For the last year her emails had been full of stuff about a girl named Kaida. Had they broken up without his hearing about it?

"How?" he blurted. Then he felt his face get hot. "That's not—I mean, I thought you were with a girl."

"I am," Ainsley snapped. She glared at him. "I just...you know, we were all back Stateside and we were in New York City for a night before flying home. We went out for a couple of drinks, and one thing turned into another, and..." She looked down at the floor. "I don't want it. I'm only twenty-seven, for God's sake. I'm not ready to be a mom. And Kaida isn't...I mean, we haven't even talked about that, not yet."

"So get rid of it," Lachlan said, shrugging. "Problem solved."

"Problem—" Ainsley glared at him. "I can't murder my baby!"

"It isn't even a baby yet," Lachlan said. "It's, like, a bunch of cells that make you puke and keep you from being able to drink."

Ainsley rolled her eyes. "Only you could be so crass."

"Pretty sure plenty of people besides me are even crasser," he said. "Fine, so...I mean, why did you even tell me that, Ains? What am I supposed to do?"

"I don't know! Make me feel better?"

Lachlan sighed. He'd already tried giving her advice and trying to make her laugh. Neither had worked. What was he supposed to do to make her feel better? "You're only telling me because Kaida would dump you if she found out."

Ainsley punched him in the shoulder. "That is *not* making me feel better."

"Ow!" He rubbed his shoulder, scowling at her. "Okay, fine." He pursed his lips, then took his guitar off its stand. "I started writing a new song two days ago," he said.

It wasn't very good yet, but he automatically hit the record on his phone before he started picking out some of the notes of the intro.

Picked out like that, the song had a wistful sound, which wasn't what he'd been going for, but he knew she would like it. He felt his way through the intro and led into the first verse.

He didn't have any words yet. He had two methods of writing a song, and if the music came first, he had to get the whole melody worked out before he knew what the song wanted to be. If the lyrics came first, he could usually come up with a hook to go with them, and that made the whole song-writing process faster, but the end product felt less organic to him.

Lachlan crooned wordlessly along with his guitar. When he had the melody down, he closed his eyes, waiting for Ainsley to join in. She would eventually. She always did. Before she was sent to Afghanistan, before she decided to be an engineer, before she signed her ROTC papers even, this was how they'd spent their free time. They'd hung out together in the basement, Lachlan writing the music while Ainsley wrote the lyrics.

That had been a long time ago. Sometimes Lachlan thought it was a whole different life ago.

"This is not the life I wanted..." Ainsley's voice came in thin, tentative. "Not the life I planned... Either I wind up haunted, or I cross that line in the sand..."

Lachlan opened one eye. It wasn't up to her usual caliber, but they *were* out of practice. His sister's eyes were closed, too, tears glistening on her cheeks. She didn't look like the war vet. She didn't even look like his priggish older sister. She looked...

"Broken," Lachlan sang across her vocals. She opened her eyes, startled, but kept on with her words of a life unplanned as Lachlan started strumming. "Out of place," he added. "Lost in the woods, lost without a face."

He felt the old rush building as they continued to sing, Lachlan creating a raw counterpuntal melody against Ainsley's more traditional lament. He used his voice like he usually used his electric guitar, and he felt the hair on his arms stand up as they built to a climax. Just as they finished, Lachlan's finger slipped, introducing a discordant note that jangled.

Ainsley broke off, laughing awkwardly. "Oof. We haven't done that in so long. You can tell we're out of practice." Her voice was stronger, and the big sister note had crept back in.

Lachlan shrugged. "It wasn't that bad."

"It wasn't that good, either." Ainsley straightened. "You did cheer me up, though. I still don't know what to do, but at least now I believe I'll figure it out. Thanks, Lach." She stood and leaned over to kiss his forehead. "You know, if you'd applied yourself, you probably could have studied music at Butler. You'd be really talented if you were trained."

She favored him with another smile, but she turned away too soon to see Lachlan recoil as a pang of hurt went through him. Ainsley walked over to the apartment door. "Come to dinner next week, doof. Don't make us order a pizza just to see you."

Lachlan hugged his guitar, grunting something that she would hopefully take as assent. Apparently it sufficed, because she left, shutting the apartment door behind her.

How could she be so casually cruel? Hadn't she felt the rush like he had? Hadn't she missed this? They'd been such a good team before. Lachlan hunched over the guitar as he realized he'd secretly been hoping she had watched his videos while she was overseas, that she'd been impressed by his following and how much he'd progressed.

He'd been hoping she would want to make music with him.

24

Squeezing his eyes against an embarrassing rush of hot tears, Lachlan straightened and strummed his fingers hard down the strings, playing as angry and hostile a sound as an acoustic six-string could produce. For just a moment, he wished Ainsley hadn't come back from the war.

"I've been making music without you," he whispered to his sister. "I'll keep making music without you."

CHAPTER 3

Martin had been standing in front of the refrigerator for five minutes.

He had leftover pasta from last night's dinner, or the weather was nice enough that he could grill a burger, but he sighed and shut the fridge. A loud meow informed him that he'd actually meant to get something for Whizz to eat.

"Chloe says you aren't allowed table scraps," he told the cat, who looked directly at him and meowed again.

Martin leaned down to rub the cat's ears. "You big liar. Fake mews, that's you. All right, if you don't tell her, I won't." He opened a can of chicken out of the pantry and dished it out onto a saucer.

He had pretended to be annoyed that he had to take care of Chloe's cat Whizz during the honeymoon, but after three days of waking up with the huge orange cat plastered to the small of his back, he knew he was going to have to admit he liked the little stinker. Whizz was built like a mountain lion, powerful muscles and huge paws, but he was a gentle giant. He liked scratches under the chin and leaning against whatever human he was gracing with his presence. Martin found he'd been sleeping better with a purring cat tucked against his ear.

In Chloe's absence, Martin also began to realize just how isolated he'd grown. He worked long hours keeping the garage open and he spent a couple evenings a week with his big sister, and he'd mostly lost touch with the rest of his friends. His pre-military friends had gone to college, gotten married, and mostly moved away from Indianapolis. Some of his Army buddies were still in, some of them had come home to families, and a couple of the best ones had never made it back from Kandahar.

Whizz's earth-shattering purr filled Martin's ears as he stood up and opened the refrigerator again. Nothing in there looked appealing, not even the pint cans of Sun King Cream Ale. He wanted a drink, no question, but he was tired of waking up with a tacky mouth and nagging headache.

"You don't mind if I go out for a while, do you?" he asked Whizz. "Geez. I'm losing it, talking to a cat."

Whizz looked up at him and meowed, making Martin laugh.

"All right. You behave yourself and don't get on the kitchen counter," he ordered. He pulled his phone out of his pocket and dialed Jake Ruiz's number.

"Yo."

"Hey, it's Martin. Wondered if you want to grab a pizza somewhere."

There was a brief pause and Martin wondered suddenly if he'd ever called Jake to hang out without Chloe being along. Then Jake said, "Sure. I gotta finish up a couple of things."

"You still at work, man?" Martin said. He glanced at the clock—seven-fifteen.

"Somebody's working without a partner this week, remember? Gotta pick up the slack for some silly chick who decided to get married."

Martin snorted. "You downtown?"

"Yeah."

"How about I meet you at Bazbeaux in half an hour? There's nothing going on downtown tonight, right?"

Jake hummed thoughtfully for a second. "Indians game, but they've already started, so the traffic won't be bad. Sounds good, as long as you don't make me put nothing weird on my pizza."

"No arugula or anchovies, I swear," Martin said.

Jake laughed and hung up.

Feeling as if he'd taken a positive step, Martin went to make sure he looked presentable, then grabbed his keys from the kitchen counter. Whizz watched him go with round golden eyes.

Bazbeaux Pizza had three locations, one of them just a couple of blocks from Martin's house, but the downtown location was closer to where Jake worked, and Martin liked driving. The Broad Ripple location had been the first, in a ramshackle house that had belonged to the local gravedigger. Martin and his sister had a running argument about whether Bazbeaux or Jockamo's pizza was the best. Martin liked both, but Bazbeaux was his favorite. Chloe favored Jockamo's.

Martin headed south along College Avenue towards downtown. The traffic wasn't heavy at that hour, so he made the drive in about twenty minutes. It took him another ten minutes to find a parking space, but he'd already given his name to the hostess when Jake Ruiz came walking in. He looked tired, but he smiled at Martin.

"I'm going to tell Chloe you missed her while she was gone."

"Lies. You're no substitute for my sister."

Jake clutched at his chest in mock hurt and Martin shook his head, chuckling.

"I've been craving a Chilope since you called," Jake said.

"Never had it. What's on it?"

"Black bean dip, salsa, green pepper, cilantro..." Jake trailed off, his forehead wrinkling as he thought.

"Why not? What's life without a little adventure?" Martin shrugged. "I like all that stuff by itself."

Jake stared at him. "Seriously? My sisters won't let me order that when we eat here. They say it isn't a proper pizza without pepperoni and shit."

Martin shrugged again. "I like to live dangerously."

Jake snorted, but when the waitress came to take their order, they got the Chilope.

They spent the next hour talking about cars and politics. Jake's sister Celia had been helping organize political marches since January, and Jake apparently had mixed feelings about it. As a police officer, he was concerned about the public safety issues involved, despite his sympathy for the causes. It wasn't a comfortable time to be a member of a minority, especially in a red state.

"Tell me about it," Martin said. "One guy I know? His sister's transgender and she tried to kill herself a couple of days after the election. Scared about how bad things might get."

"That sucks." Jake scowled at his beer. "Thank God Celi knows we've got her back, you know? But it's a double whammy, being Latina *and* a lesbian. She's been drinking more since November, and she flies off the handle at the least thing. Me and Lucy, we're just trying to keep things normal as possible at home, so she's got a safe space. Thank God she decided to put off moving out."

Martin nodded. "Good for you guys. If I can help, you know..."

"Like you ain't got your own shit to worry about." Jake was smiling, though. "Thanks, man."

Martin took a long sip of his beer and exhaled. "Is it weird that it's both worse than I expected and somehow better? I mean, the racial tension and the polarized speech and the damn travel bans and shit...that's all as bad as I thought it would be and more. But at the same time, I keep seeing these signs pop up all over, printed in three languages about welcoming our neighbors whether they're immigrants or Muslims or whatever."

"It's like the good folks out there are so horrified that they're being louder about loving people, I guess," Jake said. "Our church has been talking about what to do about ICE raids and stuff. I don't know how many undocumented we have, and I don't want to know, but I've tried to make everyone know my job is about protecting and serving, not deporting."

Martin nodded. "Good for you," he said. "People like you give me hope that we're not all going to hell in a handbasket."

The waitress stopped by the table, a smile on her face. "You guys need refills?"

Jake checked his watch. "I probably ought to head out, actually."

Martin nodded. "Yeah, just the bill, I think. Thanks."

As he drove back to Broad Ripple, thinking of an affectionate yellow cat waiting for him and the pleasant meal he'd just spent, Martin felt like maybe there was more hope for the world than he'd thought.

* * *

The June Full moon was at nine in the morning, which ruled out letting the pack run through Eagle Creek Park. Braxton's house was larger than Elliott's, and Elliott had a key so he could feed Fuzzy anyway, so he'd invited the rest of the Eagle Creek Pack over to Braxton's. Tara had declined to join them, but Maura had agreed to swing by Ximena's apartment to make sure she joined them. Since her cousin's death several months earlier, Ximena had been withdrawn, only joining the pack occasionally. Elliott was determined to take good care of her in Braxton's absence.

Murphy was the first to slouch in. He bumped Elliott's shoulder in a semi-affectionate way on his path to the basement.

"Sup." Elliott yawned. He'd stayed up too late the night before reading.

Murphy shrugged. "Life sucks and our president is a Dumpster fire."

Elliott tipped his head. "Can't argue the second part, but why does life suck?"

"'Cause that's what life does." Murphy slanted a look at him and thumped down the steps.

Elliott shook his head. Murphy had a chip on his shoulder, and Elliott was used to it, but he kept hoping things would get better. Somehow he had the feeling Murphy'd had a chip on his shoulder even before he was turned—violently and against his will. Being assaulted and having his whole life shaken up couldn't help.

The doorbell rang. Amiable and stocky, Theo Smith was Murphy's complete opposite both physically and personality-wise. He grinned at Elliott as he came inside. "Feels weird knowing Brax isn't here," he said, already tugging his shirt over his head.

"Tell me about it." Full moon *days* were always a little odd, in Elliott's opinion. The full moon was the only time a werewolf couldn't control the change. It didn't matter whether it was the middle of the day or not—the moment it hit full, the change would begin. Most Day Fulls the pack stayed in their own homes, curled up and carefully quiet. But with Braxton away, Elliott had somehow thought it was better to have everyone together.

A series of brisk knocks announced Maura Schroeder's arrival. A stately British woman, she had one hand wrapped around a thin, brown wrist, which was attached to an exhausted-looking Latina woman.

"Ximena," Elliott said, smiling at her. "Good to see you."

She gave him a wan smile, but her dark eyes were dull. "Hi, Elliott."

"I thought we'd pass the Full in the basement," he told the women. "Murphy and Theo are already down there."

As he followed the two women downstairs, Elliott thought how strange it was to think that almost everyone was here. The Eagle Creek Pack had had a rough year. It had been about a year since Braxton's father—their previous leader—had been killed. Six months after that, Estella—the pack doctor—had been killed in a fight with a necromancer and mage. Elliott and Maura had both been badly enough hurt in the fight that they'd had to spend several days healing, though they'd ultimately recovered.

Still, the pack felt fragile in a way it hadn't just a couple of years ago.

We'll make it, Elliott told himself. *Braxton's got a mate now. She might choose to be turned, and even if she doesn't, their kids will be wolves. And maybe one of the girls will move back home...eventually.*

His sisters were both werewolves, but Olivia had relocated to Fort Wayne for her job and Emily was doing graduate public health work in Louisville,

Kentucky. Elliott kept hoping they'd come back to Indianapolis, if for no other reason than they were the only blood family he had left. So far, Em sounded like she might come back, but O seemed fully invested in Fort Wayne life.

Elliott shook himself and looked around. The pack was watching him.

"Thanks for coming over," he said. Maura smiled warmly at him and Theo nodded. Murphy stuck his middle finger in the air, but he was smirking faintly, so the finger was just for show. The acknowledgment made Elliott feel better. They were a pack. Family. They'd be okay.

He felt his skin begin to twitch. "Soon," he said, and jerked his t-shirt off. Murphy whistled and then ducked, snickering, as Elliott hurled the shirt at him.

The moon reached full.

CHAPTER 4

It started out like it usually did, everything normal, just another convoy. Martin's mouth was dry from the heat and nerves, even though he went outside the wire often enough that he shouldn't be scared, just alert. But something felt wrong, and Dax was teasing him for being twitchy. The area had been quiet, after all.

Then time jumped forward, the way it did in dreams, and the air was screaming around them. No, people were screaming around him. No, the flames squealed as the truck burned.

Dax's arm was lying in the dirt about eight feet in front of Martin. Dax was lying six feet in the other direction.

Martin was gasping for breath, trying to push himself up to go to Dax, fashion a tourniquet, stop the bleeding. He scrabbled across the rocky ground, gagging at the taste of bloody mud in his mouth.

Dax gasped at him to get down.

Martin swore at him.

Then there was a shadowy figure standing just a few feet in front of them, completely motionless, shrouded in black. It was obviously watching them from beneath its dark hood. Martin knew it was laughing at him.

"Cole! Cole, get down!"

But Martin couldn't look away from that shadow. He thought he could see, deep beneath that hood, the glow of green eyes. He was too slow to react as it moved. Claws—no, blades—flashed out at him, ripping open his throat. He tried to scream—

Martin jerked awake, breathing hard. He sat up and stared around the living room. He'd fallen asleep in his recliner, the television flickering with the early news. Cold sweat trickled down his chest.

"You're home," he whispered to himself between breaths. "Winthrop Avenue. Broad Ripple. Indianapolis. Indiana. United States of America." His pulse was slowing as he consciously deepened his breathing. "Not Kandahar. Not Afghanistan. Indiana. Cornfields. Race cars. You're good. Deep breaths. You made it. You're back."

He rubbed a hand over his face, feeling his fingers tremble against his forehead. That wasn't how the dream usually ended. There hadn't been any shadowy figure, in real life or in the other dreams. Most of them were a straight recounting of the day their convoy hit an IED. Why was his brain putting something new in it?

"Winthrop Avenue. Broad Ripple," he whispered, and then jolted upright as his mouth began watering. Shit. He knew what came next.

He barely made it to the bathroom in time to hit the toilet, tears pressing from beneath his clenched eyelids as he heaved.

When he was finished, he slumped back to sit on his heels, shivering. He dragged his bathrobe from its hook and huddled into it. Rubbing his closed eyelids, Martin whispered, "Most holy Apostle, Saint Jude, faithful servant and friend of Jesus, patron of difficult cases, of things almost despaired of, pray for me."

Sometimes the novena to Saint Jude succeeded in calming him when his home mantra didn't, but this wasn't going to be one of those times. Martin shuddered and climbed to his feet. He rinsed his mouth and spat, then washed his face. He met his gaze in the mirror, scrubbed his wet fingers through his short hair, and exhaled heavily.

He wanted a drink.

The cabinet under the sink, where he usually kept his liquor, was empty—he drank too much to escape the memories, but he couldn't drink it if he didn't have it. But a glance at his watch told him it was only ten-thirty. Plenty of bars would still be open, and Martin knew a couple that weren't usually overcrowded.

Ten minutes later Martin was walking north towards the Broad Ripple Tavern—only a block or so from the loud clubs, it was a laid-back local haunt in a building from the 1920s. The closer he got to Broad Ripple Avenue, the more people he saw. Broad Ripple's nightclubs were popular for dancing and drinking the night away, despite the village's eclectic day-time feel. The dark, humid, Indiana evening was about as far away as he could get from the dream of Kandahar, and that suited him just fine.

A handsome, dark-haired guy smiled as Martin passed him on the sidewalk. Martin smiled back absently, but he still had the shadow of his dream hanging over him. He hadn't come out for a drink to be *with* someone so much as just to not be alone. It was a distinction he'd never been able to explain to Chloe, but there were times he wanted to have people around who weren't interested in actually interacting with him.

Anyway, tonight he mostly wanted to have a couple of drinks that would make it easier to fall asleep—dreamlessly—when he went back home.

He found a small, two-person table that was unoccupied and took the seat with his back to the wall. He couldn't quite shake the memory of that strange shadow with glowing green eyes. He knew it was just a dream, but he didn't want to have his back to people.

He gulped the first whiskey, then ordered a second and swirled the glass slowly as he waited for the first one to take effect. He considered the five-block walk home and decided he could always get a taxi if he needed one.

* * *

The club was hot tonight. Elliott wiped sweat from his forehead and smirked at the guy he'd been dancing with. He had to lean in to make himself heard, and for just a moment he let himself relish the grip of possessive fingers at his hip. Then he shook his head.

"Gotta go," he told the guy. "See you 'round."

The guy frowned at him, but Elliott shook his head again and walked away, threading his way through tightly packed dancers. When he reached the edge of the dance floor, he took a deep breath and shook himself.

Usually he enjoyed losing himself in the thumping base and frenetic rhythms of Broad Ripple's club scene. The sound and smell of so many people packed in together dampened his werewolf senses, making his world smaller, drawing it in around him. But he wasn't feeling it tonight. In fact, he'd been out of sorts the whole week since the Full.

He went out to the sidewalk, thought about flagging down a cab, and decided to walk a while first.

He half wished he'd asked one of the other wolves to come with him. Murphy was usually working, but sometimes he came along, and even though Murphy was pretty heterosexual, he never minded dancing with Elliott. Theo was always up for a club night. Braxton wasn't a club guy at all, but he would come with Elliott if he asked, except he and Chloe weren't coming back until tomorrow. So Elliott was by himself, not really planning to hook up so much as dance away the odd melancholy that had settled around him lately.

Look how well that had worked.

Sneering at himself, Elliott shoved his hands in his pockets and wandered along Broad Ripple Avenue, glancing idly at the window displays of the closed shops. He probably shouldn't have come back to the Broad Ripple scene to lose the melancholy—after all, this was where they'd had Braxton's bachelor party. It made sense he'd start thinking about how everything was changing.

He didn't want to go home yet. It was a modern apartment, with minimalist white walls and a balcony that overlooked a busy street. He didn't have a pet or even any plants, and he was still trying to talk Murphy into moving into his spare room. He knew the rent was higher than what Murphy could afford, even splitting it fifty-fifty, but having a roommate would be worth undercharging Murphy. Then again, Murphy was so damn prickly about being poor—as if Elliott hadn't been there himself, fifteen years ago—that hell was likelier to freeze over than Murphy was to agree to take something he saw as charity.

Then again, the Cubs did win the Series last year, Elliott thought, smirking faintly.

On a whim, he ducked into the Broad Ripple Tavern, which looked way more laid back than the clubs. It seemed like the sort of place the locals might go, if they were brave—or foolhardy—enough to venture out on a weekend. It was early enough they might still have food available, and there was probably a game on. He paused just inside the door and glanced around. One area had a few pool tables, which were heavily populated at the moment. The other side of the bar had tables, most of them occupied. Just to the left of the door was a bar area that opened to the sidewalk. It was occupied by pretty girls wearing tight shorts and smiles, and Elliott looked away.

Then a shock of recognition went through him as his gaze met that of a pale, auburn-haired man drinking by himself at a table.

Martin Cole sat with his back to the wall, a glass of what looked like whiskey in his hand. His mouth was open just a little as he stared at Elliott. He clearly hadn't been expecting to see anyone he knew.

Before Elliott could think better of it, he crossed the room to stand by Martin's table.

"Mind if I join you?"

Martin's Adam's apple bobbed as he swallowed, but he just lifted his glass in a greeting.

Heart suddenly racing, Elliott tried on a smile, pulled the chair out, and sat.

He expected Martin to say something, but instead he took a long sip of whiskey, those icy blue eyes locked on Elliott's. Well, that wasn't awkward or anything. Elliott wet his lips, searching for something to say. He was usually better at this. Then again, he still hadn't figured Martin Cole out. Most people were easy to read. Not Martin Cole.

"Heard anything from your sister?" he settled on finally. It was a dumb question. What woman on her honeymoon bothered calling her brother? But Martin didn't laugh at him, at least.

"They're coming home tomorrow," Martin said. "I didn't think you lived around here."

"No, I'm up by the Fashion Mall. But the dancing's better here."

Martin's eyes crinkled nicely when he smiled. "I forgot how much you seemed to like dancing." His teeth were very straight. Elliott's stomach swooped oddly.

Oh, God help him, he wasn't getting a crush on Martin Cole, was he? That would be twenty kinds of awkward.

Elliott smiled back. "Sometimes it's nice to just lose yourself in the rhythm. Forget about everything else for a while."

Martin tilted his head. "Funny. That's not exactly something Chloe's ever been good at. Figured it was a cop thing."

"I have to consciously turn off the 'cop thing' to really enjoy it," Elliott admitted. "Doesn't happen often. I'm not a fan of losing control in public, and I definitely don't go dancing by myself often."

"But you did tonight." Martin took another long sip of his whiskey.

Elliott shrugged and glanced over his shoulder. "I'm going to grab a drink real fast. You need anything?"

Martin raised an eyebrow, and damned if Elliott could tell what he meant by that expression. But he really wished he could. "Another Maker's, rocks."

Elliott nodded and went to the bar, where he ordered two whiskeys and a plate of pub chips with horseradish dip. The girl asked if he wanted to open a tab, so he handed over his credit card. This was the perfect opportunity to learn more about Martin Cole.

By the time he returned to the table, Martin seemed to have settled some question with himself. He was relaxed against the back of his booth, making no secret of the way he was watching Elliott.

"So what made Detective Elliott Blake decide to go dancing by himself tonight?" he asked. "Bad day at work? Bad breakup? Bad year?"

Elliott was surprised into a laugh. "None of the above. Pure ennui, I guess."

Martin snorted. "Yeah, I bet homicide detectives deal with that a lot." He was clearly using his sarcastic voice.

"Maybe not at work, but some of us do wish we had real lives outside our jobs," Elliott said. "I dunno, I'm probably just feeling useless because neither of my sisters have called me to fix something recently, and Braxton clearly doesn't need me around anymore."

"Heh. I guess I know what you mean. Chloe drove me nuts when she was rooming with me after the fire, but now that she's gone, my house feels weirdly empty."

Elliott nodded and sipped his whiskey. "That what brought you out by yourself on a Friday night?" he asked.

He saw the tension creep back into Martin's shoulders, the way the crinkles at the corners of Martin's eyes faded along with his amusement. Elliott swore to himself. He kept misstepping with Martin somehow, and he wasn't even sure how—after all, Martin had essentially asked him the same thing! But to his surprise, Martin took a gulp of whiskey and answered him.

"I have bad dreams."

Elliott sat back in his chair, brows drawing together as he studied Martin. Now that he considered it, he could see a certain hypervigilance in how Martin carried himself and sat with his back to the wall. Braxton had said something once, hadn't he, about Martin's job? Mechanic, that was it. But how did a mechanic end up with PTSD? There were plenty of ways, of course, but one came to mind instantly. Elliott narrowed his eyes.

"Army?"

The way Martin's expression dissolved into surprise would almost be comical, except for the topic of conversation. "How—" Then he broke off and shook his head. "Cop. Should've known." He sipped his drink. "Joined up right out of high school, seven years, few of 'em in Afghanistan, one tour in Iraq."

Elliott nodded. "Thanks for your service." It was automatic, though he wondered if it was really the right thing to say.

Martin gave him a crooked half-smile. "I was mostly trying to get out of Chloe's way while she got her feet under her. It seemed like a practical way to get an education."

Elliott suspected there was more to it than that, but he just nodded again. He didn't feel comfortable asking more questions, but he kept his gaze on Martin's face as he sipped his whiskey, hoping it would invite Martin to keep talking if he felt like it.

Instead Martin looked down at his drink. Elliott couldn't help noticing the way those strong hands curled around the glass, one thumb tapping the other.

On top of that came a small but distinct whiff of sweat. The conversation was making Martin uncomfortable, so Elliott verbally backed off.

"Braxton said you have your own business?"

He was rewarded with the sight of Martin's hands going still. "Yeah, Squeaky Wheel Auto Repair. A friend of mine asked me to partner with him when I got back stateside. After a while, he got tired of the uncertainties of owning our own business. He got a job at a chain and sold his half of the business to me."

Elliott nodded. "You like being your own boss? Seems like a big change from Army life."

To his relief, Martin laughed. "You think? But yeah, I like handling all the aspects of it. I have an accountant, because I'm shit at math, and I don't want to get on the wrong side of the IRS accidentally, but aside from that, I call all the shots. If I'm a success, I know it's because of me, not someone else." He finished his whiskey. "Course, if I'm a failure, that's also my fault and not someone else's."

A server brought the plate of pub chips Elliott had ordered. She smiled at Martin. "Would you like another drink?"

Elliott held his breath as Martin looked from her to Elliott, obviously wondering if he'd been maneuvered into something. But after a few moments he nodded. "Maker's on the rocks, please."

Elliott found himself smiling.

CHAPTER 5

Lachlan's cell phone rang and he jumped, jangling the chord he'd been fingering on his guitar. He swore and stopped the recording, then looked at his cell.

Ainsley. Awesome.

Biting back a sigh, he took the call. "What's up?"

"You said you were coming to dinner tonight."

"Shit." He looked at the clock. It was almost six, and Sunday dinner was always at five-thirty. "I lost track of time." He'd actually meant to be working, but someone had needed to switch shifts at the last minute.

"I guess. If you hurry you can get here by six. Mom said the roast needed a little longer, anyway." She paused and her voice grew muffled. "I think it hurt her feelings to think you weren't coming, Lach."

"You just want someone else there to keep Mom from figuring out you're preggers," he countered, but he stood up and settled his guitar in the stand. "Fine. Do I need to bring anything?"

"Just yourself, asshole." Ainsley hung up.

Lachlan sighed and glared at the poster of Kurt Cobain hanging on his living room wall. He'd thought, after their first impromptu jam session, that maybe he'd be able to get Ainsley into making music with him. He could feature her in a few songs. They almost sounded a little like Evanescence when they really got going. But Ainsley was so focused on what everyone else expected of her—get a job, move out of the basement, decide what to do about the baby she was growing—that she didn't spare any thoughts for her little brother anymore.

He went into the bathroom to wash his face and check his hair. Some part of him suggested he was being unrealistic in his own expectations, thinking she'd be the same person now as she was when she went off to war a couple of years ago. But that had been her choice, after all. She'd known when she signed up for ROTC that the country was embroiled in two wars, with no clear end in sight for either of them.

And now we have a nutjob trying to start a war with North Korea on top of all that, he thought as he locked the apartment door behind him and walked to his car. But hey, thank God Ainsley's back. She'll make everything better. He rolled his eyes.

When he let himself in the front door of his parents' house, his father was commenting loudly on the time. Lachlan shoved down his resentment. He was late, after all.

"There you are!" Their mother Bobbi had given Ainsley her red hair and good looks, but she had a cheerful carelessness about her that Ainsley definitely hadn't inherited. Bobbi beamed at Lachlan. "I'm so glad you were able to get off work this week. Now we can have dinner as a whole family." She glanced around the room, her contentment shining through her.

"Too bad he didn't bother getting here on time," Joe grumbled. "The roast better not be dried out because we waited dinner for you."

"Nonsense," Bobbi said. "It was a larger roast than I'm used to cooking lately." She turned her smile on Ainsley. "Cooking for one extra again! I'll have to get back in practice."

Lachlan didn't think he was imagining the way Ainsley paled at their mother's remark. She obviously hadn't told them yet that she was expecting, but that 'one extra' was a little too close to home.

He smirked at Ainsley, who shot him a hard look.

"Let's sit down," Joe said, gesturing them all toward the table, which was set and ready for them.

As soon as they'd settled in and said grace, Joe filled his plate and started passing dishes around the table. "Seems like you were out a lot this week, Ains," he said.

She paused in the act of dishing herself mashed potatoes. "Oh, I had two job interviews, and I wanted to do my homework on the companies beforehand." Lachlan *knew* he wasn't imagining the way she squirmed as she passed the potatoes to their mother.

"Good job, kiddo. You'll have people knocking down the door to hire you before you know it. I'm proud of the way you've hit the ground running."

Ainsley gave him a half-hearted smile. "I just want to keep busy."

"Be nice if some other people would learn that lesson."

Lachlan felt his face get hot, but he took a sip of his Coke before answering. "I keep busy enough. Knot Tide has had a wedding every weekend this month, and I had over ten thousand hits on my latest YouTube music video."

"What about hits on your resume?" Joe took a bite of roast.

"I'm not looking for a *job*. I have a job. I want a career."

"Selling pizzas?"

Lachlan took a long breath. He couldn't understand why his dad thought Ainsley was great for finding a white-collar job but looked down on Lachlan's blue-collar job when Joe had spent his life repairing appliances. "Making music," he said, trying not to clench his jaw.

Joe grunted. "That'll pay the bills."

"Maybe it will," Lachlan said, his voice rising, "if I keep working at it."

"Lach's good, Dad," Ainsley said in a soothing tone. She shot Lachlan a look that clearly said, *Shut up.* "He has a lot of talent."

"And no drive."

"Lachlan works hard on his music, don't you, dear?" Bobbi's voice was fond, and Lachlan felt a sharp rush of gratitude for his mother. "I don't really understand how it all works, and your music *is* a little loud for my taste, but we just want you to be happy, dear. I'm glad you're doing well with your music."

Joe sighed and shook his head. "I don't know how you and your sister turned out so different."

Lachlan shoved half a roll in his mouth to keep from snapping back.

"Dad, I like music too," Ainsley said. "There's nothing wrong with that."

"Liking music is one thing. But you made a ten-year plan, and you stuck to it. You got yourself a damn good education—and a practical one, none of this rock-star bullshit."

"Dad, that isn't—"

But he cut her off. "You served your country, put your life on the line, and thank God we got you back."

"Thank Jesus," Bobbi echoed.

"And then you didn't even take a vacation—you hear me, Lach? Your sister didn't even take a vacation when she got home from the *war*. She just hit the ground running. She's already out there trying to get a job."

"While living in your basement," Lachlan muttered. Over his words Ainsley blurted, "I sleep in most mornings, Dad, geez."

"You've earned that, by God!" Joe's face was ruddy. He was really warming to his subject. "This brother of yours is slacking through his own life."

"At least I pay my rent and haven't knocked up some girl," Lachlan snapped. "I work long hours at two jobs on top of writing music and managing a vlog. I'm going to go viral one of these days, and who gives a shit if I'm delivering pizzas until then?"

Ainsley was gaping at him, her freckles standing out vividly against her pale skin.

"Such high standards, Lachlan. Pay your bills and avoid having a baby mama? Why not aspire to keep off meth and out of prison, while you're at it?" Joe mocked.

Bobbi cleared her throat. "Can't we just have a nice dinner? I spent a lot of time cooking this meal, and it would be nice if we could all enjoy it." She gave her husband an imploring look. "Our children have different goals in life, that's all. We love both of you. We're proud of you for believing in your dreams."

"At least Ains works on hers," Joe protested.

Lachlan sneered. "Yeah, until she has the baby and has to raise it in your basement because no one will hire her."

"*Fuck you, Lachlan.*" Ainsley was finally angry too. Lachlan met her gaze, a taunting smirk playing his lips. If she was going to be Daddy's Little Darling, he wasn't going to pull his punches.

"Language, Ainsley," Joe snapped.

Bobbi was silent.

"You're not perfect, Ainsley," Lach said, letting his lips tug up mockingly. "Isn't it fair they know that?"

She stood, her chair almost falling backwards. "You poisonous little shit," she hissed.

"Ainsley? You—" Bobbi was blinking rapidly. "Are you—"

"It's *my* business, not yours!" Ainsley snapped. She turned on her heel and stormed out of the dining room. A moment later the front door slammed shut.

Lachlan slouched back in his seat, a sour taste in his mouth. It had felt good poking her weaknesses in the moment. Joe was staring at the empty door, his face blank. Bobbi sucked in a breath.

"Lachlan Conor Shaw, that was mean," she chided.

Joe jolted upright as if electrified. "What the hell was that?"

Lachlan huffed. "You know what? I'm out of here."

"Lachlan!" Bobbi's voice rose in pitch. "Lach, don't leave! Please, just—"

Lachlan ignored his mother as he stood up and took the same path his sister had taken a minute earlier.

"Let him go, Bob," he heard his father say. "Let him think about what a jackass he's being."

"Fuck all of you," Lachlan muttered to himself as he slung himself into his car. It was a battered, fifteen-year-old Honda that looked like shit, but it had never let him down.

And who cared if he was driving a piece of shit car now? No matter what his dad said, he was going to be a famous musician. And when the money started rolling in, Lachlan would be able to drive whatever he wanted. Maybe his father would take him more seriously if he'd moved to Nashville and started trying to get a record deal, but Lach had studied the business inside and out, and with the availability of technology these days, he knew he could make more money as an independent. Build his platform, gain a following, and once he was selling his music online, bringing in a bigger percentage than a label would give him, he could start touring.

He screeched out of his parents' neighborhood and headed towards his apartment. He detoured along Eighty-Second Street to Crown Liquors to pick up a bottle of Jack Daniels, then changed his mind and went with Red Bull and vodka instead. He had a free Sunday night, so he might as well spend it making music.

He felt like something was pulsing and growling inside him, just waiting to get loose. The best music he made was always when he was feeling something strongly. He'd written an entire album's worth of songs after his last breakup, and he knew—he *knew*—that was damn good music. He'd written some good stuff after Grandpa Shaw died, too. And as angry as he was tonight...this was it.

Tonight he was going to write music that would blow them all away.

CHAPTER 6

Martin Cole jerked awake, breathing hard. He pulled out his earplugs, wondering if it was early fireworks that had woken him.

"You're home," he whispered to himself between breaths. "Winthrop Avenue. Indianapolis. Indiana. United States of America." His pulse was slowing as he consciously deepened his breathing. "Not Kandahar. Not Afghanistan. Indiana. Cornfields. Race cars. You're good. Deep breaths. You made it. You're back."

Blood spraying across his face as the woman's eyes widened. Screams of terror. A flash of light glinting off something, and cold darkness.

"No. You're home," he said, more loudly. He couldn't banish the image, though. The woman had long, red hair and green eyes. She was wearing a black shirt and jeans. She wasn't Afghani. She was either Irish-American or just plain Irish. She had a crooked smile and a scattering of freckles across her cheeks. She met his gaze with a frank friendliness.

And then she fell. Her eyes widened and she reached out to him. Her mouth was open in a silent scream as she hurtled away from him in the darkness. Then she was gone.

Martin recoiled, staring into the blackness of his bedroom.

"No," he said, his teeth gritted. "No. You're not real, damn it."

He laid back, rolling to his side and pulling the covers over his head despite the night's barely-air-conditioned warmth. "This is a dream. This is the PTSD. *Go away.*" The relaxing exercise only worked some of the time, but Martin kept trying.

She kept staring at him, despite the way his eyes were squeezed shut. Martin squeezed his eyes shut, counting the seconds he breathed out and the seconds he breathed in. He was home. Winthrop Avenue. Indianapolis. Indiana. He was home. He could do this.

But after a couple of minutes, Martin snaked his hand out from under the covers, grabbed his cell phone, and scrolled through the touch screen to his sister's number. Then he hesitated.

Chloe and Braxton were back from their honeymoon, but if he kept calling her in the middle of the night, she would realize that Martin wasn't getting better. In fact he'd had more dreams since the events of last Halloween than he had during the entire year before that. Anyway, what could Chloe do? Martin knew it was a dream. He knew where he was. There was nothing she could say to make it better.

He ought to get a cat.

After a few minutes, Martin climbed out of bed and went to the kitchen for a glass of water. He turned on the tap and watched as the glass filled, trying to slow his breathing in a meditative manner. He'd worked with a therapist, a few dozen sessions that mostly boiled down to Martin acknowledging that he felt guilty he came home when his buddies didn't and some breathing exercises that were apparently supposed to interrupt the panic attacks.

"God, you are so fucked up," he mumbled, rubbing his hands over his face.

Tomorrow—today, really—was Independence Day—not exactly his favorite holiday since getting back from Afghanistan. He'd promised to go to Chloe and Braxton's cookout, even though he'd just as soon spend the day working. Then again, he couldn't deny some part of him hoped Elliott would be there.

Martin knew he wasn't imagining the attraction between them, even if they hadn't acted on it. And Independence Day wasn't going to be the day to act on it, either. Martin would have to make sure to be home with earplugs in and music cranked to drown out the sound of the fireworks. In a couple more days, the fireworks would be finished for the year. Maybe then...

Martin closed his eyes, his thoughts returning to the redheaded woman. *Go away*, he told her image.

He went back to the bedroom, where he dressed hastily. Then he headed outside. So what if it was two in the morning? He'd go for a run and maybe clear his head a little.

They were just dreams, he told himself as he headed down the sidewalk. Just dreams. But they felt important. He had no idea why, but he thought they meant *something*. It was probably just the PTSD causing this, but lately the dreams weren't always about roadside bombs and ambushes and Dax losing his arm in the explosion. If it was just the PTSD, he would be dreaming about Afghanistan and Operation Medusa and Kandahar Province. He wouldn't be dreaming about a young, white woman dying a bloody death.

Would he?

The Monon Trail was a well-used rail trail that ran just behind his property. At this hour, he might be asking to get mugged, but one thing Kandahar had given him was the ability to handle himself. He wasn't the skinny gay kid who ran from a fight (because one thing high-school-aged Martin had been good at was running, and he had plenty of cross-country ribbons to prove it). Post-Army Martin Cole carried himself differently than he used to, and he carried a lot more muscle and training now, too.

The greenways in Indianapolis were open twenty-four hours a day, and after living in Broad Ripple for three years, he knew plenty of people commuted to all kinds of jobs on the multi-use trails. Martin didn't see anyone on this stretch, but he wouldn't be surprised if he ran into at least one other person, even this late. He headed north, his steps quiet in the summer night. It was too early for cicadas to be singing, but there were crickets and tree frogs blaring their presence to the world, and fireflies lit up the darkness around him.

The humidity of an Indiana summer night went to work on him almost at once. The joke was that you needed gills to survive an Indiana summer, and even though Martin used to hate that, he'd grown to appreciate how different it was from the desert. He rubbed a hand over his hair and slapped away a mosquito.

He started out jogging, but as the image of those penetrating green eyes flashed into his thoughts again, he picked up his pace. Before he'd gone two miles, he was running flat out, fast enough to outrun the mosquitoes.

He finally drew up, panting, when he realized he'd reached the Monon's intersection with the Fall Creek Trail. He leaned on the railing of the pedestrian bridge over the creek. He'd passed two or three people during his run, but he was alone here. Why was that redhead so insistent in his mind? She hadn't been like a normal dream.

He stared down at the dark water. She'd had long red hair and green eyes. She'd been dressed casually, nothing to tell him anything about her. He hadn't known her. Sometimes in dreams he knew someone, even if they weren't acquainted in real life. But he remembered vividly that he hadn't recognized her at all, even in the dream. And yet…something about her had drawn his eye, had made him feel connected to her somehow.

He rubbed sweat out of his eyes. "You're imagining things," he told himself. He straightened up, checked his surroundings, and headed back towards home at a steady jog.

The sky was still dark when he got back home, but the robins had started chirping in the maple tree behind his house. He didn't care. The garage was closed today, so he could sleep in—if the dreams would let him. Martin let himself into the house, stood under a hot shower for a few minutes, then collapsed naked and only half dry into bed.

* * *

Elliott Blake parked his SUV in front of his best friend's house and frowned. Usually the Fourth of July was his favorite holiday, but this year he couldn't remember the last time he'd had a date, let alone someone to make out with during the fireworks. That had always been his favorite part of the holiday. And on top of that, he was on call, so there was no guarantee he wouldn't get pulled away from Braxton's cookout to investigate a homicide or even a stupid fireworks-related death that looked suspicious enough to call him out. Still, he knew Braxton was counting on him, since this was the first big party he and Chloe had hosted as a married couple. Elliott would look like a dick if he didn't show up, so he'd agreed to show up right at the start time and stay as long as possible.

"All right, Blake, get your head in the game," he muttered, running a hand through his hair in a vain attempt to tame it.

This would be fine. Elliott knew how to shine at a party, even though parties weren't his favorite way to pass the time. He'd seen the term ambivert thrown around lately, and he wondered if it applied to him, because he was good with small talk and social situations, but he'd far rather spend time socially with a small group of friends. Either way, though, he'd given his word about this cookout, and he would do what he'd said. He took a deep breath and got out of the car, grabbing the case of beer he'd brought in lieu of a covered dish—because honestly, he was a bachelor, and no matter what the invitation said, covered dishes weren't his thing—and headed for the front door.

It swung open before he reached it.

"Hi Elliott," Chloe said, her expression way more cheerful than he was used to seeing at work. "Thanks for coming. Braxton is in the back yard messing with the grill." She gave him a look that was frank in its appraisal. "Hey. I know this is weird. I mean, it *is* weird, right? Anyway, what I'm trying to say is, thank you. Braxton feels way better knowing you're coming."

Elliott exhaled slowly, trying not to let her hear. "Come on, Cole. You know there's nothing I wouldn't do for Brax." He should probably call her 'Wolfe' now, but he couldn't quite bring himself to do it.

She grinned at him anyway. "I know. I mean, I hoped. I mean..." She trailed off and shook her head at him. "You're his best friend, and...I get that. I appreciate that. I just—I don't want to get in the way." Her grin faded and she frowned. "I mean, I refuse to be one of those women who tries to change the guy she married, okay? Brax is your best friend, and he'll always be your best friend, and that—that isn't my business."

Elliott raised his eyebrows, but he couldn't deny that he was grateful to hear that. Elliott had never dated anyone who filled every need that Elliott's best friend did. He was just glad to know Chloe understood. "You've had six months to prove that, Cole. It's fine. So stop worrying about people getting along, and *start* worrying about whether or not your werewolf husband has any concept of how ridiculously *un*bloody most humans prefer their meat."

Chloe laughed and gestured for Elliott to follow her through the house to the back yard. "How do you even know that, Blake?" she teased.

"Hey, I've dated humans. Not to mention having to pass for human myself. I know how squeamish you normal people can be." Elliott felt his shoulders relax as they fell into their usual banter.

"I'm not squeamish," she grumped. "I just think death is a waste."

"You keep rockin' that line, Cole. Most of the homicide squad believes you." He grinned at her as she pretended to slam the back door in his face. Then he saw his best friend poking at the grill. "Brax! Remember, medium well is the baseline."

Someone who wasn't Braxton snorted in amusement, and Elliott glanced over to see Martin Cole standing at the patio bar slicing a lime. He glanced up briefly. "How's it going, Elliott?"

Elliott felt his lips curling automatically. He hadn't seen Martin since their chance encounter at the Broad Ripple Tavern, but he hadn't forgotten how much he enjoyed their talk that evening. "Living the dream," he said. "And you?"

Elliott didn't think he was imagining the faint blush that tinged Martin's cheekbones as the other man shrugged. "Not bad. Keeping busy at work, which isn't as horrible as if you all were keeping busy at work." He looked up again, and Elliott couldn't help but notice that Martin had a nice smile.

He laughed, just a beat late, at Martin's joke. "It doesn't take a large number of homicides to keep me busy," he said. "Investigations, paperwork, evidence chains, witness statements, interviews..."

Martin glanced over his shoulder at Braxton and Chloe, who were bickering genially about the fire. When he turned back to Elliott, he leaned in a little. "So here's something I'm dying to ask Braxton, but I have no idea if it's bad manners or not," he said, lowering his voice. "Chloe says you know about the werewolf thing, so tell me if you think it's rude."

Elliott's eyes widened a little. Chloe knew Elliott was a werewolf. But Chloe's brother was gay, so she would know it wasn't nice to out someone—whether as gay or as a werewolf. She obviously hadn't told Martin, and Braxton probably thought, if it occurred to him at all, that she would have told her brother. "Uh, okay."

"How does that impact his interviews and stuff? Being able to detect heart rates and scent emotions and stuff, does that mean he can tell when someone's lying? And then, if so, isn't that frustrating, to know someone's lying but not be able to prove it yet?"

Elliott found himself chuckling. He wasn't sure what question he'd expected, but it wasn't that one. "It's not rude," he assured Martin. "And actually, I can answer that for you. Yes, we can tell when someone's lying, and yes, it's frustrating to not be able to prove it, but at least it gives us a direction to look."

His grin widened as Martin stared at him. "Oh, shit. You're—I mean—" Martin paused and ran a hand over his face, covering his eyes. "Heh. I'm glad that's not a rude question."

Elliott laughed and sat down on the other barstool. "So question for you in return," he said. "How are you not freaked out by werewolves?"

Martin studied him for a moment, then shrugged. "What's to be freaked out by? My sister sees ghosts, you guys turn into a ginormous wolf once a month, and apparently Braxton knows some girl who can walk through walls when she needs to." He looked down at the lime slices and shook his head. "IEDs are scary. The racial tension in this country is scary. The Yellowstone caldera is scary. Werewolves? Not really scary."

Elliott let himself look at Martin longer, since the other man wasn't looking back at him. He had light auburn hair, almost as short as a military cut, and a strong jawline. And, Elliott realized, he was crazy anxious. Ell caught a piquant whiff of sweat, even though the day was still just comfortably warm, along with a little bit of adrenaline and nerves.

"The Yellowstone caldera is scary?" he repeated when he realized he'd been silent too long.

Martin lifted a blue gaze to meet Elliott's. "Have you been there? There's like a thousand ways to die in Yellowstone, and besides being attacked by bison and boiling alive in a hotspring, there's always the possibility the volcanic caldera under the park will blow in a massive eruption that'll disrupt crop production all the way to here. How is that *not* scary?"

Elliott laughed again when he detected a slight glimmer of mischief in Martin's gaze. Sly sense of humor, this one. He suddenly found himself wishing he'd been warmer to Martin during the wedding preparations. Maybe this would all be easier if he had.

"I don't know, I mean, at least if you're eaten by a bear at Yellowstone, people can say you had an adventurous life," he offered. "Or, well, death, I suppose."

The glimmer of mischief drained from Martin's expression. "I guess," he said, leaning down to pull a bottle of tequila out of the bar. "But sometimes I think adventure is overrated."

Elliott was grateful that the rest of the werewolf pack came around the corner of the yard, boisterous and happy. He wasn't sure what he would have said to that comment. He wasn't sure how to respond to the way Martin seemed to have retreated back into himself. It was an unexpected transformation; Elliott hadn't even realized Martin had opened up a little until then.

Damn it, do not crush on him, he ordered himself. Imagine how awkward it'll get if you fuck up a relationship with your best friend's brother-in-law.

Theo and Murphy came over to Elliott, bickering good-naturedly. At least, it was good-natured for Murphy, who would never be accused of being overfriendly. He was dressed in his usual black clothes, his straight, dark hair flopping into his eyes, but he was actually laughing. Elliott gave him an assessing glance, then smiled at Martin. "I know you've met Murphy. What about Theo?"

Martin's nod looked a little tight, but he didn't smell hostile, just wary. "We've met."

Murphy nodded in return, but Theo, being Theo, threw his arms around Martin in a way-too-familiar greeting. Elliott saw Martin's eyes widen right about the same time the anxiety scent skyrocketed.

Theo pulled back at once, his expression friendly and open, giving no hint of the concern Elliott could sense in him. Theo would have smelled the anxiety, too. He was a good-hearted guy; he wouldn't want to make Martin uncomfortable. "Good to see you again," he said, his tone easy. He patted Martin's shoulder and turned slightly away, his face toward Martin, but his gaze lowered. It was the sort of "I'm Not Here About You" posture he would have offered to a freaked-out wolf.

To Elliott's surprise, it worked on Martin even better than it would have worked on Murphy. Martin's shoulders relaxed and he nodded again, the scent of anxiety dropping. Elliott smiled, but at that moment, his cell phone went off.

"Damn," he muttered. "Sorry. I'm on call. Gotta take this." He took a couple of steps away, turning away from them, and answered. "Blake."

His good mood plummeted as his partner's voice said, "We got a body."

* * *

Elliot pulled up to the address Flynn had given him. It was a two-story house, probably built back in the seventies, and well maintained. There was a patrol car in the driveway, lightbars flashing, and Flynn's unmarked car was parked on the street just beyond the drive. The medical examiner's wagon hadn't arrived yet. Elliott took a deep breath and tried to steel himself for what he knew was waiting for him in there.

The door opened before he could knock, and the ruddy face of Brady Flynn offered a welcoming smile. "Elliott. Come inside and meet Joe and Bobbi Shaw." He lowered his voice. "Our victim was their daughter Ainsley. Just back from the 'Stan."

Elliott frowned. He liked Flynn, but they'd only been working together for about six months, since Ell's last partner retired. Flynn was, in Elliott's opinion, a little too casual and a little too eager to be liked. Elliott didn't really mind training Flynn, though; he thought the younger man would make a fine detective once he settled into himself a little more.

He shoved the thought aside. What mattered right now was Joe and Bobbi Shaw. He put on the protective booties to cover his feet and prevent the contamination of evidence. Then he followed Flynn into the living room, where two people in their late forties were huddled together on a couch that looked too big for them. The red-haired woman had her face buried against the man's chest. He held her tightly, his bearded face stricken.

"Mr. and Mrs. Shaw, this is my partner, Elliott Blake," Flynn said.

Elliott nodded to them. "I'm so sorry for your loss," he said. It was true. Certainly working in homicide you got used to dead bodies, but you were never happy to have them. He reminded himself of that fact every time he started getting bored with paperwork or wishing he didn't have to testify at a trial.

Mr. Shaw nodded, but didn't speak. His wife was sobbing into his chambray work shirt. Flynn shot Elliott an anxious look.

"If you don't mind, I'd like to take a look at your daughter's room before we talk," Elliott said.

Shaw nodded again, his face crumpling a little before he got it under control again. "Downstairs," he managed.

"Brady will stay here with you," Elliott said, to give his partner guidance. Flynn didn't look thrilled at the prospect, but he nodded.

Elliott made his way down to the basement. The stairs were carpeted and lined with photos of the family—Joe and Bobbi Shaw first, then with a little red-headed girl—presumably Ainsley—and then with a little dark-haired boy. Elliott made a mental note to ask about a brother as he reached the basement hallway. There were bloody footprints on the cream-colored carpet, leading back the way Elliott had come. The footprints of whomever had found her, he assumed. From the size, it had probably been the mother. Elliott sighed.

The door was slightly ajar, most likely left that way in a panic once Bobbi realized her daughter was dead. Elliott paused in the hallway and closed his eyes, drawing in a deep breath through his nose.

The scent of blood hit him first; he pushed that aside, sorting through the other scents. Fear, despair, human waste, vomit. But there was something else—something he hadn't been expecting.

Magic.

His eyes flew open and he scanned the hallway. Nothing out of place, no signs out here of any sort of ritual. But then, there were many types of magic. Blood magic was the easiest to identify by scent, metallic and choking, while pack magic smelled like forests and wolves. Fae magic had a variety of scents, depending on which court the fae in question belonged to, but it always had a certain throat-stinging, crystalline quality. None of the fae magics he was familiar with smelled like this, though. It smelled of...of peat and earth and just a hint of blood. He closed his eyes, overwhelmed with the feeling of being in a graveyard.

The presence of magic changed the nature of this investigation. Elliott hadn't come across many magical murders in the course of his career, despite what people might think. Relationship problems and interpersonal conflicts were the motivation behind most homicides in the United States, and guns were the most commonly used weapon.

Elliott took another deep breath, solidifying the scent in his memory. At least it wasn't the scent of the ancient blood magic wielded by Teresia, the mage who had come after the pack last year. If it had been her, he would have had to find a way to seal the crime scene and request Braxton's collaboration on the case. They'd been on edge since November, when Teresia escaped with her life—but minus one hand, thanks to Murphy. So far, she hadn't resurfaced, but Elliott went back on edge with every new case.

He pulled out his phone and texted Braxton. *Magical involvement in victim's death. Unsub isn't Teresia but might need a consult.* Then he slid his phone back into his pocket and pushed the door open wide enough to walk in.

He didn't step inside. He stared at the blood-soaked carpet at the end of the bed, where one outflung hand reached for him as if pleading for help. He swallowed back a surge of nausea. Poor Ainsley Shaw. It was too late for anyone to help her now.

Anyone except Chloe, he thought suddenly. Despite Chloe's aversion to death, Elliott thought he had her halfway talked into transferring to homicide. He wondered if Ainsley's ghost was lingering here, waiting to see if they would solve her murder.

It had to be a murder. With that much blood spilled across the carpet, Elliott didn't think it could be anything else. He took a few steps into the room. The bed had blood spattered across it, and the duvet was tugged half off the bed. Elliott frowned. How could anyone have killed Ainsley so violently without her parents noticing something? It must have happened while both Joe and Bobbi were out of the house.

He took another step and his lips curled back from his teeth as the hair on the back of his neck prickled.

Ainsley Shaw had been eviscerated.

* * *

When Elliott got back upstairs, Bobbi Shaw was still sobbing against her husband's shoulder, but her grief had settled in. Elliott clenched his jaw. He knew how she felt. He wished he didn't.

Elliott exchanged a glance with Flynn and then sat down in a chair facing the parents. "Do you think you can walk me through how you found her?" he asked quietly. He held Joe's gaze, trying to project all the compassion he felt for them. It was hard sometimes, walking the line between professional and empathetic, especially since he'd been where these people were. He still remembered, vividly, the brusque questions of the detectives who responded when he found his mother dead, the front door forced open, when he came home one afternoon.

He shoved the memories aside. Now wasn't the time. He had a job to do.

Joe cleared his throat. "Ainsley just got back from Afghanistan. I think we told Detective Flynn that."

Elliott nodded.

"She, uh, she's been sleeping in a lot since coming home. Her deployment was rough. I mean, no rougher than anyone else's, I guess, but..." Joe shook his head. "I didn't serve. I was too young for Vietnam, and too old for Desert Storm. At least, I had a wife and baby by that time, and I didn't feel I could leave them and my job to join up."

Elliott nodded again. "It's hard for us civilians to understand what our veterans go through," he said. Cops weren't civilians, strictly speaking, but he wanted to put Joe at ease by finding something they had in common.

"Yeah." Joe coughed. "Anyway. She's been sleeping in a lot. I was covering the holiday shift today, so I went to work without bothering her."

Bobbi let out a sob and Joe's hand lifted to smooth her hair.

"Bob only works part-time, so she left later than me. What time?" He glanced at Bobbi, who didn't seem inclined to answer. "Eleven, I think. She works noon to five."

Elliott kept nodding. "Works where?" He would have to verify that Bobbi had shown up.

"The Fashion Mall. It's a makeup store." Joe cast a fond look down at his wife. "She likes making people beautiful."

Bobbi let out a noise that was half sob and half wail. Joe winced.

"Anyway. I got home a little before five, and Ainsley's car was still here. Surprised me. Even though she's been sleeping late, she's been pretty regular about her exercise. She goes running most afternoons, and she's usually still out when I get home." He paused. "Was." His face crumpled, but he sucked in a sharp breath and regained control.

Bobbi let out a strangled wail. "How could we not have heard anything?" she cried. "How could we just—" She broke down again.

Joe rubbed her back. "She's an adult, even if she's living with us for the moment. We try to treat her like one. So I didn't bother her when I got back. It wasn't—" His voice wavered. "It wasn't until Bob got home—" He stopped, looking like he was choking on the words.

Bobbi sat up, drawing in a deep breath, and wiped her face. She was a pretty woman, Elliott thought, despite her blotchy face and reddened eyes. No wonder she enjoyed making other people beautiful. "I brought takeout home," she said, her voice unsteady.

"Takeout from..." Elliott prompted.

"Uh. D-Donato's on Eighty-Sixth and Ditch. Ainsley's favorite pizza." She swallowed. "Pepperoni."

Elliott nodded. "Go on."

"And I...I went downstairs to see if Ainsley wanted any." She stifled a sob, sucked in another breath, and straightened. "And that's when I saw the blood."

Elliott saw her expression waver. He nodded. "What did you do then?" he asked gently.

Slowly, bit by bit, he teased out the story of how she had gone in, touched Ainsley's face, found the skin cold. She had run back upstairs to call 911. There was no phone extension downstairs, she explained. Ainsley just used her cell phone. Joe had found her on her knees in the kitchen, screaming half-hysterically at the dispatcher.

Joe hadn't gone downstairs to verify his wife's assertion that their daughter was dead. That struck Elliott as odd, but not necessarily suspicious. Joe had apparently been focused on keeping his wife from collapsing.

"Is it just the three of you in the house?" Elliott asked when the story seemed played out.

Bobbi let out a tiny shriek. "Oh, God—Lach! We—We—He doesn't know!"

Joe looked sick, like he'd been punched in the gut.

"Lach?" Elliott repeated.

Joe cleared his throat a couple of times. "Lachlan. Ainsley's little brother." His voice was still choked. "I don't—" He broke off and shook his head. "They're so close. I don't—I don't know—"

Elliott waited, but Joe didn't continue. "Would you like me to speak to him?" Elliott said finally. He didn't specify that he would need to talk to Lachlan anyway, to rule him out as a suspect. This way he would be able to gauge Lachlan's reaction. More than half of all murders were committed by friends, loved ones, or someone the victim knew. But if Joe and Bobbi didn't know that, Elliott wasn't going to bring it up.

"Would you?" Joe looked at him with painful gratitude in his gaze. Elliott's stomach twisted at the mild deception he was committing, but he told himself that if they didn't know his motivation, he was doing them a favor.

He nodded. "I take it Lachlan doesn't live here?"

Joe shook his head. Bobbi whispered, "He has an apartment north of here. Off College Avenue in Nora."

Behind them, Flynn held up his notebook; he had an address for Lachlan Shaw. Elliott nodded. "Okay. I'll go see Lachlan, and then I'll come back and check on you. Brady will stay here to answer any questions you have."

Flynn didn't look thrilled about the idea, but he nodded. Elliott gave him an encouraging look and headed for the car.

CHAPTER 7

Before Elliott pulled out of the Shaws' driveway, he checked his phone. A missed call from Sarah Fitzgerald, which made him grimace. Two text messages from Braxton. *OK to consult.* Then a minute later he'd added, *Not thrilled about another rogue mage.*

"Neither am I," Elliott muttered. He pocketed his phone and headed for Lachlan Shaw's apartment. He hated this part of the job, and yet this was part of the reason he'd become a homicide detective in the first place.

When he was nineteen, Elliott had been living at home and attending college locally on scholarship. He'd done his best to help out around the house, since he had two little sisters and his mom worked two jobs to pay the bills. He'd been majoring in history and waffling between history education or going on to law school. He'd liked the idea of history education, but his mom always reminded him that teacher pay wasn't great.

His career plans had changed the day in April that he came home to find the front door forced and his mother dead of a gunshot wound. Being treated first as a suspect and then as a pain in the ass by the officers who answered his 911 call had been Elliott's first push towards becoming a police officer—so he could be a better kind of cop than that.

The Fourth of July holiday traffic was a bear, but Elliott kept reminding himself it could be worse; he could be trying to get somewhere around Geist Reservoir. He'd worked a case up there on Independence Day a few years ago, and even with the lights and siren blaring, he'd been reduced to a crawl through the congested roads leading to fancy, sprawling homes that backed up to the water.

Finally he pulled into the apartment complex off College where Lachlan Shaw lived. He parked in front of what he thought was the right building and checked his notes again.

Lachlan Shaw. Why did that name sound familiar? Elliott frowned at the paper for a few seconds and then shook his head.

The apartment complex had probably been built in the sixties, if he had to guess. They were stark brick buildings with outdoor walkways and open stairways built of concrete and steel. There was nothing attractive about the place, to Elliott's eye, but he had a feeling some 'modern' architect had given himself fits of joy over this design. Elliott wasn't sure exactly what the rent would be at a place like this, but if Lachlan Shaw had a good income, he hadn't spent it here.

When the door to Apartment 4B opened, Elliott found himself looking at a skinny man in his early twenties. Lachlan Shaw had dark shadows under his eyes, exaggerated by what looked like eyeliner. His face was so thin it almost looked gaunt, but when

Elliott glanced down at Shaw's arms, he saw a wiry strength there.

"Yeah?" Shaw's voice was gravel. From the way he squinted, he was probably hung over.

Or else he spent the night eviscerating his sister, Elliott thought.

He shoved it aside. There were all kinds of statistics that said Ainsley Shaw had probably known her murderer, but Elliott always did his best to treat family members as if they were genuinely grieving. He remembered how shitty it had felt when the cops thought he'd killed his own mother.

Besides, Lachlan Shaw didn't smell right to be the murderer.

He held up his badge, giving Shaw time to make his eyes focus. "Detective Elliott Blake. I'm with IMPD. Can I come in?"

Shaw blinked at him a couple of times and then his eyes widened. He shrugged and held the door open.

"You're Lachlan Shaw?"

"Yeah. What's going on?"

Elliott glanced around the apartment, taking in the huge framed poster of Kurt Cobain, a keyboard, and two guitars on stands. That jogged his memory, and at last he realized why Shaw looked familiar. "Are you with the wedding band?" He couldn't remember the band name, but this was the definitely the guy who'd played Braxton and Chloe's wedding last month.

"Yeah, Knot Tide. Did something happen to Julie or Wade? Or Steve?"

"No, I'm sorry." Elliott drew in a slow breath. Shaw smelled like alcohol, cigarettes, and sweat. Anxiety was creeping in the longer they stood there. A musky scent teased at Elliott's nostrils from somewhere in the apartment, but it wasn't Shaw. "Why don't we sit down?"

He followed Shaw as the younger man went over to drop into a computer chair. Shaw gestured at a beat-up couch. "You're making me nervous, detective. What's going on?"

Elliott bit his lower lip, drew in one more breath—Shaw wasn't lying about being nervous—and sighed. "Mr. Shaw, I'm sorry to inform you that your sister, Ainsley, has been killed. We have reason to believe it was homicide."

Lachlan Shaw had pale skin that combined with his thin frame and shadowed eyes to make him look like a consumption patient. Elliott wouldn't have thought he could get any paler, but after Elliott spoke, Shaw went so white his lips almost disappeared. Terror spiked in his scent.

And then he fainted.

Elliott had done this often enough that he was always prepared for whatever reaction the news might prompt. He hadn't expected Shaw to faint, though, so he almost didn't catch the man as he tilted slowly forward.

He shifted Shaw over to the couch and propped him up. Just a few seconds later Shaw's eyes opened and he blinked. Elliott could tell the moment the memory kicked in; Shaw's green eyes darkened and his heartbeat jumped again. "Oh, my God," the young man whispered.

Elliott gripped his shoulder for a moment and then went to the kitchen for a glass of water. He dampened a paper towel and carried it back to the living room. Shaw was slumped over, one hand covering his eyes as his shoulders shook. Elliott draped the paper towel over the back of Shaw's neck.

Eventually the torrent of grief slowed. Shaw lifted his face, tear-streaked and blotchy.

"I am so sorry for your loss," Elliott said. Shaw's eyes were red-rimmed now.

"Uh...do, um... Does Mom know? Uh, Mom and Dad?"

Elliott felt a pang of sympathy. Shaw looked like he'd had his bell rung. He was in shock now; the initial reaction was past, but the truth hadn't set in yet. He was operating on instinct.

"Yes, I've just come from their house."

"God," Shaw whispered. "H—" He choked on whatever he was going to say.

Elliott refilled the water glass and brought it back to him.

Shaw took a couple of sips and then cradled the glass in both hands. The water trembled from the way his hands shook. "How did it happen?"

"I'm afraid it's too early to be certain," Elliott lied. "We'll have to wait for the medical examiner's report. But the circumstances are highly suspicious."

"Where—"

Elliott held in a sigh. "Your mother found her in her room. We believe she was killed sometime last night."

Shaw squeezed his eyes shut. "I was going to call her," he whispered. He choked again and his skinny shoulders began heaving. "I was writing a song. I wanted her to help. We used to sing together."

His use of the past tense caught Elliott's attention, but then he considered that Ainsley Shaw had just barely returned from a deployment to Afghanistan. Lachlan probably meant before her deployment. "She sounds like a talented young woman."

Shaw just nodded. He buried his face in his hands. "Do we..." He trailed off and shook his head. "I can't."

"I understand. Is it all right if I ask you a few questions?"

Shaw's face spasmed, but he took a deep breath and nodded. "Sure." His voice was dull suddenly. "Ask whatever you need to."

* * *

Martin pulled his purple 1970 Camaro into his driveway and leaned his head back, closing his eyes. He'd stubborned his way through three hours of the barbecue after Elliott left, and that had been all he could take, even with Murphy there to talk comic books with. He'd muttered some excuses, waved off his sister's concerned expression, and made his escape. He almost wished he'd just gone in to work. The garage was closed, but he could have finished the carburetor job in peace instead of navigating an awkward social situation.

He let out an explosive breath and rubbed a hand over his face. *Face facts, Cole,* he thought. *You're what's awkward, not the situation.*

But that was just an excuse. He wasn't usually awkward in social situations. He might never be known as the life of the party, but he was no wallflower. All the same, he'd spent most of the afternoon fighting a creeping sense of dread. He couldn't pinpoint it, but he assumed it was just anticipating the coming fireworks. The only time he'd really been able to relax was when he'd been talking to Elliott Blake.

Martin shoved the thought away and got out of the car. He made his way up the walk to the side door. He'd bought out his landlady two months ago, when she'd decided she was ready to sell the house and move to a condo in Fishers to be closer to her grandchildren. He'd never really gotten around to remodeling the house, though, so it was still subdivided into two living spaces, and he didn't see any point in moving until he'd finished the remodel, so he was still in the two bedroom apartment he'd lived in since returning from Afghanistan.

Martin locked the door behind him and dropped his keys on the table, then pulled open the fridge and stared inside. He'd had a burger and eaten enough chips and salsa at the barbecue that he shouldn't be hungry, but he still felt something gnawing at his gut.

He would never admit it to Chloe, but he missed her stupid yellow cat. Chloe and Whizz had only lived with Martin for eight months or so, between the time her house burned down and she married Braxton, but Martin hadn't been able to get used to an empty house again.

Not that he would tell Chloe that. She was truly happy in her new life, surrounded by her new werewolf pack and madly in love with Braxton. No way was Martin going to do anything to spoil that. She'd spent years taking care of him after their parents died. The least he could do was take care of himself now that she was happy.

Martin had been through enough counseling to be aware he was starting to feel sorry for himself. He considered the situation for a couple of minutes, and then he closed the refrigerator and got the bourbon out from under the sink.

"Drinking won't erase your problems," he said aloud. "And it could exacerbate the nightmares." And then he poured himself a healthy glass.

Martin's back prickled and, even though he knew better, he spun to look around him.

There. The shadowy figure stood behind him, hood pulled up to hide everything but the glow of green eyes. It was watching him. Martin shivered and he told himself to confront the figure, to chase him away. He couldn't seem to move, though, so he and the hooded figures stayed where they were and stared at each other.

Then he heard the footsteps. A woman in high heels, by the sound of them. She was walking confidently, her steps purposeful but not hurried. She wasn't afraid despite the darkness or the crumbling buildings that were suddenly around them. Martin squinted up. Hadn't he just been in an alley? But these buildings looked dustier, more exhausted. He knew, not knowing how he knew, that this was Kandahar.

But he still heard the footsteps.

When he turned around, she was walking towards him. A redhead, pretty, though her eyes looked tired. She looked at him with a curious smile, her lips curving in a sexy smile that was wasted on him. No, it was a friendly smile. A smile that invited intimacy, but not physical intimacy. She knew his secrets, that smile said, and she would tell him secrets of her own in exchange.

The air behind him chilled like he'd walked into an industrial freezer. The woman's eyes widened and Martin tensed, beginning to turn.

He was too late.

Blood sprayed across his face. The woman screamed.

Martin spun, raising fists to fight whatever had hurt her. He lunged, trying to keep between the woman and the danger. But light flashed in his eyes, blinding him.

He turned again, reaching for her, wanting to push her away, make her run—

And Martin woke himself up screaming.

The room flickered blue with TV light as he took several shuddering breaths. "The hell..." he breathed, wiping a hand down his face.

His clothes were soaked through with sweat. He was in his recliner. Outside, an explosion rocked the night. Martin threw himself to the floor, heart racing, breath choking in his chest—

And then he remembered it was the Fourth of July.

He squeezed his eyes shut. "You're—home," he panted. "Winthrop Avenue." Gasp. "Indianapolis." Gasp. "Indiana."

His breathing was slowing, deepening. Another explosion boomed through the night, but he took another breath and kept from reacting.

This was the moment Whizz would have come nosing around, probably to see if he'd died. But Whizz had gone home to live with Chloe and Braxton and Fuzzy. Martin's eyes stung. He wished Whizz and Fuzzy had despised each other. He'd have had an excuse for keeping Whizz.

"United States of America," he recited. His pulse was finally slowing. "Not Kandahar. Not Afghanistan. Indiana. Cornfields."

Barbecues and hot werewolf cops.

He stiffened and said aloud, "Cornfields. Race cars. You're good."

He needed to focus on what was real. What he could touch. He could touch cornfields and race cars. He could *not* touch hot werewolf cops.

"I don't *want* to touch hot werewolf cops," he muttered, knowing it was a lie.

To distract himself, he climbed back into his recliner and reached for the remote. The pretty news anchor on Channel 13 turned her perky smile into a sad face, a clear segue into bad news. What now, he wondered. Indianapolis was the fifteenth-largest city in the United States, and the homicide rate was worse than their size warranted. On top of that, there was so much racial and political tension this year. There had been an officer-involved shooting of a black man just a few days ago, and even though the man had fled the police, it was looking like he hadn't been armed.

Do I really want to know what happened now? he wondered. Then he remembered that he'd been thinking about the golden-brown color of Elliott Blake's eyes, and decided the news was definitely preferable to thinking about an unrealistic attraction to his brother-in-law's best friend.

"—police say that twenty-seven-year-old Ainsley Shaw had only recently returned from a two-year deployment to Afghanistan. She was in the process of receiving an honorable discharge from the Army and was looking forward to life as a civilian engineer."

The camera switched from a live reporter standing outside a split-level house surrounded by crime scene tape. A photo appeared on screen of a young woman with pale, freckled skin, green eyes, and long, straight, red hair.

Martin's jaw dropped. It was the woman from his dreams.

* * *

Elliott was finally wrapping up his shift when his cell phone rang. Brady Flynn sighed and gave Elliott a look that clearly said Flynn was ready to be home in bed with his wife. Elliott shrugged and made a 'what can you do' face back at him and answered without checking the caller ID. Belatedly he remembered that Sarah Fitzgerald had tried calling him twice now.

"Blake." His voice was crisp, professional, his mind lingering on the way Lachlan Shaw had fallen apart over his sister's death.

He wasn't expecting the thrill of heat that shot through him when a rich male voice said, "Elliott Blake? This is Martin. Cole. I know it's late…"

He bit down on the pleased smile that wanted to spread across his face. "Martin, hey. What's up?" He tried to make his voice more casual, and the switch caught his partner's attention. Elliott waved a hand at him, an indication that Brady could take off.

"This is going to sound crazy." Martin's voice was hesitant, heavy. "I'm completely aware of that."

"Call you maybe?" Elliott joked.

To his relief, Martin huffed a tiny laugh. "Now I'll have that stuck in my head, so thanks for that." Then his tone grew more serious. "No, this is…" He trailed off and Elliott heard a couple of breaths.

Martin's breathing sounded anxious or stressed, but without the added input of scent, Elliott couldn't tell which. He hated talking on the phone. "What?" he prompted.

Martin sighed. "I told you I have bad dreams."

"Yeah." Noticing Brady still watching him, Elliott made a more emphatic *go-away* gesture at him. "Need to talk?"

Martin coughed. "Yeah. Uh." He paused, and Elliott strained to hear anything that would give him a clue. Sounded like the television news in the background, and a hum that was probably Martin's air conditioning, but that was it.

Realizing Martin wasn't going to continue, Elliott resorted to quoting Tennyson. "'Dreams are true while they last,'" he offered, and then immediately felt stupid. Martin probably wouldn't get the reference, because most normal guys didn't spend their free time reading British Romantic poetry.

"Shit." Martin exhaled. "I live in Broad Ripple. Can you swing by?"

Elliott's stomach lurched. Was Martin asking him over to talk, or to distract Martin from what he didn't want to talk about? He was surprised to realize he hoped Martin really wanted to just talk. Distracting him might be fun, but Elliott found he genuinely enjoyed Martin's company, and nothing would complicate that faster than trying to have a fling with him. "Sure. My shift just ended."

"I'm on Winthrop Avenue." Martin gave him the address, then added, "It's the side door. I haven't finished de-apartmenting the house."

"I'll be there in twenty."

He only realized when he ended the call that Brady hadn't left. His partner was standing near the door, his arms folded across his chest, his eyebrows raised. "Okay, do my ears deceive me, or did Detective Blake just get booty called?" There was a teasing smirk playing around his lips.

Elliott glared at him. "I did *not* just get booty called," he said. "I have a friend who's going through a rough patch. He needs someone to talk to, not someone to sleep with." He didn't add that he wouldn't mind offering both, in Martin's case.

Brady held up his hands, his smirk widening into a grin. "Okay, okay, sorry. I can tell it's personal, so I'll head out. See you tomorrow."

Elliott nodded and straightened things up on his desk for a couple of minutes to give Brady time to get to his car. The second time he dropped his stapler, he realized two things simultaneously: he was stalling, and he was terrified. He took a deep breath.

This is stupid, he told himself. Just because he told me about his PTSD dreams the other night when we were both half drunk, it doesn't mean he's into you. It doesn't even mean he trusts you. It just means his inhibitions were lowered and you were a friendly face at the right time.

He didn't want to admit—even to himself—that he wanted desperately to be wrong about that.

* * *

The scent of coffee permeated the kitchen. Martin looked at the bottle of Jack Daniels on the counter, trying not to think about all the different ways this night could end.

"Should have just called Chloe," he muttered, scowling. It wasn't really that late. She'd probably still be awake. For that matter, some of the cookout guests were probably still there. Then again, maybe that was a good reason *not* to have called Chloe. She would have dropped everything to come over, and that would have screwed up her first party as a married woman.

He wasn't even sure what had made him call Elliott Blake. It seemed logical that, as a homicide detective, Elliott would be working the Ainsley Shaw case. Elliott had been called away from the cookout for a homicide, after all.

The party had dulled a little for Martin after Elliott left, and maybe that was what had made him think immediately of Elliott when he realized the dead woman on the news was the woman in Martin's dreams.

But Chloe was his sister. They'd grown up together. She saw ghosts. She'd married a werewolf. She was obligated to believe him if he told her he'd had a dream about the dead woman. Elliott didn't have any such obligation.

Then again, Elliott was a werewolf.

Martin's cheek burned at the memory of how he'd asked his possibly-offensive question of Elliott, not realizing the guy was a werewolf, when he clearly should have realized it. After all, he was Braxton's best friend, and your best friend knew all your secrets.

Really? Like your *best friend knows all* your *secrets?* whispered a nasty little voice in his head. But that was different. Chloe had enough problems of her own.

Anything Martin had kept from her, he'd kept from her because he wanted her to be happy.

And that means not bothering her during her cookout, he told himself firmly. As his thoughts came full circle, someone knocked on his door. He went still, praying he hadn't made a really stupid decision.

"Okay, worst case," he said aloud. "What happens? Elliott Blake decides you're either crazy or a liar. What happens then? He starts avoiding you. Braxton is too nice to do the same, and Chloe loves you." He scratched his head. "Best case. What happens? Elliott believes you. What happens then?"

That gave him pause. What *would* happen if Elliott believed him? His heart pounded in his chest as he tried to imagine it.

"Only one way to find out," he muttered at last, as Elliott knocked again. He sighed and went to open the door.

He checked the peephole before opening the door. Elliott looked tired, his lips turned down. His shoulders were slumped. His dark curls look tousled, like he'd been running his hand through them. There was nothing of the self-confidence Martin had seen in him earlier today. He wondered if the case had been really bad.

Martin swung the door open. He was surprised at how quickly Elliott looked up, smiling at him.

"Hey." Elliott's voice was a little husky, his smile almost shy. Martin's chest tightened.

"Hey," he said back. He took two steps back, holding the door open.

"I'm surprised you're not still at your sister's party," Elliott said, stepping into Martin's apartment. His tone was light, as if he were only saying it to be saying *something*.

Martin shrugged. "I don't like the Fourth much."

Elliott slanted a sideways look at him. "The fireworks," he said. It wasn't a question, so Martin just nodded. "Don't blame you," Elliott added. "This may sound dumb coming from a guy who deals every day with people killing each other, but I can't imagine doing what you did, signing up to die for my country like that."

Martin's stomach flopped. "I didn't sign up to die for my country," he said. "I signed up to fix deuce-and-a-half trucks for my country."

Elliott took a couple more steps inside and then turned to look at Martin. "Okay. I guess I can't imagine leaving everything you're used to and giving up security and comfort to fix trucks halfway around the world in a country where half the population hates you when there are plenty of trucks to fix here."

Martin's lips twitched despite his discomfort. "I can't imagine trying to figure out who killed some poor joe when it isn't a war or self defense," he said, leading the way to the kitchen. "So maybe we're even."

Elliott shrugged, looking at the floor. It was a nice floor, original wood, though scuffed, but Martin had a feeling Elliott wasn't admiring the quality. Guilt pinched at him.

"Sorry," Martin said. "You want a drink?"

Elliott looked up, his lips curving up on the left side only. "Yes. Which means I probably shouldn't."

Martin huffed a laugh. "Yeah. I told myself that when I got home tonight…which is why my bottle of Jack is only half full now."

The sound of Elliott's laughter sent warmth spreading through Martin. He smiled at Elliott, who smiled back.

"Hell, why not?" Elliott said. "But I've gotta work tomorrow, so just one glass. Werewolf metabolism means it takes a lot to get me drunk, but that isn't a good excuse on a work night."

Martin nodded and poured two fingers of whiskey for Elliott and two for himself. He held out the glass. "Thanks for…y'know…getting it when I called."

Elliott's fingers brushed Martin's as he took the glass. "Thanks for calling me," he said. He held Martin's gaze, his eyes crinkling at the corners in a way that invited Martin's confidence.

"I figured you'd be done with your work by now," Martin admitted. "I hope I didn't interrupt anything."

"Nope." Elliott was turned towards Martin, leaning in a little. Martin would like to think it was because Elliott was interested in him, but Martin had some experience with law enforcement officers. He knew his sister's habits of taking in all kinds of peripheral details even when she looked like she was focused on a conversation. He wondered what Elliott Blake was deducing about him.

He gestured towards the living room. "Want to sit?"

Elliott nodded and followed Martin to the living room, where he opted to sit on the couch. He'd probably realized the recliner was Martin's, since Martin lived alone.

"Chloe says you're an Indy Eleven fan," Martin said. He knew Elliott would see this for the ploy it was—something to avoid getting right to the point. But it was also something they had in common, something they could talk about while he nerved himself up to talk about the dream.

"Long-time member of the Brickyard Battalion," Elliott said, grinning. "You like the Boys in Blue too?"

"Hell, yeah." Martin smiled back at him, his stomach giving an odd flip at that grin. "Season ticket holder."

"We'll have to sit together next game," Elliott said. "You know all about how the team got its name, right?"

"Sure, Civil War General Lew Wallace and his Eleventh Indiana Infantry." Martin couldn't stop smiling. This felt good. Normal. It was something anyone would do, not just a screwed up vet with PTSD. Or whatever it was. "I don't know a lot about the Civil War, but I know Wallace saved DC from the Confederates late in the war."

"And wrote *Ben-Hur*," Elliott added. "He was also the ambassador to Turkey, which is part of why they settled on an English Mastiff for Zeke."

Zeke was the Eleven's mascot, a big dog dressed in a zoauve uniform. Martin held up his hands in mock surrender. "Okay, I didn't know that about the mascot," he admitted.

Elliott huffed a laugh. "History nerd. I just outted myself there, huh?"

Martin chuckled. He wasn't that into history, but he'd never thought it was as boring as people claimed. History mattered too much; it shaped things that were happening today. The war in Afghanistan, for instance—there was so much history there, it was almost impossible to sort out, he thought.

In the conversational lull that followed, Martin took a small sip of whiskey and sighed, content to savor the smoky taste of whiskey and appreciate the handsome man sitting on his couch. Elliott seemed fine with cupping his glass of whiskey in both hands and staring blankly into the middle distance.

Martin wondered suddenly why Chloe hadn't tried to set him up with Elliott before now. Did she not know Elliott liked guys? Did she just think Elliott wasn't his type? She'd never been reticent about introducing her gay friends to her gay brother in the past.

Stop it, he told himself firmly. *This isn't about hooking up with someone.*

A little voice in the back of his head pointed out that if he wasn't interested in hooking up, he would have called his sister the cop, or his brother-in-law the state trooper, instead of the sexy homicide detective.

Martin squelched that little voice with another slug of whiskey.

He *wasn't* interested in hooking up. That didn't mean he was immune to attraction.

"Not that I'm complaining," Elliott said after a while. "And not that you have to talk about it if you don't want to. But I know you didn't call me to geek out about the Indy Eleven. You sounded kind of…ragged…when you called earlier."

Martin exhaled heavily. Ragged. That was a nice way of putting it. He gave Elliott a rueful smile. "I, uh. The other night, I told you I had bad dreams," he began.

Elliott nodded, his golden-brown eyes intent on Martin's.

"Usually my dreams are about Afghanistan." Martin wrenched his gaze away and looked down into his glass. "About eighty percent of them are just replays of the day the IED hit our convoy."

He stopped talking, his throat tight. He hadn't even told Chloe this. He'd tried to spare her the worst of what he'd seen in Afghanistan. At first he'd kept it secret because of how fragile she'd seemed when he left—just after she lost the baby she hadn't told him about and broken up with her boyfriend. When he got back home, he realized she had chosen to abort and end an unhealthy romantic relationship; he'd been relieved for her, but he'd wanted to spare her worrying about her little brother. And after a while, it had just become habit to not talk about what he'd experienced in country.

"Makes sense." Elliott's voice was a little rough, but his tone was gentle. He wasn't quite looking at

Martin, but his face was turned towards Martin, like he was inviting confidence but not demanding it. It reminded Martin of the way you were supposed to approach a dog you were uncertain of, and a distant part of him wondered if Elliott was using werewolf body language on him.

"My best friend, Dax." Martin coughed. "He lost an arm in that explosion. A couple of other guys died. I got out of it with a concussion and a sprained wrist." He felt his lips twist and tried to press them into submission. He hadn't earned this trauma.

"Concussions aren't anything to mess around with," Elliott said.

"Maybe not, but I still have both my arms," Martin snapped. Then he sighed. "No, sorry. You didn't deserve that."

Elliott shrugged. "I can take it," he said, and the expression on his face as he looked at Martin was inviting yet somehow vulnerable.

Martin's heart kicked at his chest, making him gasp for breath. What was Elliott doing to him? Why did the warmth in his gaze, the vulnerability of his mouth, make Martin want to run fast and hard in the opposite direction?

"Uh." Martin cleared his throat. "I haven't, uh, haven't told Chloe some of this."

"I like your sister," Elliott said quickly. "I respect her. But whatever you tell me, it's between you and me."

Martin closed his suddenly stinging eyes and kept talking. "Last night I had a really weird dream. I was standing in a street somewhere, and this girl was looking at me. She seemed friendly, but sad, if that makes sense." He could tell his voice sounded weird. He took a deep breath. "In my dream, I knew her. Once I woke up, I realized I had no idea who she was. But you know how it is in dreams."

Elliott nodded.

"I dreamed about her again after I got home today." Martin pinched at his nose, pressing his thumb and forefinger into the corners of his eyes. "She had a friendly smile, and she was walking down a street without being afraid. She had confidence in herself. Then I saw this shadowed figure, and I felt cold all over."

Without looking up, he lifted his whiskey glass to his lips and drained it. "I knew her in my dream again, even though I couldn't have told you what her name was. But she was walking towards me, and then I felt something cold at my back, and she looked past me and her face was just...terrified. And then there was blood—all over." He choked and wished he had more whiskey.

"She saw something behind you," Elliott murmured.

Martin nodded. "Whatever was there, she recognized it as danger. But she didn't have time to react. It ripped her open. She fell back, and all I could see was her green eyes and red hair. And then I woke up."

His hands were shaking and his lips tingled so much they were almost numb. He couldn't quite feel his face. He wondered how he looked to Elliott. *God.* This was why he drank.

"It's okay, Martin." Elliott's voice was a low murmur, warm and solid. "You can tell me. I won't tell anyone."

Martin shuddered, looking down at his knees. "She knew my secrets somehow. And in the dream, I knew hers. She'd failed someone she loved. And then I saw her blood spraying. I saw her die." His breath caught in his throat. "I woke up before I could do anything. Help her, fight whatever attacked her, anything."

His voice was rising in pitch and volume. He tried to clamp down on it. His breath was coming too fast. "I tried to stop it. I tried to save her. But all I saw was her eyes. Her blood."

Strong hands curled around his. "It's okay. Breathe, Martin."

Martin clenched his eyes shut, relishing the feel of Elliott's hands despite his anxiety. "She's dead. But I saw her. I saw her clearly. And once I woke up, I knew who she was."

He couldn't catch his breath. His heart was going to pound its way through his chest wall. His throat was closing around the breaths he tried to suck in. There was a long silence, punctuated only by his ragged breathing.

"You saw Ainsley Shaw's death, didn't you?" Elliott Blake's voice was low and entirely certain. Martin wanted to ask how he knew. Wanted to ask why he would think such a thing. But instead, he just nodded, his lips parted as he tried to suck in air.

"I think," Elliott said slowly, "you'd better tell me everything. From the beginning."

CHAPTER 8

Lachlan swore and shoved his guitar away from him.

"God damn it, Ainsley," he gasped. His stomach was flipping, making it hard to catch his breath.

He covered his face with his hands and panted into his palms. He couldn't understand why he kept having these panic attacks where his chest got tight and his heart tried to beat its way out of his chest. It wasn't like anything was coming after him. He was fine.

It was Ainsley who was dead.

A sob escaped him as he doubled over and keened softly into his hands. He broke off and gasped for breath. He'd had to come home to his apartment to sleep. His parents had tried to get him to stay in his old bedroom, but he hadn't been able to spend one more minute in that house—the house where Ainsley died.

How could you let her be slaughtered without even noticing? he'd wanted to howl at them. How could someone break into this house and rip her to shreds without waking you up?

But he hadn't said it. He could tell his parents were asking themselves the same questions, and so he'd choked the words back until he thought he might vomit from the words and the pain and the anger all clogging his stomach. So he'd lurched to his feet and said, "I gotta go," and bolted from the house.

His father had followed him to the door and down the front steps.

"Lach," he called, and his voice broke, which made Lachlan turn around. He'd looked at his father, poised on a knife-edge between his father's criticisms of him and his own love for his family. He hadn't said anything.

"Lach," his father repeated. "Son. I love you. You know that, don't you? Your mother and I, we love you."

And Lachlan had rushed back into his father's embrace, burying his face against his dad's shoulder and aching with all his body to be six years old again and believe that his father could fix anything.

His mother hadn't followed them. She'd been all but passed out on the couch after taking a couple of pills the family doctor had prescribed for her. Lachlan was glad. His mom always believed in him, always loved him, and never asked anything of him. His father was more critical, more tough-love than unconditional-love, but Mom would have seen this as some turning point, and Lachlan knew it wasn't.

He loved his father, but his father was powerless to fix this.

"I love you, too, Dad," he'd muttered, almost embarrassed, and when his father loosened his embrace, Lachlan had moved quickly to his car. "I'll see you tomorrow, okay?"

And his father, knowing Lachlan needed to be alone, maybe needing to be alone himself, had just nodded.

Lachlan scraped the heels of his hands over his face, drying his cheeks and pressing into his eyes until he saw sparks of light against his eyelids.

"I hate you," he muttered, and even he didn't know if he was talking to his father, to the person who had murdered Ainsley, or to Ainsley herself.

How *dare* she die when she was still this perfect war veteran who'd sacrificed her own hopes and dreams to fight for her country? How *dare* she die right after their fight at dinner on Sunday? How *dare* she leave Lachlan behind to always be the disappointment, the underachiever, the loser?

"I hate you," he whispered again, and wondered if he meant it for himself.

* * *

Martin was back at Chloe and Braxton's cookout, which was how he realized he was dreaming.

Somehow the realization that he was dreaming didn't wake him, though; it made everything feel sweeter. He was happy to be there, knowing Elliott would show up soon. He wasn't nervous about impending fireworks.

This, he thought, was going to be a good dream.

Sure enough, Elliott walked into the backyard, his gaze searching—and landing immediately on Martin. His face lit in a smile and he crossed the yard to where Martin stood.

They were deep in a conversation about soccer when Murphy showed up with some of the other werewolves. The Ruiz family arrived, everyone smiling and clearly enjoying themselves. Someone turned on a radio, and someone else turned it up.

It seemed natural they start dancing, and Martin was pleased when Elliott wrapped an arm around his waist and pulled him closer. Before long they were kissing as they danced. Martin had stopped paying attention to anything but Elliott.

That, of course, was when someone began screaming.

It was so ragged and raw that, as Martin and Elliott tensed and fell away from each other, Martin wasn't sure if the screamer was male or female.

Then he spun and saw Murphy, sprawled on the ground, back arched. Murphy was screaming. A shadowy figure leaned over him—no, not shadowy.

Blurry.

Martin ran at the figure, but even though he was running as hard as he could, he wasn't getting any closer. He clenched his hands into fists and shouted.

The figure lifted its head and he caught a flash of strawberry blonde hair. Then it whirled away from him, dragging Murphy's limp form with it.

"Elliott!" Martin screamed. "Where's Murphy?"

He woke, splayed out across his bed, the sheets twisted around one leg so tight he could barely move it. It took him several seconds to flail out of the sheets and swing his legs over the side of the bed.

He was panting, his pulse thumping in his neck. He cupped a hand against the pulse, closing his eyes and trying to will his heart to slow down. After a moment he tried for breath control. Breathe in, in, in, hold it, out.

Then he huffed in disgust. He knew what he was supposed to do. Why mess with what—sometimes—helped?

"You're home," he whispered to himself between slow breaths. "Winthrop Avenue. Broad Ripple. Indianapolis. Indiana. United States of America." His pulse finally began to slow. "Not Kandahar. Not Afghanistan. Indiana. Cornfields. Race cars. You're good. You're back."

It calmed him enough to clear a space for thinking, although his hands were still shaking as he went to the kitchen for a glass of water. Only after he'd drained the glass and splashed cold water against his face did he let himself turn his thoughts back to the dream.

Murphy. If Elliott was right, if Martin really was having visions of some kind in his dreams, Murphy was in danger. Murphy was all hard edges and sharp glares, but he was a comic book nerd, and Martin felt drawn to him somehow. Maybe it was just because he knew Murphy had helped save Chloe and Braxton's lives last fall, but it didn't really matter why. Martin needed to help Murphy.

In order to do that, he needed to call Elliott.

His pulse jumped again at the thought, but this time it was a pleasant one, despite the circumstances. He refilled his water glass and went to get his phone.

* * *

Elliott jerked awake, heart thumping, as his phone rang. He straightened, the realization creeping in that he'd fallen asleep at his kitchen table. As the ringtone started up again, he fumbled through the papers scattered across the table. He could tell it was there somewhere…

Finally locating it, he tried to answer just as it went to voice mail. The caller ID told him it was Martin Cole.

Elliott smiled involuntarily. It would be nice to talk to Martin instead of worrying about the case, which was what he'd been doing all day.

Then he realized it was almost ten at night. Martin wouldn't be calling him that late unless…

…*Unless he's lonely and wants some company?* suggested a hopeful voice in the back of his mind.

"Unless he's had another vision," Elliott said aloud. He sighed and rubbed his forehead and hit the callback button.

Martin answered on the first ring.

"Hey," Elliott said, his voice automatically softening a little at the sound of Martin's voice. "Sorry I missed your call. I couldn't find my phone."

Martin's chuckle made Elliott's chest feel odd. He really liked that sound.

"It's fine," Martin said. "I'm sorry if I woke you."

"Nah," Elliott lied. "I was working on case stuff. I just had all kinds of papers piled over the phone."

"Any new developments?" Martin asked.

"Not to speak of."

"Well… I might have something for you. I'm not sure." Martin sounded sure, though.

"Tell me."

"I was dreaming about the cookout," Martin said. "So that's why I'm not sure. This wasn't like the PTSD dreams. It was a nice dream." He coughed. "I mean, you know, everyone was talking, laughing, some people were dancing." He paused. "Anyway. It started out nice. Then someone started screaming."

Elliott wondered about that pause. What was Martin leaving out? His lips curled involuntarily. Had Elliott been in that dream? Had Elliott and Martin been talking in the dream? *Dancing* in the dream?

Suddenly he very much wanted to dance with Martin.

"Are you there?" Martin's voice sounded uncertain.

"Sorry, yeah." Elliott shook himself. *Don't get distracted!* "Someone started screaming?"

"When we turned to look, it was Murphy. He was on the ground."

"Murphy!" Elliott's heart jumped into double-time. He stood up, looking around the kitchen for his shoes.

"Yeah. He'd been attacked by something. Someone, actually. I almost saw the person. At least, I saw light red hair. They were too blurry to make anything else out."

"But you're sure it was Murphy?" Elliott shoved his feet into his shoes. "Did you try calling him?"

"I don't have Murphy's number," Martin said.

"Shit. Hang on. Stay on the line, I'm gonna text him."

Elliott pulled up his messaging app and texted Murphy, *Hey, text me ASAP.* Then he put the phone back to his ear. "What else happened?"

"That was almost all of it. I tried to run at the figure—I *did* run at the figure—but I wasn't going anywhere." Martin huffed. "Sometimes I dream that I'm driving, and I push the accelerator, but it just goes all the way to the floor and the car doesn't move. You ever have that dream? This was like that, except running."

Elliott scowled. "What about the figure? Was Murphy still screaming?"

"No, he'd stopped. He wasn't moving. The figure grabbed him and vanished. He took Murphy with him."

Elliott swiped his car keys from the hook on his refrigerator. "Murphy's not answering. I'm going to go check on him."

"Take me with you," Martin said.

The words made Elliott smile, but they also filled him with an odd sense of reluctance. "I don't know," he hedged. Murphy could be a shit, but he was pack. How would he react if Elliott showed up with Martin, a guy he barely knew, charging to the rescue?

Then again, Murphy had at least seemed to like Martin.

"Please," Martin said. "Or I can meet you. Where does he live?"

Elliott made up his mind. "Meridian, just north of Fall Creek. You're basically on my way there. I'll be there in fifteen minutes."

He called Murphy's phone six times between his apartment at Keystone and Eighty-Sixth and Martin's house just south of Sixty-Second. Every call went straight to voice mail.

He pulled up in front of Martin's house and unbuckled his seatbelt, but Martin must have been watching for him. He was hurrying down the sidewalk before Elliott had even opened the door. Martin slid into the passenger seat and gave Elliott a tight smile.

"Hey. Thanks."

Elliott took a few moments to look Martin over. His auburn hair was just long enough to be tousled and show that Martin had been sleeping. There were shadows under his eyes that Elliott didn't remember seeing at the cookout. Had that really only been yesterday? Thirty hours ago.

"Thanks for calling me," he said. He wanted to reach over and take Martin's hand, though whether it was to comfort Martin or for his own comfort, he wasn't sure.

They didn't talk much on the drive to Murphy's apartment building. Elliott had asked Murphy on several occasions if he wanted to move in with Elliott. There was an extra bedroom that Elliott was using mostly as a junk room right now, a dusty computer desk piled with bills and paperwork he kept forgetting to file. The rent was too high for Murphy if they split it evenly, though, and Murphy wouldn't hear of Elliott subsidizing his part of the rent.

Elliott was of the opinion that Murphy was too proud by half.

Then again, Elliott had never been as poor as Murphy seemed to be. Elliott's mom had struggled when he was very young; she was a single mother working two jobs and sometimes three until he was in first grade. That was the year she got pregnant with Olivia. Olivia's dad had stuck around for a couple of years, but Elliott's mom wasn't the marrying sort, and eventually she was acting as a single parent again. Soon after he left, Emily was born.

By that time, though, their mom had finished college and gotten a better job. She worked full time and started saving money. She'd put every extra penny into her 401(k) and college funds for the girls. Elliott's father had set up a college fund for Elliott, and although he lived in another state and rarely saw his son, no one could accuse him of neglect.

Elliott was so deep in thought that Martin's voice made him jump.

"Is there any chance Murphy could just be asleep?"

"Uh. Maybe, but he's a night owl, generally." Elliott frowned. "He might still be at work, I guess." Murphy had been working at the Fed Ex distribution center for a couple of years now, and he'd managed to hang onto that job even though he cycled through fast food jobs on a fairly regular basis. Elliott thought the

Fed Ex job was mornings, though, and restaurant jobs evenings.

He pulled into the parking lot behind Murphy's apartment building, headlights sweeping across a couple of figures who turned and stared in startlement. One of them was clearly a troll. Murphy had said there were some in the neighborhood.

"Is that—" Martin broke off. When Elliott looked over, he was shaking his head.

"Could you tell he was different? That was a troll."

"The green-skinned kind, right?"

"Well, gray-green, but yeah." Elliott switched off the ignition. "I don't see Murphy's car in the lot, but it might have broken down again." He climbed out of the car, Martin close behind him. "You ought to come up with me. They aren't generally aggressive or territorial, but if they realize you're a supernatural they don't recognize…"

Martin didn't argue about being labeled a supernatural. Elliott wondered if that was just because they were taking the stairs two at a time, or if Elliott had convinced him.

Elliott knew Murphy's access code for the door. Pack members always had access to each other's houses; it was a safety issue as well as a family thing. Elliott's stomach was churning as he led the way to Murphy's door.

No one answered.

Elliott scowled. He had a key, but he didn't like that he would have to use it. Was Murphy here, hurt, unable to call out? Was he taken by that figure? Was he— *Don't think it*, he told himself, and slid the key into the lock.

The apartment was empty.

"There's no sign of a struggle," Martin said. "And anyway, this kind of lock requires a key. They wouldn't have been able to lock it, would they?"

"If they took his keys, they would." Elliott's voice was grim. He checked his phone, but there were still no missed calls or answering texts from Murphy. Another call went straight to voice mail.

"Okay, would he be with Chloe and Braxton? Or other pack members?" Martin was pinching the bridge of his nose. He looked tired.

Elliott sent a quick text to Braxton and another to Tara. Within five minutes, as he did another sweep of the apartment, they both responded they hadn't seen Murphy since the cookout.

"Then we check his work," Martin said. "Do you have the number?"

"We'll go there," Elliott decided. "If something has happened to him, I want to be able to interview his coworkers."

* * *

Martin's head was starting to hurt. He supposed it had something to do with how little sleep he'd had over the past two or three days, but Elliot's growling and Martin's worry for Murphy couldn't be helping.

By the time they pulled up in front of a pizza place, Martin was beginning to wonder if Elliott had forgotten he was in the car. The other man hadn't said a word since they left Murphy's apartment. Martin knew the packmates were close, though he also knew Murphy was a little outside the closest group of werewolves. Still, Elliott had to be sick with worry.

Martin trailed Elliott into the front of the store. It was empty except for a blonde girl working the counter. She looked up and smiled at them. "Hi! How can I help you?"

To Martin's surprise, Elliott didn't turn on the charm. He just held up his badge and said, "I need to talk to Murphy O'Hare."

The girl's eyes widened. "Uh, is he in trouble?"

"Is he here?" Elliott demanded.

"He's not in trouble," Martin put in.

Elliott looked over, his eyes widening a little. He *had* forgotten about Martin, hadn't he? It would be amusing if the situation weren't so fraught.

"I'll—I'll go get him." The girl disappeared into the back of the restaurant.

"Sorry, I shouldn't have butted in," Martin said, and Elliott sighed.

"No, I shouldn't have gotten in her face. I'm sorry. I just—I worry about him. I guess I'm too used to being a big brother, taking care of my sisters. I feel like I ought to take care of Murphy, too." Elliott gave him a sheepish half-smile.

"What the hell, Elliott?" Murphy's voice was sharp. Martin turned to stare at him, relieved to see him despite the hot glare the younger man was aiming at them. Murphy was wearing a flour-dusted apron and a hairnet that made his large nose look larger. His arms were at his side, hands clenched into fists.

"Murphy! You're okay!" Elliott took a step forward and then stopped.

"Yeah," Murphy said, as if it should be obvious. "But you're not going to be in a minute."

"Why don't we take this outside?" Martin said. He didn't mean to use the voice of calm authority he'd learned in the Army, but from the startled glances Elliott and Murphy both gave him, he obviously had.

Murphy glared for a second and then stomped out the door, pushing Elliott out of the way.

Elliott and Martin exchanged a look and then followed.

Murphy kept walking, leading them around the side of the building until they were back by the Dumpster. "Okay, so. What the hell?"

"I think you're in danger," Martin said. "Maybe."

Murphy stared at him for a moment and then turned his glare on Elliott. "Trying to impress your new guy, Elliott? Show him what a badass cop you are?"

Martin felt his cheeks heat. Was he that obvious?

"Murphy—" Elliott began, but Murphy cut him off.

"No, go on," he said. "Throw your weight around some more. Want to search my car, *detective*?"

Elliott didn't flinch, exactly, but Martin could see him tensing. Hastily Martin interrupted. "This is my fault, Murphy. I had...uh..."

"Don't bother apologizing, Martin," Elliott said. His voice was heavy.

"No, don't, *Martin*. We don't apologize to Murphy for shit."

Martin raised his eyebrows and folded his arms across his chest. "Aren't you taking this Rocket Raccoon act a bit too far?" he asked.

Elliott turned to stare at him. Murphy just glowered. Elliott's eyes were wide, his mouth open a little as if he'd started to speak. His expression blanked as Murphy snorted.

As Elliott swung around to stare at *him*, Murphy's hands unclenched. "Does that make you Starlord or Drax?" he asked, grudging amusement in his voice.

"I am Groot," Martin replied.

The last of Murphy's spite vanished as he laughed. "Actually, I can see it." He kicked Martin's foot. "Ah, you're all right, Marty." He looked at Elliott and it turned into a glare again. "*You*, I'm still pissed at."

Elliott held up his hands in surrender. "I'll be in the car," he said, and walked away.

"So." Murphy eyed Martin for a couple of heartbeats. "You like him."

Martin's eyes widened before he could help himself. He sucked in a quick breath and said, "I am Groot," as blankly as possible.

Murphy rolled his eyes. "So why the hell *did* you guys show up here?"

Martin sighed. "I know this is going to sound nuts, but I honestly did think you were in danger. Maybe you still are, I don't know."

Murphy gave him an eyebrow and Martin knew he wouldn't be able to get out of a better explanation. He gave Murphy a quick rundown of the way he'd dreamed about Ainsley Shaw's murder, and then described the last part of tonight's dream. Murphy didn't need to know about the dancing and kissing, but he had a right to know there might be a murderer after him.

Finally Murphy sighed. "As long as you're not dreaming kinky things about me and some ugly person, I don't care if you dream about me. But that obviously wasn't a vision, because first of all, you were dreaming about something that already happened."

"The cookout happened," Martin protested, "but it didn't happen like that. Maybe this is another cookout."

"So get Braxton to cancel it," Murphy said. "Whatever. It's just obvious that wasn't a vision."

Martin rubbed his forehead, feeling stupid. "It's just obvious I'm not psychic," he muttered. This whole night had been a colossal mistake. He should have known it wasn't a psychic thing. He should have kept his dream to himself.

"No shit," Murphy said, but the glare he directed at Martin seemed almost, a tiny bit, affectionate. "You can't even tell how much Ell's into you."

Martin fled.

CHAPTER 9

Elliott poured himself a third cup of coffee and tapped his fingers on his desk. Kaida Akimoto had agreed to come in to the station to talk about Ainsley. He was looking forward to finally having a step forward in the investigation that he could point his superiors at. They were getting antsy that he'd interviewed people and had no leads or suspects. It was shaping up to be a high-profile case, with Ainsley's veteran status and the gruesome nature of the crime—though at least that was still out of the media, there was no guarantee how long it would stay that way.

His phone rang. It was the desk officer. "A Ms. Akimoto here to see you."

"You swear it's Ms. Akimoto and not Sarah Fitzgerald?" He was mostly joking, but he was still dodging Sarah's calls. She was like a terrier with a bone when she thought something was hinky. It was part of the reason they'd broken up years ago—but she'd never quite let him off the hook.

"You think I've slipped so much I'll let a reporter into this office?"

"I'm in Interview One," Elliott said. "Can someone show her back?"

"For you, anything, Blake," she said sourly.

Elliott grinned. "I'll owe you a dozen Long's Donuts."

"Damn right you will."

He took his coffee and the case file, complete with graphic crime scene photos, and headed for the interview room. He was seated, a blank notepad in front of him, when the door opened.

The woman who came through it was a short, Asian woman. She wasn't looking at him as she walked in; she had turned to say something to the person showing her in. It wasn't until she was inside and the door shut behind her that she turned and registered his presence.

Fear spiked tangy in her scent. He could see her muscles tense. She was going to bolt.

He didn't get up or even move. He met her gaze and then flicked his eyes away from her. She might not know he was a werewolf, but she probably did, or she wouldn't be as scared as she was. Either way, she would instinctively understand from his body language that he wasn't trying to dominate her. He made his voice as soothing as possible as he said, "Calm down, Ms. Akimoto. You're not in trouble."

The fear was thick, but a piquant whiff of curiosity spiraled through it. She didn't bolt, but she also didn't sit down. She folded her arms across her chest. She was short and slender, but her arms were muscular in a sleeveless silk shell. "I'm not? Aren't people's lovers the first one you suspect?"

Elliott nodded. "A lot of the time, sure. A lot of murder victims know their killers." A heavy, musky scent washed the room—grief. "But," he added, as if he hadn't noticed that scent, "being what I am, I have the killer's scent. I haven't caught any…weird stuff…when I'm around the family."

Kaida stiffened and pulled out the chair opposite Elliott's. "Weird stuff. You think—"

He spoke quietly. "Not many human killers do what this one did."

She sank into the chair, the musky scent growing stronger. "Was…" Her voice was calm, but he saw tears glisten in her eyes. "It was bad?"

"Bad enough." He spoke gruffly, knowing there was no easy way for her to hear it.

Her gaze was on the folder in front of him. She would know there were photos in it. Anyone who'd ever seen a police procedural on TV knew there would be photos. Elliott watched the tears spill over and slip silently down her cheeks as she met his gaze and jerked her chin at the folder.

Wordlessly, he flipped the folder open and slid a photo across the table. It was the easiest of them, a bloodless pre-autopsy photo. Ainsley's face was recognizable, even if her body had been ravaged. Elliott's throat tightened a little; he still remembered how the detective had slammed down the photos of his mother, trying to get Elliott to confess to something he would never have done.

Kaida Akimoto took it better than Elliott had himself. She lifted one hand to almost touch the photo.

118

Then she clasped her hands together and turned her head. "Please take it away."

She was weeping almost soundlessly, her face turned away from him. He saw her shoulders shaking, saw her lift a hand to dab at her eyes. He smelled grief, anger, disgust, fear. Elliott didn't think she'd done it.

"So I have to ask," he said, his voice heavy. "Where were you on July third?"

Kaida took a long, slow breath. "Chicago. I had a business meeting." She wiped her eyes with the back of one hand and squeezed the bridge of her nose. Then she fished in her purse and pulled out a business card, which she offered to Elliott. "You can call my company and they'll give you any information you need. Hotel, business associates, whatever." Her voice was dull, low. She was calm, but desperately unhappy.

Elliott nodded. "When did you last see Ainsley?"

"July first. She spent the night at my place. I'd invited her to come to Chicago with me, just to get away from her folks' place for a couple days, but she had a job interview."

Elliott nodded and kept watching, waiting for Kaida to continue. She didn't disappoint.

"My train left hella early for Chicago on the second, so Ains dropped me at Union Station."

"So it was actually July second," Elliott said.

"Well, yeah, technically. Five-thirty am July second."

Elliott nodded. "What are you?"

She stiffened, fear and anger spiking in her scent. "Excuse me?"

"You're not a werewolf. Not a witch. What? Some kind of fae?"

Kaida rested both hands on the table. "How exactly is that germane?"

Elliott had been hoping his question, coming from such a different angle as the others, would catch her off guard. He shrugged, trying to appear insouciant. "It'll help me rule you out as a suspect."

Her voice was cold as she said, "I didn't kill Ainsley."

"I hope not." Elliott met her gaze, wondering if her sense of smell was as keen as a werewolf's. Would she realize he was in earnest? "I truly hope not. But Lachlan said their folks didn't know about you. Didn't know Ainsley had a girlfriend—was a lesbian."

"Pansexual," Kaida interrupted stiffly.

Elliott tilted his head slightly. "Sorry. I shouldn't have assumed. But her parents didn't know she was pansexual, did she?"

Kaida didn't speak.

"They had no idea she had a serious girlfriend. Or...maybe not so serious, since you probably aren't the person who got her pregnant."

Kaida shot to her feet.

Elliot didn't shift, didn't raise his voice. He watched her calmly as he said, "Sit down." He could smell her anger, but there was no surprise, no fear, nothing that indicated she was hearing this for the first time. "You seem to know I'm a werewolf. That means you understand exactly how I know you aren't surprised about the baby."

Kaida sat down again and folded her hands. "Which gives me motive."

Elliott nodded. "I don't want to believe you killed her, because in the same way I can tell you knew about that, I can also tell you're genuinely grieving. So help me out, Ms. Akimoto."

Kaida held his gaze for several heartbeats, her dark eyes serious as she searched his. Elliott didn't know what she was looking for, but she apparently found it, because she sighed.

"Ainsley cheated on me. Just once, as far as I know. She was in New York City. Her company had just gotten back to the States, and I wasn't able to meet her in New York. They all went out for drinks. Her ex was an officer. They slept together—they were both drunk." She licked her lips. "He's married."

"And you found that out when, exactly?" Elliott asked.

She sighed again. "From an email she sent me the night she was killed. At least, I found out some of it then. She confessed she'd cheated. She didn't tell me about the baby."

She was telling the truth. At least, she didn't smell anxious and he didn't hear her heartrate spike. She would pass a lie detector test. There were people who could fool those, but Elliott was pretty sure Kaida Akimoto wasn't a sociopath.

He took his own opportunity to study her face, letting her see him do it. "What can you tell me about the ex?"

Kaida blinked. "Uh." She shook her head. "I know his name, that's it. David Corriden." She frowned. "You don't think—"

Elliott shrugged. "Gotta check. But unless he's some kind of monster, probably not. It's not easy, running an investigation like this and trying to keep the higher ups from asking questions they shouldn't."

Kaida nodded slowly. "Kitsune," she said, her voice quiet.

Kitsune. Elliott drew in a long, slow breath, savoring the musky, magic scent that was laced with cherry blossoms. So that was what a kitsune smelled like. "Don't leave town," he said finally. "If work tries to send you to Chicago, you'll have to find an excuse to put it off. At least until you hear from me again."

"Understood." Kaida stood, brushing her palms against her crisp slacks. "Find the bastard who killed my girlfriend."

Elliott stood, too, and offered his hand. "I'll do my damnedest."

* * *

On Friday, Lachlan went to the funeral home with his father. Mom was still drugged to the gills with whatever the doctor had given her, but Dad wasn't much better even without drugs, so someone had to step up.

These decisions weren't things a twenty-four-year-old guy ought to be thinking about. What songs to sing at Ains' funeral, whether the casket should be pine or oak or mahogany, if they should ask their pastor to officiate or have the funeral home appoint the officiant.

Lach said he thought the chaplain for Ainsley's Army unit ought to be the one to speak. After all, the chaplain probably knew her better than her family after the last couple of years. He'd thought Kaida ought to be part of the funeral planning, but he hadn't known how to contact her. He had tried calling her, using a number he found in Ainsley's cell, but she hadn't returned his calls, not even after he left a voice mail. She wasn't on social media, as far as he could tell, so he'd exhausted whatever resources he'd had to find her.

He'd never even met the girl his sister was in love with. How fucked up was that? He ignored the nasty voice in the back of his head that pointed out he could have told Ainsley to invite Kaida to dinner on Sunday. He could have asked Ainsley and Kaida out to dinner or just to hang. Instead he'd wasted the last month on resenting his sister and resisting her overtures.

How was I supposed to know some fucking asshole would fucking murder her after she came back? She was home from a war zone, for Christ's sake! She should have been safe.

"Mister Shaw?"

Lachlan jerked to attention and looked over at his father, who was staring blankly at his own clasped hands.

"Sorry," Lachlan said, looking over at the funeral director. "What was that?"

"I was just asking if your family would like to create memory boards for Ainsley. Photos and the like for callers to remember her by."

Lachlan inhaled slowly and nodded. "Yeah. Yeah, I have a lot of pictures. And she sent us some from Afghanistan. And Kaida—" He broke off, his throat closing for a moment. He felt his face ripple as he pressed his lips together. He wouldn't cry, God damn it. He *wouldn't* cry.

"Kaida." He looked straight at the funeral director. "My sister was dating a woman named Kaida Akimoto. I haven't been able to get in touch with Kaida, but she ought to be involved in this, too."

"...What?" Of course this was the moment their father chose to wake up to the world around him again.

Lachlan exchanged a glance with the funeral director. "Ains was a lesbian, dad. She was dating this chick, Kaida?" Pansexual, actually, but their father wouldn't care about the details. He would just be pissed that his perfect daughter was—in his eyes, at least—not quite so perfect.

His dad blinked several times. "How...Wha..." He shook his head. "Why didn't I know this?"

Oh, I don't know, because you would have fucking flipped out if your perfect Goddamn daughter was anything other than Goddamn perfect? Lachlan thought. Because you might have kicked the dyke out of your house? Because you and mom might have asked her where you'd failed her as parents?

Aloud, he just said, "I think she just realized it while she was away. She was getting ready to tell you guys." He bounced his knee, hoping his dad wouldn't realize he was lying.

"This was something new? Something..." His father shook his head again. "Maybe it was just a phase she was working through."

"Yeah, sure." Lachlan sneered. "Realizing who you really are isn't a phase, Dad. She'd been with Kaida for most of her deployment. She just knew you'd react like this."

The funeral director cleared his throat. "Do you have a phone number or email address for Ms. Akimoto?"

Lachlan reached across the desk and took a sticky note off the cat-shaped dispenser. He pulled up Kaida's number from his contacts and wrote it on the sticky note. "This is the number I have. I took it off Ains' phone, so I assume current."

The funeral director nodded. "I'll see if I can reach her," he said. He gave Lachlan a look they were probably taught in their funeral training. It was supposed to convey sympathy, concern, probably even friendship. Lachlan didn't care what it was supposed to convey, as long as the funeral director didn't try to gloss over the fact that Ainsley had been dating a woman.

There were half a dozen forms to sign and a check to write, but finally Lachlan guided his father out of the funeral home and back to his SUV. His dad hadn't wanted to ride in Lach's crappy old car, but he was definitely in no shape to drive himself, so Lach took the keys and hustled his dad into the passenger seat.

"You want to get something to eat?" he asked. He wasn't hungry, and he couldn't imagine that his dad was, either, but it seemed the thing to do. It was almost one o'clock, after all.

"No." Lachlan's dad slumped in his seat, staring at the dashboard. He looked like everything that had ever mattered to him in life had been destroyed.

Lachlan knew how he felt. He'd only thought his singing career was the most important thing in his life. It had taken Ainsley's brutal murder to show him how important his sister had been to him. He didn't care about eating. He didn't honestly give a fuck whether he ate ever again. But he knew there were people who were depending on him still. Maybe his parents, at least for now. The people at work. If no one else, Knot Tide needed him.

"I'm gonna hit the KFC drive through," he told his dad. "If you change your mind by the time we get here, let me know."

They ended up going back to his parents' home with two bags full of chicken and fries. Despite his own lack of appetite, Lachlan knew his parents needed to eat, and he'd decided that eating in front of them might encourage them to do that.

The women from his parents' church were sitting in the living room when they got home. Two women knitted, the third scrolled through something on her phone. The youngest of them stood up when Lachlan met her eyes.

"I am so very sorry for your loss," she told Lachlan. She gathered her knitting and stood up, but, thank Jesus, she didn't look like she was going to hug him. She was maybe thirty at the oldest and the way she shifted her feet made Lachlan think maybe she was embarrassed about her role in this.

"Thanks," he said flatly. He didn't honestly give a shit about making the other women feel better, but he did appreciate that they'd been willing to come over and check on his mom. "We have a little extra chicken, if you want."

"We're supposed to be feeding you," she replied, her lips curling up a little. "I think that's the main point of a women's circle."

Lachlan snorted, which made her lips curl up further. "Thanks for staying with my mom," he said. "You know Ainsley was a dyke, right?"

He felt a little guilty for labeling her that again, since it wasn't entirely true, but he had a feeling Ainsley would have been amused by the way one of the women flinched. The oldest woman merely put her phone down and met his gaze.

"We are not here to judge Ainsley," she informed him. "We are simply here to do whatever we can to ease the burdens on your family."

Feeling obscurely guilty, Lachlan ducked his head. "I appreciate it," he muttered. "The funeral director's going to work on arrangements, but I think the funeral will be Friday or Saturday."

The oldest woman nodded. "I'll be sure to let Pastor Stanley know," she said, and stood up.

The other two women stood as well and spent a minute shaking hands with his father. Then the youngest woman hugged Lachlan, to his surprise.

"Ainsley was a good friend," she whispered. "Look up Esther in her contacts if you need to talk."

Lachlan had stiffened automatically, not returning her hug, but he filed her name away for future reference. She backed away, looking embarrassed, and Lachlan felt a sharp stab of guilt. If she'd really been a good friend of his sister's... "Do you know Kaida?" he asked.

Esther shook her head. "I knew about her, but we've never met." She ignored the look the flinchy woman gave her and smiled at Lachlan. "Maybe we can get coffee and talk sometime."

Lachlan couldn't make himself smile, but his lips pulled to one side. "I'd like that," he said, and surprised himself by meaning it.

CHAPTER 10

When Martin got to Thr3e Wise Men Brewing Company, Chloe was already going to town on a plate of pub chips. She dunked one in the jalapeno dip and waved it at him. Martin threaded his way over to the booth she'd taken. She was sitting with her back to the huge plate glass windows looking into the brewing area; Martin liked watching them do their work.

"Hey," she said, her mouth full. "I ordered us a pizza and got you the IPA. Hope that's okay."

"You better share those," Martin said, dropping into his chair. "How's married life treating you?"

Chloe beamed at him. "Pretty good. It isn't that much different from before, except neither of us has to go home at the end of a date."

"Your cats still getting along?"

"Dude, they're so cute. They snuggle and everything." Chloe sipped her beer. "I actually caught Murphy smiling when he saw that the other day."

"Murphy? Smiling?" Martin clutched at his chest.

"I know, right?" She shook her head. "He's a good guy, really. I mean, he's a little shit, but underneath it, he's just lonely and kind of insecure. I think he's mostly an asshole to make people think he doesn't care if he doesn't have friends."

"That makes no sense. He's got the pack." Chloe and Braxton had given him the rundown on who was in the Eagle Creek Pack after he confessed his faux-pas with Elliott at the cookout. "I mean, you said they took him in right after he got bit."

Chloe made a face. "Yeah, but they couldn't give him a choice, either. Braxton's dad was still alive then, and he said Murphy could either join the pack or die. You can't have out-of-control werewolves running around. If Murphy didn't learn control, he'd probably bite more people, and that never ends well."

"Yeah, that's not exactly a way to win a guy's trust." Martin smiled as the waitress approached. After he asked her for a glass of water to go with his IPA, he turned back to Chloe. "So when's the next Full?"

"Tonight, which is why I asked if you wanted to hang out. I mean, it isn't like they're not safe to hang out with, but a human can't exactly keep up with them, and sitting around a forest in the dark by myself isn't my idea of fun, so…"

Martin snorted. "I should have known you didn't want to hang out with me because you missed me or anything."

Chloe reached over and smacked the side of his head.

"Ow! Dude, you don't have to be such a jerk about it." Martin rubbed his ear, grinning.

"I'll show you a jerk," Chloe said, grinning back at him. "So what's new in your life since I got married?"

Martin took a long, slow sip of his ale to give himself a couple moments to think. Chloe knew about his dreams, even if she didn't know how often he'd been having them lately. Did he want to tell her what Elliott thought about the new development in his dreams? Knowing Chloe, she was more likely to believe Elliott than Martin was. After all, she saw ghosts. She probably wouldn't bat an eye at the idea of her little brother being psychic.

Even if Martin didn't believe it himself.

He'd taken too long to answer, he could tell. Chloe had straightened in her seat and was watching him avidly. "You met someone!" she declared.

Martin choked on his drink. "No," he spluttered. "Sorry to disappoint." He coughed a couple times and cleared his throat. "No, it's something less exciting and more...weird."

"Uh-huh." Chloe had her head tilted to one side like she was trying to decide whether or not to believe him.

"So...it's about my dreams."

Her expression dimmed and he wanted to cringe. For some stupid reason, Chloe still blamed herself for Martin's going off to war. It was true that he'd thought he should get out of her hair for a while and live his own life, but that didn't mean it was her fault he'd decided to enlist. It was just the easiest way he could think of to pay for an education. He sucked in a breath.

"I had one that was weird, the morning of July Fourth," he blustered on. "It wasn't really about Afghanistan, and it had this red-headed woman in it. She wasn't anybody I know or anything, but in my dream she was familiar, you know?"

Chloe nodded.

"So anyway, it was a crap dream, because something attacked her, but the point is, when I woke up, I saw on the news that this woman—Ainsley Shaw—had been murdered. And the thing is, Ainsley Shaw was a redhead. She looked just like the woman in my dreams."

He took a deep breath and added, "So Elliott thinks I'm psychic."

Chloe sat back in her chair, her expression so blank he didn't know if she thought he'd gone nuts or if she was pissed at him or what. Martin chewed the inside of his lower lip as he watched her. He was surprised to see the way she started smiling—no, *smirking*. That was definitely a smirk.

"You totally *did* meet someone," she said, eyes dancing. "You have a crush on Elliott."

Martin opened his mouth to protest, but he'd never lied to his sister, and he couldn't start now. "I—uh—that isn't—"

"Yeah, it totally is," she countered. "I mean, he's totally hot, and he's bi, and he's not seeing anyone…"

"The point," Martin said loudly. Someone a couple of tables over looked his way and he lowered his voice. "The point," he repeated more quietly, "is that maybe I'm dreaming of things that are really happening. Like, as they happen. Or even before, maybe."

Chloe waggled her eyebrows. "Did you dream about Elliott, too?"

"Shut up," he said, covering his face with his hand. He usually liked being a ginger, but right now he hated the pale skin that was so quick to turn beet red when he was embarrassed—or even when he wasn't embarrassed, but his body thought he should be. Some part of him was grateful Chloe had seized on the Elliott thing, though; maybe she was trying to downplay the rest of what he'd said. He thought about what a hard time she'd had when she told him she could see ghosts, and decided that yes, she was definitely trying to make the psychic announcement easier on him.

"You like him," Chloe said triumphantly. "I think that's awesome, Martin. He's a really great guy, we already know he gets along with my husband, so that would be perfect."

"Okay, fine, I like him," Martin muttered. "Still not the point. The point—"

"Is that you might be psychic. Okay, so we'll deal with that." When he looked back at his sister, Chloe was scooping up a huge glop of dip. She popped the chip in her mouth. "After all," she said through her food, "I see ghosts. Makes sense you might have some sort of crazy psycho thing."

"Psychic," Martin corrected, only to have her smirk at him.

"That's what I said. Psycho."

* * *

Elliott woke up the morning after the Full with Murphy plastered to his back and a fern tickling his nose. He grunted and nudged Murphy.

"Get off. I gotta go to work."

Murphy mumbled something unintelligible and wrapped an arm around Elliott.

Normally Elliott wouldn't mind a post-Full cuddle, but he needed to get ahead of the Ainsley Shaw case, and he definitely needed a shower before work. "Murph," he said more forcefully. "Move. I need to get up."

Murphy grunted. "S'my first good sleep in three days, but whatever, be an asshole and make me wake up," he muttered. He sat up with a sigh.

"Sorry," Elliott said. He sat up and stretched. "I'm in the middle of a case."

"Yeah? What happened?" Murphy's tone was casual, but he seemed more awake than he had been.

"The Ainsley Shaw murder that's been all over the news." Elliott looked over at him. "You know her or something?"

"Nah. Her brother a little bit. Lach, right? He's a guitarist, played Chloe and Braxton's wedding." Murphy was inspecting his fingernails. He grimaced and started picking at one of them. Elliott could see blood crusted underneath.

"Right. How do you know him?"

"He delivers the pizzas I make."

Elliott had forgotten Murphy switched jobs just after the last Full. He nodded. "He pretty dependable at work?"

"You interrogating me?" Murphy narrowed his eyes. "How would I know? I've only been there a month."

Elliott held up his hands in surrender. "Just asking, geez."

Murphy shrugged and ambled over to the trunk where they stored their clothes. Elliott waited until Murphy had most of his clothes on and then went over to start getting dressed himself. Braxton was sitting, fully-clothed, on a log, sipping coffee from a Thermos.

The rest of the pack was beginning to stir, conversing in low murmurs. The only other sounds were a breeze whispering through leaves and the chirping of robins, always the first birds to wake.

"Good luck with the case," Braxton said, holding out the Thermos.

"Thanks." He started walking, Thermos in hand, toward the spot where he'd parked his truck.

CHAPTER 11

Ainsley's funeral was held on Monday, less than a week after she was killed. Lachlan knew his parents wanted him to come home with them after the funeral. That was at least part of why he wasn't going to do it.

Kaida showed up for the funeral, though she hadn't actually responded to any of Lach's messages. He'd known her from Ainsley's photos when he saw her: a pretty Asian-American woman with a tiny diamond in one nostril. He wasn't sure if he should talk her to her in front of other people, but he didn't want her to feel like an outsider, so he shoved his hands in his suit coat pockets and gritted his teeth. He saw the exact moment when she realized he was coming to talk to her—she squared her shoulders and straightened.

"You're Kaida, I guess," he muttered.

"And you're Lachlan." Her gaze was sharp on his face. She was shorter than he was, her hair cut in a razor-short pixie. "You have more tattoos than she mentioned, though."

Lachlan shrugged.

"The funeral home called me a couple of times," she told him. "I didn't know if I had any right to participate, though." Her voice soured. "Since she was pregnant with some dude's baby."

"You knew about that?" Lachlan blurted. Then he felt his face get hot. "She was really sorry about that. I mean, she told me. She hated that it would hurt you."

Kaida hitched her shoulder. "It would have. But not as much as having her die on me."

Lachlan wasn't sure what to say to that. He had hated his sister at times, but he couldn't imagine life without her. He thought Kaida would understand that, but he couldn't bring himself to say it aloud.

"I'm a lesbian," Kaida said. "And the only woman I'd been with in two years was your sister. So I guess I get why she'd be afraid to tell me."

Lachlan nodded. "I wish she'd introduced us before," he said.

She looked at him. Her eyes were red rimmed, her face just a little puffy. "She talked about you all the time. She said you'd be on our side even if your parents weren't."

Lachlan wasn't sure what to say. Oddly, he almost wanted to defend his parents, who had always loved their kids the best they knew how. At the same time, he knew he would have taken Ainsley's side about how ignorant their folks could be.

"It's okay," Kaida said. "I get it. My dad won't care that I like girls, but my mom will lose her shit. She wants grandbabies and thinks the only way to get them is the biological way."

Lachlan snorted.

Kaida slanted a tiny smile at him. "Thanks for laughing."

Lachlan shrugged. "I hated Ainsley sometimes," he told her. "She was the one everyone thought was a hero. Sacrificed for her country, so smart, so pretty, so talented. Everything I wasn't."

To his surprise, Kaida huffed a laugh. "I resented her sometimes, too," she admitted. "She was the dutiful daughter my parents would have loved, focused on pleasing everyone, trying to live up to the image people had of her. She was more worried about how your folks would react to having a lesbian daughter than she was about her own happiness."

Lachlan snorted. "Sounds like Ainsley."

"I just wanted her to stand up for herself, you know?" Kaida said. Then she shook her head. "No, to stand up for *us*. I wanted her to think our love for each other was worth fighting for."

"Yeah." It struck Lachlan suddenly that he liked Kaida. She wasn't trying to make Ainsley a saint. She was just talking about her as if she'd been a human. That was what his parents hadn't been able to do, even before Ainsley was murdered.

"I must sound like a real bitch." Kaida wrapped her arms around herself, folding her arms and curling her fingers into her dress.

"You sound like you're the only damn honest person I've talked to in three days," Lachlan said.

Kaida looked over at him, her eyebrows drawing in. But whatever she saw in his face, she must have believed him, because she suddenly hugged him hard.

Lachlan wrapped his arms around her automatically, like he would have hugged Ainsley. He was surprised when he heard her muffled sob. Kaida didn't seem like the kind of woman who would cry in front of strangers.

She hooked her chin over his shoulder. "I'm sorry," she gasped into his ear. "Fuck. I hate crying. I just—" She broke off and sobbed for a couple of seconds. When she stopped sobbing, her chest heaved against his, and Lachlan could tell she was trying to get herself under control. "God damnit."

Lachlan lifted a hand and patted her shoulder. He felt suddenly as if he had Ainsley in his arms again. Ains had hated crying, because she usually cried when she was pissed off and she knew people would think crying was a sign of weakness. She'd also hated the way people expected her to coo over babies when most babies were squished little people who looked exactly like squished little people and nothing like the parents you were supposed to say they looked like. Ainsley hadn't been opposed to emotions, but she'd thought it was just decent to keep your emotions to yourself.

"I'm so sorry," Kaida said, pulling away. "I don't even deserve to mourn her. I only knew her for like, a year and a half, or something."

Lachlan wanted to ask how they'd met, how they'd gotten together, if Kaida had wanted to marry Ainsley. He wanted to know if Kaida was military, if she was a reporter, how they'd met, what they'd dreamed the rest of their lives together would look like.

Instead, he said, "You're allowed to feel how you feel," and was rewarded with a dazzling smile from Kaida that dissolved into tears again.

It felt like a lifetime before Kaida pulled away from him, though it had probably only been a few minutes. She scrubbed the back of her hand across her face and glared at him.

"You're such an asshole for making me cry."

The smile he gave her hurt, even though it felt good to smile. "That's exactly what she would have said."

Kaida nodded. She wrapped her arms around herself. "I would have made your sister happy."

Lachlan wondered if he was allowed to think of Kaida like a sister, even though they'd just met. He wondered if Kaida would ever want to talk to him again. He inhaled slowly. "I believe you."

He cleared his throat. "Uh. I think they're getting ready to start. You want—" He glanced over his shoulder and, seeing the stony expression on his father's face, changed what he was going to say. "You want me to sit here with you?"

Kaida must have followed his gaze. She gave him a brittle smile. "Thanks. I really do."

* * *

Elliott had never liked the funeral part of being a homicide detective, but there was no denying it was a good place to gain insight into the case. Fifty-four percent of murder victims knew their killer. Almost a

140

quarter of them were killed by family members. Elliott didn't have the sense that Ainsley had been murdered by her parents or brother, but he couldn't peremptorily rule out the possibility.

So he put on a black suit and tamed his hair with gel and stood in the back row of the church while the chaplain from Ainsley's company talked about what a go-getter Ainsley was, how determined she was, but how she was always ready to drop everything to help someone out. The more the chaplain talked about Ainsley—not shying away from her sarcasm or quick temper—the more Elliott wished he'd known her when she was alive. That was the other down side of being a homicide detective.

He glanced across the church to where Braxton had slipped in, midway up the sanctuary. Elliott liked having another pair of eyes in a situation like this. He'd thought about asking Martin Cole to come to the funeral, to prove he still believed Martin was psychic, but he'd decided against it. For one thing, Martin wasn't a cop. For another, he was clearly still struggling with PTSD from his own deployment; Elliott wasn't going to ask him to do something that would exacerbate that. And on top of all of that, a funeral was a really creepy setting for anything that might be mistaken for a date. So he'd asked Braxton instead, and Braxton, who knew there was something supernatural involved in this, had quickly agreed.

After the funeral, they went to J&J Cafe to grab coffee and sticky buns and compare impressions.

"It's the weirdest thing," Braxton said. "I didn't have any overwhelming impressions of magic, but every once in a while, I got a tiny whiff of it. It was like..." He frowned. "Like the wind changing directions and bringing you a hint of woodsmoke. And then the wind changed again and it dissipated."

Elliott hummed thoughtfully. He'd only once caught a tang of magic, when Kaida walked past him, tears streaming down her face. He relayed the incident to Braxton. "She couldn't have been the person you were scenting, though; she walked down the outside aisle on my side," Elliott added.

"So more than one magic-user there." Braxton took a bite of his sticky bun, his dark eyebrows drawing together as he chewed.

"Or magical being," Elliott added.

Braxton nodded.

"There's, uh..." Elliott sipped his coffee. "There's something else I haven't told you." His heart rate jumped. Braxton was his best friend, but he was also his alpha, in the sense that he was the leader of their werewolf pack and Elliott accepted his authority. Elliott wasn't sure how Braxton would feel about the Martin Cole issue, since Martin was intimately connected to his wife. "And it's something I can't tell you. Not yet. I mean, not without—" He scrubbed a hand through his hair. "It's not my thing to tell you. But there's other factors in play."

Braxton sighed. "All right. I'll trust that it isn't anything dangerous."

Elliott licked his lips. "Sorry. I just—I promised."

"I'm sorry," Braxton said, his eyes meeting Elliott's. "I didn't mean that the way it sounded. I *do* trust you, Ell."

"Thanks."

Elliott drummed his fingers on the table, feeling awkward now that he'd cut off the conversation like that. He shouldn't have brought it up at all, except that he thought Braxton should know there were other issues surrounding them. *I ought to ask Martin if I can tell Braxton about this. Except Braxton's married now, and married people tell each other things, and Martin obviously doesn't want Chloe to know, but Braxton probably needs to know.* He tried to make the thoughts stop circling. No matter what, he couldn't tell anyone what he'd promised to keep in confidence. It felt good that Martin trusted him with this, that Martin wanted to talk to him about it.

Elliott realized suddenly that he was smiling stupidly at his plate. He coughed. "So. The cookout went well, I thought."

Braxton's gaze looked altogether too interested for his liking. "You mean until you got called out for a murder."

Elliott shrugged. "Until that."

"Yeah, I think it was. Murphy actually behaved himself—even hung out with Martin for a while. Theo surprised no one by monopolizing Lucy Ruiz all evening. Ximena...well. She came. That's progress."

Elliott nodded.

"You and Martin seem to have mended fences."

Elliott's heartrate jumped, his nostrils flaring a little, and he looked accusingly at Braxton. "That was an ambush," he accused.

"Guilty." Braxton folded his arms over his chest. "So. Martin."

Elliott felt his face getting hot. Shit. "Well...uh, I ran into him while you guys were off honeymooning. At the Broad Ripple Tavern. We got to talking, you know."

Braxton's lips were beginning to quirk up. He leaned back in his chair. "Just happened to run into him, huh?"

"Yes," Elliott snapped. He instantly regretted his tone. He sounded too defensive. "How was I supposed to know he'd be at the same bar as me?"

"Oh, no reason, I guess." Braxton was out and out grinning. "Though come to think of it, you *did* know he lives in Broad Ripple. And I'm pretty sure the Broad Ripple Tavern is a local hangout, more laid-back than your usual club."

Elliott could feel his face getting even hotter. He narrowed his eyes at Braxton, who laughed.

"Turnabout's fair play," Braxton said.

"Fine." Elliott glanced away and found a fascinating light fixture to look at. "I like him. But don't worry, I know he's not my usual type, and besides, I don't want to make things weird with you and Chloe. I *can* keep my hands to myself."

Braxton chuckled. "I don't know, I can see it working between you two, actually. He's way more laid back than you, PTSD aside, and I've seen the way he responds to you."

Elliott was surprised into looking over at him. "Huh?"

Braxton shrugged. "There was definitely tension at the bachelor party. And at the cookout the other day, he didn't really talk to anyone else the way he talked to you. He seemed kind of bummed after you took off."

Elliott's chest tightened even though he tried not to get too excited about what Braxton said. It was stupid to get his hopes up. A friends-with-benefits thing might work between them, but nothing more serious—and the longer he knew Martin, the more Elliott wanted something more serious.

"And he knows about werewolves," Braxton added, still grinning.

"No," Elliott said. "Just—stop. I know how easily I fuck things up, okay? So don't go there. It's just better to leave this alone."

Braxton's grin faded as he held Elliott's gaze, but he finally sighed and nodded. "All right. I won't bring it up again. But for the record—"

Elliott held up a hand. "Noted. Now can we get back to the case on hand?"

Braxton was silent for a moment. "I'd like to see the room where Ainsley died. Can you get me in? I know you didn't recognize the person's scent, but I might."

Elliott swallowed and nodded. Hopefully Braxton would honor what he'd just said. If Braxton didn't keep egging him on, Elliott could get over this thing with Martin Cole.

He hoped.

* * *

When Lachlan got home from the funeral, he started his laptop automatically. He went to the bathroom to wash his face and changed into sweatpants and a t-shirt. He turned the ringtone on his phone to silent. He knew he *should* have gone to his parents' house after the graveside stuff, but he just couldn't face it. They might have given birth to and raised Ainsley, but Lachlan was the one who'd grown up with her. He didn't think anyone had the right to mourn her the way he did.

Kaida had been a pleasant surprise, but her company, even her anger at Ainsley, hadn't filled the hole in his chest.

He nuked a mug of water with a teabag in it, biting his lip at a memory of Ainsley telling him that didn't count as making tea. He thought briefly about his sister kissing Kaida before deciding that was weird and creepy. Then he thought about the last time he and his sister had made music together.

He'd never been able to shake the idea that the song he and Ainsley had sung together was the best music they'd ever made in their lives. She was gone now. There was nothing he could do about that. But he'd recorded the last song she'd sung. A little bit of editing—not much, just enough to make it seem intentional—and he would have a hit on his hands. He just knew it.

Forty minutes later, Lachlan hit the 'upload' button and watched as the progress bar slowly moved to the right.

Lachlan had incorporated some of the vocals he'd captured from Ainsley on the first night they sang together. At the time he'd known it wasn't really kosher, but after her death, it was just 'unreleased recordings' of Ainsley's phenomenal voice.

After all, how many Gen X women—or Millennials, for that matter—were just like his sister? How many'd had plans for their lives before realizing the networks and the government had control of all the information? How many women knew what they wanted from life, only to run face-first against the patriarchy? How many women pretended to be straight to get ahead, only to finally admit they were gay when they realized happiness was more important than money or prestige?

All the same, Lachlan hadn't really given serious consideration to the fact that Ainsley's lament for how her life should have gone was truly the ballad of an entire generation. Not until Ainsley was gone. He didn't even hesitate before he hit the 'publish' button.

Then he opened a beer and started drinking.

Two days after Ainsley's funeral, Lachlan's phone woke him up with a shrill and determined tone, informing him that there'd been over fifty thousand hits on the "Ainsley's Lament" video.

Lachlan hated that she was dead, but he'd be damned if he shied away from the publicity. After all, wouldn't Ainsley want him to have a successful musical career? This was a way for him to showcase not only his songwriting ability, but also his singing voice. This was a way for him to leverage sympathy for his sister's murder into a possibly life-changing career opportunity for himself.

No, Lachlan told himself. No matter what happened, Ainsley would want him to do well.

He scrolled through some of the comments on his video. "It's like this song was written just for me," one girl wrote. Another commented, "Got goosebumps when I was listening to this." A third just commented, "OMG I'm crying."

There were a couple of comments that the song was a little rough, but they were the exception. The comments were overwhelmingly positive—and lots of people wanted to buy the song. Tears stung Lachlan's eyes as he went over to the website he had set up to sell his music and added "Ainsley's Lament" to the store.

When he checked the store stats, he realized he'd sold a couple hundred copies of his digital EP. People weren't just enjoying the lament, they were also coming to buy his music. The tears spilled over.

"Oh, God, Ains," he choked. "I'm sorry. But thank you." He buried his face in his hands. "I wish you were here to see this."

CHAPTER 12

Martin put down his crowbar, leaned away from the drywall he was demolishing, and wiped sweat off his forehead. His shirt was stuck to him, but he'd left it on because he thought that was better than being sweaty *and* covered in drywall dust.

A glance at the clock told him it was almost eight. He ought to knock off for the night. He was almost finished tearing out this wall, and then he just had one more interior wall to go. He would have to hire a general contractor at some point, once he got into plumbing and cabinets and electrical, but he could handle the demolition part.

Inviting Elliott Blake over to his house had made him realize how ridiculous it was that he still hadn't done anything about the renovations he'd planned when he bought the house from his landlady. He was living in a small apartment—comfortable, certainly, but small—and he didn't need to be. His two-bedroom apartment could easily be a three-bedroom house with an open floorplan living/kitchen/dining area. That would make it a lot more comfortable for entertaining.

Not that he had lots of people to entertain, but now that he'd realized how much he'd drawn into himself over the last few years, he could do something to change that.

And if Elliott Blake had anything to do with why Martin wanted to entertain people...well, he'd think about that some other time.

He sighed and found a place to prop the crowbar. Chloe would squawk at him if she saw how messy the house was, but he didn't see any point in vacuuming while he was in the middle of construction. With a yawn, he headed for the shower.

Forty minutes later, as he relaxed in his recliner, his phone chimed.

It was a text from Chloe: *Finally home from dinner. Guess who we ate with tonight!*

Martin eyed the message warily. Had they seen someone famous, or was she being a jerk? His fingers hovered over the entry line as he debated his response, but before he could think of anything, she proved she was being a jerk.

Your favorite werewolf! It was followed by a heart-eyed emoji and a kissy-face emoji.

Martin rolled his eyes and texted back, *Shup already.*

Honestly, she didn't need to rub it in. He'd admitted he liked Elliott. What more did she want from him?

There's an Indy11 game Saturday. You ought to ask him to it.

"Why would I do that?" he muttered aloud. "I already know he has season tickets." The text he sent back simply said, *Shup.*

It had been one of the first things Chloe and Martin had said to each other as kids, and they used it often enough that his phone no longer tried to autocorrect it to 'ship' or 'shop.' He could picture Chloe snickering at her phone and hoped Braxton wouldn't ask her what was so funny.

Then again, Braxton probably already knew Martin liked Elliott. They were married. Why wouldn't Chloe tell him?

You're no fun. Chloe replied. *Take a chance already.*

Martin sighed heavily. *Shut. Up. Already.*

There was a long pause after that one. He could see the little dots that indicated Chloe was typing, then she stopped and started a couple of times. The message that finally came through was just, *Touchy.*

That didn't seem to require a response. Martin plugged the phone into the charger on the kitchen counter. He did a quick tour of all the exterior doors, making sure he'd locked them, and headed to the back of the apartment to get ready for bed.

He'd shifted his evening routine since his discussion with Elliott about his dreams. He'd done some homework on how to sleep better and come up with articles about blue light and phone screens being bad for your sleep. Bedrooms, several articles advised, should be reserved for sleep and sex. Anything else should have another place in the house. And alcohol, they all stressed, might make you fall asleep faster, but you'd sleep poorly as a result.

Martin had implemented a lot of the suggestions in those articles, but he hadn't taken it to the extreme.

He still liked reading in bed—though he'd switched to reading only print books instead of reading ebooks on his phone. And he'd resolutely avoided his liquor cabinet all week.

We'll see how long that lasts, said a cynical voice in his mind. He shook it off and grabbed the book he was reading. It was a true crime book about the Green River Killer. Possibly not the best choice of subject matter just before bed, but he'd always enjoyed true crime books, and at least in these, he knew the bad guy had already been caught.

After a couple of chapters, his eyelids started drooping. He marked his place in the book and set it on the bedside table, turned off the light, and drifted into sleep.

Martin was standing on a dusty street surrounded by sand-colored buildings. He stood differently, carrying sixty pounds of armor and equipment. There was an M-4 in his hands. Sweat trickled down the small of his back. His skin prickled and, even though he knew better, he spun to look around him.

There. The shadowy figure stood behind him, hood pulled up to hide everything but the glow of green eyes. It watched him. Martin shivered. He couldn't seem to move. Why did this all feel so familiar? He narrowed his eyes, trying to pierce the darkness under the figure's hood.

"We've done this before," he breathed.

The green eyes blinked. Then the shadow shifted and Martin heard a clanking sound. When Martin looked closer, he thought he saw a chain around the figure's neck. It stretched into the shadows behind the figure. Was there someone else back there?

Someone was approaching. Martin could hear footsteps. He looked around, expecting a pretty redhead, though he wasn't sure why.

Instead it was a stocky white guy with sandy hair. The man wore rectangular black glasses, jeans, a white t-shirt, and a leather jacket that looked like it had gone through a war all on its own. He had a dimple and a cleft chin, and his lips were curled in a smirk. Martin wanted to clench his fists.

The M-4 creaked in his hands. He squeezed tighter, realizing something as he did.

"This is a dream."

He said the words aloud and the world changed.

Suddenly he was standing in front of the Indianapolis Museum of Art. The smirking guy was still there, arms folded across a muscular chest. He watched Martin, seemingly oblivious to the shadow monster that watched them both.

"You need to get out of here," Martin said, but even though his lips moved, he couldn't hear his own voice. He flung away his rifle and started walking toward Smirky.

As soon as he let go of the gun, the air around him chilled. Shit! That had been a mistake. He dove after the gun, hoping it hadn't gone far. He landed on the path, felt the stinging in his knees. His hands grasped after the weapon as his flesh rose in goosebumps.

The air around him had frozen. His nose-hairs were sticking together. Something was making a horrible, high screeching noise behind him, and then something clanked.

Martin got his fingers on the gun, realized it had broken in half. With an oath, he grabbed the stock. He could always swing it like a club. He turned, lifting it in readiness.

He was too late.

Blood sprayed across his face. A man screamed. Light flashed in his eyes and he lifted his hands, reaching to stop that shadowy figure —

And he was awake again, gasping and shuddering under the covers. He kept his eyes squeezed shut, suddenly terrified that if he opened them, he would see a shadowy figure standing over him, staring with green, glowing wide eyes.

"It was a dream," he whispered. "You're home. Winthrop Avenue. Indianapolis." He sucked in a breath and eased his eyes open. "Indiana."

There were no shadowy figures in the room. There was also, he thought, no purring cat coming to check on him. He took a long, shaky breath and put a visit to the animal shelter on his mental to-do list.

Only then did he check the time. It was three-forty-one in the morning. Too early to get up and entirely too late to start drinking.

Martin sat up and rubbed his hands over his face.

You could call Elliott, whispered a little voice in the back of his mind.

He could, too. Elliott had made Martin promise to call him if he had any more dreams that felt different from the PTSD dreams. Despite the Murphy mess, which had made Martin feel better about the whole thing.

He hadn't promised to wake Elliott up right after they happened, though, and he wasn't sure if Elliott would really appreciate that. After all, even homicide detectives had to sleep. Martin had seen enough of Chloe's irregular schedule to know no police officer loved interrupted sleep.

He got up and went to the bathroom, got a drink of water. His skin was still prickling unhappily, and he'd begun to shiver. "Fine," he grumbled, and took his phone back into the bedroom with him.

Maybe he hadn't promised to wake Elliott up, but somehow he didn't think Elliott would mind.

* * *

The phone startled Elliott out of a pleasant dream. He bolted up in bed, heard thudding in his chest. It took two more rings for his head to clear enough to realize he needed to answer that.

He exhaled and reached for the phone. He really hoped it wasn't an emergency. "Blake," he rumbled.

The person on the other end of the line cleared his throat, half swallowing the sound. "Elliott. Uh. This is—"

"Martin," Elliott finished, smiling. He slumped back against the bed, then frowned. "Wait, what time is it?"

"Heh. Quarter to four. Ish."

"Everything okay?" Elliott sat up again, prepared to pull on some clothes if Martin needed help. His chest gave a funny twist and he tried to shove it away. He shouldn't like Martin this much; he'd only screw things up if he tried this hard.

"I had another dream. Not a Kandahar dream. I mean, I thought it was at first, but then it—I don't know, something felt different. Off. So I realized it was a dream, and I never realize that when I'm really dreaming about the war."

Elliott found himself smiling at the way Martin was rambling. "Take a breath," he suggested, knowing Martin would hear the smile in his voice. "I've got time to listen."

He heard a huff of laughter. "I probably shouldn't have woken you up in the middle of the night."

"Nah, it's fine. I'm glad you called me." Elliott stretched out a little, relaxing muscles that the harsh waking had tensed. For a moment he considered inviting Martin over to talk in person. "So walk me through the dream. Take your time." He draped an arm over his eyes so he could focus on the sound of Martin's voice.

Martin's recitation of the dream still sounded a bit rushed at the beginning, but he was settling down by the time he got to his realization that the gun didn't feel right in his hands— "Wait, is that what clued me

156

in?" he interrupted himself. "I didn't know until I told you."

"That's how it works sometimes," Elliott said. "So you realized the gun felt wrong. What about the gun?"

"It wasn't heavy enough. It—creaked when I squeezed it." Martin sighed. "I don't like guns. I never did, but we had to have one when we were outside the perimeter. Even a mechanic has to be a killer if necessary."

Elliott wasn't sure what to say to that, so he just hummed a noise he hoped sounded encouraging.

"Anyway. I decided it was useless and threw it away, and that's when the shadow thing came up on me." Martin's voice tensed again as he described the shadowy figure and how it clanked when it moved. Then it trailed off to nothing when he finished with the spray of blood.

Elliott didn't say anything immediately after Martin stopped talking. He was okay with silence in a conversation, especially when it was a conversation as fraught as this one. He let himself mull over the dream's possible implications for a little while. Finally he took a long breath.

"So I think we have two—no, three questions," he murmured. "Is this murder tied to Ainsley Shaw's? Who is Smirky Guy? What does the shadow figure's chain mean?"

"Only three?" Martin's laugh was a little higher than normal. "I have about a million."

Elliott let a grin break across his face. "Well, I guess I have a few more questions myself, but I think those are the three we need to focus on."

And not on questions like *Is there any chance you're as into me as I am you?* or *What about getting breakfast together to talk this over?* Those weren't case-related questions, and they would only lead down a path that ended up with Elliott hurting Martin somehow and Braxton never wanting to speak to Elliott again.

He realized suddenly that Martin had been talking. "Sorry," he said, a flash of embarrassment rushing through him. "I completely missed that."

"Gee, I can't imagine why, since I woke you up at an ungodly hour." How was Martin able to conjure sarcasm at this time of night?

Elliott chuckled. "No, sorry. What did you say?"

Martin cleared his throat. "Oh. I was just...I wondered if..." He stopped speaking and Elliott felt his pulse speed up. Maybe Elliott wasn't the only one who wanted to talk this over at breakfast. *Slow down, idiot*, he reminded himself.

"I have plans this afternoon," Martin said finally, and Elliott's heart fell. Then Martin added, "But maybe Saturday we should grab lunch or something and work through some of this?"

Elliott couldn't bite back the grin that spread across his face. He knew if he said anything Martin would hear it, so he tried to frown instead. His face felt funny, but he thought his voice sounded pretty normal when he said, "Sure, I think that's a good idea." He had a full schedule today, anyway. He had to get Braxton in to see Ainsley's room.

Braxton. Damn it. Elliott sighed. He didn't want to suggest it, but this was first and foremost about trying to catch Ainsley's killer. "Um, are you okay talking this stuff over with Braxton?" he blurted before he could talk himself out of it. "I've got him consulting because there's something supernatural about this death. It wouldn't hurt to have him in on this."

There was a pause, then Martin said, "Oh. Sure, yeah."

"I mean, I haven't told him about you," he blurted. "I promised I wouldn't tell anyone, and I haven't. But I...I think, if you're willing to talk to him about it, he might have some really good insights we haven't come up with."

"I already told Chloe about the dreams, so Braxton probably knows anyway," Martin said. Elliott hoped he wasn't imagining Martin's disappointment. He *knew* he wasn't imagining his own. He'd like nothing better than to spend more one-on-one time with Martin Cole. But he had a duty to Ainsley Shaw, and that came first.

"Okay. I'll text you later to set up the details," Elliott said.

"Yeah."

Elliott hesitated. Martin didn't sound as open as he had earlier, though he didn't sound angry, either. Maybe he just wasn't ready to go back to sleep. Elliott knew *he* wouldn't be ready to go back to sleep after a dream like that. Then again, what time did Martin open the garage? Maybe he wouldn't need to go back to sleep anyway.

"Do you—" Elliott began, just as Martin said, "Well, I'd better—"

They both broke off, chuckling. "Go ahead," Elliott said.

"I was just going to say I'd better let you get back to sleep."

Elliott blinked. "Only if you'll be able to sleep, after talking about it."

He heard Martin make a quiet noise—of surprise? Or amusement? "I think I will. Thanks."

CHAPTER 13

Within a week of his sister's brutal murder, Lachlan Shaw was an internet superstar.

"This is not like I imagined," he muttered, the lyrics a fitting sentiment for the position he found himself in.

He'd already fielded calls from six bar owners, asking if he'd be available to do gigs. He'd done shows at two of the venues before, and open mike night at a third, but three of them had just laughed at him in the past when he'd tried to get in to play. Knot Tide was booked for weddings through the end of September, and he'd started referring a couple of other friends who played other wedding bands.

He didn't have record labels knocking on his door, but he was okay with that. Staying indie would allow him to keep control of the music as well as giving him a bigger share of the money.

If things kept up at this rate, he would be able to quit delivering pizzas and concentrate on making music. But it all felt hollow somehow. He'd always expected Ainsley to be right there with him.

He'd taken a week off work, and his boss had actually offered to pay him for the time, bereavement pay. Lachlan hadn't expected that, but he wasn't going to look a gift horse in the mouth. He spent the week feverishly recording and editing new music and burning CDs to sell as quickly as his computer could spin them.

That Thursday he played the first of his new gigs at a little hole in the wall called Clancy's. He'd done an open mike night there a couple of times and had been well-received. It was an intimate little venue, able to seat maybe seventy-five people, and he liked it.

The place was pretty full for a Thursday night, and Lachlan could tell he was in the zone. His fingers felt like they were on fire. The usual drone of conversation present even in the best crowd simply wasn't there. Every eye was on him as he belted out some of his favorite hard-hitting rock numbers. Then he slowed down just before he was ready for a short break. It was time for Ainsley's lament.

He'd debated how to do it, and he'd finally decided there was no way to perform it live without using her voice recording. He picked out the first notes on his guitar and what little movement he'd sensed in the room stilled.

Lachlan sang.

He gave himself over entirely to the music, from the pain in his fingertips to the raw scratching of his throat. His body curved in a bow over the guitar and his voice came out like a sob. He closed his eyes and wailed out the end of the song, letting Ainsley's voice blend and contrast with his own.

When the last notes rang out, Lachlan opened his eyes.

The people in the front, men and women alike, had tears streaming down their cheeks. Lachlan stared in disbelief as one woman, her dark, curly hair falling around her shoulders, doubled over sobbing. Behind the bar, a tall, muscular guy with a fade was knuckling the corner of his eyes. Lachlan looked around him, shaking his head.

His gaze met that of a tall, slender woman with strawberry blonde hair. She wasn't crying, nor did she look sad. She was staring at him, her gray eyes wide, but he couldn't tell if that was surprise he read in her expression. When she realized he was looking at her, she closed her mouth and curved her lips up in a half smile.

Lachlan took off his guitar and set it on the stand. He needed a drink. Preferably something with a lot of alcohol in it.

The woman met him at the bar. The muscular bartender shook himself as Lachlan approached. He was only too happy to mix Lachlan a Jack and Coke with double whiskey. "On the house," the guy told him, shaking his head in wonder.

"Cheers," Lachlan said, and took a gulp of his drink.

"You have incredible power," the woman said. She leaned one elbow on the bar, angling her shoulder to cut the bartender out of the conversation. Lachlan was about to thank her when she added, "But you wield it inexpertly."

He checked his words, mouth hanging open like an idiot. Finally he managed to say, "What?"

"Your voice." She smiled faintly. "It's like a blade, but you don't always need a blade. Sometimes a feather will do the job. Sometimes a wall."

"I suppose you're a voice coach." Lachlan had tried vocal training before, but he hadn't liked it. It felt artificial to him.

"No." She began chuckling. "Oh, no, not a voice coach. Although..." She put one finger on her chin as she surveyed him. "There *is* much I could teach you. If you are willing."

Lachlan leaned back just a little. She was so close he was getting claustrophobic. He wondered suddenly if she was trying to get him to bed. "I like to think I'm always willing to learn," he said. "If the price is right."

Her gaze sharpened. "Oh, the price is steep. It is always steep. But the rewards are well worth the exchange."

A chair screeched across the linoleum floor, making Lachlan jump. The audience was finally beginning to wake from whatever trance of sorrow they'd fallen into. He glanced around, seeing that each person was blinking and looking around as if afraid they'd been asleep.

He took another sip of his drink. "I'm not sure I know what you're talking about," he admitted.

Her thin lips curled. "I'm sure you don't," she said. There was a superiority in her voice, but it attracted Lachlan as much as it repelled him. Perhaps even more. "But I can be patient. Finish your set,

Lachlan Shaw. Sing well, *fir chaointe.* Sell your wares to the adoring crowd. But when you are done, come sup with me, and I will tell you everything."

"Fear what?"

"*Fir chaointe.*" When she said it, it meant something, though Lachlan couldn't understand. He shivered, but she only smiled. "Go sing, Lachlan."

"Wait," he said as she began to turn. She looked back at him. "What's your name?"

Her smile deepened. "Eris."

He sold all of the two dozen CDs he'd brought with him. It made him nervous to have over four hundred dollars in cash on him, plus the check the manager had given him. But he couldn't resist hearing whatever Eris had to tell him. Her hints were too intriguing. So he followed her to a small table in a dark corner where two glasses were waiting.

"I had the barman bring you another of the drink you ordered earlier," she said. "He'll be here to take our food order in a moment."

"You must come here a lot." Lachlan wished she had let him sit with his back to the wall. He felt oddly exposed here. Then again, maybe it was best if other people couldn't see his face. It had taken him a long time to get rid of all his new fans. He took a long drink.

"You are young for your talent," she said, ignoring his question. "I am certain I hadn't heard of you before this month."

He shook his head. "Probably not. My sister died and the song I wrote for her went viral. I've done a lot of weddings, but nothing like this before."

"I am sorry for your loss." She didn't sound like she was, but Lachlan didn't mind. She hadn't known Ainsley, after all, and she barely knew him. "Would she be proud of you for this success?"

Lachlan felt his forehead crinkle. "I don't know," he said, looking down into his glass. "I hope so."

Eris nodded. "But you aren't certain. Perhaps there was jealousy between you? Rivalry even?"

He frowned at her. "I mean, we were always a little competitive, but I loved her. She was my best friend."

"Best friend…worst enemy… It's always the way." Eris' smile looked wistful.

Lachlan wondered suddenly how old she was. She didn't look much older than Ainsley had been, but there was something almost archaic in the way she talked.

"Take your order?"

Lachlan jumped at the bartender's sudden appearance. He ordered a tenderloin and fries and waited while Eris ordered a salad "and another drink for my friend."

He looked down at his glass and realized it was almost empty. He'd have to be careful. He had to drive home, after all. Well, he could book a ride, but using any kind of public transportation with all the cash he had on him seemed like a risk.

"So you said you were going to explain everything," he challenged once the bartender had gone.

"I did." Eris smiled. "I said you have power in your voice. That is because you are *fir chaointe*."

"I'm what?"

"You have heard of the *Ban Sidhe*?" Eris' eyes flashed. "The fairy woman whose voice brings death?"

"Oh. Banshee. Yeah, wasn't one of the characters in *Teen Wolf* a banshee? Like Black Canary. She screamed so loud she could break glass or burst eardrums or things."

Eris tapped long fingernails on the table. "A crude description, but apt enough. The Irish words *ban sidhe* merely mean 'fairy woman,' but that is an oversimplification."

"I wish I knew what you were getting at."

Eris folded her hands on the table and contemplated him. "You have a magic voice. I do not speak in metaphor. Your voice does more than merely carry emotion. It creates it. You are able to transmit power through your song, power to make a person feel or see or think whatever you wish them to feel or see or think." She paused, her eyes narrowing as she gave him a smile that was not entirely pleasant. "Or do."

He blinked. "Magic."

"Magic." Her smile widened. "You, Lachlan Shaw, are *fir chaointe*—the wailing man. The term—the talent—is not a direct equivalent for the banshee, but close enough."

"You're saying I have magic." Lachlan lifted his glass to drain it and found he already had. Fortunately the bartender came back just then with another drink. Lachlan gulped it.

"I am saying exactly that. More than having magic, you *are* magic." She tilted her head, watching him closely, and added, "You killed your sister with your voice."

* * *

Lachlan fumbled his keys as he tried to unlock his apartment. They hit the concrete entry walk with a discordant jangle. Swearing, he picked them up and tried again, only to drop them again.

"Fuck!" He punched the door and pain blazed through his hand. He whimpered. Sucking on his scraped knuckles, he retrieved the key with his other hand and finally managed to get the door unlocked. Shouldering it open, he stumbled into his apartment. He slammed the door behind him and barely remembered to throw the deadbolt.

Someone would probably bitch at him tomorrow for making so much noise at—crap, it was past midnight. He pulled open the fridge and blinked at it for a few seconds. Then he reconsidered and opened the freezer instead. It was stuffed with microwave dinners and burritos, but the corner where the ice trays used to go held a bottle of Grey Goose. He unscrewed the top and took a slug.

The cold made him gasp, which made his throat feel even colder. Just a few moments later, though, a pleasant warmth began radiating from his stomach up to his chest. He'd had to get a ride from the gig. After what that woman had said, no way in hell was he going to sober up enough to drive himself home.

She was wrong though. Lach knew she was wrong. He hadn't wanted Ainsley dead. He would *never* want her dead. Sure, they fought. And sure, sometimes he hated how superior she acted. The way she seemed to think she was better than anyone. But that didn't mean he wanted her *dead*!

Eris' last words still rang in his ears. Lach took another long swallow of vodka. He didn't want to think about this anymore. He'd buried his sister. He had to learn to live without her. He just wanted to put this all behind him and pour his grief into his music.

His music.

Lach's throat tightened. His music was, according to Eris, the whole problem.

He'd blurted denials and anger at the woman for half an hour, spluttering through the three bites he managed to take of his tenderloin. He finally shoved his chair away from the table. "You're a liar or you're crazy," he'd said, his voice shaking. "Either way, I'm going."

Eris had looked calmly back at him, a tiny smile curving her lips. "There's an easy way to test it, you know. Just pick someone else you hate."

"Crazy," Lachlan had decided. He turned away, swaying as he leaned over to pick up his guitar.

"You'll have questions, *fir chaointe*. When you do, I'll find you."

"You can fuck right off," Lachlan muttered. He'd stormed out of the restaurant, phone in hand to order his ride.

Test it. Lach closed his eyes against the thought. Who the hell would he hate enough to want them dead? He didn't think he'd ever wanted someone dead. Maybe the bully who picked on him in sixth grade, but Lach had finally hit back and the bully had never bothered him again. Lach had been suspended, which pissed off his parents and made Ainsley proud. She'd wanted to hit the guy herself, but Lach had told her being defended by his sister would only make it worse.

"Ainsley," he whispered thickly.

What was it the woman had called him? *Fir chaointe*? What language was that, anyway? The television show with a banshee had had other supernatural creatures in it—werewolves, obviously, and kitsune, which he remembered were Japanese. But he couldn't remember what country's mythology held the banshee.

Why had that woman even thought he was killing people with his music? He'd never done anything like that before. Even that time he'd gotten into it with that Parrish guy over the battle of the bands, he'd never wished anyone ill. And Parrish was still alive and kicking, competing against Lachlan and occasionally leaving annoying comments on the YouTube videos.

"Ha. Let's see if it works." Lachlan grabbed his guitar and strummed a harsh chord and sang in a lymericky voice, "I knew a man named Parrish, who didn't even try to be fair-ish. He acted like a jerk, despite my hard work, I wish I could just make him vanish."

Ugh. Not only was it ugly, it was stupid. That woman was just a sick fan, trying to use Ainsley's death to get in good with Lachlan. It wasn't going to work.

"Why am I even thinking about this?" he muttered. He took another drink of vodka. He'd be on the floor pretty soon if he wasn't careful. He didn't have to work tomorrow, but he needed to be functional. He wanted to make a video and burn more CDs. That would be way harder if he was hung over.

"I'm not going to think about this anymore," he announced.

He opened the music app on his phone and scrolled to his Dream Theater playlist. Plugging in his headphones, he hooked them over his ears and stumbled over to the couch, hitting the light switch on his way. He took the vodka with him. Just a couple more swallows, and he could lose himself in John Petrucci's blazing guitar.

And hopefully, when he woke up in the morning, none of this would be real.

CHAPTER 14

Elliott took a deep breath and rang the doorbell at the Shaw home. He wasn't looking forward to this. Braxton gave him an encouraging thump on the shoulder just as the door opened.

Joe Shaw had two days of stubble on his chin. He smelled like cheap scotch, sweat, and despair. "Detective Blake." His voice was flat.

"Mr. Shaw, this is Master Trooper Braxton Wolfe with the Indiana State Police. He's consulting on the investigation, and I was hoping we could take another look at Ainsley's bedroom."

Joe didn't move from where he stood, blocking the doorway. "Why do you need to look here again? Shouldn't you be interviewing suspects?"

"We are interviewing people, sir, but it's possible we missed something the first time we looked at the room." Elliott was glad Braxton was standing behind him; they'd worked on cases together before, but this was humiliating. Elliott had absolutely nothing to go on, and now Ainsley's father's anger just made him feel even more ineffectual.

"What about this Akimoto woman? Did you know Ainsley had a life insurance policy?" Joe leaned in, eyes narrowing. "With the Akimoto woman's name on it. Doesn't that make her a suspect?"

Elliott hadn't known about the life insurance policy—he suspected Kaida didn't know about it yet, either—but he'd checked Kaida's alibi, which was rock-solid. "Ms. Akimoto was in Chicago when Ainsley was murdered," he said, keeping his voice as level as possible. He had a feeling part of the reason Joe was so hostile to Kaida was because he didn't like that his daughter had been dating another woman.

"She could have hired it done." Joe's fists were clenched. Elliott felt Braxton tensing behind him.

"Ms. Akimoto is not a suspect at this time." Elliott put every ounce of his authority into his voice.

"Then who the hell is?" Joe shouted. "You haven't got a damn thing to go on! My daughter has been dead for ten days and you haven't done a single thing to catch her killer!"

Elliott lowered his voice. "That's why I'm consulting with the state police, Mr. Shaw. I assure you, we are—*I* am—entirely committed to catching your daughter's killer and bringing that person to justice. I will not stop until we have answers, sir."

Joe stared at him for several heartbeats, working his jaw. Elliott could hear how quickly the man was breathing, could smell his rage as well as the chilly, sour scent of fear. Finally, Joe sighed. "You're lucky Bobbi isn't here," he muttered. "Wouldn't let you in if she was. She's shattered. Her doctor's got her on Xanax and she still can barely function. She went to stay with her sister for a while." He made a guttural sound in the back of his throat. "I wouldn't let her see you going through Ainsley's stuff."

He turned and walked away from the door, leaving it standing open. It was as much of an invitation as they were going to get, so Elliott and Braxton went inside. Joe had collapsed into a recliner in the front room and was staring blankly at the television, which wasn't on. Elliott couldn't quite keep from looking at Braxton, whose lips pulled to the side in a sympathetic non-smile.

They went downstairs.

"That is one very angry man," Braxton murmured as they walked along the downstairs hallway.

Elliott swallowed thickly. "His daughter was brutally murdered." He shook his head. "And I get the idea he's used to having things under control. This has thrown him into a tailspin—overachiever daughter dead, dutifully adoring wife absent." It was an oversimplification of the family dynamic, he knew, but he thought his assessment was fair.

"And the son?"

"Not exactly close with his dad. I get the idea they butt heads a lot. Boy's a gifted musician—your wedding band guy, actually, and very popular on YouTube—but I think his father views him as a disappointment." He paused, a hand on the doorknob to Ainsley's room. "At least, Lachlan thinks his father's disappointed in him. Shaw hasn't said that himself."

He looked back over his shoulder at Braxton. "You ready?"

"Open it."

The scent washed over them as Elliott opened the door. He stepped into the room, looking around at the room. It hadn't changed since he stepped inside the first time, except for the body missing from the middle of the floor. The bed was still unmade, one of the pillows lying on the floor. The walls were covered with framed photos of Ainsley in groups of people. The small windows at the top of the walls let in light through the open blinds.

Elliott opened his mouth, tasting that peaty, throat-stinging magic. He felt his skin prickle and he shivered. Hearing Braxton suck in a breath, he turned.

Braxton had his eyes closed, his teeth bared. He took several deep breaths and lifted a hand to his temple. Then he opened his eyes.

"This is fae magic," he said, his voice low. "Unseelie." He drew in another breath. "Not high court. It—" He shook his head. "Do you smell a graveyard?"

"That was my first thought when I smelled it the first time," Elliott said.

"I've caught this scent before, but I'm not sure when. Not that long ago. This summer. Maybe at the wedding, but it might have been on the honeymoon, too." Braxton frowned at the bed.

Following his gaze, Elliott saw a big, brown teddy bear stuffed half under the pillow. His stomach churned a little. Ainsley Shaw had been so young. A soldier, yes, and maybe a mother-to-be, but she'd had so much of her life ahead of her. Something— some*one*—had stolen that from her.

Elliott was going to find out who.

"That's all I know for sure," Braxton said. "I'm sorry."

"More than I knew." Elliott carefully unclenched his fist.

"You could ask Theo. He's more involved with the fae than the rest of us."

Elliott shook his head. "Not yet. I still haven't talked to Ainsley's ex. I might learn more when I do."

"I'm sorry I wasn't more help." Braxton's voice was soft. Elliott wondered if Braxton were thinking the same things he had been. Braxton didn't deal exclusively with homicides in his position. Part of Elliott envied him that—but he did this to keep any victim's grieving family from being treated the way he had been treated.

The day he didn't feel lessened by someone's murder...that was the day he'd quit.

* * *

Three Sisters Cafe had been a brunch establishment in Broad Ripple for twenty years or so. Since he arrived first, Martin managed to snag a table on the patio. He felt his heart give a funny jump when he saw Elliott. *You are in serious trouble,* he told himself, but he couldn't deny that he liked this feeling, scary as it was.

Elliott smiled when he saw Martin, turned his head to speak to someone, and Braxton appeared behind him. They made a beeline for Martin. Martin had taken the seat that placed his back to the wall—partly so he could watch for them, but mostly because his recent dreams of a murdering monster sneaking up behind him had him jumpy.

Elliott settled into the chair next to Martin's, with Braxton across the table from them. Braxton's expression was serious, his gold-brown eyes worried. Martin reached for his iced tea and took a gulp. It struck him suddenly how unfair it was to be a human attracted to a werewolf. Elliott could probably tell just how into him Martin was, between hearing his heartrate jump every time Elliott was around and probably being able to smell attraction or something.

Braxton smiled at him. "How are you, Martin? Haven't seen you for a couple weeks."

"Good." Martin cleared his throat. "Keeping busy at work, you know. I keep waking up and expecting to find Whizz plastered against me, though. I miss the little stinker. I may have to get a cat."

Braxton laughed. "Wait til I tell Chloe," he teased. He tilted his head. "I would have thought you'd be a dog person."

"I like dogs, too," Martin said. "But cats are more independent. I don't have a fenced yard, and I wouldn't want to have to come home in the middle of the day to let it out. Just me at the shop, you know."

"You could hire an assistant," Elliott suggested.

"Please. I'm barely paying my own salary as it is," Martin said. It wasn't really true, but it got a laugh, and he felt some of the tension leaching off.

The waitress came over to take their orders. Three Sisters was known for its delicious vegetarian fare, but they had plenty of meat options, and Martin found himself biting back a smirk at the sheer amount of eggs and meat the two werewolves ordered. Martin went with the biscuits and gravy.

When the waitress was gone, Elliott cleared his throat. When he spoke, his voice was low. "So, Braxton. You know Martin's having visions."

Braxton nodded, leaning in over the table.

"The problem is," Martin said, "I don't actually know any of the people in the visions. I mean, in the dream—vision—whatever—I feel like I know them. But I don't know them in real life. So I can't do anything to stop it from happening."

"You can tell it's murder, though?" Braxton said.

"Yeah."

"And what do you think is the nature of the murders?"

Martin blinked at Braxton, confused by the question. The nature of a murder was evil.

"I mean, are they mundane—committed by humans, ordinary murders, or—"

"Oh. I think..." Martin chewed his lower lip. "I mean, I see the faces of everyone else. The victims. But not the killer. It doesn't make sense that I'd have a vision full of people I don't know, but only see some of the faces." He twisted his lips in self-deprecation. "I mean, as much as any magic makes sense."

"But it does," Elliott broke in. "Magic has its own set of rules and rhythms. It works the same way every time. So yeah, it *should* make sense."

Martin nodded. "So maybe, since I don't see the killer's face, he's using magic to disguise himself? Or using magic to kill."

Elliott said, "That makes sense. And it jives with what I already know." Martin wondered if he was imagining the way Elliott seemed to be leaning closer to him.

Braxton nodded, his eyes grave.

"But what good does that do?" Martin burst out. He lowered his voice, embarrassed at how loud the question had been. "I mean, so I'm seeing the murder before it happens. So what? I can't stop it if I don't know the victim or the killer. So why even let me see the murder? What's the *point* of any of it?"

Elliott rested a hand on Martin's arm. Heat rushed through Martin as his breath hitched. He saw Braxton's gaze flicker down to Elliott's hand, which withdrew. Oh Lord, this was embarrassing. Not only could Elliott tell what kind of effect he had on Martin, but Braxton could, too. Martin closed his eyes briefly.

"What about your latest dream?" Braxton said. Thank God his voice sounded completely normal. "Was it before or after Ainsley's murder?"

Martin gulped his iced tea. "After. But it wasn't Ainsley. It was some dude with glasses who smirked."

Braxton nodded. "And there hasn't been anything since?"

Elliott shook his head. "A couple of shootings, which sucks but is pretty typical. Also, one of the victims was female and the other was black."

"So not the guy in my dreams," Martin put in.

Braxton waved a hand. "It wouldn't be, anyway. I think you're only dreaming about magical murders."

"Hey!" Elliott turned to look at Martin, his face lit with excitement. "Did you have any weird dreams back when Garza was trying to resurrect his daughter?"

Martin frowned, trying to remember. "Well...yeah? Maybe. I mean, remember, I had no idea there was supernatural stuff going on, and I kinda thought Chloe getting shot and having her house burned down had just triggered my PTSD. But...I dreamed this girl was following Chloe around. I don't remember her face very clearly, but maybe that was Alita's ghost?" He pursed his lips. "So I can't be sure."

The waitress came back with their food at that moment, and conversation lagged as they dug in. Martin's heart was still beating too hard. He was overly conscious of how close Elliott was. He kept having to sip his tea because his mouth felt so dry. Chloe was lucky, he thought. She hadn't known Braxton was a werewolf until after they'd kind of gotten together.

"Braxton got a good hit of the killer's scent," Elliott said after a while. "Fae. Unseelie, which is...mostly...bad guys."

"Not always." Braxton's voice was sharp.

"No, yeah, I know." Elliott dug his fork into an egg.

"Isn't that what Lucy found out she is?" Jake Ruiz's sister Lucy, who had always seemed like the steady, respectable sister compared to Celi, had learned that spring that she was Fae. Martin didn't know all the specifics, but he knew there had been a period of time when Jake and Celi—and Chloe—had been afraid Lucy would leave to go spend time with her birth family. Turned out the family she'd grown up with was the family she chose, but it had been a tense time.

"Which is why you can't just divide them into good and bad. Lucy is Winter Court, which is Unseelie. But Lucy and her mother aren't hostile to mortals."

"Plus, even the Seelie Fae are dangerous," Elliott said. "Considered through the lens of human ethics, we'd call the Seelie amoral at best."

Braxton shrugged. "This is beside the point. It's just enough to say we know the killer is Unseelie and not of the court. Possibly a solitary fairy, which narrows it down a little."

"Not enough," Elliott muttered.

"So...can't you ask someone who knows about this stuff?" Martin asked. "I mean, Lucy just found out this spring, so I get she might not know too much, but—"

"Theo would be a good person to ask," Braxton interrupted. "He's connected, and as a reference librarian, he has access to a lot more information than we do."

"Even about the Fae?" Martin asked.

Elliott nodded. "Believe it or not, there are supernatural databases out there, stuff only a certain set of people have access to. I *should* ask Theo. I need to do some more old-fashioned investigative work."

They fell silent, each of them staring at their plates as they finished eating. Martin's chest felt tight, and he thought it was mostly frustration rather than attraction. What was the point of him having visions if he couldn't be helpful? Chloe's gift of seeing ghosts had helped her solve at least one huge mystery and a couple of small ones over the past nine months. What was Martin able to do with his so-called gift? Nothing.

Finally Braxton sighed. "Ell, I think I caught that scent at my wedding."

Elliott looked up quickly. "So one of the guests?"

"Or...the wedding singer."

"Lachlan?" Elliott shook his head. "No, he was genuinely shocked to hear she was dead. I gave him the news myself. I could tell. There was no guilt in his scent."

Braxton sighed again. "Then maybe that isn't the killer's scent at all. She's his sister. His scent could have been in there from any number of visits."

Elliott stared at Braxton for a couple of moments. "So we don't even *have* the killer's scent? Shit."

"Yeah."

The meal ended on a glum note. After they paid, Braxton said he had something to get to and rushed off. Martin and Elliott walked out to the parking area. Martin didn't have the heightened senses of a werewolf, but he could tell Elliott was frustrated and discouraged. It made him look a little angry and a little vulnerable, and Martin suddenly wanted nothing more than to make all of that go away.

He licked his lips. "Hey, I'm sorry this wasn't more helpful," he said.

Elliott shrugged, not quite looking at him. "Part of the job, I'm afraid."

Martin wished he could hug him. Or kiss him. Kissing would be better. "I'll let you know if I have any more dreams." He didn't want to let Elliott leave like this, looking so down.

Elliott did look at him then, smiling a little. "Thanks."

Damn, he was gorgeous, and on top of that he was kind and smart. Martin swallowed and blurted it out before he could stop himself. "Listen, do you—uh."

Elliott cocked his head. "Do I what?" The smile still lingered around his lips.

"Do you want to...The Indiana Historical Society has this new exhibit. 'Be Heard'? It's about—"

"Being gay in Indiana. I've heard about it." Elliott's smile strengthened a little. Martin took that as encouragement.

"It opened last week," Martin said. Why couldn't the ground open up and swallow him right now? He was so bad at this! "Would you like to go? With me?"

There was a long pause as Elliott's smile spread slowly across his face. "Just to be clear," he said, "are you asking me on a date? To a museum?"

Martin wondered if this was how it felt to be a butterfly pinned in someone's collection. "Is that a dumb idea?"

"Not at all." Elliott's smile turned into a grin as he stepped closer. "You didn't answer my question." His voice was low, his gaze inviting.

"Damn cops," Martin muttered, surprising a laugh out of Elliott. "Yes, I'm asking you out."

"Good." Elliott stepped back, golden gaze locked on Martin's. "Okay, let's go out. When?"

"Next Saturday?" They could go today, but Martin was absolutely certain he wasn't prepared for that. He would need a week to psych himself up for this. What the hell had he just done, anyway?

"Sounds good." Elliott was still grinning at him. "We can meet at my place, but you're driving so I can ride in that awesome car of yours. Text me a time."

"Okay." Martin's breath was coming too fast, but he found himself grinning back at Elliott. "Okay."

CHAPTER 15

Early on the Saturday morning following Ainsley's funeral, Lachlan slipped in the front door of his parents' house. Hopefully his father would be in his den with his coffee and the *Indianapolis Star*. He already knew his mother wouldn't be there.

In times of crisis, Bobbi Shaw retreated to her sister's house. Ainsley's not getting into her first choice college had been one such crisis. Lachlan's declaration that he wasn't going to college at all had been another. And there was the crisis eight years ago, the one Ainsley and Lachlan weren't supposed to know about, when their mom had caught their dad cheating with his office manager.

Lachlan's mom definitely wouldn't be at the house.

He looked around the front hall as he eased the door closed. The pictures hanging there told the story of a perfect little family, happy parents, pretty daughter, tall son. He rolled his eyes. Pictures might be worth a thousand words, but no one ever said those words were true ones.

The pictures Lachlan had come here for weren't hanging on the walls, anyway. He'd come to collect the scrapbooks, both the ones their mother had kept when they were little and the two Ainsley had stashed on the shelf in the back of her closet. He and Kaida were hanging out tonight, and he wanted to show her a little bit of *his* Ainsley.

He retrieved his mother's scrapbooks from the living room first. She would notice they were gone as soon as she came home, but he didn't care. By that time he might be ready to give them back.

Then, scrapbooks tucked under his arm, he went down to Ainsley's room in the basement.

His steps faltered on the carpeted stairs. There were crime-scene cleanup companies—something he had just learned a week earlier—but what if they had missed something? What if the detectives had missed something?

What if they'd found something that proved what Eris told him was true?

He shoved the thought aside. She was crazy, sick in the head, just trying to get his attention any way she could. He wasn't going to let her get under his skin.

The closer he got to Ainsley's bedroom door, the harder his heart pounded in his chest. His mouth had started watering a little the way it did before throwing up. He swallowed hard and stopped walking. He couldn't throw up in Ainsley's room.

He pivoted into the bathroom Ainsley had been using and pushed the door mostly shut. He took a moment longer, despite the spasming of his stomach, to put the scrapbooks carefully on the bathmat behind him. Then he emptied his fast food breakfast and Mountain Dew into the toilet.

186

He didn't dare flush, despite the reek. He pulled back, wiping his mouth with toilet paper and fumbling under the sink for mouthwash. A swish and spit into the toilet would have to do.

Lachlan slumped back against the bathroom wall, pressing the heels of his hands into his eyes. "God, Ains," he whispered, "what am I doing without you? How the fuck did this happen?"

He threw up again before mastering himself, but finally he forced himself to his feet and pulled the bathroom door open, listening. The clock in the living room chimed the hour—nine in the morning—and fell silent. Somewhere on the second floor a door shut. Lachlan held his breath. Yes, there—the water had gone on. Dad was in the shower.

He flushed the toilet, hoping viciously that the shower would go cold for a second. Then he dashed into Ainsley's room before he could psych himself out again. He pulled the scrapbooks out from under the shoebox that hid them, added them to the pile of scrapbooks from downstairs, and bolted.

At eight that evening, someone knocked on his apartment door.

Lachlan set his guitar carefully in its holder and opened it to let Kaida in.

"Hi," she said. She was even tinier and fiercer-looking than he had remembered. Lachlan's chest tightened with a feeling similar to one he'd felt when he heard Ainsley was coming home from Afghanistan. Kaida was someone who had known Ainsley almost as well as he had.

So why did this feel so weird?

"Hi," he said back, holding the door.

She had a pile of takeout boxes in her arms. "I didn't bring anything to drink. I hope that's okay."

"No problem. I have beer, pop, water, and milk that's probably sour."

Kaida huffed a little laugh as she toed off her shoes next to the door. "Beer's good, as long as it's not an IPA."

"It's Coors Light," Lachlan said. "Craft beer is one hundred percent not my thing."

She snorted and looked around. "Where do you want this?"

"Oh." Lachlan looked at his apartment, seeing it the way she would. He had a comfortable couch for the TV and his computer desk and chair. Where Ainsley would probably have put a coffee table he just had a busted amplifier. "Um. I use the amp for a table sometimes."

Kaida's expression didn't betray her thoughts. She just carried the boxes over and started placing them on the amplifier. "You said you wanted Pad Thai, but you didn't mention anything else. I got extra spring rolls if you want."

Lachlan stepped past her to the kitchen and got their beer and forks. "That's fine."

How was he supposed to talk to her? He couldn't talk to her the way he'd talked to Ainsley. Maybe if they'd ended up getting married, he could have treated her like a second sister. But he didn't know her well enough for that. It had been easier talking to her at the funeral, where they were allies against Ainsley's adoring public.

Kaida opened her mouth when he held out the beer and fork. She looked down at them, at the food containers, and closed her mouth. Lachlan felt his stomach twist a little. She'd expected him to get plates, hadn't she? He was probably living down to everything Ainsley had told her about him.

Instead of protesting, though, Kaida grabbed a box of curry, settled cross-legged on the couch, and cracked open her beer can. She blinked once at him and shoved a forkful of food in her mouth. She chewed and swallowed and then let out a long sigh.

"Dude, that is so good. Ainsley never let me have Thai food."

Startled, Lachlan laughed. "Me neither. Drove me crazy." His laughter faltered. "I mean…" He trailed off. At the funeral they'd both admitted to resenting Ainsley, but he couldn't help wondering if that was off-limits now.

"You know, I never understood why people say you shouldn't speak ill of the dead," she remarked through a mouthful of curry. "I think it's worse to lie about the dead. If you can't speak any ill of them, how do you know you really knew them at all?"

"Right," Lachlan said. "Ainsley pissed me off all the time, but she was my sister, and I loved her. And I don't need to pretend she was some kind of saint to love her."

"Did she ever tell you about our first date?" Kaida said, her lips quirking up. When Lachlan shook his head, she continued. "The first thing she did was spill her beer on my white slacks. She swore up a storm in between apologizing and trying to blot me—in a spot I would have smacked most people for touching."

Lachlan snorted.

"We'd met several times, of course, and I'd always thought she was so poised and all, so it blew me away." Kaida laughed faintly. "And then charmed me."

Lachlan dragged over one of his mother's scrapbooks. "Ainsley was horse-crazy when we were kids, did you know that? Yeah. Begged and begged for a pony for every holiday you can think of. Even the Fourth of July, because she said the revolutionaries all had ponies, so she needed one too." He sipped his beer. "She never got a pony for real, but our mom gave her riding lessons one year for her birthday. Three lessons in, the horse stopped before Ainsley did and she fell off and broke her arm."

Kaida's eyes widened. Chewing, she motioned for him to keep talking.

"The next lesson she climbed on the horse and switched the reins to her other hand, and that was that."

"She was so determined even as a kid?"

"Determined, hell. Mom says—" Lachlan choked the word off and cleared his throat. "Mom always said Ains was the textbook strong-willed child. But it worked for her."

For a few minutes they ate in silence while Kaida flipped slowly through the scrapbook. She passed pictures of Ainsley in a Girl Scout uniform, pictures of Ainsley and Lachlan in the bathtub, pictures of Ainsley on a horse in perfect English riding posture.

"She moved on to horses, I guess," she remarked.

"Yep. She wanted to learn how to ride Western eventually, too, but Mom said English style was harder, so she could start with that."

Kaida shook her head. "That seems backwards."

"Nah, you start with the hardest thing and master it. That was Ainsley's style." Lachlan poked his Pad Thai with his fork. Who would have expected he would start missing that about Ainsley?

"We talked about moving west," Kaida said. Her voice was so soft Lachlan had to lean closer to hear. "I have family in Portland. She knew I missed them, so we'd talked about getting a place together out there."

Lachlan hadn't known that, but he wasn't surprised. "What's your family like?"

Kaida shrugged. "Two brothers, my parents, my mother's mother. It's one of my brothers who lives out in Portland, and he takes care of our grandmother. She's very active, but she doesn't see well enough anymore to live alone safely."

Lachlan didn't know what to say to that. He finished his Pad Thai, watching her turn pages. Her fingers stopped moving when she reached the picture of Lachlan and Ainsley singing together at a talent show. Lachlan had almost forgotten that night. It was Ainsley's senior year in high school, and she'd wanted Lachlan to perform with her. They'd sung "Don't Give Up" by Peter Gabriel and Kate Bush and brought down the house.

It was a good night.

Kaida touched the photograph with one fingertip. "Did she ever tell you how much she envied you?"

Lachlan's mouth dropped open. Envy? Ainsley?

Kaida looked up to meet his gaze. "You're so brave. You're not afraid to be yourself, never caring what people expect of you. She envied you that. She loved all the videos you posted."

Lachlan swallowed to clear the lump from his throat. His voice still croaked when he said, "I didn't know she watched them."

"All the time. She'd email me every link, usually with all this analysis and praise. Critiques too, sometimes, but even those, you could tell how proud she was of you." She set aside her takeout container and looked back down at the picture.

"Proud." Lachlan shook his head. "One of the last times we talked, she said I could've been successful if I'd just gone to Butler."

"That was the only way she knew to succeed." Kaida folded her hands in her lap. "Make a five-year plan and follow it, that was the Ainsley Shaw way. But she could see how you freeform and improvise your way through life, and it terrified her."

Lachlan looked Kaida up and down. "I bet you weren't in her five-year plan."

They laughed, and if Kaida's expression was bittersweet, Lachlan knew why.

After a moment he said slowly, "She was trying to figure out how to make things right with you, you know?"

"I didn't even know things *weren't* right." Kaida's voice was bitter.

"Nah, see, that was part of her planning thing. She had to figure out how someone would react before she could confess anything. S'why she hadn't told them about you two yet. She thought she knew how Mom and Dad would respond, but she wanted to make sure she had her own response to their response planned."

Kaida shook her head. "Couldn't she have just trusted me? I *love* her. Couldn't she let that carry us?"

Lachlan started at her. "Have you seen what we call love in our family?" He was surprised at the bitterness in his voice.

Kaida sniffed and Lachlan looked away, down at the scrapbook and then quickly over at a poster he had taped to the wall. His Pad Thai felt like a stone in his stomach.

What would she say if he told her what Eris had said? Kaida thought her love for Ainsley was enough to forgive her for cheating. Would she be able to forgive Lachlan for what Eris said he had done?

But she didn't love Lachlan. Without love, would she forgive him? Laugh at him? Call him sick?

Call the cops?

Stop thinking about it, he ordered himself. Eris was crazy. She was lying. It didn't make sense. For one thing, magic didn't exist. Magical beings didn't exist. For another, why hadn't anyone else he knew turned up dead before?

Wait...hadn't his dad's office manager gotten cancer or something? Could he have caused that?

Kaida shifted in her chair and looked down at her wrist, where a non-existent watch obviously belonged. "It's getting late," she said. "I should probably go."

"Yeah." Lachlan didn't stand until she did, then he shot to his feet. He followed her over to the door.

"Let's do this again," she said, and finally met his gaze.

Lachlan nodded.

"Let me know when your next show is." Kaida gave him a wry smile. "I can't leave town until they find whoever did this. I might as well support you as often as possible while I'm here."

"Sure." Lachlan wondered if she meant it. But he would do it. A text sent just a little bit before the show would be fine, and she wouldn't feel like she had to be there.

Kaida wrapped her arms around his waist and hugged him hard. "Thank you, Lachlan," she whispered. She tilted her head back to meet his gaze.

Then she turned and left.

CHAPTER 16

Elliott spent the rest of weekend alternating between flipping out about the upcoming date and brooding over Ainsley's murder. He tried to distract himself with a Civil War movie marathon, but he kept catching himself thinking about the date or the murder instead of watching the movie. Finally he turned off the DVD player and headed for the gym. He could brood about things at the gym as easily as brooding at home.

Sunday afternoon wasn't a busy time at the gym, so Elliott was able to do his circuit without sharing weights or machines with anyone. Sweaty and breathless from a final treadmill jog and feeling more confident about the date, if not about the murder, he hit the showers. He was damp and wrapped in a towel when his cell phone rang. He didn't get to the phone in time to answer, so when he saw that the caller ID said BRADY FLYNN, he decided to at least get some boxers and a t-shirt on before Brady called back.

The second time the phone rang, it was in his hand. He picked up on the first ring. "Blake."

"We have another body. Just like Ainsley Shaw."

"Where?"

"East side. I'll text you the address."

"Meet you there in twenty," Elliott said, and ended the call.

In less than a minute he was dressed and heading for the murder scene.

Brady pulled up right behind Elliott. The responding officers were standing with a woman who was obviously pregnant and had a toddler on one hip. Elliott swore under his breath as he stepped out of the car. He exchanged a glance with Brady, who had gone pale. Elliott nodded; he'd handle this one.

He introduced himself to the woman, who turned out to be Beth Parrish, the wife of the murder victim. She was extremely calm and dry-eyed, but Elliott could hear how fast her heart was beating. She shook his hand and then lowered trembling fingers to clench at her side. Holding it together for her little girl, Elliott decided.

"And who is this?" he asked, smiling at the girl.

"This is Hayden."

"I'm free," the girl informed him, holding up three fingers.

Elliott widened his eyes. "Wow. My friend Brady has a little girl who's almost three. Do you want to hang out with him, Hayden?"

Brady gave him a grateful smile and took charge of Hayden. When Elliott looked back at Beth Parrish, she was giving him a similarly grateful look.

"Why don't we go inside?" he suggested.

Beth jolted upright. "Please, no." Her voice was quiet. "What about the back porch? I can't—I just—" She lifted her fingers to her cheek and dropped them again. "Jo is—inside."

"I'm so sorry," Elliott said, mentally kicking himself for his gaffe. He should have asked about that first. "The back porch is fine, Mrs. Parrish."

She led the way around the house. By the time she turned to face him again, her face was wet. "I can't let Hayden see," she whispered. "I feel like I'm going to explode."

"I understand." Elliott spoke softly, trying to instill as much understanding as he could. "I lost my mother when I was young. The hardest part was being strong for my younger sisters."

At the same time, he'd been grateful to have Em and O to be strong for. He couldn't fall apart because they were his responsibility. He had to show he could take care of them, or CPS might have decided to get involved. They were both minors when their mother was killed.

Beth sniffed loudly and wiped both hands over her face. "I'm so sorry. I found him like that and...all I could think about was getting Hayden out of the house and not...not..."

"Take your time." Elliott put a gentle hand on her elbow and guided her to a patio chair. "Would you like a drink of water?"

She sniffed again and shook her head. "How does this work? Do you ask me questions or do I just tell you?"

"Which would make you more comfortable?" he asked.

She huffed. "Neither is going to be comfortable."

Elliott nodded. "Okay. What happened?"

Beth Parrish and her daughter had just come home from a week at her mother and father's house in Virginia. Jo had stayed in Indianapolis because of commitments, but they had talked on the phone Thursday night. "I thought it was weird he didn't text me Friday or Saturday," she said, "but I figured he was taking advantage of having us away." Her expression was rueful. "He won't keep alcohol in the house, but with me and Hayden gone, he was going to have a poker night with some of the guys. I just assumed he was hung over."

"What guys would those be?" Elliott said.

"Some of the vets. Jo started a nonprofit called Homes and Hope. They rebuild houses for homeless vets. Some of the guys he's helped in the past turn around and volunteer with the organization, and they've become close. A chosen family, you know?"

"I'll need a list of their names at some point."

Beth blinked at him and then nodded. "When I got here, I got Hayden out of her car seat and we went up to the house. The front door was ajar. It was weird, but I thought maybe it just hadn't latched when he got home. I knew he was home, because his truck's in the garage. So I just pushed it open."

She stopped talking and covered her face with one hand. Her shoulders began shaking. He could hear her heart beat faster again and her breathing was audible and shaky. He waited until she composed herself and looked up.

"He was dead," he said.

Beth nodded. "He was lying on the living room floor. His guitar was on the floor next to him. And there..." She closed her eyes. "There was so much blood."

Elliott waited a couple of moments. "What did you do then?"

"I got Hayden out of the house and called 911."

"You didn't go inside?"

"Not beyond the doorway." Beth's eyes were full of tears as she looked at him. "I knew he was dead. No one can lose that much blood and still be alive." She took a long, shaky breath. "We got married just before his first deployment. I spent three years expecting to get that call, you know? Dreading it. Praying it would never happen. But knowing it was a possibility."

She dragged her fingers through her blonde hair, pushing it away from her face. "He's been home six years now. I never expected something to happen here. I thought we were home free."

Jo Parrish had been surprised by death. He was eviscerated just like Ainsley, and, also like Ainsley, he hadn't seen it coming. The shock on his face was unequivocal. The living room was thick with the smell of blood, but underneath it, Elliott could catch strains of peat and earth. It was the same scent he'd encountered in Ainsley's room. If it was Lachlan Shaw's scent, why would it be here?

Elliott smacked himself on the forehead. This couldn't be Lachlan Shaw's scent. If it was, Elliott would have smelled it at Lachlan's apartment. And why hadn't he thought of that right away? He wasn't bringing his A game. He was letting himself get too distracted by this thing with Martin.

Martin. Elliott sighed. He couldn't let himself be distracted by romance, but he also needed to keep Martin in the loop on this case. He moved over to the wall, where several framed pictures showed a sandy-haired man with glasses smiling at the camera. In some of the pictures he was with Beth and Hayden; in others he was in the desert with half a dozen other fatigues-clad soldiers. In one picture he stood in front of a truck with a "Homes and Hope" graphic on the side. He had a triumphant smile on his face. Elliott pulled out his phone and snapped a picture of that one. He attached it to a text message for Martin. *This your dream guy?* he typed, and hit send.

He slid the phone back in his pocket and looked around the room, stepping around the crime scene guys as they worked. By all appearances, Beth and Jo Parrish had a happy marriage. The house wasn't spic-and-span clean, but it was as tidy as any house with a three-year-old living in it could be. Nothing seemed to be in disrepair, which made sense; a man who ran a construction-related business wouldn't let his own home get run down.

After making a couple of calls to check Beth's alibi, and inadvertently becoming the person to tell Beth's parents that their son-in-law was dead, Elliott had developed a splitting headache. He checked his phone and saw he had two text messages and a missed call from Martin. He raised his eyebrows and opened the messages.

What's his name? Is he dead? said the first. *He was the one in the dream.* Elliott blinked, trying not to be surprised. After the Murphy dream, he'd wondered…but Martin *was* psychic, after all. He smiled; he probably didn't have the right to be proud, but he was. He scrolled to the second message. *Who is he? Are you okay?*

Elliott found himself smiling at his phone. Martin was the one having murder visions and he still took the time to ask if Elliott was okay? He typed back, *I'm okay. This is the job. I'll fill you in later.*

With a sigh, Elliott peeled the protective booties off his shoes and headed outside, where dusk was falling. He would have to talk to as many of the Homes and Hope people as possible, but first he needed to ask Beth a few more questions.

He found her sitting in the passenger seat of Brady's car. She was clutching a bottle of water like it was keeping her afloat. Hayden was nowhere to be seen.

"My neighbor took her," Beth volunteered when she saw Elliott looking around. "She babysits Kay a lot, so we thought it was best."

Elliott nodded and crouched next to the open passenger door. "Mrs. Parrish, can you think of anyone who'd want to hurt your husband?"

"No!" Beth stared at him. "I mean, he *helps* people. He puts everything into Homes and Hope, and people admire him." She shook her head in an unfocused way. "Some of the neighborhoods the houses are in are kinda sketchy, but...he's always had a good relationship with the neighbors. When he buys a foreclosed house, he tells the neighbors what he's doing and why, and explains how they aren't *flipping* houses. They're rebuilding them to let a homeless veteran buy it on contract. A lot of the neighbors love the program. They get involved, bring cookies over to the guys as they work and stuff."

"What about the vets he works with?" Elliott said. "Are any of them..." He caught himself and rephrased what he'd been about to say. "Do any of them concern you?" Asking if they were dangerous was wrong-headed on two levels. First of all, they were veterans, so they all knew *how* to be dangerous; but it was biased of him to think they were more likely to be dangerous to others, even if they did have PTSD.

"I mean, a lot of them have symptoms of Post Traumatic Stress Disorder," she said. "Jo did himself, which is why he started the program. He found it helped to spend time around people who understood. But they love Jo. I can't see any of them hurting him." She rubbed the bridge of her nose and shook her head. "No. None of them concern me."

"Can you think of any clubs or groups Jo belongs to?" Elliott asked. "A veterans support group, the American Legion, anything where he might have come into contact with people you don't know?"

"We go to the Legion sometimes, but we know most of the people we see there. Some of them volunteer with Homes and Hope." Beth pushed her hair away from her face. "He's got a garage band with a few of the vets. They're all good people. I'm not saying otherwise. But they play at bars sometimes. Even at the Legion. Maybe they've seen something? You should ask some of them."

"I will." Elliott stood up. "What kind of hours is Homes and Hope open? Would I find someone there tonight?"

"Maybe." Beth's gaze wandered across his face and down to the mailbox at the end of the drive. "Probably. They do most of their work on weekends."

All right. "Thank you for your time, Mrs. Parrish. When I talked to your parents, it sounded like they would be leaving Virginia to come here. Do you have anyone local you can stay with tonight?"

She nodded. "My cousin lives in Greenwood."

"Okay. Nikki over there is with us. Do you want her to go inside and get anything for you? A change of clothes or stuff for Hayden? A blanket or stuffed animal?"

"Yes, thanks." Beth pushed herself out of the car. "I'll go talk to her."

Elliott had given her a card earlier, and Brady would have given her a card, too, but people tended to misplace things at a time like this. Elliott held out another card. "If you can think of anything, no matter how small and insignificant it might seem, give me a call, okay? Don't feel like you're bothering me. Right now I'm going to be spending all my time trying to find out who killed your husband, so your phone calls are important."

She nodded. Her face was closing down. He could tell the truth was setting in but she was still in denial. His stomach twisted. There was nothing he could do about Beth Parrish's grief. But he could find Jo Parrish's killer. And his next stop was Homes and Hope.

* * *

Homes and Hope's office was a metal pole barn structure with a regular door and a garage door in the front. The garage door was rolled up and music was playing as Elliott walked up the drive. He could see half a dozen people inside.

He took a deep, bracing breath. This was going to suck.

All conversation ceased as he walked in. A man in a wheelchair turned it to face him. A tall black man stopped hammering something and looked up. A white woman and a Latina woman stopped sorting through a large bin of wood.

Elliott held up his badge. "Detective Elliott Blake, IMPD. Is there someone who's in charge here?"

The black man put down his hammer. "Is this about the music? I didn't think it was too loud." He snapped off the radio.

The music was loud enough to hear, but it wasn't overly loud for a summer Sunday. Elliott shook his head. "I'm not here about a complaint. I'm looking for people who know Jo Parrish."

One of the women laughed. "That would be all of us. But there's no way he's in trouble."

When Elliott didn't reply, the silence took on a sharp quality.

"What's this about?" the black guy asked.

"You are?"

The black guy's look grew less friendly. "James Tipton, USMC."

Elliott regretted his tone, which had obviously made the man feel like he was being treated like a suspect. He hadn't wanted this to be confrontational. "Mr. Tipton, I'm afraid Jo's wife found him dead this afternoon. I'm here on a homicide investigation." He waited for the gasps and exclamations to die down and then added, "I'm hoping you all can help me."

"What happened?" James took three steps closer to Elliott. "When? We thought he must have changed his mind and gone to Virginia with Beth."

Elliott shook his head. "I'm afraid I can't tell you much. We don't have a time of death yet." Though from the scent, he thought Jo had been dead at least twenty-four hours. "I'm trying to find out who would have wanted to hurt him."

"No one. You're talking about a guy who doted on his family and spent all his time trying to help people." Tipton's fist was curled at his side.

"Sir, I know this is hard to imagine. But it happened. It...doesn't look random. As difficult as it is, I need you all to think about anyone who might have had a conflict with Mr. Parrish." Elliott looked around at the shocked, scared faces. "I'll need to talk to each of you," he added. "It doesn't have to be tonight, but if we can arrange a time, I would appreciate it."

Tipton's shoulders slumped. He looked down and seemed surprised by the curl of his fist. He lifted the hand, opening it to rub over his face. "We have a sign-in sheet. Jo tracks volunteer hours for a grant he got. That'll give you contact info for everyone who's here tonight. Well, for everyone who's worked here recently."

Elliott nodded. "That'll work."

"Why don't the rest of you head out," Tipton said, gesturing at everyone. "I'll stay here and talk to Detective Blake."

"Are you sure you'll be safe?" the Latina woman asked.

Tipton looked over at Elliott and held his gaze. "Of course I'll be all right. Detective Blake isn't here to hurt me, and I'm unarmed."

"Aside from a dozen hammers and nailguns and whatever," the Latina woman countered.

To Elliott's surprise, Tipton chuckled. As soon as the sound left his mouth, his expression blanked and he looked shocked at himself. After a moment he shook his head. "I don't think a brown cop is gonna shoot me, Cris. I'll be fine. Go home."

Elliott watched Tipton as the others filed out of the building. He liked that Tipton had acknowledged his skin color. Elliott was light enough that a lot of black people didn't recognize him as biracial, though he was certainly dark enough that most white people didn't think he was white. It was a truth that made him feel like he was straddling a very awkward rift between black people and the police, especially in the Black Lives Matter era. Elliott fully supported what the BLM movement was trying to do, but he didn't always feel comfortable saying so around the office. It made him think his choice to be a cop had given him a certain amount of privilege—blue privilege instead of white, but still real.

Tipton pushed a button to close the big garage door and went to a fridge in one corner of the room. "You want a Coke?"

"I'm good, thanks," Elliott said.

Tipton nodded, grabbed a Coke for himself, and came over to sit down. "So someone murdered Jo." His face twisted and he sucked in a breath. "You're sure it was—murder? He got depressed sometimes."

"This wasn't a suicide," Elliott said. He wasn't sure if that made it easier or harder.

Tipton exhaled. "Was he shot?"

"I'm not at liberty to share all of the details," Elliott said. "But it appears a blade of some kind was involved."

Tipton shook his head. "This isn't right, man. Jo's a good guy. Helps other people because it helps him feel better to do that. I can't figure anyone wanting to hurt him."

"I'm very sorry for your loss," Elliott said.

"So what questions do you have for me? I want to help you catch whoever did this."

"Can you think of anyone he was having trouble with?" Elliott said. "Whether it was someone who volunteers here, someone in the neighborhood, or a supplier or contractor of some kind?"

"I don't know about anyone who was giving him trouble." Tipton cracked open the Coke can. "I know he was concerned about a couple of people. Cris—she's had temper issues lately, but she..." He trailed off. "This is between us, right?"

Elliott nodded. "As long as it doesn't have bearing on the case."

Tipton shook his head. "Cris self-harms. She's not a danger to anyone else."

Elliott sighed. "Okay. Jo was trying to help her?"

"Jo didn't feel qualified to help her, man. None of us do. Jo was trying to get her to get help, though. He's always open about how much counseling he's been through, telling us that sometimes it isn't enough to hammer a few boards together, that sometimes you have to talk it out with someone who knows how to deal with all that."

"Good for Jo." The more he heard about Jo Parrish, the more Elliott liked the guy. Just like Ainsley, he was someone who'd come home safe and was trying to rebuild a life that got shaken to pieces by war. Jo went a step further by actively trying to help other people do the same. He wondered if Martin had known Jo.

"There was one guy Jo was worried about. He just started showing up a few weeks ago. Just got back from a deployment." When Tipton saw Elliott was paying attention, he went on. "This guy, Dave, I know he had a lot of issues. I think there was marriage trouble, and he was having a hard time adjusting. And then..."

"Go on."

Tipton shifted back in his seat. "Dave knew the girl who was murdered."

Elliott lifted his head in sudden understanding. "David Corriden," he said. "Ainsley Shaw's commanding officer." Finally a direct connection to Ainsley's murder, one besides the fact that she and Jo Parrish were both veterans. And David Corriden still hadn't returned Elliott's phone calls. He would have to prioritize that ASAP.

"And her ex-boyfriend before he got married, from what I hear. I don't know the guy well, okay? But he's taking her death hard."

"How hard?" Elliott asked.

"I know he wasn't the one who broke it off with her. He rebounded pretty quick, all the way to the altar, okay, but I think he never really got over her."

"Do you think he and Ainsley were still involved?"

"I mean, they were still friends. I didn't know her. Never met her. I just know Dave talked about her all the time."

Elliott raised his eyebrows. "Did he talk about Ainsley more than he talked about his wife?"

Tipton looked like that should have been obvious. "Well, yeah. After the news broke about her murder, he was a mess. He showed up here drunk one time. Jo took him in the office and made him sleep it off on the couch."

Elliott straightened. "Thank you for your time, Mr. Tipton. Could I get a copy of that sign-in sheet you mentioned?"

"Sure thing." Tipton stood and led the way to the office. He ran a copy of two sheets of paper and handed them over. "I hope you find out what happened," he said.

Elliott scanned the pages quickly, but none of the names stood out except David Corriden's. "Me too."

* * *

By Wednesday Martin had to drag himself out of bed. He hadn't had any weird dreams since Friday, but his sleep had been restless and he'd had trouble even falling asleep.

He was in the middle of rebuilding a transmission on a Chevy S-10 for a guy who was hoping to keep the truck alive for a couple more years. It was something he could probably have done in his sleep—ha ha—normally, but that day he kept fumbling wrenches and dropping nuts. Just after lunch, he took the skin off two knuckles trying to catch a part before it hit the ground and busted.

Martin swore and sucked the blood—and grease—from the offended knuckles. This was ridiculous. At this rate, he'd end up dropping a tire on his foot or falling into the pit and breaking a leg.

"Wouldn't trust myself to change someone's oil right now," he grumbled as he poured peroxide over his knuckles.

What was affecting his sleep so badly? Was it the fact he'd cut back on his drinking? He knew he'd been using that as a crutch to fall asleep for months, but he hadn't realized it was that serious. Or maybe it was the realization that his dreams might not be PTSD. *Might not be?*

He scoffed at himself and dabbed his fingers dry. "They aren't PTSD. Or at least they aren't *just* PTSD. If they were, Jo Parrish would never have shown up in them."

He stuck bandages on his knuckles and headed back to the office. There was no point in trying to get anything else done on the transmission right now. He'd only have to redo it all tomorrow if he tried.

Maybe he was subconsciously avoiding sleep because he didn't want to dream. But could your subconscious do something like that? He had no idea.

For that matter, until he came back from Afghanistan, he hadn't given sleep much thought at all. It was something you did when you were tired. On deployment, you learned to sleep wherever you were, no matter if there was gunfire in the distance or your cot was creaking every time you breathed.

Sleep had only become difficult once he had a soft bed of his own.

And no one to share it with, added a voice in the back of his mind.

Maybe it was time for him to do some investigation of his own. Elliott had admitted flat out that he was no expert on psychic stuff, except that he knew it was real. Martin wasn't an expert, either, but that didn't mean he couldn't become one. Elliott had a murder to solve, but Martin had nothing more pressing than the shop work.

There had to be some Chilton's equivalent for dreaming, and he needed to find it.

Martin was reasonably comfortable with computers. He could use the internet to order the parts he needed and file his taxes, and he was adept with inventory and invoicing software and the diagnostic software required by newer vehicles. But one of the werewolves was a librarian, and from Theo, Martin had learned that librarians actually got entire degrees on how to search for information.

No sense wasting a perfectly good librarian, Martin thought, so he closed the shop an hour early and headed for the library.

He found his way to the reference desk and loitered nearby for a few minutes, looking around for Theo. But the stocky werewolf didn't appear, so finally Martin went up to the tie-clad man who sat at the desk.

"Hi there," the man said, smiling at him. His name tag proclaimed him to be Kyle. He was appallingly cheerful. "Is there something I can help you with?"

He was also, Martin realized, very nice-looking, in a fresh, clean-cut kind of way. "Is Theo here?"

"Oh, sorry, he's off this week. Are you a friend of his?"

"Yeah, uh, well." Martin shrugged. "We have a friend in common. I just knew he worked here. I'm actually looking for some information."

"You're in the right place. We have lots of that." The man's hazel eyes actually twinkled. "I'm happy to help you find whatever you need."

"Sure, okay." Martin rubbed the back of his neck, suddenly feeling scruffy even though he'd scrubbed to get the grease off his hands before coming here—an instinct left over from elementary school, when they'd been made to wash their hands before getting library privileges.

"So what kind of information are you looking for?" Kyle clicked a couple of buttons on his computer and then poised his hands over the keyboard, watching Martin avidly.

"Sleep." Martin gave him a sheepish smile. "I guess that's pretty broad."

"A little bit, but we'll see what we get." He started typing. "Are you looking for information on the science of sleep? How to get better sleep? The effects of not sleeping enough? I have about five thousand results here, so we'll have to narrow it down a little."

Martin scoffed in astonishment. Five thousand books just about sleep?

"Those are across the whole Indianapolis library system," Kyle explained, correctly interpreting the noise. "I'll start by limiting it just to the books we have here."

"Well, I live in Broad Ripple, so…"

"Okay, I'll add in Glendale branch. That takes us to…about seventeen hundred." He smiled at Martin, displaying a dimple on one cheek. "That's progress."

Martin shook his head. "Now I know why you need special training to do this."

Kyle laughed. "What kind of information are you looking for?" he asked again.

"I guess…how to get a good night's sleep. What might keep you from sleeping well."

"Okay, let's see…Looks like we've got self-care, health aspects of sleep, sleep disorders…" Kyle started writing on a notepad. "What I'll do is write down the Dewey Decimal number of some of these books, and then we'll take a look at the shelf and see what looks useful to you."

"Thanks." Martin shoved his hands in his jeans pockets, winced at the pressure on his sore knuckles, and took that hand back out.

"I've got a few books here that look like they're good general books on sleep, some books on beating insomnia… oh, here's one on the power of sleep and dreams."

Martin cleared his throat. "That one sounds good."

Kyle looked over at him, eyes bright with interest. "Dreams?"

"Yeah, I guess dream meanings, interpretation, why we dream, something on that would be good, too." Martin wondered suddenly if librarians were like doctors and priests. Could they tell other people what you'd been asking about, or were they sworn to secrecy?

A good question for Theo, the next time he saw him.

"Mm, here's one on the science of dreams." He wrote on his notepad. "Beauty sleep... Don't need that one." He shot a sly smile at Martin. "Here's one on anxiety and dreams."

Martin, who suddenly wondered if he was being flirted with, nodded. "Anxiety, like it causes dreams?"

"And insomnia, looks like." The man fixed his gaze on his computer, his shoulders tightening a little.

"What about..." Martin paused, licked his lips, and then lowered his voice. "What about PTSD. Would that affect sleep?"

Kyle hummed thoughtfully and looked back up at Martin. "There are at least two titles here that suggest it would, yes." He'd lowered his voice, too. "Or, well, one is about PTSD and one is specifically about combat trauma."

"I'd like to look at those," Martin said, surprised at how firmly his voice came out.

"Okay." Kyle rolled his chair away from his desk and stood. "I'm going to show you where the books are shelved—616.85212 is the place to start."

"Careful, I might have to start throwing engine diagnostic codes at you if you're going to speak a foreign language," Martin said, feeling a smile pressing at his lips.

Kyle looked back at him, eyebrows raised. After a moment he smiled. "Mechanic, then? I was wavering between that and cage fighter." He gestured at Martin's bandaged knuckles.

Martin chuckled. "Mechanic's a safer bet."

He followed the librarian through the stacks, wondering why it always happened this way—you met someone interesting as soon as you'd already met someone interesting.

Of course, this guy could be just being helpful. Martin wasn't always certain he was being flirted with—or that he was flirting. He liked to joke around with waiters in restaurants, but more than once he'd been accused of being a flirt when he just thought he was being friendly.

"Okay, so this whole section here is going to relate to sleep in some way," Kyle said. "Sleep in general is here in 616, and then the numbers after the decimal point break it down into more specific issues. So 616.5 is where you'll find natural remedies and alternative medicine approaches to sleep. Insomnia is there," he added, pointing. "Now, dream interpretation isn't in this section. It falls more under psychology, I guess, so those books will be in 154.6—that's down that way." He gestured. "Want me to show you?"

"I think I've got the gist of how the system works," Martin said. "I just wasn't sure how to search the computers for what I needed."

Kyle beamed at him. "That's what I'm here for." He held out the slip of paper. "I'll be here for another hour or so, so let me know if I can help with anything else, okay? Sometimes it takes a couple of tries to find the right fit, but I'm good at what I do."

Martin raised his eyebrows. "I believe you." He took the paper and smiled.

By the time he finished looking through the books in the sleep and dream sections, he'd found half a dozen he wanted to check out and another three that had turned out not to be exactly what he needed. There were signs asking people not to reshelve the books, and since Martin only had a vague notion of all the rules of the codification system, he carried them back to the reference desk.

Kyle was helping a teenager who was showing him something on her phone. After a couple of minutes she walked away and Kyle turned to Martin with a smile.

Martin held up the books. "Thank you for your help. I think I found some that will help." He pulled out the three he didn't want. "These weren't right, but I knew I wasn't supposed to put them back. What should I do with them?"

"I'll take them. We have a cart back here." Kyle's fingers just barely brushed Martin's as he took the books. "Can I help you with anything else today?"

Martin pulled his hand back and scratched his neck. "I'm still not entirely sure what I'm looking for, so..." He shrugged. "You've really been helpful."

"Well..." Kyle drew the word out, then turned and picked up two books that were sitting on his desk. "Based on your earlier topics, I did a little more searching and realized these books were checked in but hadn't been shelved yet. They wouldn't have been exactly where you were looking, anyway." He slid the books across the desk. *Adventures in the Strange Science of Sleep,* read one subtitle, and *Sleep Thieves: An Eye-Opening Exploration into the Science and Mysteries of Sleep* was the other.

Martin blinked. "Thank you," he said, touched. "You didn't have to go to so much trouble."

Kyle shrugged. "It's a slightly different angle. I thought it might give you some ideas."

"I'll check those out, too," Martin promised. He took the books and smiled at Kyle. It seemed inane to thank him again, so he just added, "Have a good night."

"You too," Kyle said. He smiled. "Sleep well."

CHAPTER 17

Lachlan hadn't intended to do any more shows until he decided if he believed what Eris had told him about his music being magic. He'd kept writing and recording, because he figured the magic—if it was real—must not work unless it was live. Otherwise he'd have had thousands of followers before Ainsley died.

Before he killed Ainsley.

Before he murdered his sister.

You didn't murder her, he told himself. You couldn't have murdered her. You didn't want her dead. You never wanted her dead. And even if you had, you had no idea you could make that happen. You wouldn't have used a gun or a knife or anything to kill her. So this doesn't count.

A large part of him wished he had told Kaida about what Eris had said. A larger part of him was afraid she would either laugh at him or hate him. Or maybe both. After all, he'd laughed at Eris. He laughed every time he thought about her ridiculous claim that magic was real and he had it.

Then he started doubting himself again.

So he'd decided it would just be easier to avoid live shows, even if one event coordinator had told him he was self-sabotaging what could be a skyrocketing career if he would just embrace it.

But on Wednesday he'd gotten a call from Sam at the American Legion, asking for an emergency fill-in because the band he had lined up for Saturday had canceled. They had a sick band member or something, and Sam couldn't find anyone else at such short notice.

Lachlan caved. How could he say no to playing at the Legion? After all, those were Ainsley's people. Whether or not he'd accidentally killed her—*accidentally*—he still loved her. She would want him to do this show.

So Saturday afternoon found him setting up and doing a quick sound check at the Legion. He'd tried to get a couple of his Knot Tide bandmates to play with him, on the theory that no one had ever died at one of the weddings they'd played. But everyone had plans, which was why they hadn't booked a wedding for that Saturday.

He was on his own.

He made one last trip out to his car, where he chugged an energy drink. When he headed back inside, Eris stood on the sidewalk, her arms folded across her chest.

"I knew I was right about you," she said. Her red-gold hair was pulled back, her gray eyes narrowed in what looked an awful lot like triumph. "Have you finally embraced this power?"

"You again." Lachlan tried to brush past her, but slender fingers dug into his arm.

"Your power is strong, but raw," she hissed. "You did well to eliminate a rival, but now you must learn to shape this. You need a bigger vision."

Lachlan stared at her. "I don't know what you're talking about, lady. I didn't do anything about a rival." He shook her hand off his arm. "I just want to make music."

"Exactly. And *you* created this opportunity to make music." She lifted her chin as he gazed at her in astonishment. "With your magic."

Lachlan shook his head. He hadn't even *wanted* to do this gig. He just did it for Ainsley.

Eris gestured at the American Legion sign, at the people filing into the building. "Weren't you a late fill-in? Didn't you think to question why?"

Lachlan scowled. "What are you—"

She seized his elbow and spun him to face the entryway. A large poster hung next to the door. ACCEPTING DONATIONS FOR JO PARRISH FAMILY FUND—SIGN UP FOR MOTORCYCLE RIDE TO BENEFIT HOMES AND HOPE.

There was a picture under the words of a muscular veteran leaning against his truck, a group of people surrounding him. In the background was a metal building.

Jo Parrish. Lachlan knew him. They'd actually gotten into it one time at a battle of the bands thing, when Parrish thought Lachlan had messed with his guitar. Lachlan, who would never have done anything underhanded like that, had taken offense, and they'd shouted at each other. Lachlan's bandmates had dragged him away before the beefy guy had been able to pound on him.

Eliminating a rival…

"Son of a bitch!" Lachlan rounded on her, fists clenched.

"Your magic chose him." Her lips were curled in a mocking smile. "All well and good, but you need to learn to choose your victims for yourself. You can control the magic. Direct it."

He wanted to hit her. "Shut up!" he hissed. "I'm just here to sing." He spun on his heel and stalked towards the entrance.

Eris' laughter followed him.

* * *

Martin pulled into the parking lot of Elliott's apartments and shut off the engine. Was he really doing this?

He'd spent the whole week shocked at himself for asking and shocked that Elliott had said yes. At this point he'd probably been dwelling on what might happen so much that even the best date would pale in comparison to the fantasy.

It had taken him until Thursday to work up the courage to tell Chloe he'd asked Elliott out. He'd expected her to crow in triumph and tease him. Instead he'd just gotten a quiet, "I'm proud of you," that had managed to both comfort him and make him even more nervous than he had been.

He'd changed his clothes three times, finally settling on black jeans and a charcoal gray button-down shirt. It had been so long since he'd gone on an actual date that he kept wondering if he should have dressed more casually—or maybe more dressy. Maybe he should have added a tie.

"Shut up," he whispered. He couldn't let his social anxiety win, or he'd end up dying alone and eaten by the cat he hadn't even adopted yet.

He got out of the car and tried to force confidence into his stride as he made his way to the stairs. Elliott's apartment was on the third floor, which made Martin grateful he'd kept running. He wouldn't want to be breathless when he knocked on the door.

Elliott swung the door open just a handful of seconds after Martin knocked. He had gone a little more casual than Martin, with black jeans and a white t-shirt that set off his brown skin. His black curls were tousled and his lips were curved in a welcoming smile.

Martin's heart kicked into overdrive.

"Hey," he said. His smile felt funny. Was it too wide? Not wide enough? *Damn, enough with the overanalyzing,* he told himself.

"Hey." Elliott cleared his throat. "I forgot to tell you, I'm a member of the IHS, so we can park in their lot free if there's room."

Martin hadn't forgotten Elliott was a history nerd, but he hadn't thought about this possibility. "Great. Um...you ready, or..."

"I'm ready." Elliott stepped out into the hall and locked his apartment. "How was your week?"

Martin shrugged. "Aside from brooding over the fact that I couldn't stop another guy from getting murdered?"

Elliott curled his fingers around Martin's elbow. "Hey. I thought I told you not to beat yourself up about that. How are you supposed to find people you don't even know?"

Heat radiated from Elliott's touch up to Martin's chest. "Easier said than done," he managed.

"Okay, I get that." Elliott sighed. "But you're going to have to figure out how, or else this is going to drive you crazy."

Martin cracked a smile. "Short walk," he pointed out, and led the way down to his car.

The "Be Heard: LGBT Experiences in Indiana" exhibit was a moving one. Local photographer Mark A. Lee had taken black and white portraits of the Hoosiers who shared their experiences in an oral interview project. The portraits were intimate, the stories were touching or heart-breaking, or sometimes both. Many of those interviewed had military backgrounds.

There were others in the exhibit room, which was on the top floor of the Indiana Historical Society. The large portraits were accompanied by telephone handsets with recordings of the interviews. Martin saw one woman clutching the handset with both hands, tears on her cheeks.

He knew how she felt. Each of the stories was moving in its own way. He found himself blinking back tears after one veteran's interview.

By the time he and Elliott were through touring the exhibit, speaking rarely and only in hushed voices, Martin felt as if he truly had a community to belong to. He wanted to know these people who had been brave enough to tell their stories. He wanted to thank the older interviewees for paving a way for people like Martin and Elliott.

When he stepped up to the guestbook, he couldn't think of anything meaningful to write. He leafed through the pages, seeing where other visitors had come from and reading their comments. Finally he just scribbled his name and, "Thank you."

He turned and found Elliott standing a couple of feet behind him. His lips were pressed together, his eyes a little glossy, but when he saw Martin looking, he smiled.

"Pretty powerful, huh?" he said.

"Very." Martin stepped away from the railing. "Did you want to sign the guestbook?"

"Sure." Elliott's stance blocked Martin from seeing what he'd written until he stepped back again. Martin couldn't help but glance down, and his lips curved in an involuntary smile as he saw, "I'm glad we chose this for our first date—so we can honor those who went before us in this movement."

First date. That implied there would be others.

Elliott glanced at him sort of sideways. "I'm glad you suggested this." He tilted his head in invitation and then started for the elevators.

"Me, too." Martin wondered if he should admit that it meant more being able to see it with someone he knew understood. But that wasn't the whole truth, was it? It meant more being able to see this exhibit with Elliott in particular.

Elliott punched the button to take them to the canal level. Downtown Indianapolis' Central Canal Walk was a popular place to picnic, socialize, and relax. It could get dangerous after dark, but at three in the afternoon, it was an ideal way to continue their date.

"I'm nervous, too," Elliott blurted once the elevator was in motion.

"Huh?" was all Martin could think to say.

Elliott's gaze darted to Martin's face and then away. "I—you remember what you asked me at the cookout? If werewolf senses helped in an investigation? I guess they sort of give me an unfair advantage right now. So...I'm nervous, too." He turned to look fully at Martin. "But I'm having a good time."

Martin couldn't contain the smile that spread across his lips at those words. "Okay." He huffed a laugh. "I'm glad to know you're fair. I'm having a good time, too."

The elevator opened to the food court, which opened directly onto the canal. "Guess I should have asked if you wanted to walk," Elliott said.

226

"I want to," Martin replied. "I love this part of town."

They walked past people playing games on their phones, busking, and inline skating. On the water of the canal, families pedaling rental boats competed for space with mallards. Elliott and Martin walked slowly, talking a little about the exhibit and a little about their own experiences growing up queer in Indianapolis.

"I was lucky," Elliott said. "My mom was a single mother and totally sex-positive. Sex ed started when each of us was about six, I think. She flat out said she knew I was curious, and if I ever had questions, to just ask her. She said no question would get me in trouble." He shrugged. "I guess it was natural that when I was fourteen I asked her if it was okay for a boy to like other boys."

Martin watched the play of emotions across Elliott's face as he spoke. Amusement followed wistfulness, and then both were chased away by grief. A moment later, the smile was back.

"What did she say?"

"She said it was fine. Asked if that meant I didn't like girls, and then explained what bisexuality was when I said I liked both." Elliott laughed. "I think she was more okay with it than I was, at least to begin with."

"Good for her." Martin sighed. "I hope my folks would have been okay with it, but I never got the chance to find out. I guess you probably know Chloe's and my parents were killed in a car wreck when I was in high school. Chloe was of age, so they let me stay with her, but..." He shook his head. "I kept wondering if me coming out would get her in trouble, like CFS would blame her for me being gay."

Elliott made a noise of disagreement, but Martin didn't let him interrupt.

"Hey, I was young and closeted. Chloe was trying to get through college and still support me, and..." Martin trailed off as a realization hit him. "And...I guess I thought my being gay would just make that harder for her." He glanced over at Elliott and shrugged. "I came out to my best friend, and he was decent about it, but we drifted apart after I enlisted. I don't think it had anything to do with me being gay. At least, I hope it didn't. I was just—off to Basic, and he was off to Purdue, so."

"I'm sorry it sucked for you," Elliott said.

Martin shrugged. "To be fair, Chloe took it great when I got back. I mean, part of it has to be that she was glad to get me back alive, but still. She said she wished I'd told her sooner, but she understood why I hadn't."

He glanced over at Elliott, who was watching him. Elliott just nodded for him to go on.

"And then she started trying to think of anyone she knew who might be gay, so she could try to set me up."

Elliott snorted. "Nice."

"She was." Martin smiled. "She is. I'm glad she's happy." He gulped. "Whatever happens, you know, with this..." He waved a hand between them. "I don't want us to jeopardize what she and Braxton have."

"Won't happen." Elliott's voice was deep and firm. He waited a beat and then added, "Because they'd probably both kill us before it got to that."

Martin laughed. "Good point."

They reached the northern terminus of the canal walk, just south of Eleventh Street, and with a glance at each other headed on around to the east side of the walk. As they walked under Tenth Street, Elliott gestured up ahead. "I've heard good things about Burgerhaus. You want to get an early dinner?"

Martin's stomach flipped pleasantly and he smiled. "Sounds good."

When they were seated on the patio and supplied with local craft brews from Daredevil Brewery, Martin leaned back in his chair and looked across the table at Elliott. He was good to look at, with the smattering of freckles that showed across his light brown nose and cheeks, his dark curls ruffled by the breeze. Martin didn't even mind being the object of Elliott's return scrutiny. He thought he cleaned up all right, and he'd been told a couple of times in his life that he looked a little bit like Michael Fassbender. There were worse people to be compared to.

While they were waiting on their burgers, they talked about books. Martin was charmed by the fact that not only was Elliott a history nerd, but he loved cop shows, as long as they were British—*I can't tell if they're screwing up since I don't know British laws*—and disaster flicks, no matter how egregiously bad.

"So, okay, favorite movie of all time," Martin said.

"*A New Hope*," Elliott said promptly, and Martin rolled his eyes.

"Favorite movie outside of Star Wars and other obvious classics," he amended.

"Are there any other obvious classics?"

"Well, George C. Scott's *Patton* comes to mind," Martin said. "And *The Princess Bride.*"

Elliott tipped his head, conceding the point. "Okay, it's a toss-up. Either the first Jurassic Park movie or *Twister.*"

Martin nodded slowly. "Solid choices."

"Bachelor number two, same question," Elliott said, grinning.

"*Pacific Rim.* It's Voltron meets Godzilla, with Idris Elba."

Elliott fanned himself. "Enough said. I haven't seen it."

"We will correct that," Martin promised. "I've heard it's seriously pretty on a 4K TV, but I haven't sprung for one of those yet."

Elliott's grin widened. "You're in luck. I happen to have one."

Martin was almost relieved that the waitress interrupted then, bringing their food. His chest felt tight. He was starting to think he was too happy right now. The floor was going to fall out of this any time now, maybe right around the time Elliott realized just how emotionally messed up Martin was.

Somehow, he couldn't make himself care. He was enjoying this too much.

They ate in near silence, but it was a comfortable one. Martin was savoring this feeling. He couldn't remember when the last time was he'd felt this way. He'd dated a little during his time in the Army, but never seriously. And since he'd come home, he'd been too skittish to settle into a relationship. Every time he started thinking about spending the whole night with someone, he'd thought about the possibility of waking up screaming and scaring the guy off. It was easier to leave before that happened.

Easier, but it had never made him happy.

"Penny for your thoughts," Elliott said softly.

Martin looked up. He stuck a fry in his mouth, wondering how he could even explain any of that. In the end, he decided to go with something that was less about him and more about Elliott. "How do you balance it all? Being a cop, biracial, bisexual, *and* supernatural?"

Elliott blinked at him for a moment and then shrugged. "How do you balance being a gay Army vet with PTSD whose sister sees ghosts?"

"Yeah, but I still have white privilege on my side," Martin said. "That gives me superpowers." He waited for Elliott's eyes to widen before he gave him a slow, sly smile.

"You—" Elliott snorted. "Smartass. I honestly thought you had no sense of humor when we first met."

Martin lifted an eyebrow. "Well, I save it for people who're actually willing to listen to me."

"Ouch." Elliott took a slow sip of his beer. "Guess I deserve that. I was so pissed about the best man thing."

"You're kidding," Martin deadpanned.

Elliott gave him a flat, unamused look, but he couldn't hold it, and pretty soon they were both chuckling.

"Really, though," Martin said after a while. "Don't you ever just get tired of being different?"

"No." There was no hesitation or uncertainty in Elliott's statement.

Seriously? Martin tilted his head to one side, letting his skepticism show.

"No, look." Elliott straightened, sipped his beer, and leaned in. "I know I'm not perfect by a long shot. But the only one of those things—cop, biracial, bisexual, werewolf—the only one of those things I *chose* was being a cop. I didn't get to decide about any of the rest of it. It's not my fault if people can't deal." His brows drew together. "Do I get tired of the way people treat me sometimes? Hell, yeah. But I would never want to be someone different just to please all the bigoted assholes out there."

Martin sighed. "I wish I had that much strength," he muttered. He took a long sip of his beer. "If I found a genie in a bottle, I'd probably wish away the PTSD *and* the gay."

"Why not wish away homophobia instead?" Elliott teased, his voice soft.

That startled a chuckle from Martin. "Well, yeah, I guess as long as we're wishing…"

"I like who you are, Martin." Elliott sat forward, his golden-brown gaze intent on Martin's. "PTSD and sly sense of humor and comic book nerd and all. And I'm pretty sure your sister and brother-in-law do too. For that matter, *Murphy* likes you, and he barely likes anyone."

Martin snorted in amusement, though his chest was feeling pleasantly tight again. He looked at Elliott, who was smiling faintly back at him.

"Wanna get out of here?" Elliott said. His smile strengthened when Martin said yes.

* * *

The show started out all right. Lachlan had created a setlist comprised mostly of covers, with original pieces sprinkled in sparingly. He didn't know what the American Legion crowd liked, but he'd assumed it involved southern rock and country. He could stomach the southern rock, but there was no way in hell he would touch country with a ten-foot pole, so they'd have to deal.

Maybe that was part of what set him on the defensive, though he later decided it was mostly Eris—and the knowledge that Eris had been right.

He should have canceled the show.

Instead he played songs by the Black Crowes and Def Leppard and threw in "Suspicious Minds" before launching into "Ainsley's Lament." He'd suspected that would be the song people might recognize, since it had gotten some local radio play in the last week. He'd even sucked it up and played some Allman Brothers and Lynyrd Skynyrd, though he knew he wasn't as strong on those bands.

It was when he decided to do Johnny Cash's version of Nine Inch Nails' "Hurt" that things started falling apart.

It was a damn good song. Even Trent Reznor had admitted Cash took the song and made it his own. And as much as Lachlan loved the NIN version, he thought the Cash version would go over better at this venue.

But as he reached the first chorus, his fingers started tingling and he felt something hook behind his stomach and twist, and the music took over. The words tore out of him, his throat aching as if he had something caught in it. By the end of the song, he had his eyes squeezed shut as he sang, the last few notes dangling on his guitar strings.

The first thing he saw when he opened his eyes was a gray-haired guy wearing a Make America Great Again hat. The man had covered his face with his palm, his shoulders shaking as he sobbed. Next to him a woman the right age to have been in the first Iraq war hunched over, clutching her stomach like she was going to puke.

There was no applause.

Lachlan cleared his throat. "I, uh. I'm gonna take a short break."

"Keep singing!" A woman shouted from the back of the room. Lachlan knew it was Eris, but before he could refuse, others took up the cry.

"Keep singing! Don't stop!"

Lachlan coughed. "Uh. Okay. How about someone get me a Jack and Coke up here, then?" He decided to move a little more contemporary and started picking out Everlast's "What It's Like." It had been one of Ainsley's favorite songs, and it sounded good coming after "Hurt."

It was an angry song, though, and the music—or the magic—took control completely. He followed one angry song with another, and threw back drink after drink. The anger made him thirsty and the alcohol fueled the anger. He wrapped up the set with "Famous Last Words" by My Chemical Romance—a stripped version, with the electric guitar and Lachlan's voice raw and crackling.

As he let the last note morph into the squeal of feedback, adrenaline and pleasure rushed through him. Lachlan threw his head back, letting the noise ring out and relishing the electricity flashing along his veins.

The note died. Into the silence came a single sound—Eris' laughter.

Then all hell broke loose.

* * *

On the walk back to where they'd parked the car, Elliott walked just a little closer, his fingers brushing Martin's twice. It could be accidental, or it could be teasing. Martin's breath was a little short by the time they got back to the car.

It was a quiet ride back to the apartment. Martin's heart was thudding in his chest. He was pretty sure Elliott was going to invite him up, and he was pretty sure he was going to say yes, and the possibility excited and terrified him all at once. This wasn't like the people he'd met and dated casually in the last few years. This was someone who was important to Chloe and Braxton—someone Martin would have to see at least occasionally for the rest of his life. There was no room for screwing up here.

Elliott didn't actually invite Martin up. He just got out of the car, walked around, and opened the driver's door. His lowered lids and soft smile were all the invitation Martin needed.

He followed Elliott upstairs, mouth dry, hands shaking a little. It was so stupid to be this nervous. He just couldn't seem to quell it.

The minute they were inside, Elliott's hands were on Martin's hips. He pulled Martin closer without hesitation. Martin buried his fingers in Elliott's curls, their first kiss sending sparks through his veins. *Oh, this was everything he'd hoped for and more.*

Elliott breathed Martin's name against his lips and Martin parted his lips obligingly, inviting Elliott to deepen the kiss. Elliott had pressed him back against the door and Martin found they were just the right height. He slid an arm down to curl around Elliott's waist, pulling him closer.

He was breathless when Elliott finally pulled back a little. "Hang on, hang on," Elliott whispered. He was panting. "We need to slow down."

Embarrassment flooded Martin. Had he been too forward? Too desperate? It *had* been a long time—

"No," Elliott said, laughing at the look on Martin's face. "God, no. I just—I don't want to rush this." His cheeks darkened a little.

This was too perfect. Martin's heart was doing weird things in his chest. He was falling so hard. He was *letting* himself fall.

"Ell," he whispered, leaning in to brush his lips against Elliott's again. He didn't know how to say any of what he was feeling, any of what scared him. He just *wanted* so damn much—

The pain hit him so fast it knocked his breath out.

One minute he was on the verge of pleasant hyperventilation, and the next, his head had been seized in a vice that squeezed so hard his vision went black.

Martin groaned, his entire body going rigid. His fingers slid from Elliott's hair and flew to clutch at his own temple. The attraction and excitement and terrifying happiness were wiped out by a wail of grief and anger and the discordant clash of furious guitar.

"Martin?" Elliott's voice was tense. His hands gripped Martin's hips to hold him up now, instead of holding him close. "Martin? What is it?"

Panic clawed its way up from Martin's stomach, gripping his throat. He croaked, trying to speak, but all he could do was gasp. His vision was pulsing red now, and he could feel the rage building inside him—no, not inside him, not Martin—inside—*the shadowy figure.*

He only got a glimpse, but he realized suddenly that the grasp on his throat wasn't panic, it was something—someone—else. It was his keeper. It was the person who held the other end of his chain.

"Martin, breathe," Elliott ordered.

"Hold me up!" Martin gasped, reaching out blindly. He couldn't see anything of the apartment now. His vision was locked on the shadowy figure, lit by red and blue strobe lights. He could see a pale face, green eyes wide. Someone was screaming. Angry voices shouted at each other. Sirens wailed in the distance. A guitar rose into eardrum-shattering feedback.

And so low he almost didn't hear it, a woman laughed in glee.

"Martin."

"Gonna be sick," he mumbled, feeling the chain tighten around his throat, keeping the bile down. His stomach was churning. The apartment wasn't coming back into focus like he wanted. He just kept seeing that shadowy figure—and someone behind it, tugging on the chain.

Elliott's hand pressed against his lower back, guiding him to move. Martin stumbled but did his best to go where Elliott guided him. "Kneel down here," Elliott said. He took Martin's hands and brought them down to press against cool porcelain.

Martin managed to vomit into the toilet, coughing and heaving as tears sprang into his eyes. The tears cleared his vision, though—just in time for him to see what a humiliating mess he'd made of the best date in his life.

The tears might not all be reflexive.

"Is this PTSD?" Martin heard water running and then a cool washcloth pressed against the back of his neck. "Did I do something wrong? I didn't mean to trigger anything—"

Martin managed to shake his head before heaving again.

"Vision," he whispered finally. "Never..." He gulped and sucked a couple frantic breaths. "Never had one awake before."

"Okay." Elliott's voice was calmer suddenly. Was it because he hadn't caused this? Or was it just the cop instincts kicking in? Martin had seen his sister turn on the calm before. "Here." Something smooth and cylindrical pressed into his hand. A cup. "Rinse."

Martin rinsed and spat a couple of times. Then, when Elliott filled the cup again, he drank a few tentative sips.

"It's okay, Martin." Elliott's whole demeanor had changed. Even the way he touched Martin conveyed control and reassurance. "Let's get you to bed."

"M'so sorry," Martin mumbled.

"No need. This is all new to both of us, yeah?" Elliott helped Martin to his feet and guided him out of the bathroom to a bedroom with blue carpeting. "I wasn't actually trying to get you into bed on our first date," Elliott murmured as he lowered Martin to the bed.

It made Martin chuckle despite the weariness that was swamping him.

"Good. Let's get your shoes off, at least. Then you can lie down for a while. See if that helps." Elliott knelt in front of Martin and suited actions to words. He looked up at Martin and brushed his fingers against Martin's cheek. "I'm sorry that hit you so hard, but I'm glad I could help you."

Martin blinked, feeling his lips curve into a tiny, stupid smile. "Me, too," he managed, swinging his feet onto the bed and slumping down.

Elliott brushed fingers through Martin's hair. "Let me know if you need anything."

Martin smiled a little wider, but he was already too close to unconsciousness to answer.

CHAPTER 18

Elliott paced the living room for twenty minutes, scowling and trying not to take it personally that Martin had passed out on him. He knew it was a vision. Martin had said so. Martin wouldn't make that up. He wouldn't use it as an excuse if things were going further than he wanted.

"Don't be stupid," he muttered to himself. Between the scent of desire and the sound of Martin's racing heartbeat—twin to Elliott's—he knew that Martin was just as into him as he was into Martin. Not only that, but Elliott had scented a real surge of adrenaline and fear when the vision hit. Maybe Martin was a little awkward and introverted, but he was honest. It was just Elliott's low opinion of himself that made him feel like Martin didn't want him.

He dropped onto the couch, clutching at his head in annoyance. Of all the times for his self-confidence to desert him, it had to be now.

He was well aware of his own good looks and charm. He was a good conversationalist, and he was a good kisser. He made good money and had a nice apartment.

But none of that was a basis for a real relationship, and that was what he wanted with Martin.

Would he settle for being friends with benefits? Well, he had in the past, plenty of times. He'd had fun dating people casually, rarely going for an exclusive relationship. When he did settle into an exclusive thing, it rarely lasted more than five or six months before falling apart. He knew some of it was his schedule, and some of it was his fear of settling down. He'd talked it over with Braxton enough to be aware he was afraid of losing a life partner the way he'd lost his mother. But it wasn't something he could just rationalize himself out of, and so he'd gone all in as a serial-dating commitment-phobe.

Until now.

Now he wanted commitment. He wanted all of Martin's attention. He wanted to be the first person Martin wanted to talk to in the morning and the last person Martin wanted to talk to at night. Because that was how he felt about Martin. He wasn't sure how it had happened so quickly, but he had fallen head over heels for a smart, introverted mechanic who just happened to have visions.

Groaning, Elliott pushed his shoes off, swung his feet up, and collapsed backwards across the sofa. There was no way he would try to share the bed with Martin; consent was important to him. Besides, as much as he wanted to be the guy who woke up next to Martin, he didn't want it to start like this, after Martin was incapacitated by a vision. It had almost looked to him like a migraine attack. Olivia suffered from classic migraine, and there were times she would do little more than slap a hand to her forehead before dashing to the bathroom to throw up. As soon as she was done being sick, she grew nearly incoherent and passed out. After a few hours of sleep, she was right as rain, but in the meantime, she was completely incapacitated.

Elliott wished Martin had been able to tell him what he'd seen before passing out. It would give him something to work with while he lay here, brain churning in circles. It might be enough to draw him away from doubting himself and the wisdom of trying to date his best friend's brother-in-law.

Then again, Braxton had encouraged him. He'd said he could see Elliott and Martin working. Elliott would have to believe in that, even if he couldn't believe in himself.

At some point, Elliott drifted into sleep.

He woke up when something crashed and someone swore.

Blinking and rubbing his face, Elliott sat up to see Martin rubbing his elbow, a sheepish expression on his face.

"Hey," Elliott said, his voice gravelly from sleep.

"I didn't mean to wake you. I ran into the door." Martin stopped rubbing his elbow and scratched at the back of his neck.

"I'm glad you did. I mean, not running into the door. Waking me up." Elliott swung his legs down and rubbed his face again. "Are you feeling better?"

Martin nodded. "I'm sorry about—"

"It's good," Elliott interrupted. "We're good."

"No, I..." Martin rubbed his nose, lips twisting. "I had a good time. I've never had a vision when I was awake before. I'm pissed that it interrupted."

"It looked like it hurt," Elliott said.

Martin's lips pulled to the side. "More than I've ever noticed a dream-vision hurting."

There was a brief pause while Elliott enjoyed the fact that Martin was confiding in him. He couldn't tell what Martin was thinking, but just as Elliott opened his mouth to speak, Martin moved further from the bedroom and towards the door.

"Wanna sit?" Elliott said hastily.

"Oh, I don't..."

Elliott gulped. "Please," he said, his voice soft. It almost hurt to ask, but he didn't want Martin leaving like this, when things felt awkward between them.

Martin shifted on his feet, eying Elliott, and then came over to sit next to him.

Elliott turned to face Martin, tucking one leg under him. "Do you remember the vision?"

He thought Martin looked a little disappointed, though he wasn't sure if it was the question or what he was about to say that disappointed him. "I remember...screams. Anger." He shook his head. "Whoever's killing people is really angry. And—grief, too."

Elliott could hear Martin's heartbeat pick up. He reached out and rested a hand on Martin's knee.

"People yelling. A woman laughing." Martin looked down at Elliott's hand. After a moment, his heartbeat slowed again and he placed his hand carefully over Elliott's. "I heard sirens and saw police lights. Or ambulance lights." His heartbeat jumped again. "Ell, I saw his face!"

Elliott's chest tightened a little. Martin had called him Ell. He'd called him that earlier, too, he remembered. He pushed it aside. "The killer?"

"Well, the shadow. The one with the chain on his neck." Martin frowned. "He had green eyes. The chain was choking me. Him. Us."

"You felt what he felt?" Elliott leaned closer.

Martin nodded. "Anger and grief, and the choking."

"And you said people were yelling. Between that and the sirens, this had to be somewhere public. Or at least with a lot of people."

"There were guitars. I heard rock music."

"Okay. This is good. Helpful."

Martin smiled ruefully at him. "If only it hadn't spoiled our date."

Elliott's return smile felt a little too warm. "I don't think it was spoiled."

Martin ducked his head, but Elliott could see his smile widening. For his part, Elliott's stomach was doing odd swoopy things, but his brain was kicking in, too. He wanted to kiss Martin and stay awake all night talking. He also wanted to call a couple of guys on the force and see if he could chase down this lead.

"I should head home," Martin said. He looked back at Elliott, eyes twinkling a little. "You could sleep in your own bed that way."

Elliott bit back the first comment that came to mind—*you could sleep with me*—and said, "Are you okay to drive?"

"Sure. The headache's gone."

Elliott frowned. Maybe it *had* been a sort of migraine attack. "Have you ever had a headache along with a vision?"

Martin shrugged. "Maybe. I don't know." Elliott kept frowning at him and Martin laughed. "I'm fine," he insisted. I just want to go home and sleep."

"Okay," Elliott said slowly. He stood up, tugging Martin to his feet before dropping his hand. He noticed then that Martin had already put his shoes back on. Had he planned to sneak out without saying goodbye? *Shut up*, he told himself. *Even if he did, it would be because he's considerate, not trying to ghost you.* He walked to the door with Martin, wondering why he felt so uncertain about everything.

Because this matters more than it ever has before, whispered a voice in the back of his head.

They paused at the door. "I really did enjoy today," Elliott said, glancing over at Martin.

"Me, too." Martin tilted his head a little.

Elliott realized after several seconds that Martin was waiting to see if Elliott was going to kiss him. *Stupid*, he told himself, and stepped a little closer. He lifted a hand to touch Martin's cheek, wondering why Martin hadn't initiated it and then mentally kicking himself again. He brushed his lips against Martin and then made a soft noise of surprise when Martin kissed him back more forcefully. Oh, that was reassuring.

"Thank you for today, Martin," he said, meeting the other man's eyes. "I'll call you."

He was already trying to think of who'd been on the overnight roster this weekend who might have worked whatever event was the subject of Martin's vision. He thought he saw an odd flicker in Martin's blue eyes, but Martin nodded, so Elliott decided he'd imagined it.

"See you," Martin said, and let himself out.

* * *

On Monday Elliott gathered several incident reports from things that had happened over the weekend. There was a stabbing at a bar on the south side of downtown, a possible gang-related fight at another location on the east side, and a few others. He had just finished reading the report of an odd near-riot at the American Legion when his phone rang. He glanced hopefully at the caller ID—had Martin decided not to wait for his call?

The caller ID's SARAH FITZGERALD was accompanied by a photo of a smiling brunette with scarlet lipstick and glimmering green eyes. She was bewitching and beguiling, and Elliott would trust her with his life.

He just wouldn't trust her with a case.

Sighing, he answered.

"You've been dodging my calls," she accused.

"Guilty as charged." He had to fight a smile. She was so damn relentless. It was one of the things that had first drawn him to her. It was also one of the reasons they'd broken up.

"You know you can't hide forever, Blake."

He let her hear him sigh. "Coffee?"

"I'll see you at Mo'Joe in ten." She hung up on him.

Brady Flynn looked up from his computer, where he was painstakingly typing up a report from that morning. "Are you leaving?"

Elliott did *not* want Sarah getting Brady in her sights; he'd never be able to hold out against her professional mixture of sympathy, charm, and downright nosiness. "Just got a meeting. Won't be gone long. Want me to bring you back some good coffee?"

"I'd give my right kidney for good coffee right now." Brady gestured at the computer. "I have six more reports to write up before lunch."

Elliott chuckled. "Back soon."

When he stepped into Mo'Joe Coffee House on West Michigan, Elliott felt like he'd stepped back in time. As a Criminal Justice major at Indiana University, he'd spent hours studying here. After his mother's murder, he'd taken as many classes as possible at IUPUI—Indiana University Purdue University at Indianapolis—to be available to his sisters. Mo'Joe was a big student hangout.

"Hey, handsome."

Elliott turned toward the voice and was greeted by a tight hug. Sarah was a petite brunette, five foot four without heels, and she looked like a student herself. Her long hair pulled back in a ponytail, she was dressed in jeans, a red top, and Converse sneakers.

"I swear, you just stopped aging at twenty-four," he said, smiling at her.

"I ordered your coffee for you," she said, holding out a cup.

"I'm great, thanks, and how are you?" he said. But he took the coffee.

She rolled her eyes at him. "Come on, I know you're on a tight schedule. You work too much."

"You haven't even seen me in six months, how do you know I work too much?" He followed her to a table, where a sleek tablet computer and a couple of notebooks sat next to a cup of coffee and a pastry that he knew would be a raspberry tart.

"Because you always work too much." She settled into the chair. "Sit."

Another reason they hadn't worked out was that being around Sarah made him feel like he was still working. She had a sharp mind and quick wit, and as great as their chemistry had been, he'd always felt poised on the brink of spilling something he shouldn't.

"You know I can't tell you anything," he said. It was his usual opening line in their dance. He sipped his coffee, unsurprised that it was mostly black with a hint of caramel and cream. Sarah was great with details. "I shouldn't even be here."

"And you know I can't let a story like this go." She propped her chin on her hand, giving him a placid smile.

Elliott took another sip of coffee. They had an entire routine they usually went through, and he always ended up giving her one or two tidbits on condition of anonymity. This case was too sensitive for a lot of reasons, though. He wasn't going to offer her anything, and he didn't really feel like playing along this time. She looked innocent, but he knew better. Despite her good intentions, she'd never fully appreciated his position that details shared with the press could compromise a case.

And despite his good intentions, he'd never fully understood why she was so driven to her role in the Fourth Estate.

The business of the coffee shop went on through their mutual silence. The cash register chimed, an espresso machine whirred and chortled, and a dozen other conversations took place around them. After their silence had stretched out long enough to make Elliott consider getting up and leaving, Sarah sighed.

"I saw your press conference after the Shaw murder. You did a good job."

"Flattery won't work," Elliott said, despite the warmth her words generated in his stomach. When they'd met he'd been an awkward rookie, unused to speaking in public or dealing with confrontational reporters.

Then again, he'd planned to be a history teacher — a job that required zero reporter confrontations.

"Is the killer targeting veterans? I heard there was a near riot at an American Legion post Saturday night. Something like twenty people taken to the hospital, half a dozen arrests. More than one person arrested was carrying a big damn knife. I know Ainsley Shaw was stabbed to death."

His satisfaction that the actual manner of death was still a secret was squashed by her first words. He didn't like that she'd made the same connection he had. So far he didn't have anything to definitively connect the Legion brawl to the killings, except that it took place at nearly the same time as Martin's vision.

He sipped his coffee and didn't speak.

She huffed. "Why won't you talk to me, Elliott? Let me help you! Don't we want the same thing?"

"I don't know, do we?" he snapped. The way her brows drew together poked at his conscience. He dropped his gaze. He knew better, and she didn't deserve to have him taking his frustrations with the case out on her. "Sorry. I know you care about the people you write about."

She nodded. "And I remember why you went into this line of work."

"This is not about my mom." He spoke quietly, and this time it was Sarah who looked away.

The door to the coffee shop jangled as it opened. Elliott pushed his chair back. This was pointless. "I gotta go."

"Come on, give me something, Ell," she said. "You want to catch this guy. I want to help these families express their pain."

"Then why aren't you talking to them?"

"I *am*!" Her eyes flashed. "That's how I know Joe Shaw is pissed off. He doesn't think you're doing enough." Her voice was sharp, but the hand she placed on his wrist was gentle. "I know that isn't true. The Elliott Blake I know doesn't give up on a case."

Elliott slid his hand out from under hers. "Joe Shaw thinks his daughter's girlfriend killed her, and I know that isn't possible. The man's grieving, but easy answers won't fix it."

She leaned forward, her gaze sympathetic. "Have you told him that?"

"Man doesn't need to hear my damage on top of his," Elliott said.

She shrugged. "He'll know you empathize."

"He doesn't need empathy. He needs justice." Elliott looked down at his coffee, which suddenly tasted too sweet. He finished it anyway.

"Can I print any of what you just said?" she asked.

Elliott met her gaze. "You know the answer to that."

She didn't reply to that. He couldn't see her tablet screen, but the top notebook had her distinctive blocky, all-caps handwriting on it. It was easy to read upside down: AM. LEG. TIED TO MURDERS? WHY VETERANS? SHAW - PARRISH - ???

Finally he drew in a slow breath. He spoke formally and precisely. "At this time we are considering any and all leads. We believe the killer is someone who knows his victims; however, no family members are currently suspects."

"That's a very nice statement, detective," she said, her voice snide.

Elliott met her gaze without speaking for several heartbeats. Then he went to the counter, ordered two black coffees to go, and left the shop.

* * *

Dax's arm was lying in the dirt about eight feet in front of Martin. Dax was lying six feet in the other direction.

Martin gasped for breath. He needed to go to Dax, fashion a tourniquet, stop the bleeding. His mouth was full of wet grit—blood and dirt and maybe a little vomit. Dax wasn't screaming. It was the strangest thing. Dax ought to be screaming.

Martin scrabbled across the rocky ground, gagging at the taste in his mouth.

Martin jerked awake. The first sensation he was aware of his legs slipping against each other wetly. His stomach wrenched and he wondered—as he always did—if he'd pissed himself. Then he realized it was sweat.

He threw the covers off.

"Winthrop Avenue," he whispered. "Broad Ripple. Indianapolis. Indiana."

It was so damn hot. He would have thought he was still in Afghanistan if it weren't for the humid prickle of dampness across his chest. But the desert wicked all the moisture from your skin. It was unforgiving.

"Winthrop Avenue," he began again, but his throat closed on the mantra.

His mouth watering, Martin threw himself from the bed and ran for the bathroom, where he vomited chamomile tea.

It wasn't until he lifted a shaking hand to flush the toilet that he realized how quiet the house was.

Martin wiped a palm over his face, wondering if meditation would help after you tried—and failed—for a lucid dream. He hawked and spat a couple of times and flushed the toilet again. His knees felt shaky, but he pulled himself to his feet, bracing himself on the vanity and blinking at his reflection.

His eyes were the same blue they'd always been, except deeply shadowed underneath. He thought the lines next to his mouth were deeper than they had been. But maybe that was because he felt so Goddamn old.

He turned on the tap, splashed water on his face, and straightened. He didn't bother blotting it.

"Breathe," he told himself, switching off the bathroom light.

The air conditioning wasn't running. Not only that, but it *hadn't* been running, from the stuffy feel of the house. It was almost the end of July. There was no way the AC shouldn't be on. Had it broken?

Martin stripped out of his sweat-soaked boxers and pulled on another pair before padding to the laundry room that housed his breaker box. Sure enough, the breaker had tripped. He would have to get an electrician out to look at all the wiring. He'd never had this problem before, but if he was going to return the house to a single-family unit, he might as well make sure the wiring was up to snuff.

The air kicked on as soon as the breaker clicked into place. He went to the kitchen. He wanted a cold drink of water, but he ought to try another cup of chamomile tea. It was supposed to be a natural sleep aid, after all. He filled the kettle and started the heat.

It had been a week since his research trip to the library. In that time, he'd had nothing but the usual dreams, until tonight. He'd skimmed all of the books he'd checked out from the library, though the only book he'd read cover to cover was the one on the long-term effects of combat trauma. He'd dismissed the dream interpretation books as bunk.

Tonight's dream wasn't anything prophetic, for that matter. It was his damage showing, plain and simple. He thought about the bottles of liquor he'd moved to the empty portion of the house. It would be so easy to justify just one drink.

"Except it's never just *one*, is it?" he muttered.

He could call Elliott. Elliott would understand. He would listen, make comforting noises on the other end of the line and be sympathetic. His voice would be gravelled with sleep and make Martin wish that, despite the heat, he could climb in bed with Elliott and take comfort from the simple closeness.

But no. This wasn't a vision. It was a dream. It was post traumatic stress disorder reminding him of the worst day of his life. Elliott already had enough crap to deal with. He didn't need more.

Martin sat at the kitchen table and leaned across it, listening to the noises the kettle made as it heated. There was no reason to call Elliott except for the purely selfish desire for comfort. A glance at the microwave told him it was just shy of midnight. No police detective would appreciate being woken up at this time of night if there was no body involved.

"Ah, God," Martin whispered, squeezing his eyes shut against the hot prickles that rushed to them. "Help me."

His parents had been devout Catholics. Quiet in their faith, they had nevertheless modeled it for their children, and Martin had never questioned it. His crisis had been about his sexuality and not his faith. He'd spent a couple of years thinking there was something wrong with him—he'd never considered something might be wrong with the religion drummed into him.

Eventually he'd come to reconcile the two, believing that he was, indeed, created in God's image and that God made no mistakes—and also that he had been created gay. Still, he'd felt more often than not that there were no rote prayers that felt right for his own life.

No prayers, perhaps, except the Lord's Prayer. When nothing else—not even the prayer to Saint Jude, not even prayers to Mary—helped, Martin fell back on the Lord's Prayer. It didn't always seem to relate to his situation in the moment, but he always told himself that if it was good enough for Jesus, it was good enough for Martin Cole.

This night, face pressed against the sticky laminate of his kitchen table, Martin whispered the Lord's Prayer until his kettle whistled.

Just the smell of the chamomile tea made him gag when he poured it. But Martin had determined to give each of the sleep remedies and rituals a try. He had a strong preference for visions coming to him in dreams instead of interrupting dates that were going well, so he wanted to create as healthy a sleep environment as possible.

His heartbeat had slowed the longer he prayed. He took his mug of tea back to the bedroom, where he turned on the ceiling fan. It was too hot for hot tea, but the only thing worse than hot chamomile tea was cold chamomile tea. He'd learned that the hard way.

Eventually, one corner of the sheet dragged across his waist, Martin fell back into sleep.

He was in a forest. Murphy was sitting against a tree, facing him. Nearby Martin could hear a voice that made him smile, made him feel as if a strong hand grasped his. He couldn't quite hear the words, but that didn't matter.

He looked across a flickering fire to see his sister, her knees drawn up in front of her. It was hard to tell in the shifting light, but she looked pregnant. Martin narrowed his eyes, leaning forward.

The fire crackled and blazed and Chloe was gone.

"Martin." The word was a caress. An arm wrapped around his shoulders. Martin turned, lifting his face for a kiss, but he was alone.

The fire was gone. There were no voices. No sounds at all, except the howling of wolves. When Martin looked up, the moon was full.

He rubbed his eyes, looking for the wolf that ought to be resting its chin on his knee, looking for brown skin and dark brown curls he wanted to touch.

Instead he saw Dax's arm, lying in the dirt eight feet in front of him.

Dax. Where was Dax?

Martin twisted, staring around him. Dax sprawled on a concrete pad six feet in the other direction.

Gasping, Martin scrabbled across the rocky ground, gagging at the taste in his mouth. He needed to stop the bleeding.

Dax wasn't screaming. Dax ought to be screaming.

Martin woke himself trying to scream, the only sound escaping his throat a quiet whimper.

He climbed out of bed and stomped out to the living room. The side table next to his recliner held the books he'd checked out from the library. He swept them from the table with a snarl.

"This is bullshit!" he screamed. "Whatever you're trying to tell me, just fucking *tell* me already!"

The spurt of rage left him shaking. He doubled over, staring at the books. He should give up on this. He should stop trying to dream. Take his doctor up on the offer, made four months ago, of an Ambien prescription. He'd fall asleep without trouble using the drugs.

He should walk away from this.

Martin dropped to sit on the floor and buried his face in his hands.

Images from Chloe and Braxton's wedding drifted into his memory. The two of them standing at the front of the church, faces radiant with joy and hope. The two of them waving goodbye as their limo drove them to the airport. The newlyweds back at their home, welcoming guests to their first cookout.

The pack as Elliott described it, always having each other's back, always supportive despite disagreements, full of acceptance.

The taste of Elliott's kisses.

When Martin straightened, his face was wet but his features were resolved. He couldn't walk away from this. Even if he could turn off the visions, he shouldn't. And he couldn't ignore them. They were a tool, maybe even a gift from God. They shouldn't—couldn't—be ignored.

The clock told him it was quarter after three. Martin drew in a long breath and sighed. Then he went to change into work clothes. He had time to tear out those ugly cabinets in the other apartment's kitchen before he had to be at work. He might as well make use of this time.

CHAPTER 19

Elliott didn't like Thursdays.

He'd never been able to pinpoint why, but it seemed like Thursdays always lasted longer and were more chaotic than other days in the week.

This particular Thursday, however, he was anticipatory to the point of glee.

He'd finally gotten ahold of David Corriden and made an appointment for him to come in. Corriden had been on some administrative assignment in Washington, D.C., for the past week. Elliott had also managed to convince Kaida Akimoto to return for a second interview.

And, like any good detective, he'd scheduled the two appointments to overlap by ten minutes.

Kaida was steadier than she had been when Elliott first met her, but she was also sadder. Elliott spent some time asking about her year and a half dating Ainsley before switching to what Kaida knew about Ainsley's past dating life.

"I know the name David," Kaida said, her hands folded on the table. "Ainsley didn't like talking about exes, but she had cared deeply for him, and I didn't resent it."

"You didn't resent it?" Elliott leaned forward, giving Kaida a confidential smile. "Come on, Ms. Akimoto. I'm dating someone right now, and I honestly want to snap at anyone who looks twice in their direction."

Kaida raised an eyebrow. "In *his* direction, you mean," she said, meeting his gaze.

Damn it. Elliott was always careful to speak generally about his partners when he was at work, but as a lesbian, Kaida would know all about deliberately obscuring her partner's gender. Elliott tipped his head. "All right, his direction," he said, trying to make his voice sound agreeable.

"How long have you been dating?" Kaida asked.

Elliott bit back the retort that he was the one asking the questions. That would sound defensive, since they both knew it already. "Not long enough," he said, giving her a rueful smile. "I admit, I'm not completely secure about it yet."

Kaida nodded. "Ainsley and I had been together long enough for me to know she was the one." Her voice was soft. "I don't suffer from a dearth of confidence, Detective Blake. I know I'm a catch. I have a good job, I make good money, I'm not hard on the eyes, and I don't really get jealous. I'm also punctual to a fault, terrible at small talk, and don't suffer fools gladly; but the upshot is, I knew Ainsley would eventually realize we were good together. I was willing to give her time."

"How much time?" Elliott wished he knew how to adopt an attitude like that. He knew he was handsome and charming and good at his job, but he also didn't believe that equated being a good partner. For that matter, he tended to think that his impatience and the way he jumped in emotions-first were entirely detrimental to a healthy relationship.

Kaida shrugged. "She had just barely gotten back from the war. I decided I would give it at least a year before I walked away. I knew she would have a lot of issues to work through. Even people who seem well-adjusted may hide damage from trauma that surfaces later. I would hate to walk away from the best relationship in my life just because she made some mistakes while working through that."

Elliott closed his mouth and tried not to stare at her. Kaida Akimoto was either the most level-headed person or the most generous person he'd ever met.

Or maybe she was just the most in-love person he'd ever met.

After a moment he said, "I wish I could learn that lesson myself."

Kaida smiled. "I don't know," she said. "It's one of those lessons I think you have to learn the hard way. Don't we all have that one who got away?" She looked down at her hands. "But I was determined not to let Ainsley be another one who got away." She glanced up at him. "I don't mean that in a creepy way."

Elliott already knew that. He could sense her deep sorrow and deep love, but there was nothing of greed or possessiveness in her scent.

Coming to a decision, Elliott nodded. "Thank you for coming to talk to me again," he said. "After evaluating everything, I wanted to let you know that I do not consider you a suspect in Ainsley's murder. I have expressed that to Ainsley's father as well as to the press. Not using your name, of course, but making it clear that, while Ainsley definitely knew her killer, she was not related to or in love with that person."

Kaida nodded. "I will do anything I can to help you with your investigation, Detective Blake."

"I appreciate that." Elliott drew in a slow breath. "You know what special skills I have. I don't know exactly what sort of special skills or knowledge you might have, but if anything occurs to you, I would appreciate a heads-up."

Kaida met his gaze. "I think your skills are likely more useful than mine, but again, I will do *anything* I can to help you."

Elliott walked her to the front of the station. He wanted to be there when she saw David Corriden coming in to talk to Elliott. The security cameras would probably tell him what he needed to know, but he might as well employ all his senses.

David Corriden was a tall man, at least six feet and probably a couple of inches taller. He had tanned skin and brown hair and eyes. He wore a preoccupied frown as he brushed past Kaida in the hallway. Kaida sidestepped and muttered, "Excuse you," before continuing on her way.

Elliott detected no trace of recognition in either of them. If Kaida had recognized Corriden, there should have been a scent tell, if nothing more physical than that. And Corriden had barely glanced at her as he walked past, but it had been an air of indifference, not one of ignoring.

Elliott took his leave of Kaida and turned to follow Corriden.

"Mr. Corriden," he said, and the man came to a screeching halt. He turned slowly, gaze searching for whoever it was that knew him.

Elliott strode forward, hand outstretched. "Detective Blake," he said. "I was just coming to meet you."

Corriden blinked and then nodded, shaking Elliott's hand. "I'm sorry I wasn't in town to get your calls earlier," he said.

This close, Elliott could see that Corriden's eyes were red-rimmed and shadowed. The man was carefully clean-shaven, but his lips were chapped as if he'd been chewing at them.

"Not at all," Elliott said. "Will you come with me to the interview room?"

He led the way to Interview Two. While he had spoken with Kaida in Interview One—and used that room to interview *all* supernatural suspects—he knew there were no careful spells laid over Interview Two. Anything said there, whether it was about the supernatural or a more mundane crime, would be recorded.

Once they'd gotten the preliminaries out of the way, Elliott laid it out for Corriden.

"I know you dated Ainsley Shaw for a significant length of time," he concluded. "I know that you also knew Jo Parrish. You were a member of his veterans group. I'm sorry to be so blunt, Mr. Corriden, but I need you to convince me you aren't the killer."

"I can't." Corriden's voice cracked. "I'm sorry. I didn't do it. But I can't account for all of my time. I'm sorry."

Just the admission that he had no iron-clad alibi was a point in favor of Corriden's innocence. Elliott leaned forward. "You loved Ainsley."

"For five years," Corriden said.

"You dated that long?" Elliott knew damn well they had only dated for two years, but he wanted to know what Corriden would say.

Corriden ducked his head. The knuckles of his hands turned white as he clutched them together. "I never stopped loving her. I accepted that it was over between us. I moved on with my life. But I never stopped loving her."

Elliott tilted his head. "That seems a little unfair to—"

"Kelly? Yeah. It was." Corriden shook his head. "It is. But Kelly loves me, and I do, truly, love her. Not the same way as I loved Ainsley. Me and Ainsley, that was…consuming. Devouring. It was the sort of love that makes you focus all your attention and time on the other person, without any room for anything else." Corriden met Elliott's gaze. "My love for Kelly isn't like that. But it's real."

Elliott nodded slowly. "Does Kelly know that?"

Corriden opened his mouth and then paused, rubbing a hand over his head. "Maybe."

"She's okay with that?"

"I don't know." Corriden scowled, his fingers twisting the wedding band on his left hand. "She married me. I do my best to show her how much I love her."

"Even if it isn't a devouring love." Elliott was careful to make his voice flat, non-judgmental—so careful he knew Corriden would hear it as Elliott judging him.

"I have always tried to prove my love for Kelly," Corriden flared.

"Except that one time in New York." Elliott let his gaze meet Corriden's. "When you cheated on her."

Corriden looked away.

"Does Kelly know about that?" Elliott pressed. "About New York? That it was Ainsley?" He drew in a breath. "About the baby?"

Corriden's gaze snapped to Elliott's. "*The baby?*"

Oh, fuck.

All the air sucked out of the room. Elliott felt a prickle of sweat on his forehead. Somehow he had just assumed Corriden knew about the pregnancy, which was not only lazy but just plain sloppy. Of course Ainsley wouldn't have told him; she would have assumed Corriden would want her to have the baby, and it was clear she'd at least been considering abortion. She had probably wanted to keep her options open until she knew how Kaida would react.

"Ainsley didn't tell you," Elliott said finally.

He saw Corriden bite back his first and second response to that statement. Corriden's self-control impressed Elliott, and the lack of an accompanying scent of fear or excitement made Elliott believe Corriden hadn't killed her.

"She…" Corriden wiped a hand over his face. "She had no obligation…" He shook his head. "She liked Kelly. They'd met. She was thinking of—and she had a girlfriend." He kept shaking his head. "It wouldn't have changed anything."

Elliott didn't even open his mouth to respond. He took a slow breath, watching Corriden, and was unsurprised when the man fell apart.

Corriden lunged across the desk, but not to strike at Elliott. He buried his face in his arms, shoulders shaking. His voice muttered for a while, mostly Ainsley's name, before trailing off into a quiet wail.

Elliott let him cry. While Elliott had always believed a woman should have total control over her own body, up to and including whether or not to give birth to a child she carried, he also understood how a man could feel grief over that decision. It didn't have to take away from the woman's decision, and it didn't imply any control on the part of the man. It just meant that man might grieve a little differently from any woman who decided to have an abortion.

Elliott didn't know Corriden, didn't have any indication of the man's religious beliefs or desire for children. But he could at least give the man a chance to deal with that knowledge before pressing him.

Finally, when Corriden had stopped shaking and was snuffling and wiping his face, Elliot said, very quietly, "I'll need to speak with your wife."

Corriden went very still, his expression blank. There was still nothing but grief and pain in his scent. Nothing to indicate fear or guilt. "That will kill her."

Elliott had the feeling Kelly Corriden was a stronger person than her husband imagined, but he said only, "I know you believe that, Mr. Corriden. But I need to talk to Kelly myself."

Corriden buried his face in his hands again. "I know I don't deserve her," he said brokenly. "But I do love her. Please don't do this."

"I would be remiss if I didn't." Elliott sighed. "My job is not to save your marriage, Mr. Corriden. It is to solve two murders. But I won't mention the baby—or your cheating—if Kelly doesn't bring it up."

Corriden lifted his face from his hands and blinked several times at Elliott. He looked miserable, and his scent confirmed that he was not only grief-stricken and hurting, but he was now afraid. It wasn't the overwhelming, sick-making fear that the man would give off if he were the killer, though. It was the right and natural fear of a man who thought he might get caught in infidelity.

Elliott couldn't understand cheating. Loyalty was something that came naturally to him, he supposed, but he'd also never been cheated on. There had been relationships where he'd never asked for exclusivity because he knew he wouldn't receive it, and there had been one relationship where he'd been torn between two people at the same time and unable to choose. In the end, he'd ended up alone.

The closest he could come in his personal experience, to that of the Ainsley-David-Kelly love triangle, was his relationship with Sarah. He loved her, and probably always would. But they'd had their chance, and had proven to be incompatible. He couldn't imagine even being tempted to be with Sarah again, because he had met Martin. He wasn't in love with Martin, but he definitely had a serious crush; he enjoyed being with Martin, talking to him, listening to him, just looking at him. His time with Sarah was over. His time with Martin… well, he could only hope that would be a lasting thing.

"Thank you, Mr. Corriden," Elliott said finally. "I would appreciate it if you would stay in town for a while. And please don't discuss this meeting with your wife until after I've spoken with her."

* * *

Martin spent several days after the interrupted date tearing out the kitchen in his house. He compared his own appliances with his former landlady's and put the extras on Craigslist and then solicited recommendations for a general contractor from his Facebook friends...and absolutely did not think about how he could have done things differently during the date when the vision hit him.

He finished one of the books about the science of sleep and dreams and—in the next to last chapter—found a folded slip of paper with Kyle's name, phone number, and email address. The discovery sent a little thrill through him. He might have made a fool of himself in front of Elliott, but at least Kyle found him interesting enough to slip him his number. He tucked the note into his wallet.

In the meantime he finished the transmission rebuild at work, handled the usual number of oil changes and minor jobs, and hired a general contractor. He had no dreams, PTSD or otherwise, and developed a Pavlovian reaction to chamomile tea; even the smell of it made his mouth start watering—but not in a good way. More like he was about to throw up.

He gave the rest of the tea blend to the woman who bought his refrigerator and dishwasher.

On Wednesday, to Martin's surprise, Elliott called him.

"Hey, I'm so sorry I didn't call you sooner," Elliott said. "I've had a journalist *and* my supervisor hounding me about this case, and I finally managed to track down a couple of people I'd been playing phone tag with, and—"

"It's fine," Martin cut in. He was smiling and shaking his head. Why did he always expect the worst out of situations like this? Elliott had a high pressure job, unlike Martin's, and he'd probably been trying to figure out what Martin's vision might mean. "How are you?"

"Exhausted," Elliott said. "But glad you're not pissed at me."

That made Martin laugh aloud. "Here I was afraid you were pissed at how I ended things on Saturday."

"I already told you I wasn't," Elliott said. Martin could hear the smile in his voice. "I wasn't just being nice. Listen, I unfortunately don't have much time to talk—I have an appointment in twenty minutes. But I didn't want to put this off any longer. I'd like to take you dinner Saturday. There's a great Japanese restaurant near me, if you like that."

A tingle of pleasure went through Martin. "Yeah, I do. What time are you thinking?"

"Maybe seven? Blue Sushi Sake Grill at 86th and Keystone. I'll make the reservations and let you know for sure."

"Sounds good."

"I had a good time Saturday. I really am sorry I didn't at least text you sooner." Elliott's voice was low and warm, and Martin couldn't help but remember the feel of Elliott's lips against his.

"It's fine. You're busy."

"Not too busy for you," Elliott said.

As they said their goodbyes and hung up, Martin's stomach was flipping pleasantly. Oh, God, this was getting out of control. He liked Elliott so much it was scary and wonderful. More wonderful than scary, since that meltdown Saturday hadn't scared Elliott off, but...

"Shut up," he told himself. "This is awesome. Enjoy it."

He had to repeat those instructions to himself several times over the next few days, every time he suffered an attack of nerves over the whole thing. He finished going through another of the sleep books and decided the science ones had more helpful stuff in them than the woo-woo books. The vague dream interpretation stuff didn't seem to carry much weight when he was dreaming about such specific people.

Chloe texted him an invitation for Saturday dinner and Martin's, *Sorry, I already have plans. What about Sunday?* provoked no teasing about dates with werewolves, which made him wonder if she was giving up on that or just saving it for when she could deliver it in person.

Friday morning he woke drenched in sweat after a run-of-the-mill PTSD dream about the ambush in Kandahar. Once his mantra kicked in and his heart slowed a little, he realized he was *relieved* it was a normal PTSD dream.

"This is seriously fucked up," he muttered. The clock told him it was four-thirty, so he got up, went for a run, and headed in to the garage early. He spent the whole day thinking about the guys who'd been involved in the ambush, wondering how Dax was doing. After work that evening, he sat down at his computer and emailed Dax before moving on to the next part of his renovation project—putting in a new half-wall and permanent support column to replace the wall he'd torn out earlier.

Saturday he met with the contractor he'd chosen and finished the drywall work on his new half-wall. Then it was time to clean up and get ready for their date.

They met at Elliott's apartment and walked to the restaurant, which shared a parking lot with Elliott's apartment complex. "I get takeout from here more often than I want to admit," Elliott said as they strolled. "I *can* cook. I just don't bother a lot."

Martin laughed. "No judgment here. I'm the same way, except it's usually pizza instead of sushi."

When the waiter came to take their order, Elliott looked over at Martin. "You have any preferences?"

Something in his demeanor made Martin think Elliott had a plan, so he shook his head. "Why don't you order for us?"

Elliott ordered shrimp tempura and cucumber maki. "I want a yuzu whisky sour for me," he added, "and..." He glanced at Martin.

"Green Kukicha tea," Martin said.

"And a flight of sake for us to share," Elliott finished. As the waiter walked away, Elliott leaned across the table. "Fun fact—the kappa they named their maki for? Totally real. There's one that lives somewhere down on the Central Canal. I see him from time to time. You ever run into one, bow. It'll be compelled to bow back and that should keep you out of trouble."

Martin blinked at him. "I'm starting to wonder just how many of the fairytales are real," he admitted.

"Enough of 'em." Elliott shrugged. "Never met a vampire, though. People who practice blood magic, but no vampires." His expression darkened.

"Blood magic. Like that necromancer last year." Martin hadn't been involved in the fight against the necromancer—Chloe hadn't even told him about it until it was all over—but he knew Braxton's pack had lost someone in that fight.

"Yeah." Elliott shook his head and gave Martin a smile that looked a little forced. "Shouldn't have brought it up. How was your week?"

Martin drew in a slow breath, deciding not to press Elliott on the topic. If Elliott wanted to talk about it, he could, but Martin didn't need to pressure him. A little bit of flirting might cheer them both up. "It got a lot better after this hot guy I know asked me out midweek," he said, smiling mischievously.

Elliott's smile looked a lot less forced at that. "Oh yeah? Tell me more about this hot guy."

"Hmm, I'm pretty sure he's a workaholic, but he's got an important job, so I understand that," Martin said. He tilted his head, studying Elliott. "And he might—*might*—be a bigger Indy Eleven fan than I am, so he's obviously got good taste."

Elliott laughed. "Man, flattery will get you everywhere."

Pleased, Martin nudged Elliott's leg with his own and leaned back in his chair. Mission Cheerup accomplished. "How was *your* week?"

"Eh. Started looking up midweek for me, too." Elliott paused as their server brought their drinks and promised their food was almost ready. "My sister Emily emailed that she's going to be in town the first week of September. She's going to run with the pack for Full—oh, that's September sixth. Anyway, she'll be staying at my place that week. I think you guys might have met at the wedding?"

"Yeah. She lives in Louisville, right?" Martin remembered her as a pretty, full-figured girl with long, dark hair and a turned-up nose.

"Yep. I'm trying to talk her into coming back to Indy after grad school."

Martin wondered if there was a polite way to ask if Elliott and Emily were full siblings or not. Elliott's skin was a lot darker than Emily's, but that didn't necessarily mean anything. "Tell me more about her," he said instead. If things worked out between him and Elliott, he'd eventually learn all of that stuff—if it mattered to Elliott. If it didn't, it didn't matter to Martin, either.

Elliott launched into an enthusiastic description of Emily's public health studies and her passion for equal access to healthcare. It was obvious he was proud of his sister, and over the shrimp tempura, Martin discovered that was partly sibling affection and partly because Elliott had been responsible for raising his younger sisters after their mother's murder.

"They caught the real killer eventually," Elliott said, his gaze firmly on the half-drunk sake flight. "An addict looking for drug money who was surprised to find someone home." His voice took on a bitter note as he tapped his fingers against the table. "But not before they tried to pin it on a black man."

Martin reached over and rested his hand on Elliott's. "Your dad?"

Elliott snorted. "After I proved I had an iron-clad alibi—a professor and sixteen other students who were more than happy to vouch for me—they moved on to Dad pretty quick." He looked at their hands and turned his to curl his fingers around Martin's. "My folks were together for several years—me and Olivia are both their kids—but he wanted to get married and Mom didn't. Eventually they split up, and he married a nice lady out in Colorado. He was a good father, came to visit us a lot, flew us out to visit him once for Christmas. He's the one who put me and O both through college."

"He sounds pretty cool."

Elliott wouldn't meet Martin's gaze. "Just—I didn't want you to think he was that 'absent black dad' the conservatives always like to talk about."

"Hey." Martin squeezed his hand lightly. "I don't have any preconceived ideas about your parents except that they obviously did a damn good job raising you."

Elliott's shoulders relaxed. "Sorry. Things are just—I've been pissed off since last fall, you know? So many assholes out there."

"Tell me about it." Martin squeezed his hand again. "You don't have to talk about stuff if it's too hard."

Elliott finally met his gaze. "Yeah. But I don't mind telling you this stuff. I...I'm not good at this, this relationship stuff. But I want to know you, Martin, and I want you to know me. The real me, not just..." He trailed off. "You know."

Martin gave him a lopsided smile. "Yeah. I know." He caught his lip between his teeth, then added, heart pounding, "And for the record, I think you're doing pretty good at this relationship stuff."

Elliott huffed a laugh. "Don't speak too soon."

Martin took his hand back so he could continue eating, but he felt more relaxed as their conversation turned to Olivia's job in Fort Wayne and the pack she ran around with up there, which included a couple of doctors and a triple-A baseball player. That led them to sports—they both preferred the Indianapolis Indians and the Eleven over Indy's major league teams—and hobbies. Martin eventually mentioned that he'd started renovating his house, and that topic carried them to the end of dinner.

The July air was warm and humid as they walked back. Elliott caught Martin's hand in his, sending a pleasant chill up Martin's arm. "I don't really want to say good night yet," Elliott said softly as they reached Martin's car.

"Me neither." Martin searched Elliott's gaze, wondering what sort of invitation this was.

Elliott shrugged. "Someone told me a guy who has a 4K TV really needs to see *Pacific Rim*. I hear it's kinda Voltron meets Godzilla?"

Martin gave him a slow grin in return. "Did you seriously buy a movie just because I wanted to see it on 4K?"

"Nah, what kind of weirdo does something like that?" Elliott scoffed. "I just like watching movies that make my TV look sexy." He smiled and tugged Martin's hand gently. "Want to come up?"

Martin stepped closer. "Yeah, I do." He wasn't sure if Elliott really wanted to just watch the movie or if he had more in mind, but he found he didn't care either way. It had been a good night.

* * *

The last Sunday in July was the Indianapolis Microbreweries Festival, and Lachlan finally got to live a lifelong dream of playing a concert at Military Park.

Military Park was the oldest park in Indianapolis. Fourth of July celebrations had been held there in the 1820s. The park had been used as a military training ground in the 1830s and 40s, and then in the 1850s it had hosted the Indiana State Fair. For the past thirty years, Military Park had been part of White River State Park.

Dozens of microbreweries, including Sun King, Daredevil, and others that weren't as regionally well-known, set up booths around the fourteen-acre park. Three music stages were set up in different corners, and Lachlan was given the opening timeslot in the stage furthest from the gate.

He'd texted Kaida about the show, and she'd said she would be there. He'd just told his father he had a wedding, because even a show like this wouldn't impress him; Lach would have to have a major record deal in hand before his dad would believe he had made anything of himself.

The Knot Tide members had been happy to rearrange their schedules to play for him, though he'd been very specific that they weren't Knot Tide today. The were the Lachlan Shaw Band. To his surprise, no one had grumbled about it.

It was a hot, muggy day, more like mid-August than July. Sweat was trickling between Lachlan's shoulder blades as he checked the tuning on his guitar. He'd already had a pint of Sun King Cream Ale and two bottles of water, but he was feeling dry again.

"Hey, Jule, would you grab me another pint of something?" he asked. The keyboard player headed off with a nod. It was fifteen minutes to showtime and Lachlan's stomach was suddenly roiling.

Kaida arrived in a group of people, but there were only a couple dozen people around when the band struck up their first song. They played a few covers before Lachlan broke into his first original number. That was when he caught sight of Eris.

Shit. Whenever that woman showed up his music went crazy.

Lachlan tried to steady his thoughts. He'd play a couple of power songs. He looked over at Julie. "Let's skip the next couple and go to 'Welcome to the Black Parade,'" he said. She nodded and passed the word to the others, then struck her first notes. Bryce struck up a military beat on his snare to back Lachlan's voice, and then Damon came in with his electric guitar. Lachlan threw himself into the song and could feel the power building as he carried on.

By the time they got to the final chorus, the crowd had grown to at least fifty people. He could see them singing along with him and exulted. This was *him* doing this, drawing them here and making them sing. Kaida was much closer to the stage than she had been, as if she'd worked to keep a clear view of him. He couldn't quite read the expression on her face—was it pride? Concern? He wished he knew her better so he could tell.

Amid the cheers at the end of the song, he saw Eris slipping through the crowd to stand at the very front of the stage. He tried to ignore her as they leapt into a song by Chris Cornell, but as he finished that song, he was struck with a coughing fit. Julie covered for him by announcing a quick break.

Eris held up a pint glass. Glaring at her, Lachlan knelt and took it, drinking deep.

"The detective suspects you," she hissed in his ear. "Target him. Sing your sister's lament and think of his investigation going awry. Perhaps you'll even drive him away entirely."

"Screw you," he muttered, but he took another long gulp of the beer she'd given him. As he straightened, he worried. *Had* Detective Blake decided Lachlan had something to do with Ainsley's death? But how could he have decided that? Lachlan had been playing a wedding in full view of two hundred people at the time the coroner said Ainsley had been killed. Whatever magic had been in play, how could Blake know about it? He hadn't treated Lachlan like a suspect.

His stomach was churning again as he told the band they were going to open the next set with "Ainsley's Lament." He gave Damon the chords and Bryce said he'd come in on the second verse. Then he turned and focused on the crowd. It was at least a hundred people now.

"This song is dedicated to my big sister Ainsley. Please help us find the person who killed her," he said, and started singing Ainsley's part.

Think of Blake's investigation going awry, he told himself. Send him stumbling after some stupid clue. Make him chase his tail.

To his utter shock, as they approached the part where Lachlan's counterpuntal part kicked in, Kaida leapt onto the stage. She leaned into his microphone, her face just inches from his, and belted out, "Broken! Out of place. Lost in the woods, lost without a face."

Her dark eyes held Lachlan's, refusing to let him look away. He managed to keep singing, but as he stared at Kaida, he couldn't help feeling as if he were singing directly to Ainsley. He felt tears prickle at his eyes at the thought of his sister and everything she had lost.

As they wrapped the song, he finally broke Kaida's gaze and saw the fury on Eris' face. Only then did he remember that he'd been trying to thwart Blake's investigation. It was too late now. As Eris started to pull herself onto the stage, Kaida whispered, "Sorry, Lach," in his ear and darted past him to jump off the back of the stage.

Shit! She'd *tricked* him!

But the rage twisting Eris' pretty face into ugliness scared him. He had to stop her from chasing Kaida. What could he do?

He struck a chord and improvised. He'd always been a closet Taylor Swift fan, even though he'd never considered performing one of her songs. But her song "I Know Places" was the only song he could think that dealt with being chased and escaping without getting caught. He could almost feel the band's astonishment at his back, but after the first four lines, Bryce kicked in with the beat, and by the time Lachlan reached the chorus, Julie jumped in with backing vocals.

He heard Eris' shriek of frustration over the music, but he didn't care—he could *feel* Kaida running faster, twisting and turning and escaping pursuit. And when they crashed to an ending, he was greeted with a huge roar of approval at his gritty interpretation of the song.

The swell of jubilation that followed carried him through the rest of his set. By the time he and the others finished, they were drenched with sweat and Lachlan had tears sliding down his cheeks, but he was happier and more heart-broken than he'd ever been.

"Oh my God, that was amazing," Julie said, throwing her arms around him. "Lach, you're totally on the verge of liftoff here, man. I am so fucking stoked for you!"

"Thanks, Jules," he choked out. He was excited, too, but he couldn't help imagining how much better this would all be if Ainsley was with him.

Bryce and Damon pounded his shoulders, too, and then audience members were crowding around him, waving money for his CDs and telling him how amazing he was. His heart thudded so hard it felt like it would pound out of his chest, his shirt clung to his ribs, and he couldn't catch his breath. It was wonderful and horrible, and it was almost everything he'd ever wanted.

It wasn't until they'd been shooed off by the stage manager, who had another act to set up for, that the others packed up and headed out. Lachlan hadn't had a chance to pack up his guitar and amp while he was signing CDs, so he lingered.

He was winding the amp cord around his arm when Eris finally approached.

"You fool." Her voice was low and shaking. "You shouldn't have let that trickster interfere!"

"Trickster?"

"The woman. She will ruin everything. And then you protected her!" Eris' hands were clenched into fists at her side. No...only one hand was clenched into a fist. Lachlan blinked at the other hand, which looked like it wouldn't close properly. Had she hurt it somehow?

"Of course I protected her," Lachlan said. "I didn't know what you were going to do to her. And she had every right to sing with me." A moment after the words left his mouth, he realized he shouldn't let Eris know who Kaida really was. What if Eris decided to hurt her?

A chill ran down his spine as he realized he was afraid of Eris.

"What I was going to do to her?" Eris' laughter was mocking. "I am not the one who killed your sister, siren."

"I didn't do that on purpose!" he hissed. "Keep your voice down."

"Why? Are you afraid that police detective is here somewhere, watching you?" Eris' voice rose into a singsong. "Oh, siren, wailing man, *fir chaointe,* where is your sister?"

"So you're going to turn me in?" he snapped. "Fine. I'd love to see how you'll convince them magic is real! For all I know, *you* killed her and you're just trying to make me crazy!"

Eris just kept laughing.

"Stay away from me, you crazy monster!" he shouted. "Just—stay away." He slung his guitar case over his back and walked away.

CHAPTER 20

Thursday Martin had scheduled the garage to be closed for repairs to his hydraulic lift. He ended up calling an HVAC guy to come fix the air conditioning on the same day. To take advantage of the slow business day, he had arranged to meet Elliott for lunch.

It was still early days, but Martin couldn't help feeling optimistic about how things were going. Elliott had started texting him at random times during the day. Sometimes a couple of hours would pass between texts, since Martin often had grease on his hands, but the sporadic flirtation had definitely brightened Martin's week so far.

Parking downtown wasn't fun, but Elliott had suggested they meet at Rebar Indy, which was just across the street from the City-County Complex. Since Elliott was the one who had a full schedule, Martin thought that was only fair.

When he walked up to the bar on Delaware Street, Elliott was slouched against the wall outside, hands in his pockets. Martin's breath hitched in his chest. With his tousled dark curls and sunglasses, Elliott looked like a movie star. His breath hitched again when Elliott saw him and smiled.

"Hey, there you are." He reached out and squeezed Martin's hand briefly, then held the door for him.

"Sorry, you know what parking's like."

"Preaching to the choir," Elliott agreed.

Once they were settled at a table and had ordered their meal—breaded tenderloins for both of them, Coke for Elliott, and unsweetened iced tea for Martin—Elliott leaned on the table, turning his smile on Martin.

"It's nice to see you. How's your day going?"

"Good. I have to get back in an hour to meet the lift guy, but the AC is fixed already." It was the third of August, and temperatures were soaring into the upper 80s. Mixed with a heavy dose of humidity, it made for weather that made most Hoosiers wish for a dry heat.

Between Iraq and Afghanistan, Martin had spent four years in dry heat. He had to concede that sweating actually worked properly if it wasn't humid, but all things considered, he thought dry heat was overrated.

"How about you?" Martin asked. "How are your sisters?"

"Good. Olivia just bought a new car." Elliott scoffed. "Can you believe she went all over Fort Wayne and ended up driving all the way down to Kokomo just to find a Jeep with a manual transmission?"

"You're kidding. Have Americans gotten so lazy they won't even do their own shifting?" Martin rolled his eyes. He was always surprised at how rare manual transmissions were these days.

"The dealer told her it's just not as economical to make manuals, since most people prefer automatics.

But I taught my sisters to drive, and I made sure they both knew how to drive a manual transmission and change flat tires."

"Go you," Martin said, grinning at him. "Every woman should know how to use a tire iron."

"Both for changing a tire and for self-protection," Elliott agreed.

"I can't believe how hard it is to find parts to repair some of those cheap standard transmissions these days," Martin said. "I had a lady in with a Geo Metro awhile back, and the gearbox was crazy tight. I wanted to replace the whole thing for her, but it took me six weeks just to locate one. I did what I could in the meantime, but..." He shrugged. "Some of the cars I work on, once they're over fifteen years old, there are people trying to keep them running, but they don't count as classics yet."

The conversation lagged once their sandwiches arrived, but eventually Martin ventured the question he'd been biting back. "So...no news in the case?" he asked.

A pang of guilt struck him at the frustration that creased Elliott's expression. "No news. Just more dead ends and more questions. I've spent the last three days talking to anyone I could find who's ever had a connection to Jo Parrish and his veterans support group. Only two of them had ever met Ainsley Shaw, and one of them hadn't seen her since they were at college together."

Martin felt bad for asking. But he didn't want to seem uninterested, especially since he was supposed to be helping with the case. "Sorry," he murmured.

Elliott shrugged. "I have an appointment with Ainsley's dad tomorrow. Not looking forward to that, since I don't have any new information for him."

"Have you—" Martin began, then cut himself off.

"What?"

"No, you probably already thought of it." Martin sipped his tea.

Elliott tipped his head to one side. "Maybe, but I'm always happy to hear ideas."

"Well, have you tried asking Lachlan Shaw for any ideas? It sounds to me like he and Ainsley were a lot closer than Ainsley was to her parents. I mean, if she was willing to come out to him but hadn't come out to her parents, she had to trust him."

Elliott nodded slowly. "I asked him the standard questions when I first talked to him, but I haven't spoken to him since the day of the funeral. It would probably be a good idea to go back and ask again." He rubbed a hand over his face. "I can't believe it's been a month."

Martin couldn't imagine what the past month had been like for the Shaw family. At least in war, you generally knew what had happened and why. Something like this, it felt so personal and yet so senseless. Not to mention how damned unfair it seemed that she'd made it home only to die once she should have been safe.

"You'll figure it out," he said softly. "You're a good detective. You'll catch the guy who killed her."

"How do you know?" Elliott muttered.

"I know because Chloe thinks you're a good detective," Martin said. "Chloe likes you. She respects you. She wouldn't feel that way if you were a shitty cop."

To his relief, Elliott laughed. He looked at Martin, eyes sparkling with amusement and something that made Martin's pulse jump. "I'm glad to know your sister has some use for me, even if she won't come work with me."

Martin snorted. "Anyway, I have confidence in you. And I can tell how important solving this case is to you."

"Yeah." Elliott tapped his fingers against the table, watching Martin's face. "What about you?" he asked, his voice soft. "Any more dreams?"

Martin glanced away. "Not the kind you want to hear about."

"Hey." Elliott's fingers rested on Martin's hand. Surprised, Martin looked back at him. Elliott's brows were drawn together. "You can tell me about any of them, whether or not they have to do with the case," Elliott said. He gave Martin a crooked smile. "You told me the first time before we even knew there might be a connection, remember?"

Martin studied him, searching for any sign of pity or annoyance. No matter how hard he looked, though, he saw nothing but compassion and interest. "Well...heh." He ducked his head, smiling faintly. It was true he'd confided in Elliott before he really meant to—and that Elliott had been supportive from the beginning. "No dreams about the case," Martin said. "Only one PTSD dream, which is progress."

"Good."

He expected Elliott to pull away, but instead Elliott's fingers curled around Martin's. When he looked up again, Elliott squeezed his fingers and then finally pulled away.

"I hope I haven't made you feel like I'm only interested in you for how you can help me with the case," Elliott said. "Or even mostly interested in you for that." He smiled slowly. "I'm interested in you for a lot of reasons, but most of them aren't that altruistic."

Martin chuckled, amused, embarrassed, and a little turned on. "No, sorry. I just...I guess I hadn't really thought it through all the way. How talking to you about the PTSD had helped, even before you decided I had some kind of super power."

"I'm glad it helped. I wish I could help more."

Martin shrugged. "I don't know how much anyone or anything can help. It's something I lived through. It's something I can't forget. So it's something I have to live with."

Elliott nodded.

They fell silent again, but it felt like a comfortable silence. Martin found silence preferable to people offering empty phrases meant to comfort him. He liked that things with Elliott felt secure enough to just sit together without talking—without needing to fill the silence with meaningless chatter.

The conversation about trauma had definitely sobered Martin, but he felt mostly content as they finished their meal. Having a mid-week lunch date felt more settled, as if they had gotten past the initial chemistry check and had decided they were both interested in making things work.

After paying for their lunch, they lingered on the sidewalk in front of the bar. Elliott didn't seem to want to go back to work, and Martin was happy to steal a few more minutes.

"Let me know if there's anything I can do to help with the case," he said finally. He wondered if it was his turn to bring up the idea of a date this weekend. Were they alternating? Then again, his only idea was to suggest they go to the Eleven game together, and since they had season tickets in different sections, he sort of wanted Elliott to be the one to bring that up.

"Elliott!" said a bright feminine voice from behind Martin. "Twice in one week? How are you?"

Elliott looked past Martin, his sheepish smile fading into a wary expression. "Sarah. Are you following me?" He gave it a beat before he grinned. Martin wasn't certain whether he was joking or serious.

"I wouldn't have to," said Sarah, walking past Martin to hug Elliott. "You've always loved this place, even when it was the Legal Beagle."

Whoever Sarah was, she'd known Elliott for several years, if she'd been to the Legal Beagle with him. That establishment had closed a couple of years ago, Martin thought. He told himself he wasn't jealous, but Elliott was frowning at her. When Elliott's gaze flicked briefly to Martin's and then back to Sarah's face, Martin had to admit that he was maybe curious about her, even if he wasn't jealous.

"I'm kidding." Sarah had followed Elliott's gaze to Martin's. She smiled at Martin. She was pretty, with a keen quickness in her eyes that made Martin uneasy. "Believe it or not, this is purely coincidence. I told Kate and Amanda I'd pick up our lunch while they're on a conference call."

The suspicion on Elliott's face didn't fade, and Sarah rolled her eyes. "When did you lose your sense of humor, Ell?"

He huffed. "I can just never tell with you."

Sarah shrugged. "So what's up? Any new developments on the War Killer?"

"Do *not* give him a stupid nickname, Sarah." Elliott's voice was sharp. "You know better."

Martin looked from Elliott to Sarah. *War Killer?* What did that mean?

"If you would just give me something solid to work with, I wouldn't have to improvise." Sarah's voice had sharpened to match Elliott's.

Elliott scowled at her. "Is this just a game to you?"

Sarah was half a head shorter than Elliott, but she planted her fists on her hips and matched him glare for glare. Despite her annoyance, she was speaking quietly, though, which intrigued Martin. "I'm trying to cover an important news story, Elliott. I'm trying to help the families of these victims honor—"

"You're trying to break the story of a serial killer who doesn't exist!" Elliott's voice was low and furious. "You need to back off and let me work. You *know* me, Sarah. You know you'll be the first person I call when I can tell you anything."

"Do I? That promise was a long time ago."

Martin swallowed and then cleared his throat. "Listen, Elliott, I'm going to take off. I need to—I have that meeting."

Elliott's expression changed from anger to apology. "Martin, wait," he said, reaching out. "I'm sorry—"

"Martin!" Sarah's voice was sharp. "Are you a part of this investigation? Do you think this is the work of a serial killer who hates veterans? Maybe he has a grudge against someone who served and he's taking it out on other people who served?"

"Leave him out of this," Elliott snapped.

"Can't Martin speak for himself?" Sarah asked, her voice bright.

Martin took a step backwards and then forced himself to stop. He didn't like the direction this was going. *Did* Elliott think the shadowy figure in Martin's dreams was a serial killer? Was Martin somehow having visions of a psychopath? "I don't know you," he said, trying to make himself sound calm and matter of fact instead of just plain rude. "Why would I tell you anything?"

"Goodbye, Sarah." Elliott's voice was hard. He cut between Sarah and Martin, effectively pushing her out of the conversation.

"Someday you'll need my help and wish you hadn't spent so much time trying to keep things from me," Sarah snapped. She swung around and stormed into the bar.

As soon as she was gone, Martin took another step backwards and then turned away from Elliott. "The hell was that?" he muttered, shoving his hands in his pockets. He wanted to shout, but he choked down his temper. This wasn't Elliott's fault; he was clearly as unhappy at being ambushed by Sarah as Martin was.

Elliott sighed and started walking, looking at Martin in invitation. "My most obnoxious ex," he said as Martin fell into step. "I should never have dated a reporter."

"Your ex," Martin repeated. That explained a lot. The familiarity, the tension, even the easy way Sarah seemed to push Elliott's buttons.

"Yeah. It was a long time ago."

Martin hummed thoughtfully. The encounter had started out pleasant enough, he thought; they must have parted on decent terms. It was only when Sarah brought up the case that Elliott started getting defensive.

"I know you knew I'm bi. We talked about that. Is it going to be a problem after all?"

Martin looked at Elliott in surprise. The other man's shoulders were hunched, his voice tight. What was he expecting, that Martin would suddenly be disgusted when confronted with the evidence that Elliott liked women as well as men?

"No," he said. His voice didn't come out as evenly as he had hoped. Elliott's lack of trust hurt, even if it shouldn't. Martin knew there were a lot of bisexual people who felt attacked or neglected by the rest of the LGBTQ community. It shouldn't surprise or hurt him that Elliott might fear that reaction from him.

But it did.

Elliott's shoulders hunched further. "Great, so when you acted all cool with it before, that was just, what? Why would you do that?"

"Stop." Martin looked at Elliott in disbelief. "I just said I don't have a problem with you being bisexual. Further, you don't need my validation." He shook his head, trying to sound reasonable and soothing. "Elliott, it isn't a thing, okay? Not with you and me. It's fine."

"I'm sorry I didn't just ignore her," Elliott snarled. "I try to keep things friendly, but clearly this didn't go well." He glowered at Martin. He was so tense he was practically vibrating.

Martin huffed. "Are you deliberately misinterpreting me? Or is it just happening because you're mad at Sarah?" Well, shit. So much for trying to sound reasonable.

"Are you annoyed at me about the bisexual erasure thing, or are you just jealous?" Elliott snapped back.

As soon as the words left his mouth, Elliott's expression changed. He sucked in a quick breath, but Martin had already stepped back.

"Wow. Okay, *that* was uncalled for." Martin's stomach was churning. He *had* been a little jealous at first, but mostly because it seemed Sarah knew Elliott so well. But he wasn't a jealous person in general, and the accusation pissed him off. He tried to rein in the anger that was creeping up to choke him.

Elliott and Martin stared at each other for what felt like a year. In reality it was only long enough for a single car to pass them on Delaware. Martin's eyes felt hot and his mouth had gone dry. He didn't like fighting. He didn't like having to swallow the anger boiling up inside him, but he knew it wasn't good to let it out, either.

"I'd better get back to work," Elliott said finally.

"Yeah," Martin replied. "I think that's a good idea."

He drove too fast all the way back to Broad Ripple.

* * *

Martin spent the rest of the afternoon pushing his temper into submission. When the lift repairman gave him the bill, Martin had to close his eyes and count to ten so he wouldn't blow up at the price. In actuality it wasn't much higher than the man's estimate had been—which was what made Martin bite his tongue until he could get the check written out and watch the man leave.

He kept thinking about the look on Elliott's face as he spat out that comment about jealousy—and the look on his face ten seconds later, when what he'd said actually sank in. He kept wishing he'd snapped back something about Elliott projecting his own insecurity on Martin—and then being grateful that he'd actually managed to take a breath and speak fairly rationally instead. It felt supremely unfair to be accused of jealousy when he thought he'd been perfectly nice to Sarah.

He was grateful he'd allowed Thursday *and* Friday for the repairs. His regular customers knew the garage was going to be closed until Monday. As soon as the repairman left, Martin locked up, set the alarm, and went home.

The garage was less than a mile from his house, but he didn't even have to detour to hit up a liquor store on his way home. He didn't even pretend he was doing anything healthy or intelligent. He just walked straight back to where the rum was shelved.

When he got home he paused, keys in hand, and listened for the sound of Whizz dashing across the hardwood floors to greet him. It took several moments for him to remember that his sister had taken her cat back more than a month ago.

He closed the door and slumped against it, closing his eyes. "I really need to get a cat," he muttered. Cats got a bad rap. They were selfish as hell, and nine times out of ten they ignored you when you called them, but having a purry cat on your lap was therapeutic.

With a muttered curse, he locked the door behind him and made a beeline for the kitchen.

Forty minutes later he'd killed a frozen pizza and a third of the bottle of rum. He knew, he *knew*, that feeding the anger was a bad idea. Hell, he might not even have the right to be angry at Elliott. But he'd turned on the news, which was never a good idea these days. He'd found himself shouting at the television about immigration and transgender bans in the military, and the news that a suicide bomber had killed two soldiers in Kandahar had made him throw the remote at the television.

He threw back another shot of rum and buried his face in his hands. He'd spent two and a half tours enjoying his time in the military, glad he'd signed up and made such good friends, learned discipline, learned a trade. He'd spent the last six months dealing with the fallout from the IED, but he'd always thought things would be fine once he got home.

He was just so damn tired. He'd served his country, but nothing back home had changed. People in Indiana still hated gay people and people of color — anyone who looked or acted different from the straight white evangelicals who populated the state. He hadn't thought he was going into the Army with high ideals, but he'd had them, all the same.

And it felt like every single day, lately, his country tore those ideals down just a little bit more.

"Fuck this," he muttered, and swallowed another shot.

What was he doing, trying to build a relationship with someone? Martin was damaged. He'd let people down. He'd failed to protect his best friend. Why would anyone want to be with someone like him?

"Oh, God, the maudlin's kicking in," he muttered. He looked at the bottle of rum, wondered how much he was going to hate himself in the morning, and threw back two more shots in quick succession. Maybe if he drank enough, he could at least pass out without dreaming anything tonight.

It was, he thought, a theory worth testing.

Someone was moaning. Martin jerked and looked around, peering through darkness and trees to see if someone needed help.

It was hot, humid. Mosquitoes whined in his ear. Frowning, he squinted.

What was he doing out in a forest in the middle of the night?

Another moan reached his ears. That was a woman, he thought, and she was in pain. Voices rose, male and female both, but he couldn't hear what they were saying. Then the man shouted, "No!"

A moment later, a woman began screaming.

Martin shoved himself to his feet—why had he been lying on the ground in a forest?—and started running towards the sound. He had to help whoever that was.

Clenching his fists, he realized he had an M-16 in his hands. It didn't seem right to be carrying an assault rifle in a forest. He was used to deserts. This was all wrong.

"Just tell me and this can end," said a woman's voice.

Martin stumbled into a clearing. Two shadowy figures were looming over a third figure—a woman writhing in the dirt. One of the shadowy figures held a golden chain that wrapped around the other shadow's throat. She was pulling at it, eliciting gagging noises.

Martin threw himself to his knees next to the woman. She looked up at him with tear-filled hazel eyes. "Elliott?" she whispered. She obviously couldn't see him well, perhaps just the shape of him. Her long, brown hair was plastered to her forehead and cheeks, partly with sweat, but mostly with blood. Her lower lip was swollen. A bruise darkened her jaw.

"Tell her I didn't talk," she said.

Martin reached out to take her hand, hunched himself over her to protect her from whatever the shadowy figures were going to do to her.

"You!" snarled a furious feminine voice. "You have interfered one too many—"

"No!" the woman screamed, her eyes opening wide. She looked past Martin, using what he could tell was the last of her strength to throw him away from her.

Martin woke up as he hit the floor. The impact knocked the breath out of him.

Staring at the floor, choking and trying to suck in air, he realized he'd fallen out of bed.

He was fully clothed and soaked in sweat. He shifted his legs around, trying to roll onto his side. He was in his bedroom, the lights blazing. He didn't remember going to bed, but he must have.

He rocked onto his hands and knees and stared down at the throw rug, his vision refusing to focus. "Shit," he muttered, lifting one hand to wipe over his face. His hand was shaking.

His whole body was shaking, actually.

He couldn't remember exactly when the dream had started. Had it been when the woman started moaning, or had that just been when he realized he was dreaming? He knew there had been some sort of interrogation, but he couldn't remember the details. He knew the two people interrogating the woman had been at odds with each other. But how did he know that?

His stomach lurched and he groaned, lowering himself back down to lie on the floor.

What had he been thinking about before he fell asleep?

Oh, yes. The argument with Elliott. The sorry state of the world today. The futility of hoping for anything more than what he already had.

But mostly the argument with Elliott.

"Shit," he muttered, and shoved himself back up to his hands and knees. He had a feeling he was going to throw up, and he really wanted to be in the bathroom when that happened. With tremendous effort he hauled himself to his feet and staggered half a dozen steps towards the hallway before he lost his balance and rammed into the wall.

"When I finish this remodel I'm going to have a master bath," he mumbled.

Pushing off the wall, he took a few more steps before his stomach rebelled. He hunched over, clutching at the door frame, and emptied his stomach on the hardwood floor of the hallway.

"Shit," he muttered. He couldn't think. He'd clearly had more to drink than he'd thought.

Finally he lowered himself, hand-under-hand, down the door frame, to kneel on the floor. He leaned against the wall, staring blankly at the puddle of vomit. He couldn't handle this by himself.

He needed help.

Some part of him whispered that he should call Elliott. Martin ruthlessly crushed that part and decided to call the only person who had never let him down.

Chloe.

Thank God he'd had his phone in his pants pocket. The phone rang five times before Chloe answered with a breathless, "Hello?"

"Clo?" he mumbled. With a rush of shame, he heard his voice as if it were someone else's. He sounded entirely trashed. Would she even recognize it? Would she think she was being prank called?

"Marty?" Her voice was sharp suddenly, alert, alarmed.

"Yuh," he muttered. He knew what he was trying to say, but the words weren't coming out right. "Sorry. C'n you c'mere?"

He heard a voice in the background and Chloe hissed. "Where are you? Are you okay? Martin?"

"So...*fucking*...sick." He sounded as drunk as he felt. Tears prickled at his eyes. He'd tried so hard to spare her this, seeing how broken he was, all the darkness left inside him. He hadn't wanted her to feel like she'd failed him.

"Braxton—" Chloe said, her voice clear.

"No, wait," Martin interrupted. He panted, trying to catch his breath and keep from throwing up again.

He didn't want anyone else involved in this. Not even her husband. Oh, God, her husband; that was so weird. It had been just Chloe and Martin against the world for so long.

He heard Chloe suck in a breath. Maybe she was listening to him gulp air. Maybe she was just praying for patience. "Martin Jonathan Cole," she snapped, "talk to me."

Martin sighed, wishing he hadn't called her; but he knew better than to hang up now. "I'm trashed, Clo. Can you come over?"

There was a pause. "To your house?"

"Yeah." Martin gulped against a sudden swelling of emotion. "Will you bring Whizz?"

There was an even longer pause. "God give me patience," Chloe muttered.

"Chloe?" Martin's voice was very small.

"Half an hour," she said. "Will you be all right until then?"

He could hear Braxton asking questions in the background. He squeezed his eyes shut. "Yeah."

* * *

He must have dozed off again. The next thing he knew, someone was stroking his hair.

"Clo?" he mumbled.

"Marty." His sister's voice was thick with emotion. He was glad he couldn't tell what emotion it was.

"Don't, okay?" he whispered. He wiped his eyes, pissed at the way his emotions were leaking out. His sister had a key to his house, and he hadn't seen any reason to ask for it back after she got married. He was glad now. "I know I'm a mess. I screwed up."

"Hey, shhhh," Chloe said. She petted his hair for a couple more seconds. "Let's get you back in bed."

Martin wasn't sobering up, but he was definitely regaining some of his senses. He tried to help as Chloe wiped his face with a wet cloth and held a glass of cool water to his lips.

"Din't mean—" he began, but Chloe pressed her fingers to his lips and he stopped talking.

"I didn't bring Whizz," she said. "I'm sorry, but I was afraid I'd have to take you to the ER when I got here. You really didn't sound good."

Martin couldn't quite prevent a whimper from escaping his throat.

"It's okay, I'll bring him over tomorrow if you still miss him," she promised. "You stay right there. I'm going to put some fresh sheets on the bed, okay?"

Fuck. "Did I piss the bed?" he slurred.

It made him feel a little better that Chloe laughed. "No, I'm pretty sure this is just sweat. But it won't be comfortable. Give me a second to find dry sheets."

"Hall closet." He closed his eyes. The world felt like it was tilting under him, and in that moment, he actively disliked that feeling.

He listened as Chloe opened the door, which squeaked just a little on its hinges, then shut it. He heard the snap of sheets being flipped open. Then Chloe grunted as she climbed around the bed, tucking corners into place. His stomach growled, but Martin tried to ignore it. He wasn't sure he was through vomiting.

Chloe narrated some of her labors. "Please tell me this bottle wasn't full when you started," she said at one point. A little later she said, "I suggest moving the laundry room closer to the master bedroom in this remodel."

Martin, who was trying to avoid either passing out or vomiting again, didn't bother replying to most of her commentary. He knew at some point he would have to answer her questions, and he definitely wasn't looking forward to that. He might as well save his words for when they were absolutely needed.

Finally, though, Chloe was grabbing his hand and tugging him to his feet. She was only a couple of inches shorter than he was, and probably stronger, since she had a regular weights workout, so she didn't really have any trouble getting him off the floor. Martin tried to help, but he was just sober enough to realize how unwieldy he really was.

He flopped gracelessly onto his bed, squinting at his big sister as she drew crisp, clean sheets up under his chin. "Are you tucking me in?" he mumbled.

"Shh." She pulled a thin, waffle-weave blanket up next. "Yes."

Martin slid a hand up to clutch at the waffle blanket. He couldn't remember the last time he'd used it. It was light green and a loose weave. Something about it made him think about his mother.

Chloe crawled onto the bed next to him, lying down on top of the blankets. "Want to tell me about it?" she murmured. Her fingers were petting his hair the way he remembered from the weeks after their parents' car accident.

"No," he mumbled. Her fingers smoothed his eyebrows and stroked over his hair. "Yes." He sighed. "No."

Chloe didn't speak. She was a cop, so she was good at the whole interrogation thing, even if she wasn't a detective. When he'd been a senior in high school he'd been afraid to put so much as a hangnail out of line, because Chloe was, first of all, hyper aware of her role as his guardian, and second of all, incredibly skilled at drawing the truth out of him.

After a while Martin sighed. "It's too tangled up," he mumbled, thinking of how angry he was at Elliott and how quickly the national news had amplified that anger. "Don't know if I can explain."

"You don't have to," Chloe said softly. She draped an arm over his chest, resting her pointy chin on his shoulder. "But it might help."

Martin took a breath. "I don't like myself right now."

"That's okay. *I* like you." Chloe kissed his cheek. "I *love* you, Marty."

He hated it when she called him Marty. Except he also sort of loved it. He didn't know how to explain it, so he just ignored it.

"I know," he whispered.

They were silent for a long time. Martin's breathing evened out and his stomach quit churning so powerfully. Maybe he could tell her this without throwing up, he thought.

After a long time, Martin sighed. "I had a fight with Elliott."

He felt Chloe take a slow breath, but she didn't speak for a while. He wondered if his big sister was learning patience, or if she was just savoring this.

"You guys are more serious than I thought," she finally said.

"That isn't why I got shitfaced," Martin said, his voice louder than he'd meant it to be. "Well…it's part of it, but."

He broke off, not knowing how to explain it, how everything had tangled into a vine of epic proportions, how his anger and guilt and desire and hope and fear had all blended together. As he sucked air, his big sister tightened her arms around him, not demanding explanations or answers. Martin's heart pounded until he finally couldn't take it any longer.

"I couldn't save Dax," he blurted. "I couldn't help him. I couldn't stop the—I—" He choked. "And after the explosion people died but I couldn't do anything about it. I didn't sign up for that! But they were my friends, Clo—they were my best friends, and I couldn't do anything, and I—"

His words cut off in a sob. He didn't know how to explain it to anyone who hadn't been there. But his sister knew something about sacrificing for her job. She'd technically been killed in the line of duty, after all. She'd done more, if he were honest, than Martin had.

"I think about how I can't protect you, how I could lose you," he blurted at her, "and it makes me sick. You ought to be safe. Everyone who defends this country ought to be safe. I shouldn't have to pick between my duty and the people I love. I shouldn't even have to think about losing the people I love. It isn't—"

He broke off, breathless.

It isn't fair, he was going to say.

But life wasn't fair. Loss wasn't fair. He didn't know anyone who felt life had treated them fairly.

"And you don't want to lose Elliott, either," whispered his sister.

And he didn't want to lose Elliott, either.

Martin's throat tightened until he couldn't even suck in a breath. His chest clutched, making him tense. He felt his heart pounding double-time inside him. He squeezed his eyes shut against the thought of a bloody, injured Elliott. It was untenable. Unimaginable.

"I'm scared, C," he whispered finally. "I'm scared to—"

He broke off, unable to finish. His big sister tightened her arms around him. Martin relaxed into her hold, trying to give himself a minute to think.

"I'm scared to act like I deserve more than this," he finished.

"Why?" Chloe breathed.

"Because at least I came back!" he said. "Isn't that enough?"

He felt Chloe sigh. "Those guys who died. Ridley, Maddox? Were they assholes?"

Fury surged through him. "What?"

"Is Dax an asshole?" she asked, implacable.

"Chloe, what the fuck?" Martin asked, tensing and trying to pull away from her. "No! They're my friends! And they died and I didn't!"

Chloe hummed, low in her throat. "And if they weren't assholes," she murmured. "If they were really your friends…don't you think they'd be glad that you lived?"

Martin opened his mouth to argue and then swallowed his words.

All of the emails he'd ever gotten from Dax had urged him to move forward with his life. Dax had told him once, in so many words, that he shouldn't feel guilty for what had happened.

"I let them down," Martin whispered, eyes stinging.

"They loved you," his sister countered. "They would forgive you."

"I can't forgive me."

Chloe made a noise that almost sounded like a whimper. "I know," she whispered. She squeezed him tightly. "Marty, it took me years to come to terms with some of my own decisions. The abortion, the…" She made a strangled noise. "But we can't change the past. All we can do is move forward from where we are."

Martin's eyes were stinging so badly he squeezed them shut. He wanted to let go and sob, forget about anything except how miserable he was. He hesitated, trying to control his breathing, but finally the feel of his big sister's arms tightening around him was too much to resist.

He let himself cry, thinking of everything he had lost and the people he had failed. After a while he made himself think of the people he *hadn't* failed, the people who had relied on him to bring them home. Finally Martin relaxed into his sister's embrace, closing his eyes and imagining her arms buoying him up.

His pain, his loss, wasn't fixed. Maybe it never would be. But he felt better for having told her. Maybe he could redirect some of the energy he'd dedicated to hiding his trauma. Maybe he could spend it on actually recovering.

Chloe squeezed him, propping her chin against his shoulder so it poked into him. "You are gonna hate yourself so hard tomorrow," she murmured. "Seriously, though, was this bottle full when you started?"

Martin grunted an affirmative. He wasn't even annoyed when she made an "I-told-you-so" noise at him. But a few moments later he tensed.

"Clo," he blurted. "I forgot about the vision."

"Vision?"

He related it to her, the woman lying in the forest clearing, the two people torturing her. He even told her about the woman thinking he was Elliott.

Finally Chloe squeezed him again. "Okay," she whispered. "I'll have Braxton bring wedding photos, greasy food, and coconut water tomorrow. You're going to have the devil of a hangover. In the meantime, though, get some sleep." She petted his forehead. "I'm here. I'll take care of you."

Martin had spent too many years relying on his older sister. He relaxed into sleep.

CHAPTER 21

Elliott knew, when someone knocked on his door, that it would be Murphy with the pizza. He couldn't help hoping it might be Martin, though. That hope died as soon as he opened the door.

"Your neighbors always look at me like I'm going to mug them," Murphy grumbled, shoving past Elliott. "Even when I have a pizza box in my hand and it's obvious I'm just the delivery boy."

"You're too sensitive," Elliott said, smirking at Murphy's back. It was true that a couple of his neighbors were a little too rich and white, but he liked his apartment building. "If you'd just agree to move into my spare bedroom, you could educate them about how unscary you are."

"Whatever. I'm not moving in with you. You'll just kick me out when you decide to get all gay married with Martin Cole."

That sent a pang through Elliott's stomach. He couldn't deny that was a nice thought, but he'd probably screwed that up by being an idiot at Martin for no good reason today. Then again, Martin had been unreasonably angry about meeting Sarah, in Elliott's opinion. How was he supposed to know it wasn't jealousy?

And if Martin hadn't been angry because he was jealous, why had he been angry?

You could have just asked him, dumbass, he thought at himself.

"All right. What are we playing? GTA or Halo?"

"Halo," Elliott said, locking the door and following Murphy into the living room. Murphy already had the gaming system turned on. A half-eaten slice of pizza sat on the open lid of the pizza box. "Want a beer?"

"Sure."

Once they got settled on the couch and finished eating, they got serious about the game. Elliott kept trying to lose himself in the action, but he just kept thinking of things he should have said—or asked— when he was arguing with Martin. Or when he was trying to get Sarah to back off. Or—

"Dude," Murphy said. "That's the third time I've killed you. Not that I mind or anything, but you're extra crappy at this tonight. What gives?"

Elliott rolled his eyes. "Just a continuation of the crappy day I've had."

Murphy glanced sideways at him and killed Elliott's character again.

Elliott swore. "I had a lunch date with Martin." He squeezed off a few rounds. "We ran into Sarah."

"Ouch. Of all the exes to run into." Murphy's character darted around an obstacle and killed Elliott again.

"She's hounding me on this case. It's a bitch."

"Yeah, two people killed now, right? Not just Lachlan's sister."

Elliott nodded. "And supernatural stuff involved," he said. "Fae of some kind."

"So ask Theo."

"That's a good idea. He knows that stuff." Elliott shrugged. "And I have a couple of other people I need to talk to."

Murphy glanced at him again. "So what you're really twisted up about is Martin. You've got it bad, dude." He killed Elliott again.

"Damn it! You know, you're shit at making me feel better," Elliott complained.

Murphy snorted. "You wanted that, you shoulda called Brax."

"And tell him I screwed things up with his brother-in-law?"

Murphy laughed out loud at that. "Dude, you are so fucked."

Elliott dropped his head into his hands. "You're an asshole."

"Yeah, duh." Murphy sighed and the game noises stopped. He must have paused it. After a couple seconds he kicked Elliott in the shin. "Just send him flowers and apologize for screwing up, dumbass. Whatever happened, he's a decent guy, and I can tell he likes you, so you'll work it out."

Elliott lifted his head, thinking about that. Flowers. That was actually a good idea. He'd send them to Martin's house, since he wasn't sure if the garage was open tomorrow or not. And maybe they could get things patched up enough to go to the Indy Eleven game on Saturday. "Thanks, Murph. That's a good idea."

Murphy cackled and killed Elliott again.

* * *

Chloe dragged Martin out of bed just a little before eleven Friday morning. "Get in the shower. You'll feel better," she ordered. Head throbbing, he slumped his way obediently into the bathroom. As he turned on the water, he could hear her clattering in the kitchen.

When he shuffled out to the kitchen fifteen minutes later, Braxton was sipping a cup of coffee at the kitchen table, three paper fast food bags in front of him. He gave Martin a quick once-over and winced. "I hear someone ordered a greasy breakfast," he said, and slid one of the bags across the table.

Martin collapsed into a chair and unwrapped a breakfast sandwich with egg, bacon, and cheese. His stomach did a slow roll to one side at the smell, but he knew it would help, so he forced himself to take a bite. As soon as he started, he realized how hungry he was.

"Here," Chloe said, placing a cardboard drink box in front of him. "I read something a while back that said coconut water is really good for curing hangovers."

Martin made a face at her.

"It's a scientific stupidity treatment." She smirked at him.

"Rude," Martin muttered. But he took several gulps of coconut water. It wasn't a beverage he would start drinking regularly, based on the taste, but if it eased the banging and throbbing in his head, it would be worth it.

Chloe went into the living room, where Martin could hear her talking to herself. He glanced at Braxton, but his brother-in-law was staring down into his coffee. He looked like he was thinking hard about something, so Martin just ate a second sandwich without interrupting his thoughts.

"Braxton brought all kinds of good things," Chloe said, coming back into the kitchen. She was carrying her huge yellow cat and plopped him down on Martin's lap.

Martin groaned as Whizz started purring at him. "I'm so stupid," he mumbled. "Hey, Whizz. You're such a cute kitty." He rubbed Whizz's ears and suddenly, despite the hangover, he felt like he was possibly one of the luckiest people in the world to have such a good family.

"Chloe will be happy to tease you about your apparent attachment to Whizz later," Braxton said comfortably. "But at least she doesn't kick a fellow when he's down."

Chloe snorted.

"I'm told our wedding guests are in danger," Braxton continued. He reached down beside him and pulled a huge white photo album onto the table. "I hope the breakfast and Whizz have fortified you enough to work through an entire photo album."

Martin nodded. "It was weird. A lot of my vision-dreams have started out in Kandahar and then moved somewhere else. This one just started out straight in a dark, humid forest. There were two people arguing about something, and a woman was screaming. They were hurting her, torturing her." He rubbed a hand over his face. Whizz started kneading his legs, claws poking lightly through Martin's jeans.

"Did you recognize any of them?" Braxton asked.

Martin shook his head and then regretted it as the throbbing kicked up a notch. He swallowed a whimper. "Not exactly. The two people torturing her were just shadowy. One held a golden chain that controlled the other. It was a woman who held the chain, I think. But the woman they were torturing... I don't know her name or anything, but I knew her face. I'm pretty sure she was at the wedding."

"What did she look like?"

"Brown hair, I think hazel eyes?" Martin closed his eyes, calling her face back into his memory. "She was bruised, and there was blood on her face. Her hair was long, probably at least shoulder-length." He opened his eyes and looked at Braxton. "She couldn't see, I don't think. She thought I was Elliott."

"Hmm." Braxton opened the cover of the photo album. "I can think of probably two dozen women with brown hair who were invited to the wedding."

"Pretty sure the only brown-haired woman who mattered at the wedding was your wife," Chloe said, leaning over Braxton's shoulder to grin at him.

"I'm so lucky you're not the jealous type," he remarked.

Martin made a gagging noise and they both laughed.

"All right, let's see..."

They spent the next half hour scrutinizing the photos. Martin found two photos that might have been the woman in his vision, but they were both taken from behind. Her face was turned so he could see her in profile, so it was hard to say if it was her for sure.

"She's talking to Peggy in this one," Braxton said. "And these two... I don't know their names, but I think they're all Fort Harrison Pack. I'll give Peggy a call and see what I can find out."

Martin nodded and then frowned as something else occurred to him. "The other thing...I'm starting to wonder if the killer really wants to do this. I think maybe he's being controlled by someone, and she's the one making him kill people."

"You think that's why there was a chain?" Chloe said, leaning forward.

"That, and I think he was arguing with her. Maybe it was about whether to hurt the woman?" Martin's head was starting to let up a little. "I don't know."

Braxton shifted in his seat. "Elliott said there was some kind of fight or disturbance that might be related somehow to the case."

Martin felt his cheeks get hot as he thought of how the vision had interrupted their date. Skipping the parts about making out with Elliott, he recounted the vision he'd had of shouting and anger and wailing guitars. "I think there were a couple of incidents reported that he was investigating. Maybe talking to some of those people? But they weren't his cases, so I'm not sure."

Braxton nodded.

"So Braxton's going to check with Peggy and see if we can identify Mystery Victim," Chloe said. "And in the meantime, *you* really need to tell Elliott about all this." She gave Martin a hard look.

He could only meet her gaze for a couple of seconds before he looked down at Whizz, who had gone to sleep in his lap.

Braxton cleared his throat. "Let up now, C," he said softly. Martin looked at him in surprise, and Braxton gave him a crooked smile. "We'll leave Whizz with you overnight," he said, standing up. "See you tomorrow at the game?"

Martin nodded and watched as Chloe stood and grabbed the photo album. "Thanks," he said softly. "Both of you."

Chloe leaned over and kissed him on the top of the head. "Keep hydrating. And please don't scare me like that again, m'kay?"

"Shup," Martin muttered.

He saw Chloe grinning as she followed Braxton out of the house.

CHAPTER 22

Friday afternoon Elliott was straightening his desk and starting to think about calling it a day when his phone's text notification chimed. His flowers had been delivered to Martin's house, according to the flower shop's notification. He pressed his lips together, praying they would be enough to convince Martin to give him another chance.

Before he had a chance to finish that thought, his phone started ringing.

He almost dropped it in startlement. Fumbling a little, he managed to see that it was Martin calling him. He exhaled nervously and slid the answer button.

"Hello?" he said.

"So you just ticked something off my bucket list," Martin said, his voice husky.

Elliott blinked. That wasn't the way he'd expected the conversation to start. He smiled. "What, apology flowers?"

Martin laughed. "Well, getting flowers from a romantic partner, anyway. I'd never really considered the motivation behind them."

Elliott huffed. "I'm such a dumbass," he muttered.

"No way, the flowers were definitely a smart idea," Martin said.

Elliott thought the fact that Murphy had thought of flowers before he did was what proved he was a dumbass, but he didn't feel like arguing the point. Seeing Flynn watching him, he waved at his partner. Flynn smirked and said, "Have a good weekend," before leaving.

"Listen," Martin said. "Are you busy tonight?"

Elliott's heart started thumping, even though he told himself not to get his hopes up. "Just wrapping things up at work here."

"Want to come over? I have a grill and some nice steaks and now I need someone to share them with."

Elliott chuckled. "Give me about an hour. I have to finish a couple things, and you know what traffic's like at this hour."

"Sounds good," Martin said. Elliott could hear the smile in his voice. "See you soon."

Traffic was even worse than usual, even though Elliott stuck to the surface streets to avoid the I-65/70 collector that always bottlenecked that time of day. Broad Ripple could be a nightmare when it came to evening rush, though every time Elliott went to Martin's house, he understood why Martin liked it so much.

By the time he knocked on Martin's door, his mouth was dry and his stomach was jumping with nerves. On the phone, Martin had seemed like everything was okay, but maybe he'd just decided hard conversations should be held in person.

Then again, all of Elliott's other apprehensions about this relationship had proven to not apply. Maybe he should quit shooting himself in the foot.

Martin swung the door open and stepped to one side, tilting his head in invitation. As soon as Elliott was inside, Martin shut the door behind him and then pressed Elliott against it, kissing him with great concentration. Elliott felt his knees weaken a little with relief—and possibly something more.

"Hi," Martin whispered when he pulled away. His gaze was warm on Elliott's.

"I am so sorr—" Elliott began, but Martin stopped him with another kiss.

"You're forgiven," Martin said firmly. "And I'm sorry I lost my temper. It…isn't an excuse, but this book I'm reading says people with combat trauma often have anger issues. I know I need to work on it, but I thought it would help you understand a little bit."

Elliott nodded, stunned. He hadn't even thought about Martin's PTSD manifesting like that. It made sense, though. Past trauma couldn't be controlled or changed, which would have to make the person suffering it feel powerless. Anger was a natural reaction to feeling powerless.

"So anyway, I'm sorry," Martin said.

"You're forgiven too," Elliott said. "Heh. I guess you can tell I've had a couple of relationships fall apart because of my particular sexual orientation. I wasn't straight enough for one girl, and I wasn't gay enough for one guy, so… You didn't deserve to have me doubt you, though. I just…"

He held Martin's gaze for a couple of heartbeats, trying to nerve himself to just say what he felt. When Martin's piercing blue eyes were focused on Elliott like that, it felt like the rest of the world had disappeared.

Elliott sucked in a breath. "Martin, I like you so much," he blurted. "It scares me. I guess I keep waiting to find out what's wrong with you." He laughed in embarrassment.

"What—" Martin's eyes widened. "Shit, what *isn't* wrong with me?" he said. "I lose my temper, I'm introverted and distant, I drink too much—"

"*Not* the point I was trying to make," Elliott said, smiling crookedly at him.

Martin cleared his throat, glanced away, and then met Elliott's gaze again. "Um. I like you an awful lot, too." He grinned, though it looked a little uncertain to Elliott. "And I know what you mean about being scared." He took a deep breath. "I...I think I probably need to get back into some sort of therapy. I just..." He shook his head. "I just figured it out last night—Chloe helped me figure it out—that a lot of my fear is because of losing my friends in the war after we'd already lost our folks." He gulped so loud Elliott could hear it.

Elliott's heart was thudding in his chest and his stomach churning. Why was it so difficult to be honest like this, even with someone he liked and respected as much as he did Martin? He licked his lips.

"I'm terrified," Martin whispered. "I'm terrified of losing the people I have left. I've spent the last couple of years keeping people at a distance. Even my sister, to an extent."

Elliott was still leaning against the door. He slid a hand down to rest on Martin's hip, wishing he could offer more comfort. What were the magic words that could put Martin at ease?

"Thing is, maybe it took all of this," Martin said, looking away, "meeting you, taking a closer look at my dreams, at my PTSD, falling for you, having to—"

"Falling for me?" Elliott interrupted.

Martin looked sideways at him. "Duh."

Elliott grinned and pulled Martin in for another kiss. Martin relaxed into it for a few seconds, but then pulled away, shaking his head.

"Okay, but I'm not done," he said. "It took all that to make me realize how much I need to change about my life. I have a lot of broken places that need me to work on healing them."

Elliott smiled at him, watching Martin from half-lidded eyes. "Just for the record, I'm crazy about you, too, and I promise, I'm not going anywhere." He lifted a hand to touch Martin's cheek. "You deserve more than you've been allowing yourself to have."

Martin's lips twitched. "Thanks," he whispered. Elliott realized that, above the sound of his own pulse in his ears, he could hear Martin's heart racing. When Elliott lowered his hand to take Martin's, he could feel it tremble in his.

"Thank you for trusting me with all this," Elliott said. "I know it can't be easy."

Martin sighed and leaned against Elliott, pressing his forehead to Elliott's neck. "I decided if I wanted this to work, I had to be honest with you," he muttered.

Elliott closed his eyes, relishing that contact. He wrapped an arm around Martin's waist, holding him closer. After a while he heard Martin's pulse slowing and felt his breath deepening. Good. He was starting to feel more relaxed. Elliott hadn't liked being responsible for Martin's discomfort.

"I guess it's my turn to be honest," he murmured. Martin tensed a little, but Elliott lifted his free hand and stroked it through Martin's hair, gratified to feel Martin relax against him again. "I don't trust romance very easily. I don't mean I'm jealous, I just...I guess I always expect things to go wrong. I've done a spectacularly bad job of picking people to get involved with in the past. And if something seemed to be going too well, I sort of self-sabotaged." He sighed. "I'd pull back, start...over-scrutinizing things. Find reasons to end the relationship before my partner ended it first."

He could feel Martin tensing again. Elliott turned his head and kissed Martin's temple. "I'm telling you that so you'll call me on it if you see me at it," he said, and pulled back enough to meet Martin's gaze. "Because I want us to work out."

Martin beamed at him. He didn't smile easily, but that smile, when it did come, was enough to knock Elliott breathless.

Over dinner, Martin filled Elliott in on his latest vision and the theory that the next victim would be one of Peggy's werewolves. Elliott found he was relieved that Braxton was taking care of that. He had enough other leads to chase down, and since Martin's visions weren't an official part of the investigation, it might be better for Elliott to not follow them up personally.

"Something interesting I learned this afternoon," he said, setting his fork down. "Lachlan Shaw was doing a concert at the American Legion when that fight broke out. Jo Parrish's band was supposed to play that night, but…well, we know what happened there."

Martin narrowed his eyes. "So that's a direct connection between Lachlan and Parrish," he said. "Not to mention…well, Chloe's always saying how often it's a family member or friend who kills a person."

"It pisses me off," Elliott confessed. "I was the one who told Lachlan Shaw about his sister. He didn't smell like the killer. He smelled of grief and shock. I would have sworn he wasn't guilty."

Martin hummed, tapping his fingers against his jaw. "Wouldn't that make sense if my latest vision is right? If he's being controlled, he *isn't* really guilty."

Elliott opened his mouth and just barely bit back the statement that Martin hadn't planted the IED but still felt guilty about his friends who were killed. Instead he shook his head. "There would still be *feelings* of guilt. No matter whose idea it is, even if Lachlan is essentially the sword being wielded, instead of the mastermind…it's still his power that's killing." He sighed. "Maybe. If it *is* Lachlan."

Martin nodded. "Maybe…Look how long it took me to realize my dreams weren't just normal PTSD dreams. I didn't realize they were visions. It took me telling you about them and you deciding I was psychic for me to even believe that."

Elliott considered that. If Lachlan hadn't known he was responsible, there wouldn't have been any guilt. And clearly he had loved his sister; the grief had been genuine. It was a decent theory, and it made more sense than he liked.

"I liked Lachlan Shaw," he muttered, and sighed.

"Ann Rule liked Ted Bundy, too," Martin said.

Elliott blinked at him.

Martin shrugged. "I read true crime. In *The Stranger Beside Me*, she writes about working with Bundy and how likable she found him."

"Are you suggesting Lachlan Shaw really *is* a serial killer?"

"Well…" Martin drummed his fingers on the table. "Are there other unsolved murders in the last couple of years? Maybe his powers were just starting to manifest. Maybe bad things happened to other people with a connection to him before Ainsley's death."

Elliott narrowed his eyes. He would have to go in to the office tomorrow and run a few searches. Just because he disliked the idea of Lachlan Shaw being the killer didn't mean it wasn't possible. He would have to pursue it, especially since Martin had suggested it.

"I'm going to talk to Lachlan Shaw tomorrow," Elliott decided.

Martin tilted his head. "Before the game? Because…Braxton and Chloe are going. I thought maybe we could—"

Elliott beamed at him. "Of course. I'll swing back by here and pick you up after I've had a talk with Lachlan Shaw."

* * *

Elliott wasn't able to locate Lachlan Shaw Saturday morning. The man wasn't at his apartment, his parents' home, or his work. Frustrated, Elliott put the word out at work that he wanted to talk to Shaw, but he wasn't willing to spook Lachlan by having someone watch his place.

He spent a couple more hours tracking down witnesses from the fight at the American Legion before knocking off work in time to change his clothes and pick Martin up at his house.

They got to the IUPUI campus just before seven, giving them half an hour before kickoff.

The Michael A. Carroll Stadium, informally known as The Mike, was full of people. Elliott had heard the announcer say there were nine thousand and some people here tonight, which filled him with satisfaction entirely apart from the fact that he was here with a guy who clearly loved the Eleven as much as he did.

"Let's hope they can repeat their victory from last week," Martin said, grinning at Elliott as they waited in line for concessions. The Eleven had played in

Edmonton the week before and beat them one to two. This week FC Edmonton had traveled to Indy, so hopefully the Eleven would press their home pitch advantage.

"I hope so," Elliott said. The spring season for the Eleven had been disappointing; the Eleven had finished eighth in the North American Soccer League standings. It had been a crushing disappointment after the success of the 2016 season, when the Eleven had gone to the finals and ended up second in the league after an overtime loss. Added to the Eleven being passed over for the Major League Soccer expansion that spring, it made for a disheartening fall season.

"I keep forgetting to ask you who your favorite player is," Martin said as they inched forward.

"Kléberson," Elliott answered promptly. "Man's got skills."

Martin tilted his head. "True. But Don Smart's good, too." He grinned. "I'm a Smart fan myself. Well, and Éamon Zayed, because, hello, hottie."

Elliott laughed. "Okay, if we're going on looks alone," he agreed. "Though Zayed's definitely a strong footballer." He shrugged. "I dunno, I just have a weakness for Kléberson."

"That's valid," Martin said. He finally reached the front of the line and ordered a hot dog and a Battalion Pale Ale. Then he glanced over at Elliott. "And whatever he wants," he added.

Elliott slanted a look at Martin, then ordered the same thing. The Battalion Pale Ale was a new brew done by Lafayette's People's Brewing Company and named in honor of the Brickyard Battalion—the Eleven fan club Elliott was a member of. Elliott hadn't expected Martin to pay for his food, though; he wondered if they should have a talk about who paid for dates. Maybe alternating? It had been a couple of years since Elliott had dated anyone long enough for that to be an issue. Maybe Martin would have an opinion.

Before he could bring up the topic, Martin grinned at him and headed for their seats. Elliott had traded tickets with a friend so he and Martin could sit with Braxton and Chloe near center field instead of with the Brickyard Battalion. It would probably be a good spot for Elliott and Martin, but Braxton wasn't a loud, obnoxious fan, so Elliott could understand why Braxton had selected the seats he had.

Chloe and Braxton were sharing a bag of popcorn. Chloe raised her eyebrows at Elliott and threw a piece at him. Elliott ducked, trying to catch it in his mouth, and failed miserably, but it got a laugh from the others. He left the space next to Chloe for Martin.

"How are things going?" he asked.

"Better now," Chloe said. Martin grunted; Chloe must have nudged him.

"Good," Braxton said. "Peggy hasn't called me back, though. I'm still waiting to hear if she can tell me who our mystery woman is."

Elliott nodded. "D'you know what the Fort Harrison folks do for day fulls?"

The moon would be full at two-twelve Monday afternoon. The Eagle Creek Pack generally hunkered down at their homes, since wolves running around in the middle of the day were likely to be spotted. But maybe Peggy's pack did things differently.

"Not sure."

"Okay, you can't do anything about it until you hear back from Peggy," Chloe said. "So enough with the shop talk. You'll make Martin feel left out."

Martin snorted. "Hey, pot? Meet kettle."

"Ooh, buuuurn," Elliott teased. "All right, Cole, what do *you* want to talk about?"

Chloe tilted her head, shooting him a mischievous look. "Did Martin tell you he borrowed my cat the other night? He actually called me and asked me to bring Whizz over for a visit. I'm pretty sure he's got a visit to the animal shelter on his to-do list."

Martin was glaring at his sister, but it didn't have any heat. He ducked his head, cheeks reddening. Gingers were so charming, Elliott thought, and grinned.

"So you're going to have a cat next time I come over, huh?"

Martin sighed. "Maybe. I didn't realize I wanted a cat until Chloe made me provide shelter for hers."

"Excuse me? My house burned down. It isn't like I had a choice."

"Ouch. And here I thought you liked me." He nudged her. "Anyway, I thought maybe I'd go to the shelter and see about adopting one. An older cat, not a kitten. Kittens are cute, but so much work."

"But *so* cute," Elliott said.

As the game got started, they continued debating the merits of kittens versus older cats, and Braxton voted for older cat while Chloe joined Elliott in advocating for a kitten. Elliott had a feeling she was just trying to be obnoxious, but it was entertaining.

At half-time the score was still tied at zero. The second half was just getting started again when Elliott's cell phone rang.

"Hey," his partner said. "I'm really sorry, but…we got a body."

"We're not on call this weekend," Elliott said, shooting an apologetic glance at Martin. He walked away from their seats to find a place he could talk without annoying people.

"Well, McGuire and Voss are working a shooting on the northwest side, and they're going to be there for a while," Brady said. "McGuire called and asked if we could take this one. I don't think it's related to the Shaw case, but—"

Elliott sighed. "Fine. Let me make some arrangements here. Where am I meeting you?"

"I'll text you the address," Brady said. "Thanks, Blake."

"You and McGuire are both gonna owe me, Flynn," Elliott retorted.

When he hung up, he looked around and saw that Martin had followed him.

"Sounds like you have to go," Martin said, his gaze on Elliott's.

"I'm so sorry," Elliott said automatically. "We aren't on call, but my partner's really keen. He told a couple of the other detectives we would give them a hand."

"No worries," Martin said. "This is what you do. I already knew it wasn't exactly a nine-to-five job." He started walking back towards the gate they'd come in. After a moment he glanced back at Elliott. "You coming?"

Elliott hurried to catch up. "You don't have to leave because of me," he protested. "Stay and enjoy the game. That way I won't feel like I totally missed out." He'd dated so many people who weren't okay with the demands of his job. It felt weird for Martin to just accept this without complaint.

"I can at least walk you out," Martin said. "Just be careful out there." He made a face. "As careful as possible, anyway."

Elliott couldn't help smiling at the understanding Martin was showing. "I'll be careful," he promised. "Go enjoy the rest of the game."

Martin paused before they got to the gate. "Hey, Ell. Come by my place whenever you're done tonight." He smiled at Elliott. "Seriously. Even if you just need to crash as soon as you get there, that's fine. Let me see you, okay?"

Elliott's stomach flipped pleasantly. He smiled back at Martin. "Okay," he promised. He held Martin's gaze for a couple of moments before heading out to his car.

He was just about to climb into the driver's seat when his phone chimed. It was a text from Braxton. *Martin's a keeper, in case you didn't know.*

Elliott couldn't fight the smile that spread across his face. *Duh,* he texted back.

There was no way he would do anything to ruin his chances with Martin Cole, as long as he could help it.

CHAPTER 23

After lunch on Monday, Lachlan was sitting in his living room, fine-tuning a song he'd been tinkering with, when someone knocked on his door. Guitar strapped to him, he went over and opened the door. As soon as he saw Eris, he tried to slam the door again. She freaked him out.

He wasn't fast enough.

Eris thrust her arm out and the door burst inward, bouncing against his elbow and making him stumble back against the kitchen counter. He clutched his guitar closer to protect it.

"You are making music without a focus," she said, her voice cold. She shut the door behind her and, he noticed with a chill, locked the deadbolt.

She was going to kill him. Lachlan stared at her, eyes wide.

"Why would you make music without a focus for your power?" she said. She studied him through narrowed eyes. Her light red hair was swept up in a bun. It made her look like a librarian or a schoolteacher.

A damned dangerous librarian, he thought.

"Answer me!" she snapped, and Lachlan jerked as he felt a blaze of command burn through him.

"I was just trying to write a song," he said. "Just get the words and music right. I can focus it later."

"You should have a focus in mind when you are composing it," Eris said. "It will enable you to put more of your power into the song."

"Look, I don't *want* to kill anyone," he said. "I'm all about some of the other stuff; it's awesome making people cry when I sing the lament, and making people fall in love would be cool. But I don't like people ending up dead. I *loved* Ainsley."

Eris smirked at him. "And yet, some part of you obviously hated her as well," she pointed out. "If you hadn't felt that way, she would not be dead."

Lachlan's throat tightened and the spaghetti he'd eaten for lunch threatened to come back up. "That's not true."

"You know it is, *fir chaointe*." Eris leaned in so her face was very close to Lachlan's. "You killed her, and you killed your rival musician. And now you will kill for me."

Her words were soft, slipping into his ears with a seductive sweetness. As they did, he felt something golden and slimy trickle down his windpipe and into his lungs, spreading like smoke inside him. Lachlan jerked and clutched at his chest, staring at her.

"What did you—" he choked out.

Eris' laugh shimmered like bells. "A compulsion, *fir chaointe*. You squander your power, so I shall have it for myself."

He coughed, wanting the stuff out of him, but even as he did, he realized it must not be a physical thing that had invaded him.

"Go sit," Eris said.

Lachlan's legs twitched. He tensed his muscles, trying to refuse to move. Cramps seized his thighs, making him drop into a half crouch.

"Go. Sit." Eris enunciated the words more clearly, and Lachlan had no choice.

He marched into the living room and sat in his computer chair. As soon as he was sitting, the cramps eased. "You're a bitch," he told her.

Eris laughed again. "You will sing now," she said, placing a photograph of a brunette woman in front of him. "Sing of her beauty and replace it with pain."

"I won't—" Lachlan began, and bit his tongue viciously as it tried to begin singing. He swore at the pain and the coppery taste of blood.

"You will sing eventually. Why must you fight me? This doesn't have to hurt."

"Screw you," Lachlan wheezed. He wished he hadn't answered the door. He wished Kaida were here to distract him from doing what Eris demanded. She'd managed to stop him somehow last weekend. He hadn't heard from her since, except for a text to let him know she was all right and thank him for protecting her.

Kaida, I need your help, he thought.

He wondered suddenly if he could sing something that would let her know he needed her. He had thought his power would only work on people who were listening to him, but maybe now that he knew about his power, he could use it even at a distance.

Come to think of it, was that what Eris had planned for him? The woman in the photo definitely wasn't anywhere in his apartment.

Cramps struck his stomach, doubling him over. He gagged at the pain.

"Stop fighting me, Lachlan Shaw, and sing," Eris whispered. When she said his name, something hooked under his skin and tugged.

Lachlan sang.

As he sang of heartbreak, loss, and injury, the guilt that always lived in his stomach, gnawing at him, lessened. The cramps faded. His grief over Ainsley's death began to retreat—never gone entirely, but he suddenly felt as if he had just relaxed into a warm, soft bed after a long day of hard work.

His voice soared. He closed his eyes, concentrating on what he sang, and as he did, he formed a picture of that woman in his mind. He could almost feel her as the pain struck her. He imagined that he heard her cry of pain echoed in his words. He flinched, his eyes flying open.

"There!" Eris pounced. "What was that?"

"I..." Lachlan coughed. His throat hurt.

"Answer!" Those golden hooks tugged inside him.

"I think I hurt her. I think she screamed." He glared at her, the guilt seeping back in. This woman had never done anything to him. Why should he hurt her? "Why are you doing this?" he demanded.

"We are testing your power against supernatural entities. Until now, your victims have all been mortal."

Mortal. Did that mean he *wasn't* mortal now? Lachlan frowned. "But what about Ainsley? If I'm magical, wouldn't she be, too?"

Eris shrugged delicately. "Never having heard her sing, I don't know. Alas, we will never know." Her lips curved in a cruel smile. "But I intend to use you to crush my enemies, and they are not mortal."

"Lady, you are psycho." Lachlan tried to stand up. He wanted her out of here.

"Sing again," Eris ordered. "Burn her eyes out."

Lachlan clenched his teeth closed, glaring at Eris. This wasn't right. He didn't want to blind or torture someone. He didn't want to serve Eris. At the moment, he wasn't even sure if he wanted to keep singing. Maybe he should give up music entirely, if this was how it was used.

"*Sing.*" He felt Eris pour power into the word, and the power forced his mouth open.

He sighed and fingered the guitar strings. As soon as he did, he felt that warm comfort wrapping around him again. He had no idea what song would burn someone's eyes out, so he picked out a few bars before settling into "Three Blind Mice." It seemed stupid, but the 'song' he'd used to accidentally kill Jo Parrish had been equally stupid, and that hadn't stopped it from working.

The music usually gave him energy, revved him up. But as he sang the nursery rhyme a second time, Lachlan felt as if he'd turned on a tap—the power was pouring out of him, and he wasn't sure how to stop it. Was that because of that golden power Eris had used? Had she latched her power onto his somehow?

Wetness hit his cheeks as he listened to the woman's screams inside his head. He was crying. His fingers stumbled on the strings and he faltered. The power ceased its flow. Lachlan slumped in his seat, panting and looking up at Eris.

He hated her.

She arched an eyebrow. "Now what?"

"I…" He coughed and licked his lips. "I think she can't see. I felt the power going out of me, and I could hear her scream."

Eris huffed. "I should have arranged to observe her in person. Relying on your dubious senses isn't enough."

"Why do you hate her so much?" he rasped. His throat felt like it was on fire.

"Hate her? I don't hate her. She doesn't matter. She was just convenient. She crossed my path yesterday while I was looking for a suitable test subject."

Lachlan narrowed his eyes. "You're sick."

Eris shrugged. "I will have to find her now to see if your work lasts through her change. They often heal as they shift back to their human forms."

"They?" he asked, curious despite himself.

"Werewolves."

"Were—wait, they're real?" Lachlan's voice broke and he began coughing. Why had this been so much worse than usual? Why did he feel so tired?

"Anything you can dream of is real," Eris replied. She began pacing slowly.

"So why do you hate werewolves enough to kill them?" He wanted to drink something hot and go to bed, even though it was barely two in the afternoon.

She whirled on him, thrusting her hand in his face. "Time and again the packs here have thwarted me. The last time, they stole *this* from me." Her voice was a hiss. "I can never regain that hand or the power it bled from me, but I can and will destroy them."

Cringing, Lachlan stared at her hand. It was the one he'd noticed was a little odd-looking. Waved in his face, it became obvious the hand was a prosthetic. Had a werewolf bitten her hand off? Did that mean she was a werewolf, too? Or had she been protected because she was already obviously something magical—or monstrous?

"You may rest now." Eris straightened and turned her back on him. "But you may not harm me, and you will not attempt to remove my compulsion. You are mine now, *fir chaointe*. You will fare better if you accept that."

She walked out of the apartment without another glance at him.

CHAPTER 24

Elliott's phone rang at noon the day after the full moon.

Braxton's voice was tight. "Ell. We have a situation. You know where Peggy lives?"

"Noblesville somewhere. What's up?" Elliott shoved his chair back from the table, where he'd been looking over crime scene photos from Jo Parrish's house.

"You know Martin's vision? One of Peggy's werewolves was attacked just before the full."

Elliott stood so fast the chair fell over. "Shit! Who'd he kill?"

"She isn't dead. But we need to get to Peggy's *now*. I'm on my way to pick up Martin. Can you meet us at Peggy's?"

"Yeah. Text me the address. I'll leave now."

Elliott's thoughts whirled as he slapped the beacon light on his dash and pulled into traffic. The werewolf—whose name he still hadn't gotten—was it Peggy? The werewolf wasn't dead. For that matter, evisceration probably wouldn't kill a werewolf, unless it were done with silver instruments. But it would hurt like hell, and while a werewolf's faster metabolism was a blessing in many ways, it would still take a long time to heal something like that.

She wasn't dead. But she might be wishing she were.

He wondered if the werewolf was a veteran. Had Sarah been onto something when she suggested the killer was targeting vets? A surge of nausea hit his stomach—that could mean Martin was in danger. Elliott shouldn't be involving him any more.

"Don't jump to conclusions," he told himself. "Talk to Peggy first."

Allisonville Road angled northeast from Indianapolis along the east side of the White River. He hadn't even passed Conner Prairie—a living history museum complex about eight miles northeast of Indy—when a text came through. With a couple of taps to his car's touchscreen, he had the navigation programmed. He was only halfway to Noblesville. Peggy's house was in a neighborhood on the west side of town, which meant staying on Allisonville until it turned into Noblesville's Tenth Street. Route firmly in mind, he concentrated on navigating the traffic— despite the beacon, there were always a few inattentive drivers who didn't pull over fast enough. Elliott rarely wished he drove a car with an actual lightbar, but there were times it would come in handy.

Fifteen minutes later, he pulled up in front of a two-story house with gray siding and blue shutters. Two cars were already parked in the driveway, so he parked on the road in front. Almost before he'd climbed out of the car, Braxton's car pulled up behind him.

"You made good time," Elliott said.

"Chloe had better never complain about *my* driving again," Martin said, giving Braxton a wide-eyed look.

Before they had time to say anything else, the front door of the house flew open. "Get in here," snapped a tall woman with pink-streaked black hair. "Now."

It hadn't been Peggy who was attacked, then, Elliott thought with relief. It was hardest on a pack if their leader were hurt or killed. Any death was hard, of course, but the leader kept everyone together, acted almost as a parental figure to the pack, just as the alphas of a wild wolf pack were the literal parents of the rest of the pack.

The front door was barely shut behind them when Peggy whirled on them. "You know what would be awesome? If people would have the decency to *tell folks* when they're starting a supernatural war!"

Peggy was in Braxton's face. Braxton winced. He had to look up a little to meet her eyes. "As soon as we knew your pack might be targeted, I tried to let you know. I left you two voice mails and texted."

"You could have been more explicit." Peggy had been the leader of the Fort Harrison Pack for at least fifteen years, despite her relative youth. She was good at it.

"It took us time to figure out what might be coming," Braxton said. "Martin's been having visions, but he's pretty new with this, and it doesn't help that unless he has a vision of someone he already knows, he has to find a way to figure out who the person is. We spent an hour going through photos of the wedding to figure out who it was." He frowned. "I'm still not sure, in fact. I don't know all of your pack members, but I thought—"

"Cindy is blind right now," Peggy said. "*Blind.*"

Elliott, standing next to Martin, felt him flinch. Elliott's temper flared. "Don't blame Martin! He's done everything possible to help! He's still learning about all this."

Peggy's furious expression faded into apology. "Oh, hey, no," she said, turning to look at Martin. "I'm sorry if you thought I meant that." She frowned. "You're Chloe's brother, right?"

Martin nodded. "I really am sorry I didn't—"

Peggy held up a hand, cutting him off. "I'm not pissed at you, Martin. I'm pissed at the freaking *homicide detective* who didn't tell us he was working a supernatural murder case."

"I told my alpha!" Elliott protested.

Peggy snorted. "Your what now? Braxton, is there something you're not telling us? You and Chloe already breeding?"

Braxton rolled his eyes. "Shut up," he muttered, and the other two werewolves snickered.

"How can you *laugh* at a time like this?" Martin burst out. "One of your pack was blinded and I couldn't stop it and you're joking around?"

Peggy hugged him. Elliott was close enough that he sensed Martin stiffen at that. Peggy pulled back, keeping one hand on Martin's shoulder. "We're joking because it's better than crying," she said, her voice gentle. "We do know how serious this is, and we are *seriously* going to have a come-to-Jesus meeting in a minute, but we can't do much to help Cindy. We'll just have to wait and see if her eyes heal."

She let go of Martin when he nodded. She looked at each of them in turn, and then finally said, "Why don't we sit down. I have a pot of tea and some pop in the fridge if you need a drink. I want to make sure we're all on the same page, and I want us to have a strategy going forward."

Braxton sighed. "It isn't that the killer has been targeting supernaturals," he said. "It's a supernatural killer. Elliott looped me in as a courtesy, but he didn't have any reason to think it would affect either pack."

"Who's dead, then?" Peggy said, leading the way to the kitchen.

"Ainsley Shaw and Jonathan Parrish," Elliott said. "As far as we know, it's just those two."

Peggy whistled. "*Just* those two? The two the press is starting to hint might be victims of a serial killer targeting veterans?"

Martin flinched. Braxton must have seen it, because he rested a hand on Martin's shoulder briefly as they sat at the table. Elliott was too pissed off to comfort anyone.

"Sarah!" he snarled. After everything he'd done to downplay the connections and the serial killer idea, she'd run with it anyway. Damn it. She didn't know everything. She couldn't. She'd never known anything about the supernatural. And a good thing, considering how she felt the public deserved to know every damn thing that happened.

Braxton groaned.

"I swear, I don't believe this is a serial killer," Elliott said. "I'm starting to like Ainsley's brother for it. He knew Parrish. But he was also genuinely shocked and grieved when I told him his sister was dead. It threw us off—threw *me* off."

Peggy sighed. "All right. I want to hear everything, but first—Cindy's asked to see you. She said she thought you were trying to help her somehow, when she was attacked."

"Not me," Elliott said. "I think she sensed Martin."

"In my vision, she couldn't see me," Martin explained. "She called me Elliott, though."

Peggy darted a speculative look between them and nodded. "Martin, then. You'd better come talk to her. It'll do you good to see her condition, too."

Elliott buried his face in his hand as Martin followed Peggy out of the kitchen. He hoped Martin was ready for their relationship to be public, because Peggy had figured it out.

* * *

Peggy led Martin back to a hallway in the back of the house. She stopped at a closed door and turned to look at Martin.

"This isn't your fault, Martin," she said, studying his face. "You're not the person doing this."

He couldn't hold her gaze. He looked away, his throat tight. "I'm not the person stopping it, either," he managed. He hadn't been able to save Dax. He hadn't been able to save Ainsley or Parrish. He hadn't even been able to protect this latest victim. She had probably survived, Braxton said, because she was a werewolf.

A hand settled gently on his shoulder and lingered just long enough to get him to look at her.

"You're still doing something. That's what matters. You're not throwing this—" She made a face. "I won't call it a gift, because I know sometimes it feels more like a burden than a gift. But you're not throwing this talent away. You're trying to understand it and use it to make a difference. That's important."

Martin huffed a strangled noise. He meant it to be a laugh but was afraid it came out more like a sob. "Don't take it out on Elliott, either. He's doing his best, too."

Peggy tilted her head. "He needs to work on communication." She sighed. "This is Cindy. She's as drugged as we can get her—our pack doctor still hasn't found painkillers that are truly effective, and we're too worried about side effects to let her drink herself painless."

The noise Martin made that time was definitely more like a sob. "That doesn't work anyway," he said. "It just delays the pain."

Peggy gave him a sympathetic look. "Spoken like a man who's learned that the hard way."

He hitched a shoulder, and that was apparently answer enough, because Peggy turned away and tapped on the door, pushing it open as she did so.

"Cin? Got someone here to see you."

The room was dim, lit only by the sun coming in around mostly-lowered blinds. A slender form lay on the bed. Peggy nudged Martin inside and then closed the door behind him.

It had startled him when she hugged him, and then she kept touching him. It was weird. But after a while he remembered that Braxton and Elliott had both remarked on how tactile werewolves were. That thought made him reach out as he knelt next to the bed. He rested his fingers gently on the woman's wrist.

"Hi," he said quietly.

He heard her take a deep breath. "You're not Elliott." Her voice was rough, like her throat hurt. Martin's stomach twisted as he realized she'd probably been screaming.

"No, I—" He broke off and glanced back at the door to make sure it was closed. "I'm his boyfriend. My name's Martin."

She breathed a laugh. "That explains it. You have his scent on you." She sighed. "Was it you during the—attack?"

"I'm sorry we couldn't protect you," Martin said.

Her other hand closed around his. "You tried to."

"Not good enough."

She snorted. "I'm not dead. Also, I'm a werewolf. Usually people need protecting from us."

Martin couldn't help smiling. "Nice try. My sister married one and I'm dating one. I know better."

"We met before, didn't we?" she said. She tugged his arm to her face and pressed her nose against the inside of his elbow. "Yes, now I know your scent. Braxton Wolfe's wedding. You were the best man."

"I'm Chloe's brother," he said, impressed. "Can you all remember every scent?"

"I can recognize a scent. But I need context to properly place it. I already knew that you're close with Elliott, so I was associating your scent with the Eagle Creek Pack." She swallowed. "Martin, I think I know some stuff that can help you."

"Help me?" For a moment he thought she meant she could help with his visions. But that didn't make any sense.

"Catch them."

"Them." Martin sucked in a breath. "There are two of them?" Had his theory been correct? Was he right about the woman controlling the killer?

"A man and a woman." Cindy shifted her weight, turning more to face him, even though she couldn't see him. "He's young. A singer. His power is his music."

Martin nodded. "Lachlan," he whispered. So they had been right about that. It would make Elliott angry at himself.

"And her," she said. "He's terrified of her. She controls him, has a spell or compulsion or something on him."

"So he didn't want to hurt you?"

"He did it, didn't he?" Cindy's lips twisted in a bitter smile. "He wasn't willing, but he still did it. I could feel his unhappiness, but no matter how much he hated it, he did this to me. He isn't innocent."

"No," Martin agreed. "What can you tell me about her? Or—wait. Will you tell Elliott instead? He's the one who can do something official about this."

"Go get him. I'll tell you both." She shifted again and hissed. "And I don't care what Peggy says, bring me a bottle of whiskey. I can deal with the pain in my eyes. It's the way my ribs feel like they've been torn open that's killing me."

"No promises on the latter, but I'll go get Elliott," Martin said.

As it turned out, Elliott was waiting at the end of the hallway for Martin to signal him. He had a bottle of Jack Daniels in his hand.

"How you doin', girl?" he asked softly as he settled on the edge of Cindy's bed.

She croaked a laugh. "I've seen better days," she said.

To Martin's surprise, Elliott groaned. "Bad," he said. That made her laugh again, and then Martin felt stupid for not catching the pun sooner.

"So tell us what happened," Elliott said.

As Cindy described the attack, she had to pause several times to catch her breath. Martin curled his fingers lightly around hers, not sure if she would take comfort from someone she didn't know. She squeezed his fingers so hard it hurt and started talking again. After that, she didn't let him go.

"I didn't see her, exactly. I saw her filtered through his magic. It was—I don't even know how to describe it." Her voice crackled as she spoke. "She had hungry eyes and smelled like old blood. Her hair was red. And—" Cindy paused, panting. "And she only had one hand."

Martin felt Elliott go still next to him. Still squeezing Cindy's hand, he looked up at Elliott, who was staring blankly at the wall.

"Ell?" He placed his other hand on Elliott's knee, but Elliott didn't even acknowledge it.

Finally Elliott closed his eyes. "Teresia," he whispered. "It's the blood mage we fought last year."

* * *

When Elliott left the back bedroom of Peggy's house, clutching Martin's hand, his mind was racing.

"Do you know what this means?" he whispered to Martin as they walked back towards the kitchen. "This means your vision about Murphy—it wasn't wrong, Martin. It couldn't have been. Teresia—Eris—whatever her name is, she's got more reason to hate Murphy than any of the rest of us. She helped Marcineau turn Murphy against his will. Murphy's the one who bit off her hand last fall."

Martin stopped walking, tugging Elliott to a stop. Elliott looked at him, surprised, but Martin wrapped his arms around Elliott, hugging him tightly. With a shaky sigh, Elliott let himself relax completely into that embrace.

"We'll find her," Martin murmured. "Now we know she's directing this. We know there's a singer—probably Lachlan—involved. We'll find her and we'll stop her."

Elliott looped an arm around Martin's waist, pressing his face to Martin's shoulder. "I can't do this without you," he admitted. Just the thought of going up against Eris again made his knees feel shaky. She used ancient blood magic, and her motivations were entirely opaque to him. Last fall she had killed one pack member and half-killed Elliott and Maura. If it hadn't been for Murphy biting off the hand she was using to cast her spells, Elliott might not have survived.

"I know she hurt you pretty badly." Martin's fingers stroked his hair. "I knew a lot less about werewolves then. Now, knowing you were still limping around three days later... She scares me, Ell. But we'll take her down together."

Elliott allowed himself a couple more moments of comfort, then took a deep breath and straightened up. "Okay," he said, meeting Martin's gaze. "Okay. Let's go tell the packs."

CHAPTER 25

The day after the full moon, Kaida finally responded to the panicked texts Lachlan had sent her after Eris left his apartment. Her first text wasn't encouraging: *What do you want?*

Lachlan had helped her after the concert at Military Park. Why was she so unhappy with him now? *Just to talk. Please.*

That lady scared me. I don't want to come to your apartment. What if she's still hunting me? Kaida texted back.

I will meet you anywhere. Some part of him couldn't believe he was turning to a woman he barely knew for help. Then again, she had loved Ainsley. She'd wanted to spend the rest of her life with Ainsley. That wouldn't happen now—thanks to Lachlan, though she didn't know that—but couldn't she scrape up a little sympathy for Ainsley's little brother?

For a long time the only response was the set of dots that indicated she was typing. He didn't know how many answers she deleted, but finally he got, *Holliday Park Ruins. 3 pm.*

Thank you, he answered. He grabbed his acoustic guitar—he was afraid to go anywhere without an instrument now—and headed out. It was just after noon, but he would rather be early than miss her.

He couldn't stop thinking about that woman, whoever she was, that had screamed and screamed while he sang her blind. How could he find out what had happened to her? Would she be all right? She was a werewolf, and Eris had seemed to think she would heal. But how could he find out about that?

He spent an hour haunting the Ruins, taking selfies with his guitar that he could post on social media. One part of him couldn't believe he was still thinking of his singing career at a time like this—but he kept taking the selfies. The Ruins were three limestone figures said to represent the white, Asian, and African races working together. Lachlan had never been to see them before, and now he almost wished Kaida hadn't chosen this spot to meet. He got the sense that if he sang for them, they might stand on their columns and dance.

Instead of playing any particular song, he found an out-of-the-way spot to sit and noodle around on his guitar. It always made him feel better when he lost himself in his music. It didn't work as well this time, when his throat still felt raw from the day before, and now that he knew the power he wielded. He stuck to major keys, trying to make people feel happy and maybe a little nostalgic without being peppy or energetic. He didn't want to give the stone figures ideas.

And look how much his life had changed in the past month, that he could even consider that.

One of his guitar strings broke, snapping his fingers painfully. Swearing, Lachlan looked up to see Kaida approaching across the grass. She was dressed in business casual and wore a somber expression. When she saw him watching her, she stopped walking, one foot still raised.

After a moment she put it down and turned her head to look around. Lachlan looked around too, trying to see what she saw. Screaming children played in the fountain under the watchful eyes of mothers and limestone figures. Groups of people walked along the paths around the park. Traffic noise came from Spring Mill Road.

He saw her shoulders move, in a sigh maybe, and then she started walking again.

She came up alongside him and stopped walking at least ten feet away.

"Kaida," Lachlan began, and she bared her teeth at him. It was so startling he didn't finish.

"What are you?" she demanded.

Lachlan's heart started racing. He'd known that somehow Kaida must have realized what was happening. He'd known it intellectually, at least. He hadn't quite realized how threatening a short, pixie-haired woman could be, on an emotional level.

He licked his lips and finally said, "She calls me *fir chaointe*. It...it kind of means banshee, except a boy."

Kaida sighed. "Siren." She looked sidelong at him. "I could feel what you were doing with that song. Lachlan, that was *wrong*."

"That why you decided to jump in with an impromptu duet?" he asked. He wanted to hunch his shoulders in and cower at her. He wasn't sure what made him feel that way, especially since he could sing her into liking him—maybe. But he didn't want to use his magic on her. He didn't want to use his magic on anyone.

He was a musician. He didn't want any magic but the power of music itself.

Kaida shrugged and edged a couple of steps closer. "I'm a trickster. So I tricked your magic. Besides, I loved Ainsley. I knew she would have stopped you doing that, if she was there. So I did it instead."

Lachlan sighed, looking down. "Ainsley *couldn't* stop me," he told Kaida.

Silence stretched between them. It took several moments for him to work up the courage to look back at her. When he did, he saw the awful realization dawning in her eyes. She would recoil in horror any second now.

"I didn't know I was doing it," he blurted. "I didn't even believe it until I found out Jo Parrish died. I swear I didn't do it on purpose. I can barely even control it now. I didn't—"

She took four swift steps and slapped him so hard his head swung to the left. He tightened his grip on his guitar and swallowed against sudden nausea.

"You did this? You took her away from me?" Kaida's voice was shaking and cold enough to send a shiver down his back. She slapped him again, making his left cheek sting to match the right. "*You?*"

Lachlan started crying. There was nothing elegant or subtle about the tears. They gushed from his eyes as he sucked at a breath, his grief suddenly as fresh as it had been a month ago. Why hadn't he killed himself already? He didn't deserve to live, not after destroying his sister's life—and from what? Envy at her success? Petty jealousy of their father's love? The knowledge he would never sing as well alone as he did with Ainsley?

His shoulders hunched and shook as he curled himself around his guitar. He wanted the earth to swallow him whole.

Slim, strong arms slid around him. He couldn't hear Kaida's voice over the sound of his harsh, ugly sobs, but he felt, suddenly, as if her arms were offering him strength. He felt her cheek against his and realized she was crying, too.

"I loved her, Kaida," he choked out. "She's—I mean—we're supposed to fight. That's what brothers and—and—sisters do. Isn't it? I never thought—" His words crammed into his throat, stopping his speech. He panted, not trying to control his emotions, but just to ride them out. His guitar was pressing painfully into his stomach, but he didn't even care.

"How did you realize you were responsible?" she asked quietly.

The whole story spilled out of him, from his anger and resentment that Ainsley wouldn't even think about singing with him, his shock and horror at Ainsley's death, his guilt over capitalizing on her voice to publish "Ainsley's Lament," and finally to meeting Eris. At some point Kaida sat down next to him and took the guitar from his hands, placing it carefully in the hard case he carried it in. By the time he reached yesterday, when Eris came into his apartment and forced him to use his magic to blind someone, he was crying again. Finally he ran out of words and stared at the happy people walking around the park.

"Why did you decide to tell me?"

He looked over at Kaida and registered the tears slipping down her cheeks.

"I wanted to tell you the night you came over," he said slowly. "But that Sunday...when you sang with me..."

She sighed. "You could tell I felt your power," she said.

Lachlan nodded. "Eris was furious. You saw her, didn't you? I played the first song I could think of about people being chased and getting away."

"And it was just a coincidence that you picked one about dogs and foxes?" Kaida asked. At his surprised expression, she gave a tired little laugh. "I could hear that song all the way to my hiding place, Lach."

"I—I mean, it was literally the first song I thought of, that's all."

Kaida's lips quirked. "I'm kitsune. I can be a fox, if I want to."

"I really am in an episode of *Teen Wolf*," he muttered.

"It's not quite the same." Kaida's voice was dry. "But I did sense what you were doing. And I sensed her rage and her malice. I did what I could to thwart it. Not much, perhaps, but—"

"She was trying to hurt the detective," Lachlan cut in. "She wanted him blinded to the truth."

Kaida snorted. "Detective Blake is a werewolf. You should tell him what's happening." She turned and pinned him with her gaze. "Tell him *everything*, I mean. He can help you."

"This lady has a serious hard-on for werewolves. For all I know, he's the reason why. No way am I going to tell Blake about Eris." Lachlan's breath came faster just thinking about it. "Not to mention the fact he would throw me in prison faster than—"

"He probably already knows you have something to do with it," Kaida argued. "Even in human form, they can pick up the tiniest trace of scent and use that to find the suspect."

"Then why hasn't he come looking for me?" Lachlan said. "No. Right now he doesn't have any idea it was my fault, and I want to keep it that way."

"You really think you'll be able to?" Kaida straightened. The look she gave him was so disappointed Lachlan almost wanted to do as she asked.

Almost.

"I'm not telling him. The less he knows, the better."

"And you? What are you going to do, Lachlan?"

"I'll tell Eris I won't do it anymore. If she tries to make me, I'll scream at her."

Kaida didn't look convinced, but after several moments she shrugged. "I can't force you. Even if I could, I wouldn't. I don't believe in using force." Her lips twisted unhappily. "Fine thing, for a pacifist to fall in love with a warrior, hm?" She dashed away her tears and frowned at him. "I won't force you. But I think you should tell Detective Blake. If anything happens to you, I am going to tell him. But it would look much better if you told him yourself."

Lachlan shook his head, and finally Kaida walked away.

* * *

He wasn't sure how much time had passed when he heard a very displeased Eris say, "Are you attempting to hide from me, *fir chaointe*?"

Lachlan lifted his face, knowing she would see right away how tear-streaked and puffy and wretched he looked. He was exhausted and terrified of her, and he twitched to look around for Kaida before realizing he shouldn't give her away if she were still around.

Eris seemed taller and stronger than he'd ever seen her, though Lachlan thought that was probably an illusion because of how powerless he was currently feeling. He talked a big game to Kaida, but seeing Eris, he felt as if something had clamped down on his tongue. He wondered if a soundless scream would work, if it were his intent that mattered.

But he'd never intended Ainsley to die, had he?

"I can always find you." Eris folded her arms across her chest, staring coolly down at him. "I told you that your power is mine. Today I will make it so permanently."

Lachlan blinked at her. He tried to open his mouth to say something rude, but his lips wouldn't part.

Eris laughed as his eyes widened. "You cannot speak because I do not permit it. But I do wish for you to stand and walk, and so you will."

He'd taken six steps before his brain caught up with the fact that his body was moving without his permission.

Where are we going? he tried to ask, but his lips didn't move. He was just screaming inside his own head.

Eris led him to one of the trails. As they approached a family out for a hike, Lachlan mentally prepared himself to beg them silently for help. Eris stopped walking.

"Oh, no, that won't do," she said, clicking her tongue. She smiled at him, lifting a hand to cup his cheek, and he felt his face melt into lines of enjoyment. His eyelids drooped a little. "There," she whispered. "No use fighting me, my wailer. I am *very* good at compulsions." Her smile twisted cruelly. "Just wait until you see Murphy. He was such a lovely experiment."

Who the hell was she talking about? Lachlan tried to glare at her, but he couldn't make anything obey him. He suspected that if Eris told his heart to quit beating, it would stop in obedience. If she was this powerful, why the hell had she needed him?

He endured the rest of the hike, unflinching when his foot slipped at one point and splashed into a little creek they were crossing. His boots were waterproof so he didn't even have the reassurance of feeling water seeping against his skin. Lachlan was beginning to believe he was nothing more than a puppet—and to fear he might never again be anything more.

They passed under Meridian Street, cars rumbling overhead, and Eris turned sharply to the right, picking her way down to the White River. At the edge of the water she paused, made a few gestures, and then waded out into the current. Lachlan had no choice but to follow.

When they reached a small island in the middle of the river, Eris halted beside a plastic storage bin. "Here we will do our work," she said. "The river will bind our magic naturally, and the current will wash away my scent. Now, I'm afraid, things will get bad for you."

Lachlan stared at her.

"You don't appreciate the power you have. You don't appreciate the guidance I have offered. In fact, you have done nothing but struggle against my will." Eris sighed, though her expression was delighted rather than disappointed. "You are very strong, and your power dislikes being forced to submit. Since you will not willingly submit, since you force me to force you..." She shrugged. "Well, if I am to use brute force, I will use it for my own good."

Lachlan stared in horror as she drew a long, long knife from the storage bin. It didn't look like a butcher knife. A cleaver, maybe. He wondered if Eris controlled every function of his body. He couldn't even piss himself in fear. He could do nothing, in fact, as she approached him, knife upraised.

In his head, Lachlan began shrieking. He knew no one could hear him. He knew it was futile, that Eris controlled his power as certainly as she controlled his body. But he sent every plea he could think of out into the world, up into the heavens, praying to a God he'd just about decided had given up on him. And then he retreated deep, deep within himself.

He felt the pain as her blade sliced off his left hand. He smelled the thick, cloying scent of his blood as it gushed out of him. He heard the rush of the river flowing past him. Threading through it all was Eris' voice, rising and falling in a chant that made the air feel sticky around him. But none of it felt real. He couldn't close his eyes, but his vision was beginning to darken.

Was he dying? He hoped he was dying. He didn't want to go on living like this, a slave to Eris' evil impulses. He hoped Kaida would forgive him.

Lachlan, hold on. The voice in his head wasn't Eris'. It wasn't his own. It wasn't even a voice he recognized. But it knew his name. *Hold on. For Ainsley.*

He tried. He really tried. But as Eris chanted on, Lachlan's world went dark.

* * *

The Eagle Creek Pack had reconvened to Martin's house, which—though still messy from the unfinished remodel—was a good central location. Martin had opted to ride back from Noblesville with Elliott, while Braxton picked up food for them and called Chloe to join them. Peggy had refused to leave Cindy, but she'd agreed to send several other wolves to join them at Martin's.

Elliott was helping Martin clear off the kitchen table while Martin got glasses out of the cabinet. Martin had just heard Chloe let herself in with a shouted greeting when a shriek split the air. The glass dropped from nerveless fingers as Martin clapped his hands over his ears. He doubled over, trying to block it out, but the shriek grew and reverberated inside his head. As Martin squeezed his eyes shut, the shriek resolved itself into words.

Please someone anyone help me she's taking my magic she's going to kill me she's evil help help help—

Martin felt hands on his shoulders. His knees felt weak. Were the hands holding him up?

Then pain like he'd only felt once before sliced through him. The shriek lost all coherent thought as agony flared in Martin's left hand. Martin screamed too, clutching it against his stomach.

"What's wrong with him?" demanded a female voice.

"I don't know." A man, closer.

A pressure was building inside Martin's head. He could feel the guilt rising to remind him that Dax's arm would be lying on the ground near him when he opened his eyes. He would see one of his best friends in the world bleeding in the dirt. He would—

"Martin, Martin, stay with me." The man's voice again, warm, scared. It sent a wave of comfort through Martin.

No. No, this was Indianapolis. Not Afghanistan.

The hands holding him were Elliott's hands. The woman was Chloe.

And the shrieking voice—was it only in his head? "Lachlan," he gritted out, trying to push the message like a lifeline to the agonized young man. "Hold on."

"What?" Elliott's hands tightened on him. "I'm holding you. I've got you, M."

Martin opened his eyes, but he didn't see Dax. He didn't see Elliott.

He saw an island in the middle of a river. Lachlan Shaw lay on the ground, twitching a bloody stump that used to be his left hand. Bile rose in Martin's throat, but he swallowed it down. He could be sick later.

A tall woman with cold eyes and strawberry blonde hair stood over him, her expression triumphant. Her face and arms were streaked with blood. She lifted her hands, flexing them both, and shouted in jubilation.

Martin imagined himself kneeling over Lachlan, though some part of him knew that he was nowhere near the young man. "Hold on," he said. "For Ainsley."

It was a mistake. The woman's head turned and she saw him.

"You!" she snarled. "I have had enough interference from you!"

The power she hurled at him was blood-red, and when it hit him, the world went away.

* * *

"Don't let him fall on the glass," Chloe shouted as Elliott grabbed for Martin. His heart was pounding too hard, his hands shaking too badly. He couldn't catch Martin in time, so he fell with him instead, landing on his knees in the shattered remains of the glass Martin had been holding.

Martin was pale, his breathing fast. Elliott could see his eyes moving under his eyelids. Blood trickled from his nose.

"What the hell is this?" Chloe was kneeling at Martin's head, stabilizing it and cradling it to keep it from the floor.

"Vision," Elliott said. "But stronger than the last one I saw." He leaned down, wincing as glass bit into his knees. "Martin, stay with me," he muttered. "Please."

Martin had bitten his lip when he fell. Elliott's throat tightened at the sight of the bright splash of blood on his mouth. He pressed his thumb against it, dabbing the blood away. He wished he could push Martin's pain away as easily.

God, what a stupid, terrible time to realize he'd fallen in love.

"He's seizing!" Chloe said as Martin's body stiffened and began jerking.

"I can see that," Elliott snapped back, working to roll Martin on his side to ease his breathing. "Get something under his head."

She whipped a dish towel off a cabinet handle and stuffed it under her brother's head. "Did this happen with the last vision?"

"No, last time he just passed out." Elliott had had first-responder training in first aid for seizures, and he knew they could do nothing but time the seizure and wait for Martin to come out of it. But watching someone you'd never met suffer through a seizure was very different from watching someone you loved.

At some point he realized Chloe was mumbling a prayer—the Hail Mary. Elliott had been raised Catholic, even if he'd lapsed years ago, but as his voice joined hers, he realized there were some things you never forgot.

After two minutes and fourteen seconds, Martin's body went still. For one terrible moment Elliott thought—but then Martin sucked in a breath. Elliott and Chloe did, too, and he realized they'd both been holding their breath with him.

"Go make sure the couch is clear," Elliott ordered Chloe. She would argue. Martin was her brother, after all, and Elliott had barely known him for a few months. But to his surprise, she left the room without a protest.

"I'm sorry I didn't catch you," Elliott whispered, brushing his fingers through Martin's hair. Glass rattled down onto the hardwood.

It felt like forever but was probably only a couple more minutes before Martin opened his eyes. They were unfocused and glossy with tears, but they were open.

"Thank God," Elliott breathed. He cupped Martin's cheek. "Are you back with us?"

Martin blinked a couple of times. Finally his eyes focused on Elliott's face. His voice was raspy as he said, "Elliott, I know where she is."

CHAPTER 26

Martin had never thought he would be this content to have a werewolf pack in his living room and a headache so bad it made him want to cry. His head was in Elliott's lap, and Elliott had one hand shielding Martin's eyes from the light as people talked around them. Elliott hadn't said much since he'd helped Martin to the couch and settled there with him, but Martin hadn't needed words. Elliott had been there, grounding him, pulling him back.

Elliott was still there. He'd seen all of Martin's broken places and he was still there.

Martin's head was pounding, but in the past hour he had grown increasingly confident that his psychic abilities were like a throttle that had been stuck in the closed position. Something about his interaction with Lachlan had unstuck the throttle. His passing out had closed the connection, and when he came around, the choke and throttle were both closed—but Martin was confident in his ability to open that throttle back up as soon as he needed it.

"All right," Braxton said, and the riot of voices quieted. "This is a council of war, but we've got to make it quick. Martin pierced Eris' veil of protection, and we know where she is and where she's hiding. Martin, can you fill us in?"

He probably ought to be embarrassed that he was dishing out intel while Elliott stroked a hand over his hair. Turned out, he didn't give a crap about that. It felt too good for him to care. Martin cleared his throat.

"I don't know what her name really is," he said. His voice was still raspy from the screaming Elliott and Chloe both told him he hadn't done. Sympathetic pain from being in Lachlan's head, maybe? "She's been Teresia and Eris both, but neither of those is her true name. She has a name that she thinks of as her own, but I couldn't get a grasp on it."

"Okay, so don't plan on using anything that relies on her true name," Braxton said.

"They're at Holliday Park right now. Lachlan's memories of their route were piecemeal, but I know they went under Meridian and turned to go to the river."

"Where that blood-magic trail led you last year," Elliott put in.

"There's an island in the river. She had it veiled somehow, but I could see it because I was following Lachlan's screams."

"I thought Lachlan was the bad guy," Murphy said. "Why do we care if she's chopping up a bad guy?"

"Because that's making her more powerful." Martin coughed. "She's trying to fuse the hand she stole from him onto the arm you mauled last year."

Murphy swore, sinking down onto the floor.

"Lachlan isn't helping her willingly now. In fact, he wasn't helping her willingly when she used him to attack Cindy James."

"That doesn't make it okay," Theo said.

"No, but I think it means you can turn Lachlan against her, if he has any power or control left."

"I don't want him dead," Elliott said. "If we can keep him alive—his parents don't deserve to lose both children in the course of a summer."

"They don't deserve to have one child murder the other, either," Theo argued.

"No, but I still think Lachlan didn't mean to kill his sister." Elliott cleared his throat. "He certainly didn't *know* he'd done it when I notified her she was dead."

"You honestly want to redeem this guy?" That was Tara, an exuberant redhead who had been oddly subdued since her arrival.

"I don't know. But if nothing else, we need to arrest someone for these murders." Elliott sighed.

"We'll deal with that when we get there," Braxton said. "If we can kill Eris, we need to do it. But if we can keep from killing Lachlan, let's do that, too. Either way, we'll call IMPD, but only once we're on scene. That'll give us time to mop up and do damage control before they show up. I'm pretty sure with the evisceration and her chopping Lachlan's hand off, we have a really good argument for some sort of crazy magic ritual attempt gone wrong. Richard Chase was an American serial killer who drank the blood of his victims and cannibalized their corpses. We can stage Eris' killing to look like something similar."

"All of that is reliant on us capturing her," Elliott said.

"Right." Braxton sighed. "Okay, we know what we're up against. We know where we're going. Let's get there."

The assembled werewolves rose from where they'd been sitting on any available surface and made their way to the door. Elliott didn't make any move to join them. Braxton paused in the middle of the room and looked at Elliott and Martin. Martin supposed he was communicating something to Elliott with that look, but Martin wasn't about to let Elliott stay with him. He knew whatever went down, Elliott would feel guilty for not being there. That wasn't a good thing to have between them.

Whatever Elliott's expression said, Braxton nodded and went out the door. Chloe went with him, but probably only to say goodbye. Then only Murphy was left, lingering just inside the door.

Martin wrapped his hand around Elliott's hand that had been shielding his eyes. He sat up with a groan and said, "Kaida's going to call you, I think. At least, part of what Lachlan was shrieking was for her to do that."

"Okay." Elliott helped him sit up, but didn't move otherwise.

Martin turned and met Elliott's gaze. "You have to go, you know. This is your case."

"Screw that—" Elliott began, and Martin pressed a finger to his lips.

"No. You're a cop. That's part of who you are. And trust me, if you're not there with Braxton and your pack, you'll regret it."

Elliott's eyes flashed gold. "Is that a prophecy?"

"No. It's the voice of bitter experience." Martin gave him a sad smile. "Trust me."

"I hate leaving you." Elliott's voice was low. "Right after that vision, and you—"

"I'll go with you," Martin interrupted. "At least, I'll try. I know I'm new to this, but something broke loose today, in a good way. I don't know if it was my PTSD or Eris' tampering or what, but it was like my throttle had been stuck in the closed position, and suddenly it isn't anymore."

Elliott's eyebrows rose. "So, what, you want to ride around in my head?"

It hurt, Martin discovered, to roll his eyes. "No, but I should be able to sense you. If you need help, call for me."

"You need to focus on recovering after what just happened."

"I'll do that after you guys get Eris," Martin promised. "Right now I just have one mother of a headache. I can handle that."

Elliott's gaze was serious as he moved closer to Martin, lifting a hand to touch his chin. "Martin, if anything had happened to you..." He trailed off, and suddenly Martin realized that he knew what Elliott wanted to say. *Is this how it felt, being able to scent my interest and hear my pulse react to him?* he wondered. He leaned in and kissed Elliott. Maybe this was love, but he wasn't ready to hear it yet. He definitely wasn't ready to say it yet.

"It won't," he said. "You're the one going into danger. *You* be careful."

Elliott looked miserably at him for a moment and then kissed him with more desperation than before.

Martin heard footsteps. "I'd tell you to get a room," said Chloe's amused voice, "but I guess technically you own this one."

Martin pulled back, flipping off his sister and smiling at Elliott. "Go on," he said softly. "Murphy's waiting on you."

"Oh, no, you are *not* leaving my brother like this," Chloe said, the amusement vanishing.

Martin looked over at her. "Cee, it's his case. You're a cop. You ought to understand that. And—she tried to kill him once already."

Chloe growled at him.

"I thought your husband was the werewolf," Martin teased.

"Shup," she said, and huffed her way into the kitchen.

Martin kissed Elliott again. "Don't die," he said.

"Hey, Cole, take care of him til I get back," Elliott called.

"Shut up, Blake," Martin said, grinning. "I'll be taking care of you."

Elliott managed a smile and then turned and followed Murphy out of the house.

"When you're done being mad at me, bring me some aspirin and a can of Coke," Martin called at his sister. Then he settled himself more comfortably on the couch and closed his eyes. It was time to see if he could follow what the pack was doing.

* * *

Murphy was waiting in the passenger seat of Elliott's car by the time he got out there.

"You two are sickening," he said when Elliott slid into the driver's seat. "It's kinda nice."

Elliott side-eyed him. "Who are you, and what have you done with Murphy?"

Murphy shrugged. You deserve to be happy. And he's a decent guy, even if his skills took a while to get up to par."

"I don't know about that," Elliott said slowly as he turned the car towards Kessler Boulevard. "I'm not totally thrilled that you're going with us. I think Martin's vision from before, the one about you? That might have been of this. Today."

Murphy scoffed. "I would rather be literally anywhere but in this car on my way to this fight. But you assholes don't get to harp at me for a year and a half about pack being family, and then try to keep me at home for this."

Elliott glanced over at him, frowning. "Just—you already saved us from her once, Murphy."

"Yeah, I'm a little pissed she found a way to fix that, by the way."

"Damn it," Elliott snapped, glaring. Before he could finish whatever he'd planned to say, his phone started ringing. The screen of his car informed them it was Kaida Akimoto. "Just—be careful, Murphy," he ordered, and answered the phone.

"Detective Blake?" she said over the car's audio system.

"Kaida. You're on speaker. My packmate Murphy is with us." He saw Murphy mouth, 'packmate' at him.

"I think Lachlan's in trouble," she said. "He won't like that I'm telling you this, but—"

"Let me save time and tell you what we know," Elliott cut in. He rattled off everything from Martin's vision. As he did, he drove west on Kessler to the intersection with Spring Mill Road, where he turned north.

"Wow. Your psychic is good," she said. "Okay, well, I saw her as I was leaving the park, maybe an hour ago? I waited a little and then doubled back to see if Lach's car was still in the lot, and it is. His guitar is on the ground where he was sitting. But—no Lachlan." She made a noise that sounded like a sob. "I—I'm not in her league, Detective Blake. I'm sorry. Tricks, cleverness, I'm good at that. But I'm not strong enough to go head to head with her."

"It's fine," Elliott said. "We've got two whole werewolf packs aimed at her, and if we don't act quickly enough, IMPD will be following."

"Be careful, Detective," she said.

"Thanks for calling me, Ms. Akimoto."

The call ended as Elliott turned off Spring Mill Road into the park. It was almost five, so the nature center would be closing. That was good. There would be fewer people around, hopefully. And at least whatever Eris was doing was technically not in the park. Hopefully they could keep any innocent bystanders away.

He opened his trunk for the equipment belt he carried. Like a patrol officer's belt, it had handcuffs, pepper spray, a flashlight holster, and a gun holster. Since he was going in as Elliott Black, Homicide Detective, he would take all the human weapons he could.

"Promise me you won't take any unnecessary risks," he ordered Murphy.

"No problem," Murphy said. He turned to go, then hesitated and turned back. "Ell. If—if anything does happen to me...can you take care of my mom? She's..." He sighed. "She's sick. She wouldn't take it well if..."

Elliott waited until Murphy looked up at him, meeting his gaze. "I swear your mom will be taken care of," he said quietly. "But be careful. Don't make me act on that promise."

He saw Murphy swallow and then the younger man turned and loped for the trees.

* * *

Elliott hated the part of the plan that came next. He made his way along the trails, identifying himself to any people he encountered and telling them the park was closed, effective immediately, and that they should go home.

"We believe we're facing a hostage situation along the river," he told a frightened man who had been out jogging.

"I thought I heard a scream at one point, but I didn't hear it again, so—"

"It's fine," Elliott said. "Just get clear of the park, and we'll take care of it."

He didn't like being so public about it, because if this went badly, he would be the obvious person to blame. And that would paint a target on his back as far as Sarah was concerned. She would know he'd been holding stuff back from her, and their casually professional friendship would be over.

Once he'd done everything he could to clear the trails, he headed for where Braxton and the packs would be ready to move in on his arrival. He approached the riverbank as stealthily as he could, knowing the whole while that he was making much more noise than he would as a wolf.

Where was the island? He gazed blankly at the river, which was very obviously free of islands. Then something flashed at the corner of his vision. He looked toward it, stepping forward as it flashed again. And then the island was in front of him. He drew his weapon, aiming at the ground, but holding it ready to jerk into position if necessary. Glancing around, he saw several wet wolves surrounding the island. They hadn't left the river yet, thinking Eris was using the waterline as her first line of defense.

As soon as Elliott arrived, Braxton emerged from the brush to his left. He looked steadily at Elliott for a few moments. Elliott met his gaze, then closed his eyes, reaching for any sense of Martin. *Are you watching us?* he thought. *Do we move in?*

He felt a warm assurance that he knew wasn't coming from himself—he was nothing like so confident as that feeling—and then someone on the island shrieked. Elliott's eyes snapped open and found Braxton's.

"Go," he said, and Braxton ran into the water, gun at the ready.

He disappeared into the stand of willows ringing the island just as the shrieking died down. Elliott decided it must have been Lachlan, not Eris, because a woman shouted something in a language he didn't understand. He saw a flash of red light through the undergrowth.

"Eris, this is over!" Braxton shouted. "You have two werewolf packs aligned against you, you're completely surrounded, and the police are on their way. Surrender now and it'll go easier for you."

"Surrender? To you!" Eris laughed. "I will never surrender."

"Why are you doing this?" Braxton was still speaking loud enough for his voice to carry, but he sounded reasonable. "The packs here have lived at peace for decades alongside the fae folk and other supernaturals. The Crossroad Accord has held since

1821, and we had no quarrel with you until you started it."

Elliott realized he was holding his breath and made himself let it out. He *hated* being on the outside, staying human for this fight. This wasn't how he did things. But he was the officer of record, and he had to be fully human whenever the police showed up. Speaking of which...

While Braxton had Eris occupied, Elliott called dispatch for backup. "I've tracked down the Shaw-Parrish killer and she has a hostage. I'm going to need backup and a water team just in case." He gave detailed directions to their location and added, "Send a bus, too. The hostage is wounded, and he'll need medical attention ASAP."

Once that was arranged, he turned his attention back to the conversation.

"—have no ambition," Eris was saying. "We should be *ruling* this world, not hiding in the shadows!"

"This way of living works," Braxton argued. "Why change it?"

"Perhaps it works for you. Marcineau thought differently. The Bitterroot Pack thinks differently. There are plenty of werewolf packs who are ready to take their rightful place alongside the Unseelie and magic-users to rule this world."

"Maybe so," Braxton said. "But I'll never stop advocating for peaceful coexistence with humanity. And I'll fight to stop anyone who wants to subjugate them."

As he said 'fight,' the werewolves were to break cover, darting in from all directions to take Eris down. Elliott slid into the river, trying to move quietly enough that the fight would cover his noise. He wasn't supposed to be on the island, but there was no way he would let his pack fight without him.

Elliott. He jerked to a stop midstream. It had sounded like Martin was right there with him. He sent an inquisitive thought back. *Be careful. I'll try to shield you from her sight, but I can't make any promises.*

That was acceptable to Elliott, and when he got the sense that Martin had nodded the go-ahead, he climbed up onto the island.

The wolves were harrying Eris, darting in from opposite directions to keep her attacks unfocused. She was throwing spells around, but in the glance Elliott risked, he saw that her spells were mostly missing. Her left arm was sheeted with blood. The hand was curled into a claw.

He almost tripped over Lachlan. The younger man was sprawled on the ground, his chest rising shallowly. His eyes were open but unfocused. Elliott glanced at the fight again and knelt by Lachlan's head. He pressed two fingers to his neck to check his pulse.

"You killed your sister," he said quietly.

Lachlan just blinked. Elliott wondered if Eris had stopped his voice to keep him from using his power against her.

"I know you didn't mean to. But you killed Jo Parrish, and I'm not sure that was an accident."

Lachlan blinked again. His lips parted and a faint groan escaped.

"All right. We're going to get you to safety," Elliott promised. He didn't like not actively fighting, but they didn't want Lachlan dead. If Elliott carried him back across to the shore and got him well away from the island, it would look like he'd defused the hostage situation. When IMPD arrived and—hopefully—found Eris dead, that would be the end of it. At least as far as the authorities were concerned.

A furry body crashed into Elliott, snarling. He bit back a cry of surprise, but it didn't matter. Eris had seen him.

"Detective Blake," she callled, "you have been a nuisance."

A blood-red ray of magic pulsed at him. Elliott tried to duck, but he was too slow. Just as the ray struck, that same furry body interposed itself— mostly—between Elliott and the spell.

"Murphy," he screamed, clutching at his foster brother. He felt like his skin was on fire where that ray had touched him, but he managed to roll them both away from Lachlan and Eris. Murphy was yelping, his body twitching. "I told you to be careful," Elliott choked, dragging Murphy further into cover.

CHAPTER 27

Martin jolted and fell off the couch as he felt the spell hit Elliott and Murphy. He heard Chloe exclaim something, but he kept his eyes squeezed shut, ignoring the new pain in his shoulder. He was throwing every ounce of energy he had into protecting Elliott. He couldn't afford distraction.

"Hold on," he whispered. "Get Murphy out of there. Get Lachlan out of there if you can."

He felt Elliott relax a tiny bit when Martin's words reached him. Elliott's gratitude swelled and enveloped him, like slipping into a hot tub. Martin smiled with his body to show Chloe he was all right. Then he wriggled his hips a little to settle his back solidly on the floor.

He could sense the spell—or, more properly, curse, he thought—wrapping itself around Murphy. It had glanced Elliott, and that would bear looking at, but for now, Murphy was the one who was in danger. Martin didn't know the first thing about spellcrafting, but he knew instinctively that he could break this with his power. It would be clumsy and probably painful, but it would hopefully save Murphy's life.

He drew on every memory he had of interacting with Murphy—calling up the angry young man at the bachelor party, the skulking fellow with snarky remarks, the comic book nerd with strong opinions, and the proud working-class man who was struggling to make ends meet. On some level, Elliott must have felt what Martin was doing, because he supplied the image of a devoted son leaning over his mother's hospital bed. Martin wrapped all of his memories with that one, binding them together. Then he imagined himself flicking his wrist, sending those memories flying between Murphy and Eris like a floorpan heat shield.

The curse didn't shatter, but as Martin held those memories in place, supplemented with his power, he felt the heat of the curse lessening. He tried to keep breathing deeply as he channeled as much energy as he could into the heat shield. Finally the pain radiating off Murphy's consciousness faded enough that Martin could touch him directly.

"Hold on, Murph," he whispered. "Ell's going to get you out of there."

* * *

As soon as Elliott felt whatever Martin had done take hold, he grabbed Murphy and dragged him through the river to the shore. The smell of wet dog assaulted his nostrils, but underneath it he could detect Murphy's pain and fear and the adrenaline that kept him running.

"I got you," Elliott promised as he wrangled the unresponsive canine—thankfully not more than one-thirty despite being soaking wet—onto the shore and through the weeds choking the river's edge. "Once you're under cover, I think Martin can hide you."

He wasn't sure why he was speaking to Murphy. He knew better than to expect an answer. That had been a nasty spell, whatever it was. His side was throbbing from the bit of it that had brushed him.

As soon as he had Murphy settled, he plunged back across the river to retrieve Lachlan. As he did, he heard Braxton squeeze off four rounds. Elliott dropped into the water, keeping his and Lachlan's face just above the surface. There was a yelp and a scream of rage from Eris. Braxton shouted, "Stop!" and fired several more rounds in quick succession.

Elliott could hear an approaching motor. That would be the water unit. He hoped the wolves could slip away in the opposite direction. He hadn't considered that having both sides covered would leave the packs no egress.

Lachlan twitched and then began thrashing in his arms.

"Hey, hang on," Elliott gasped, securing his grip. "I've got you. I'm not going to let you drown."

"I didn't mean to kill her," Lachlan sobbed, clutching at him with his remaining hand. His voice was barely audible and rasped painfully. "I didn't even know until after Parrish. I thought—I thought Eris was full of it. I thought—"

"Shh. We'll go over all of that later," Elliott said. "For now, I want you to tell no one about what happened here." He paused. "Except Kaida, if you want. She cares a lot about you."

"You aren't—" The words sounded like they were tearing out of him, and then Lachlan choked. He began coughing.

"I said don't talk," Elliott said, dragging Lachlan onto the shore. "We need to get a tourniquet on that arm." He tugged his shirt off and began twisting it into a rope. "Lie down here. Raise your arm if you can."

He could hear sirens approaching. Someone splashed into the water behind him. Elliott glanced over his shoulder and saw Braxton approaching, blood streaking from a cut on his cheekbone. He was frowning.

"She got away," Elliott said, looping the tourniquet in place.

"Went into the river," Braxton said. "I hit her twice, but I'm not stupid enough to think a couple of bullets will stop her." He lifted his hand and Elliott saw the gruesome prize he carried. "The surgery didn't end up the way she wanted it to, but somehow I don't think Lachlan would want this reattached, even if they could."

Lachlan opened his mouth and then closed it again. He shook his head. He looked back at Elliott. "Better not," he rasped.

"That voice sounds worse every time you talk," Elliott said, frowning. "Is that something she did to you?"

Lachlan nodded. "Think so," he mouthed.

Elliott sighed and looked up at Braxton. "Go check on Murphy. We need to get him away from the scene before the grunts get here."

"I've got Tara and Theo on that. The Fort Harrison Pack is already across the river and heading for Marott Park. Peggy's going to pick them up there." Braxton leaned over Lachlan. "We're going to get you some medical help, and then we'll talk about getting you some magical help," he said. "But here's how this is going to go. Eris was the killer. She had an unhealthy obsession with your music because of that lament you wrote for your sister. She was killing people in some kind of fake magic ritual, and that's why she cut off your hand. You're just an innocent bystander in all this."

Lachlan's eyes widened. "I'm not," he rasped, trying to sit up.

Elliott rested a hand on his chest. "Yes, you are," he said firmly. "What do you think it would do to your folks if they lost you, too? You were responsible for her death, but you didn't intend it to happen. That's manslaughter, not homicide. Not to mention trying to explain how you could have killed your sister when you had a rock-solid alibi." He glared at Lachlan until the younger man subsided.

They could hear shouting and doors slamming. The responders had done the smart thing and parked at the Blickman parking lot on the east end of the park. The boardwalk from that parking lot, which had wheelchair accessible fishing, would be an easier route for the Stryker from the ambulance.

"I don't like how this went down," Elliott said. "She had a backup plan in place."

"An escape route, anyway," Braxton agreed. "And she'll be back. I'm pretty sure we can count on that."

The ambulance crew arrived then and Elliott could turn over responsibility for Lachlan's care. He gave them a terse report on Lachlan's condition and then walked with Braxton to where he'd left Murphy.

There was no sign of Murphy, either as wolf or man. "They'll take him back to Martin's," Braxton said. "And we'll hope that whatever she did wasn't permanent."

"Martin shielded us both from the worst of it," Elliott said. "He's got a true handle on his power now." He felt a gentle nudge in the back of his mind and grinned faintly. "And I'm pretty sure he already knows exactly what went down."

Braxton raised his eyebrows. "There goes your werewolf senses advantage," he remarked.

Someone shouted Elliott's name and he turned. Brady Flynn was leading the charge, followed by a dozen patrol officers.

Elliott sighed. "Now we get to try to explain this."

CHAPTER 28

"He did it to himself, you know," Martin said, leaning on the doorjamb next to Elliott.

Elliott turned from watching the bed and frowned at Martin.

"Lachlan," Martin elaborated. He slipped an arm around Elliott's waist, pulling him closer. "He's the one who destroyed his own voice. He didn't want that power, and he found a way to get rid of it."

"That's fucked up," Murphy croaked. He was shivering under a pile of blankets, sweat beading his face.

Elliott turned his frown back on Murphy. "You're supposed to be resting," he said.

"Like I can rest when you two lovebirds are staring at me like I'm in a zoo." Murphy sounded tired, but Martin knew he wasn't imagining the tiny note of pleasure in his voice. Somehow Martin's concern, or the fact that Martin had insisted on Murphy staying in his spare room, had convinced Murphy that he was honestly wanted. Martin could sense the absence of the shield of reserve Murphy had always kept between him and the rest of the pack.

He could also sense something more sinister gripping Murphy, though he hadn't been able to discern what harm it would cause. His mental image of Murphy was shot through with reddish-brown, and every once in a while the color pulsed, as if it were tightening its grip. Martin could describe the issue but not diagnose it, and Elliott had only been able to say for certain that Eris' blood magic was the cause. Braxton, having gotten a whiff of the magic, turned pale and left to make a phone call; Elliott had speculated that it reminded him of his father's death, but hadn't known for sure. None of them had any clue what sort of effects the apparent blood-curse would have.

"Peggy's sending her pack doctor over, but she said we'll probably need someone with serious firepower," Martin told Murphy. "The doctor wants you to rest until he gets here. Do you need water or anything?"

Murphy coughed and shook his head slowly.

Martin nodded and tugged Elliott out of the door. "We'll let you rest, then," he said, and pulled the door mostly closed.

"It's my fault he's hurt," Elliott said as they walked away, his voice quiet.

Martin stopped walking and squeezed Elliott's hand. "It's Eris' fault he's hurt," he said. "And Murphy chose to protect you. That's what pack does, isn't it?"

"Doesn't make me feel any less guilty."

"Trust me, I know. But keep telling yourself the truth. It is *not* your fault. You tried to protect him. And if you want, you could probably tag along to a couple of support group meetings." Martin wasn't sure yet how he felt about it, but he'd found a local PTSD support group and had also made arrangements to start helping out with Homes and Hope. If nothing else, it couldn't hurt, and he could maybe help other people while he was trying to heal himself.

He wasn't fixed, he knew. He was a long way from that. But he'd finally faced his fears and weaknesses, and he'd been honest with Chloe and Elliott about them. He hadn't tried to hide his brokenness, and he thought that was at least the right first step on the journey of fixing himself. There might not be a Chilton Manual for psychics with PTSD, but maybe—just maybe—Martin would write one himself.

Elliott tugged his hand. "What's going on in there?"

Martin smiled, surprised that Elliott had to ask. Then again, maybe gratitude didn't have enough physiological symptoms for a werewolf to detect. "Just feeling grateful that we're all still here."

"Let's keep it that way," Elliott said. He darted a glance back at Murphy's room, but Martin lifted a hand to his cheek and turned him back to face Martin.

"We'll deal with that as soon as we know what we're dealing with," he promised. "But until we have a diagnosis, we've done all we can for him."

Elliott's troubled gaze lightened a little as he looked back at Martin. But he didn't smile, and Martin picked up a whisper of self-doubt from him.

"Really?" Martin arched an eyebrow at him. "I've already made sure there's room in my new living room for your kickass 4K TV. Don't go backing out on me now."

The self-doubt was swamped in a wave of happiness, though Martin wasn't sure if that was his own emotion or Elliott's. He'd have to work on figuring out how to separate the two.

Smiling, Elliott walked back towards the front of the house, tugging Martin along with him. Over his shoulder, he said, "I hope you don't mind being werewolf central from now on. I'm pretty sure that's a thing that happened."

Martin smiled. "As long as werewolf central means you're sticking around, I wouldn't change a thing."

* * *

Though his headache had lessened considerably, Martin didn't have the energy to cook that evening. So after the rest of the pack had dispersed to their various homes, he ordered a pizza.

After taking the delivery, he sat at the kitchen table, looking around at the disarray. The dishwasher wasn't hooked up yet, so the sink was full of dirty dishes. There were cushions and pillows scattered on the living room floor where the werewolves had lounged, both during the council of war and during the debrief after. And now...

Now he could hear the shower running as Elliott cleaned up from the aftermath of the fight.

Martin smiled down at the table, letting his eyes unfocus a little. If anyone had told him the day of Chloe's wedding that he would not only form a friendship with Elliott Blake, but that he'd fall head over heels in love with him, he would have laughed. And maybe three months wasn't long enough to know for sure if what they had was forever, but Martin had a feeling it was. He was tired of distancing himself from people just to protect himself from loss. He would throw himself wholeheartedly into this—and if what he was picking up from Elliott was accurate, Elliott would, too.

Martin wasn't sure if he could actually read thoughts word-for-word at this point, except in cases of extreme duress like Lachlan had been under. He wasn't really in any hurry to find out. He had made the opposite choice from Lachlan's—he would develop his abilities as much as possible—but too much power could still be a bad thing. Especially if that power was mind-reading. What if *reading* minds turned to *controlling* them? It was more power than anyone should have.

No, he wouldn't mind telling the occasional fortune when it came to his close friends and family, but he wasn't going to be adding that to the garage's list of services any time soon.

Hands settled on his shoulder and then Elliott's damp curls brushed his temple as Elliott pressed a kiss to his cheek. "If you'd told me the pizza was here, I'd have showered faster."

Martin hummed, realizing belatedly that he hadn't jumped because he had sensed Elliott's approach. He tilted his head back to smile at Elliott. "I wanted to make sure I got my half eaten before you were done," he teased. "I know what werewolf appetites are like."

Elliott growled at him, lunging at the pizza box, as Martin fell back in his chair, laughing.

"Let's take this to the couch to eat," Elliott suggested, hefting the box. "I'm not sure I'm going to want to move again tonight."

As they got settled, Murphy's voice rose sharply just as Martin felt a stab of fear and anger from the spare bedroom. Elliott tensed, but Martin held him back. After a moment, Elliott subsided onto the couch again.

"Doc Mackenzie still in there with him?" Elliott asked.

"Much to Murphy's dismay. But Mackenzie's nurse is on a two-week vacation, so there's no one else to monitor Murphy's condition." Martin grabbed a slice of pizza and slumped back.

"So they're both staying here, too?"

"Sorry." Martin licked pizza sauce off his finger. "I don't think Murphy should be on his own while he's dealing with this."

Elliott grunted. "I guess, since we don't have a pack doctor or spellbreaker, the best place for him is with the pack psychic."

Martin didn't look up from his pizza, but from the corner of his eye he could see the glance Elliott darted at him. "Pack psychic?"

"Something Theo said. Apparently there's historical precedent for the pack having human attaches—and psychics are highly prized." Elliott sucked in a breath. "It isn't because of your sister, or because—"

"Because I'm with you?" Martin said, turning to look at him.

Elliott set the pizza box on the floor and sat sideways on the couch. "Martin, you saved our pack today. You figured out what was going on with your magic and you seized control of it and—" He broke off, his gaze intense. "Regardless of us being together, you would be a damn powerful asset to any werewolf pack. Braxton will probably be pissed that I said anything, because he wanted to approach you himself, but—"

"I'm glad you told me," Martin said, smiling at him. "This seems like the sort of decision we ought to make together. Doesn't it?"

Elliott's kiss—and the accompanying surge of joy—was answer enough.

EPILOGUE

Lachlan drifted sleepily on a haze of morphine, breathing along with the beep of his monitors.

This late, the hospital was quiet, the only light coming from the hallway door, which was partially cracked. He could hear people talking outside, since the nurses' station was just across from his room. From the cheap couch by the bed he could hear his mother's faint snore; she was still pretty medicated herself. In the stiff-looking vinyl chair next to her, Kaida Akimoto slept silently, curled into a ball under a spare flannel blanket.

Lachlan couldn't hear his father pacing, but he knew that's what Joe Shaw was doing.

In a complete one-eighty, his father had blamed this whole thing on Ainsley. Maybe it was because Ainsley was gone and Lachlan was still here. Maybe it was a coping mechanism. Maybe it was just because Joe Shaw was a bigoted control freak who hated the thought of his daughter dating an Asian lesbian.

Whatever the reason, his dad hadn't been happy once Kaida arrived. Lachlan's mom had fallen all over Kaida, weeping and hugging her, all the while thanking Kaida for calling the police and saving Lachlan's life. Lachlan's dad had fidgeted and huffed before muttering that Ainsley couldn't have been much of a dyke if she'd gotten pregnant. When his wife shot a glare at him, he stood and stormed out.

Lachlan had been furious at him—or at least as furious as the morphine allowed him to be. He'd rasped an apology at Kaida and called his dad a dick, earning himself a glare from his mother. But it hadn't mattered.

Lachlan was pissed at his dad, maybe even hated him sometimes, almost as much as he loved him. But Lachlan's anger would never cost his father's life.

He'd lost a hand and ruined his voice, and whatever power was left to him would never make its way to the surface again. Lachlan had no idea what would come next in his life, but he knew it wasn't the morphine that made him feel more at peace than he had in months.

It was that gentle brush of approval he'd felt from that voice in his head, telling him to hold on and keep going.

AUTHOR'S NOTE

Whew. This novel was a difficult one to write. Partly because I love Martin and Elliott both so much that I wanted to make sure I got their story right. Partly also because of what happened in November 2016. I was so shocked by the results of the US election that I had to put this novel on hold. It was difficult to know exactly what impact the new administration's policies would have. I knew they would be bad, but I wasn't sure how bad.

I also could not have anticipated the wave of resistance that washed across the US in the wake of the presidential inauguration in January 2017. That resistance and resilience made it much easier to return to this story.

I have to admit that I took a few liberties with time in this novel. There was no way I could write Martin and Elliott's story without talking about the beautiful "Be Heard: LGBT Experiences in Indiana" exhibit at the Indiana Historical Society. That exhibit actually didn't go up until autumn of 2017, so I moved it up a few months.

I read a lot as part of my research for this book, and I want to acknowledge one book in particular that shaped this novel and Martin's journey. *Combat Trauma: A Personal Look at Long-Term Consequences* by James D. Johnson was not only a fascinating and moving book about Vietnam veterans and PTSD, but it also shaped very directly the way Martin reacted to some things.

Last of all, I want to thank you for reading my novel. If you enjoyed this, would you please take a moment to leave a review of my book at Amazon or Goodreads? Writing just two or three honest sentences is one of the best things you can do to support any author.

Thanks!

Stephanie

Acknowledgements

Shades of Circle City was written during NaNoWriMo 2010. *Circle City Psychic* was supposed to be written during NaNoWriMo 2016, but as I mentioned above, it got derailed by current events in the US. I want to thank countless other creators who reminded me that it was okay to put a project on hold, as well as those who reminded me that—now more than ever—art matters. My fellow IndyScribes constantly challenge me to be a better writer. Peggy insisted on werewolves in *Shades* and became one in *Psychic*.

A huge debt of gratitude is owed to Garrett, who acted both as sensitivity reader and critique partner. Garrett is also an awesome writer. Read his books.

Jo Parrish and Cindy James were both huge donors to my friend and editor Rhonda Parrish's Giftmas fundraiser last year. As a reward, they got to be brutally mauled by Lachlan in this book. If you, too, would like to be killed off or turned into a werewolf in a future Circle City Magic book, keep an eye out for more online charity events!

Jillian Storm has been one of my dearest friends since we met on LiveJournal fifteen years ago. She gave me so much encouragement during the writing of this novel (including emails demanding more scenes) that I can't even express how grateful I am.

My ever-supportive parents gave me a love of words and story-telling. My best friend Tiffany is Team Edward all the way, but hopefully won't hold my preference for werewolves against me. My cats Eowyn, Strider, and Eustace Clarence Scrubb were always more than willing to chew up manuscript pages or sit on my keyboard.

And most of all, I am grateful for my readers. You enable me to keep telling stories that are close to my heart, and I would love to hear from you. Please email me at stephanie@stephaniecainonline.com.

About the Author

Stephanie A. Cain writes epic and urban fantasy. She lives in Indiana, where she works at a museum. She enjoys hiking, reading, birdwatching, and general geekery. She has three cats, which she is well aware puts her firmly in crazy cat lady territory, and way more dice than she needs. She can be found online at www.stephaniecainonline.com.